No Legal Grounds

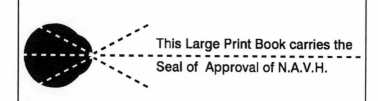

This Large Print Book carries the
Seal of Approval of N.A.V.H.

No Legal Grounds

James Scott Bell

THORNDIKE PRESS

An imprint of Thomson Gale, a part of The Thomson Corporation

THOMSON

GALE

Detroit • New York • San Francisco • New Haven, Conn. • Waterville, Maine • London

LIBRARY OF CONGRESS CATALOGING-IN-PUBLICATION DATA

Bell, James Scott.
  No legal grounds / by James Scott Bell.
    p. cm.
  ISBN-13: 978-0-7862-9708-5 (hardcover : alk. paper)
  ISBN-10: 0-7862-9708-5 (hardcover : alk. paper)
  1. Lawyers — Family relationships — Fiction. 2. Threats — Fiction.
3. Fathers and daughters — Fiction. 4. Teenage girls — Fiction. 5. Large
type books. I. Title.
PS3552.E5158N62 2007b
813'.54—dc22

       2007013779

Published in 2007 by arrangement with The Zondervan Corporation LLC.

Printed in the United States of America on permanent paper
10 9 8 7 6 5 4 3 2 1

Every society is founded on the death of men. In one way or another some are always and inevitably pushed down the line of death.

Oliver Wendell Holmes

■ ■ ■ ■

PART I:
OLD FRIENDS

■ ■ ■ ■

ONE

1.

Hey, buddy! Long time! Tracked you down after reading your blurb on the Prominent Alumni page. Prominent! You made it, buddy. I always knew you would, though it was all pretty crazy back there freshman year. Remember that? Wild times, oh yes. How'd we ever make it out of the dorm!

So I found your law firm website and then you and here I am! I'm in town! We have a lot of catching up to do. Call me, man. Can't wait to see you.

Sam Trask vaguely remembered the name at the end of the email. You remember guys named Nicky, even if you don't think about them for twenty-five years.

Nicky Oberlin. That's how he'd signed the email, along with a phone number.

The tightness in his chest, the clenching he'd been feeling for the last few weeks, returned. Why should that happen because of one random email? Because it presented a complication, a thing that called for a response. He did not need that now, not with the way things were at home.

Sam took a deep breath, leaned back in his chair in his Beverly Hills office, and tried to relax. Didn't happen. He kept seeing his daughter's face in his mind. She was screaming at him.

A quick knock on his door bumped Sam from his thoughts. Lew poked his head in. "A minute?"

Sam motioned him in. Lew Newman was Sam's age, forty-seven, and wore his sandy hair short, which gave his sharp nose and alert eyes added prominence. When Lew was with the Brooklyn DA's office he was known as the Hawk, and Sam could see why. He would've hated to be a witness about to be pecked by the Hawk's cross-examination. He was glad they were partners and not adversaries.

"We're going into high gear against the good old US of A this week," Lew said.

Sam nodded. "Got it on the radar." The FulCo case was by far the biggest Newman & Trask had ever handled. Potentially a billion at stake. That thought gave Sam's chest another squeeze.

"Cleared everything else?" Lew said.

"One matter to take care of."

"What's that?"

"Harper."

Lew rolled his eyes. "Hasn't that settled?"

"I'll take care of it."

"Please do."

"I said I would, okay?"

Lew put his hands up. "Just asking. I get to ask, don't I?"

"Of course. Sorry."

"Need you, buddy. I know things haven't been the best with —"

"I can handle it, Lew."

His partner nodded. "How's Heather doing, anyway?"

Sam did not want to talk about his daughter, not now. "We're working on it."

"Good. She'll pull through. She's a good kid."

Sam said nothing.

"So on Harper —"

"Lew, please —"

"Let me just say this once, okay? We do have a business to run, and —"

"You want me to get rid of the Harper file ASAP."

"That would be nice. Can you settle?"

"Not right away."

"Why not?"

"I need more discovery or it'll be under-valued."

"Come on, Sam. What about your value to the shop?"

Always preoccupied with the cost-benefit analysis, Lew was. Maybe that was what really had changed for Sam in the last four years. After his conversion, a little of the drive for the dollar had gone from his life.

As if sensing he'd stuck a foot over the line, Lew said, "Look, I trust your judgment, of course. But a quick settlement surely is going to be within the ballpark, give or take, and what's the problem with that?"

"No problem at all. Girl goes blind, we can toss her a few bones and move on."

"Come on, I don't mean that. Just think about it for me, will you? Harper off the table. I love you, sweetie." He made a golf-ing motion. "How about eighteen next week?"

Golf was always the way Lew made up. "Sure."

"I love you more," Lew said, then left.

For a long time Sam swiveled in his chair, as if the motion would gently rock his thoughts into some cohesive order. But it wasn't happening, because Sarah Harper was not a case he wanted to expedite.

12

The tightness came back. Come on, he scolded himself. No heart attack. You're not even fifty years old yet. Guys like you don't die before fifty. He kept in shape, ran three miles every other day, didn't have too many extra pounds. But he knew there was no guarantee. One of his old friends from UCLA Law had just gone to the cooling rack after playing pickup basketball.

One minute Tom had been a hard-charging partner at O'Melveny, and boom, the next he's an obit in *California Lawyer.* It could happen to anyone.

Sam rubbed his chest and looked back at the monitor. Nicky Oberlin. He tried to remember the face that went with the name. Didn't come to him.

Truth was, a lot of that first year at UC Santa Barbara up the coast was lost in a brain fog. He was still a long way off from a sober life then, and most of what he remembered of freshman year was a dorm known for grass and beer and late-night parties.

So this blast from the past was hearkening back to days he'd just as soon forget.

Was he the guy who came into his dorm room one night, hammered to the gills, and tried to roll out Sam's bed — while Sam was still in it? A lot of crazy things happened back then. It was a wonder any of them

13

passed their classes.

Yeah, that might have been Nicky, a little guy with a moustache. But then again . . . brain fog.

And in the fog, like the trill of a night bird, a faint vibration of unease. Oberlin had sent this to Sam's private email address. It wasn't posted on the firm's site. It would have taken some doing to find it. Apparently, Oberlin had. Which bothered him no end. It was like . . . an intrusion, and by a guy he really didn't know.

He closed his eyes for a moment and expressed his favorite prayer of late, for wisdom. Having a seventeen-year-old daughter who seemed determined to throw her life down the toilet necessitated divine intervention on a daily basis.

Now he needed wisdom for his professional life. The Harper family had come to him in their hour of greatest need. He would not drop the ball.

He took a deep breath. This was not what he thought life would be at this point in his career. He thought he'd be at the pinnacle of his profession, able to coast along at a hardworking but smooth pace, with his wife and kids along for the ride.

Instead, he was tighter than a hangman's rope and wondering if the American dream was imploding on him.

He didn't need any more tasks or obligations, no matter how small. With a touch of his index finger he deleted Nicky Oberlin's email.

He hoped Nicky wouldn't take offense.

2.

Heather Trask wondered if he would be the one.

He had the right look. She liked long hair that hung down wavy, especially if it was blond. He had great style too, judging from the way he tapped the table with his hands. He played drums for a band called Route Eighteen.

And he clearly had his eye on her. Always gave her a half smile whenever their eyes met.

Would he be the one, her first time, so she could get it over with?

Roz, who was holding court as usual at an outdoor table at Starbucks, was already well schooled in the guy department. She'd burned through three boyfriends in the last year. Heather hadn't had even one yet. Roz was older than Heather by only two years but had a worldliness Heather could only admire.

Heather also loved the way Roz could cut

15

and color her hair any which way, without a thought. Right now it was short and hot pink. Heather wasn't quite ready to chop her shoulder-length tresses and go from brown to a more luminescent tone. Maybe she would once she got out of the house.

Maybe then she'd feel like she really fit the puzzle. The pieces at home were all jumbled. She wasn't a piece there; she was a hole. The church thing wasn't going to happen for her, and her parents' disappointment made her feel like an alien presence in the home she grew up in.

Depression washed over her again. She'd been feeling so much of the dark side lately. She was using it in her songs, which Roz said were bordering on genius. Still, it was like a big, black weight on her, and she was sick of it.

Her mom and dad's solution? God. Jesus. Church.

Why couldn't she get into religion? It just didn't click, the tumblers didn't fall. Something was wrong with her brain. It wasn't a Trask brain, and she could see that thought in her parents' pained eyes with every new confrontation.

She needed to get out of there. They'd be much happier and she could finally see if there was something in this world that made sense. She could get on with things she should already have gotten to at seventeen.

So, she wondered, would her first time be with the drummer?

There were eight of them around the black iron table, crammed in and chattering away through a haze of cigarette smoke. Heather didn't really like smoking that much but did it anyway. Image. The hard part was covering up the smell when she got home.

Big Red cinnamon gum was good for the breath part. As far as her hair and clothes, well, she just told her mom it was because she'd been at Starbucks at an outside table. You just couldn't get away from the smoke out there.

She didn't think her mom totally bought that, but at least she didn't press the issue. Her dad was the one who would've made the big deal, but he was always so busy he never noticed.

"They could've taken the geek-rock crown from Weezer," she heard Drummer Boy saying. "But they turned to slacker romanticism."

Oh, no. Was he one of those pretentious, know-everything-about-music types? The kind who couldn't shut it once you got them started?

"Their last CD was nothing but lo-fi jangle and lush fuzz."

Yep.

"Detached and boring," Drummer Boy concluded loudly.

Just like you, Heather thought.

Drummer Boy brought his chair over to her side. He smiled at her and said, "Are you Jamaican?"

"What?"

" 'Cause j-makin' me crazy."

She closed her eyes.

No way he'd be the one.

Maybe she should just let it be random and hope for the best.

Or maybe there wasn't going to be any *best.* What would she do then?

3.

"Don't worry, I'm not one of *those* kind of wives, complaining up and down about how much time her husband spends at the office."

Sam took a root beer from the refrigerator, turned to face his wife. "But a little complaining every now and again never hurt, right?"

"Is that what you think I do?"

"Not in so many words, but lately . . ."

"Lately what?" She put her hands on her hips.

Uh-oh. Sam called that the Gesture, but not to Linda's face. The Gesture always raised his macho hackles. His wife was smart and insightful, and she could usually see through him. Drove him crazy sometimes. And when she was angry, and her hazel eyes caught the light, they sparked like flint on stone.

"Hints," he said. "You drop hints."

"What, would you rather I hit you right between the eyes?"

"Maybe a little more directness *would* be a good thing."

"Maybe I don't want to add to your stress, okay? Did you ever think of it that way?"

"Of course." He stepped over to her to kiss her. She gave him her cheek. "Don't pout," he said.

"When you deserve these lips again, you'll get them."

"How about I bribe you with my stunning culinary skill?"

"I'm listening."

"I'll cook up some steaks."

"You get one lip for that," Linda said. "Both if the steaks come out right."

"You drive a hard bargain."

"Take it or leave it."

"Take it. Now pay me on account."

She kissed him. A short one.

"You have inspired me with visions of things to come," Sam said. "I shall cook masterpieces."

"For you, me, and Max."

"Where's Heather?"

Linda paused. "She's out."

"With who?"

"Let's not."

Dead giveaway. "Not that Roz girl."

"Sam, I know —"

"I thought we told her —"

"Sam, please. We've been through it with her and it just leads to more anger."

Indeed, his circuits were charged. They sizzled with a high current whenever the subject of Heather's associations came up. "Who's in control around here? I don't want her seeing that girl."

"Heather is seventeen and pigheaded, like someone else I know."

She said it in a lighthearted way, but Sam wasn't into being light at the moment. "What if she wanted to go out with a serial killer?"

"Sam, Roz is hardly a serial killer."

"She's trouble, is what she is."

"That's a little harsh."

"Is it? I saw her at Starbucks one day,

hanging out with a bunch of lowlifes."

"How did you know they were lowlifes?"

"Come on."

"What happened to the presumption of innocence?"

He ignored the dig. "Where do they go, these two? They go to concerts — who knows what kind of music these bands are playing. The lyrics. Have you heard some of the lyrics out there?"

"Is this from the man who used to be a poet?"

"Hey, we didn't write anything like they're doing today."

"You know who you sound like?"

"Who?"

"Our parents."

"That's depressing." Sam went to the living room and plopped on the sofa.

"Don't pick up the remote," Linda said.

He picked up the remote. "I'm just going to check the news."

Linda snatched the remote from his hand, sat next to him. "I'm just as concerned about our daughter as you are. So we need to talk about how to handle this. We need to be together when Heather gets home."

"We have to rehearse? Is this a play or something?"

"It's called parenting."

Sam shook his head. "I think I've got it figured out."

"What?"

"Parenting."

"Oh, do you? Pray tell, what's the secret?"

"Lowering your standards," he said.

Linda hit him with a pillow.

Sam put his head back on the sofa. "You're right."

"Hm?"

"It is complicated, isn't it? I mean, I'm in the delivery room one day and out comes this innocent little package."

"Yes, I was there too."

"Innocent and pure and it's the greatest experience of my life. And I say to myself, I'm going to protect her and love her and be there for her, and when she's little she can't get enough of me. Then one day she turns thirteen and it's like some mad scientist flips a switch in her brain."

Linda stroked his arm. "It's called growing up."

"It's called the pits on a platter, is what it's called. I feel like an innocent bystander. I was standing there, trying to love her like always, and now I'm being shut out of her life."

"As my mom used to say, this too shall pass."

Sam felt the mild pressure of tears behind his eyes. "I just want her to be happy. I want her to make the right choices. I want —"

"Sam?"

"What?"

"What you want is to make it all happen yourself."

"No —"

Linda sat up. "I know you. It's good what you want for her, but you can't make it happen. You have to let God in on this."

"Like I don't know that?"

"But do you?"

"Sure I do."

She gave him the *come on now* look, but not the remote.

4.

In the study, Sam tried to get thoughts of Heather out of his head by preparing for tomorrow's deposition. It would be the crucial moment in the Harper case. His questioning of the expert who would testify that the emergency-room doctor had not made a terribly wrong diagnosis would set the stage for everything to come.

In a medical malpractice case, the testimony of experts was the key to the trial, because juries looked upon them as the high priests. Most jurors, in a medical emergency, would be willing to entrust their lives even to an unknown doctor. They entertained a willing suspension of belief that a doctor might be subject to the imperfections of mere mortals.

Lawyers who sued doctors, on the other hand, were often seen as bottom-feeders, responsible for everything from higher insurance premiums to acute acne.

Sam knew he would have a double burden if the case went to trial. In his opening statement, he planned to face the issue head-on. He would be up front with the jurors about tort reform and frivolous lawsuits.

Last trial he had, in fact, he'd asked the jurors on *voir dire* if any of them disagreed with the proposition that most lawyers are greedy ambulance chasers. Only a seventy-year-old grandmother, whose son was the DA of Kern County, raised her hand. But Sam walked through that door to elicit pledges that the jurors would treat the case before them with an open mind.

And although he'd won that case, for a fifteen-year-old boy who broke his neck diving into a river at an unsafe resort, the experts from the other side almost swayed the jury the other way.

Which was why the deposition of the experts was so important. If they came off as credible and competent, the basis of liability could disappear like a dandelion in the wind.

So Sam went over his questions carefully, designing them to build in a solid, inexorable fashion. He'd have to be on every one of his toes, because Larry Cohen, the insurance company's lawyer, would protect the doctor with every bit of legal firepower at his disposal.

Cohen was a near legend in the litigation community. At sixty-one, with a full head of silver hair and the frame of a football player — he'd been a standout linebacker at Colorado State — Cohen had not lost a case in twenty years.

It was Sam's hope that by undermining Cohen's expert in the depo, the Harper case could be settled for a fair amount. Then everyone would be happy — Lew, the Harpers, even Cohen himself, for it would be another file off his desk and wouldn't count as a loss in court.

Two hours flew by like two minutes. The only interruption was Max, his twelve-year-old. Max still liked to give his old man hugs before going to bed, and Sam took every one. Who knew how long that would last? In a few months Max would turn thirteen, and then what? Would the same mad professor that got to Heather flip a switch in his son's brain too?

How he prayed not.

Sam took a break at ten thirty and jumped online. He scanned the headlines at Google News, then made a quick stop at his email.

In the middle of the list he saw another message from Nicky Oberlin.

Hey man, just following up. Hope you got my email! We have GOT TO get together, my friend! Don't let me down! Call me now!

A faint queasiness rolled through his stomach. A feeling, ever so slight, that he was being pushed. Sam never liked being pushed.

He deleted the message, hoping this would be the last time he would hear from Nicky Oberlin.

Still, his eyes lingered on the screen for a long moment after the message vanished into the ether, as if another of its kind would suddenly appear, only this one not so friendly.

Two

1.

Sam took a sip of water, pausing to let the doctor sweat a little. It was hot in the conference room anyway. Sam wondered if this was entirely a coincidence. He knew Larry Cohen was an expert at making other people sweat. Maybe this was all on purpose.

It mattered not a bit to Sam. If Cohen wanted to play games, Sam himself would turn up the heat.

"Dr. Eisman," Sam said, putting down the Styrofoam cup on the slick maple conference table. "You have a lot of opinions about this case, don't you?"

The distinguished gray-haired doctor sitting on the other side of the table nodded. "I have some opinions, Mr. Trask, yes."

Sam cast a quick glance at the senior partner of Cohen, Stone & Baerwitz, a man well known around town to bask in sartorial splendor. He wore a three-piece suit — which looked like it cost a thousand bucks a crease — silk handkerchief, gold watch fob, and pinky ring. Not the outfit he would wear in court, of course. Cohen always wore a rather drab suit and no jewelry in front of a jury, lest they mistake him for the insurance company's rich mouthpiece.

"Yes, Doctor," Sam said. "A lot of opinions. As an expert, is that correct?"

"As an expert, yes."

"And as an expert, you are supposed to base your opinions on something, aren't you?"

"Of course."

"I see. I'd like to talk about that now."

"Go right ahead."

The doctor looked at Sam with professional defiance. It was a challenge: Find something to question me about, if you can. Put up or shut up.

Sam picked up the file folder that had been sitting on the desk in front of him. Slowly, with dramatic flair, he opened it. He wanted Cohen and Eisman to think it held a secret memo, some potential legal dynamite that would blow their case out of the water.

In truth, all it held was a photograph of Sarah Harper.

Sarah, at sixteen, had been a rising figure skating star. Local experts were taken with her precision and pixie charm. Olympic gold began to seem more than just a dream.

But after an intense practice one day Sarah suffered a severe headache that almost knocked her out. It came back the next day. And the next. She tried to ignore the pain, but when nausea and vomiting hit her for two straight days, her father took her to the emergency room. The doctor diagnosed her as having lupus cerebritis, an inflammatory condition. He put her on steroids and told her to take it easy for a while.

Sarah dutifully took the steroids, but the symptoms persisted. She went to see the same doctor two more times. He never attempted a fungal culture, kept her on the same regimen, then finally "signed her off" to an internal-medicine specialist who undertook an immediate antigen study. That's when the truth came in. Sarah Harper was overwhelmingly infected with cryptococcal meningitis.

It was too late for treatment. A week after the test results, she lapsed into a coma. When she came out of it she was blind, and without the use of her left leg.

Sarah's father was referred to Sam by one

of Sam's friends, Frank Porter, who told Pete Harper that Sam was one of the best trial lawyers in LA and a straight shooter besides. Sam knew he was good, but also that Larry Cohen had a definite idea who was the best — Larry Cohen.

It came down to this expert, Eisman, who was going to testify that the emergency-room doctor had made a correct diagnosis under the conditions and was in no way at fault for what happened to Sarah.

Sam continued to look at the photograph of Sarah, then slowly closed the file and put it down. "You are of the opinion that Sarah Harper had lupus cerebritis, is that right?"

The doctor sat up a little straighter. "That's right."

Sam looked the doctor in the eye and tried to read his expression. It was defiant, resolute. He looked exactly like what he was: a hired gun, an expert who made good money on the side testifying for insurance companies. But many such experts were generalists, not up on the specifics of a particular case. If you put tripwires in their blind spots, they could stumble.

Sam had a hunch and went for it. "Isn't it true, Doctor, that you have never made a diagnosis of lupus cerebritis yourself?"

The doctor didn't answer immediately. He

took in a deep breath and looked at Larry Cohen. Cohen's jaw twitched.

And Sam knew he'd played it perfectly. They thought the file contained Eisman's complete medical background.

Sam said, "Your answer is?"

"I would agree to that," said Eisman.

"You would agree that you have never in your lifetime made a diagnosis of lupus cerebritis, is that right?"

Eisman sighed. "Yes."

Larry Cohen's cheeks started to take on the hue of broiled salmon.

"In fact," Sam said, "you have never studied anything about lupus cerebritis, have you, Doctor?"

"That's incorrect."

"Incorrect?"

"Yes, sir."

"You want to add anything to your answer?"

Looking a bit bewildered, Eisman said, "No, I do not."

Sam smiled, knowing his next hunch would play out as well. "Then allow me to clarify, Doctor. You never studied anything about lupus cerebritis *before* being hired to testify in this case, isn't that correct?"

The defiance melted from the doctor's eyes. "I suppose."

"It's not a supposing matter, Dr. Eisman. It's a yes-or-no question."

"He's answered," Larry Cohen interjected.

"No, he hasn't," Sam said, picturing the faces of future jurors as this part of the deposition was read in open court. "Isn't it true, Doctor, that your study of lupus cerebritis began when Mr. Cohen retained you as an expert in this case?"

"That's correct," Eisman said.

"And so you must agree that you are not in any way an expert on lupus cerebritis."

"I do not regard myself as being necessarily an expert on this condition."

"Necessarily? Are you or are you not holding yourself out as an expert on lupus cerebritis, Doctor?"

Eisman's Adam's apple bobbed. "I am not."

"And yet your opinion is still that this is what Sarah Harper was suffering from when she saw Dr. Natale in the emergency room on March 7, and not cryptococcal meningitis?"

"That is my opinion."

Sam picked up the file folder again, looked at Sarah's photo, then closed it once more. "Let's explore another of your opinions, Doctor. You say Sarah Harper never had cryptococcal meningitis while she was under the care of Dr. Natale."

"That's my opinion, yes."

"Well, what is the basis of that opinion?"

Larry Cohen interrupted. "There is no need to use that tone of voice, Mr. Trask."

"Do you have an objection, Mr. Cohen?"

"It's just a request, Counsel."

"Noted," said Sam, not altering his tone. "Now let's look at the basis, Doctor. Number one: You have never diagnosed cryptococcal meningitis, have you?"

"I have not, sir."

"Number two: You have never before treated cryptococcal meningitis, have you?"

"No, sir."

"Number three: You have never studied cryptococcal meningitis before signing on to this case, have you?"

"Wait a minute!" Eisman perked up. "I probably studied something about it in medical school."

"Medical school? How long ago was that?"

"I graduated in 1975."

"Excuse me, Doctor. Are you saying you *might* have studied cryptococcal meningitis back in medical school, but you're not sure?"

"It's entirely probable."

"*Probable* is the best you can do?"

"Well, possible."

33

Sam Trask glanced at Larry Cohen, who looked liked he'd swallowed pickle juice. "Maybe now would be a good time to take our break."

2.

"Not bad," Cohen said, slipping out of his coat and placing it on an ornate wooden rack inside his office door.

Cohen sat behind his desk, his chair slightly elevated so he could look down on whomever he faced.

"Why don't you come work for me?" Cohen smiled, gestured toward the grand view outside the window. "I can offer you all this."

Sam resisted the urge to say *Away from me, Satan!* and merely nodded. "Thanks for the offer, but I'm happy where I am."

"In a two-man boutique? You could do so much better. And by the way, I wouldn't make this offer to your partner."

Sam said nothing, preferring to let Cohen get over his blather so they could get down to business. Still, a small part of him wondered what Cohen meant.

"I mean," Cohen said, "you're the quiet, smart one. Not a hothead. Hotheads get a lot of publicity, but they end up burning themselves. And their clients. I'm not joking about the offer."

"No thanks, Larry."

"Idealist, are you? Clinging to the myth of the underdog versus the big, bad insurance company?"

"Maybe we should get to the offer."

Cohen nodded. "Sure. I'm offering not to go to trial and leave your client with a big fat nothing."

A negotiating ploy, Cohen playing off his well-deserved reputation as one of the most successful insurance defense lawyers the country had ever seen. Sam knew he had to take that detail into consideration.

Sam waited for the offer.

"Nine hundred," Cohen said.

The nerve endings inside Sam's chest started vibrating. "That's way too low," he said.

"It's what it is." Not giving an inch.

"I'll give you time to reconsider."

Cohen leaned forward, hovering over his desk. "You don't quite get it, do you? I've been doing this for thirty-five years, you think I'm bluffing? It's all about information, Sam, you know that. I know about you and your partner. I know you have bigger fish to fry, that a trial would distract you from that. And I know this case inside and out, and I know how to win trials. You really want to take that risk?"

In his mind's eye, Sam saw Sarah Harper, blind, shaking her head in court, wondering why the jury had returned with a verdict against her claim.

"I'll give you twenty-four hours to discuss it with your client and get back to me," Cohen said. "After that, no more offers. We go to court."

3.

Sam drove to the upscale neighborhood of Hancock Park just to find a place to park his car and cool down.

He hated bullies, and Cohen was the classic bully of the litigator type. He had the deep pockets behind him and could throw his weight around all he wanted. Didn't matter what justice demanded.

Problem was, Cohen had the trial skills to back it all up.

Sam tuned the radio to smooth jazz and took a couple of deep breaths. Rationally, he knew he had only two options.

He could convince the Harpers that the insurance company's offer was the best they were likely to get. They wouldn't be pleased, but Lew would be. He could put this one behind him and get on to bigger and better things.

Bigger? Better? And what was Sarah Harper? Canned ham?

But Larry Cohen truly was formidable. To go through all the time and effort of a trial and come out empty would be worse than settling for what amounted to chump change from a huge insurance company.

Was he afraid to go up against Cohen? Maybe a little. But he could overcome that, he was certain. Once the trial juices started flowing, he'd be all right.

What to do?

Take it to the Harpers. Just lay it out for them and see what they say. Maybe they'd jump at it.

He checked his email on his BlackBerry. A few scattered messages, a little spam. And another from Nicky Oberlin.

Hey hey, good buddy, haven't heard from you! I'm bummed. Maybe a little hurt! I really want to get together. Not just about old times, but maybe I can offer to help you out. On that case you're handling. See, I've got resources! And it'd be great to help out an old friend.

So come on! Mail me back or call me

and let's meet and I'll tell you all about it and let's go from there. Grab a coffee or something. Whattaya say?

Offer to help? What was that all about? And how did Nicky know about any case? Was he referring to Sarah Harper, or something else?

Or just blowing smoke?

Sam thought about shooting back an email, asking for an explanation. But maybe a quick coffee was just the thing. He'd meet with the guy, get it over with, never have to see him again.

And if Nicky did turn out to be a "resource," that would be a bonus.

Sam emailed him, saying he'd be at the Starbucks at Topanga and Ventura on Tuesday morning at eight. What he didn't write he hoped Nicky would read between the lines: Take it or leave it.

4.

Sam called Linda on the way home. "Hey, let's have dinner together tonight, the four of us, sitting around the table."

"Um . . ."

"I want to be with the whole family tonight. It's really important to me."

"Sam, Heather's going out."

He squeezed the steering wheel, cocked his head so he could speak directly into the mic hanging from his ear. "Tell her no."

"She's not five anymore."

"Don't tell me that."

"Sam, what's wrong?"

"I just wanted to have dinner, all of us. Forget it. I'll see you in a few."

He clicked off, deciding that silence was the best defense against his mood. It did not improve any when the traffic across the valley became an automotive glacier.

But his thoughts kept coming back to his daughter and the trouble they'd been having lately.

Lately? He should have seen it coming years ago. The little signs of rebellion that he had never really dealt with. Some of it was before his conversion to Christianity, which should have brought more clarity.

But teenage girls continued to befuddle him. Growing up with two older brothers, he had little experience with the day-to-day life of females. They were a different breed, maybe even species.

He recalled the time he'd commented on Heather's dress when she was fourteen. She and her mother had taken pains with it, as it was Heather's first school dance. It was red, and when asked what he thought, Sam smiled and said, "It's very red."

He thought it was a nice little comment, but Heather burst into tears.

Different species.

But he had been determined in the last year to understand, console, counsel his daughter, even though she resisted it. The experiment in parental responsibility had not gone well.

Once, he found a picture in her room that she'd clipped from some teen magazine. A half-dressed boy with tattoos, ripped abs, and a come-hither look. He asked Heather if "this idiot" was her idea of what a man should be like.

Not a good language choice. And for the first time in her life, Heather screamed at him in absolute, undiluted anger.

Sam didn't take it well. He screamed back at her, louder, until she melted in tears.

Befuddlement, and guilt. He was afraid he had broken the delicate inner structure of his daughter.

If that turned out to be true, God would certainly forgive him. But would he ever be able to forgive himself?

His head was pounding when he walked through the door. Max poked his head out of the den to greet him. "Hey, Dad."

"Hey."

"I'm playing chess."

"Who with?"

"Chessmaster."

"How you doing?"

"Pretty tough right now, but Buzz is help-ing me."

Buzz was the dog Max had picked out at the Van Nuys shelter two years ago, a mix of beagle and unknown. It was a family joke that Buzz had super intelligence but was too humble to communicate it to anyone.

"Great," Sam said. "When you're done, have Buzz balance the checkbook."

"Right on."

Linda greeted Sam with a kiss, lips pursed with a certain amount of wifely concern.

"Is Heather still here?" he said.

"She's in her room."

Sam started for the stairs.

"Sam, wait."

"What?"

"Maybe you'd better let it go this time."

"Let what go?"

"Whatever you were planning to say to her."

"I just want to see my daughter for a second, is that so bad?"

"Take a breath. Come into the living—"

"Don't talk to me like a child, Linda."

She shook her head. "I didn't mean —"

"I'm going upstairs."

5.

"What is it?" Heather said.

Sam came through the door, feeling half-victorious. At least she had allowed him to enter her room. Heather turned back to her mirror and her makeup. He wished she didn't use so much. She was naturally pretty. Why hide it under garish muck? Her soft, nutmeg-colored hair complemented her clear tawny eyes. A waiflike nose gave her an appearance which, when she was five, was the very definition of cute. Now it was just part of a dark ensemble.

"Wanted to say hi to my daughter," Sam said.

"Hi."

"You going out?"

"Uh-huh."

Sam nodded, waiting for more, which didn't come.

"Where you going?"

"Just out. Friends."

"Just hangin'?"

"Right. Hangin'." Her voice was slightly mocking. "Anything else?"

Sam wanted to hug her and have her hug him back like she did when she was little, when she thought Daddy was the greatest man in the world. He wanted to go back in time and undo half the hours he'd spent churning out legal work and not being with her.

Fantasies.

He almost stroked her hair but decided it would only annoy her.

"When did we stop talking, pumpkin?"

After a short pause, Heather said, "We talk."

"No, I mean really talking. I miss that."

"Don't worry about it." Heather started putting on earrings, big silver hoops.

"You know, I would love to spend more time with you."

"Don't feel the ol' parental guilt, okay? Don't worry. I'm not going to go out and become an ax murderer."

"Oh? I was really worried about that."

Heather, looking at him in the mirror, didn't return his smile.

"Really, though, let's go out to dinner sometime, huh?" Sam said.

"Come on, Dad, you're worrying too much."

"This isn't about worry, honey. Honest. I just want to spend some time with you. I do feel bad about it."

Heather went to her dresser and got some other form of makeup. She went back to the mirror, not looking at Sam. He thought she might be embarrassed, like he was, but he was going to push on. He had to. He could feel his daughter slipping away into adulthood, too quickly to cast a backward look at her father.

Sam said, "I know I work an awful lot and haven't been around as much as I would have liked, especially in the last few years. I know that. And I'm really sorry."

"Come on, Dad."

"Remember when we did softball?"

"Of course."

"That was one of my all-time favorite years. That season you were ten, and you played on the boys' team. You were the only girl."

"Yeah, and I played right field. That's where they always put the kids who can't play."

"But you worked at it. You and I worked at it together, at home. We practiced, and you got better, and that last game you got four hits."

Heather was lining her eyelids with dark purple. "I've got to kind of get ready here."

She had dropped a familiar, unspoken sign between them again: *We Reserve the Right to Refuse Service to Anyone.*

"Hey, humor your old man, will you? Are

44

we on for dinner? I promise I won't embarrass you, like the time I did that cheerleading stunt in front of your friends."

Heather didn't change expression. "If you want."

"Next Friday night?"

"Um, can't do it then."

"Why not?"

"Rehearsing."

Her band. Right. Wonderful.

"What about next Thursday then?"

She paused. "Fine."

It was begrudging, but a small victory, and now it was time to retreat. "Thanks, cupcake. The Trask family sticks together, right?"

She said nothing.

Retreat now!

"Love you," Sam said, and quietly left the room.

THREE

1.

Tuesday morning, Sam walked into Starbucks and saw a man immediately sit up, smile, and wave.

Sam did not recognize him, but it was clear he recognized Sam.

"Nicky?"

He stood and shook Sam's hand. "You look great, man."

"It's all an illusion."

Nicky was short, a little thick around the waist, and had an advanced case of male pattern baldness. His features were orbical — round eyes, round nose, round cheekbones. He wore a white golf shirt that stretched over his belly before tucking away in his tan slacks.

"No, I mean it," Nicky said, giving Sam's form an admiring glance. "You have to work out."

"When I can."

"Gotta do the same." Nicky patted his stomach. "The all-beer diet is a fraud."

"I figured that one out a long time ago."

"Only martinis and scotch for you, I bet."

"Nah." Sam didn't elaborate, not knowing if he would come off as holier-than-thou.

"You don't do the booze thing?"

"Not anymore."

"Not like freshman year, huh?"

Sam tried to laugh it off but said nothing. A safe harbor of silence seemed best at this point. The more distance he put between himself and those days at UC, the better.

Nicky already had coffee, so Sam ordered a grande latte and brought it to the table Nicky had staked out. He felt the smallest bit of unease at Nicky's smiling face. It was almost too much. He just wanted to have a ten-minute conversation and then get to the office.

"Remember that time," Nicky said as Sam sat down, "Rick Reimer and Jeff Green had that Risk tournament with the vodka rule?"

Sam did remember, now that he mentioned it. Risk was a game of world domination played with dice and cards. Players tried to take over countries using a combination of troop moves and luck.

"Yeah," Sam said, "if you took over a country you had to take a shot of vodka."

"Only certain countries. Afghanistan, Argentina, and Australia. The big A's, we called 'em."

"We were clever then."

"You remember that tournament? It went on for a week, right before finals."

"Was it before finals? The timeframe is a little hazy for me."

"You kicked butt in that tournament, as I recall. You were blasted most of the time too."

"I was a real role model, wasn't I?"

Nicky's hands moved around his coffee cup in a nervous, jacked-up way. "I always thought you would be the guy I'd want as my right-hand man if I was interested in world domination. You ever see that cartoon show *Pinky and the Brain*?"

Sam recalled it. It had been a favorite show of his daughter's when she was eight or nine. He nodded.

Nicky laughed. "The dumb mouse, Pinky, asked at the end of the show what he and the Brain were going to do, and Brain says, 'What we always do — try to take over the world.' I really loved that."

Sam tried to imagine an adult man loving *Pinky and the Brain*.

"So what do you do, Nicky?"

"Besides think about old times? A little of

this, a little of that. The construction thing. You know that new building they did in Warner Center?"

"Yeah, just completed."

"I worked on that."

"Very impressive."

"Ah, I'm just a cog in the machine, not a big wheel like you."

"Wife? Kids?"

"Nah." He shrugged. "I guess some guys aren't cut out for marriage, you know?" He bobbed his eyebrows. "I do okay, if you know what I mean."

That saddened Sam. Here was a guy, almost fifty, who was still talking about *doing okay* with women. But Sam kept up an expression of conviviality.

"What about you, man?" Nicky said. "Bet you snagged a great lady and turned out some perfect kids."

"I've been blessed, yes." *Great choice of words! You're blessed and he's not. Rub it in, why don't you?*

But Nicky didn't seem to care. He kept a sunny smile. "Blessed, huh? Would that be by God?"

"Sure."

"You a church guy now, Sam?"

"Kind of surprising, isn't it?"

"A real kick in the biscuits."

49

Sam tried not to wince at the phrase. It seemed, well, childish. *Arrested development* flashed through his mind.

"Never would have predicted church for you, if you know what I mean." Nicky bobbed his eyebrows again. That was getting annoying fast. "Back in the dorms, you were quite the ladies' man."

Sam cleared his throat. "I was pretty stupid back then."

"Stupid? No way. You had it goin' on."

"No."

"Still do, I'll wager."

"That's all changed."

"Nah, not you, Sam."

"Yeah, me. I didn't have it goin' on a few years ago."

"What happened? Nothing bad, I hope."

"I'll spare you the details."

"Why? I'd like to hear."

Sam shifted in his chair. Talking about his faith was something he was supposed to do, wasn't it? So why was he hesitating?

2.

"I almost hit my wife one night," Sam said. "I'd never, ever gotten close to doing that. But I was under a lot of pressure over a case, and I was handling it by drinking more and more. I got into a huge argument with

Linda, and she stood up to me. One thing about my wife, she's got backbone."

Nicky was listening intently, and it put Sam a little more at ease. Maybe the message was getting through.

"Anyway, I lost my mind and raised my fist to her. It was, and still is, the absolute low point of my life. The look on her face. She woke up the kids and put them in the car and drove away. I thought I'd lost them all forever."

The pain of the memory hit Sam as if it had happened the night before. He took a long breath. "Linda had become a Christian a few years before this, and I saw it as just a thing she was interested in and let her go to church. But that night, I knew I needed whatever she had.

"So I drove to where she went to church. I guess I expected the church to be open, and I could go inside and sit down and ask for God to show me what to do. It was locked up, of course. But there's a cross on the sign in front of the church, and it was lighted, so I just knelt in the grass by the sign and waited."

"Waited?"

"You know, for God to talk to me. And he did."

Nicky's eyes widened.

"In the form of the pastor, Don Lyle. He was working late, just leaving his office. He saw me there. And when I told him who I was and what I had done, he opened the Bible and tussled with me for a couple of hours." Sam smiled. "Then we went into the church and I stripped down to my skivvies and he baptized me right then and there. When I came up out of that water I felt brand new, clean, completely forgiven."

"Heavy."

Sam hadn't heard that term in a while, but it applied.

"What about you, Nicky? You indicated there was a way you could help me."

"Right, right."

"You mentioned a case. What was that all about?"

"Your case, Sam."

"I have several cases —"

"The ice-skater." Nicky raised his eyebrows.

"May I ask how you know about that?"

"Internet, dude. How I found you in the first place."

"What, you did some background on me?"

"Oh, easy stuff. Wanted to see how well you were doing. Making UCSB proud!"

Sam forced a chuckle. "So what did you mean by help?"

"You know, maybe research or something like that. I'm a cyber king, dude. I'd love to give you a hand."

"Well, that's real nice of you to offer, but we have paralegals to —"

"I'm not talking about normal channels, Sam. I can dig into places you've missed. Let me show you."

And open up a can of trouble. Wouldn't it be great to have Larry Cohen find out someone was rooting around in *places you've missed.*

"Thanks," Sam said, "but —"

"No thanks? I got it." Nicky sat back in his chair.

"It's not that I don't appreciate —"

"You have a card, Sam?"

Sam hesitated. Then he fished a card out of his wallet and gave it to Nicky.

"Very slick," Nicky said. "Raised letters and everything."

"Makes us seem more important than we are."

"Yeah," Nicky said, "that's what lots of people think."

A tick of unease hit Sam. He looked at his watch. "Hey, Nicky, I hate to say, but I've got to run."

"So soon?"

"I'm sorry. Lawyering." He stood. "Everybody wants a piece of me. It was sure great to see you, Nicky."

Nicky stood up and put out his hand. "Let's do this again."

"Sure." Sam shook Nicky's hand, hoping Nicky would pick up on the noncommittal tone in his voice.

Nicky held the grip. "I mean it."

"Right. Bye, Nicky."

Nicky slipped Sam's card into his shirt pocket. "We'll be in touch," he said.

3.

I hope not, Sam thought.

And he kept hoping not as he drove over to see Pete Harper. There was the faintest scent of desperation about Nicky Oberlin. Not that guys couldn't find themselves a little down from time to time. But he had the feeling Nicky was putting out the first feeler to recruit Sam as part of the Nicky Oberlin reclamation team.

Sam had enough going on with the Harper case and FulCo, not to mention his own family. Nicky would have to recruit someone else.

The Harper place was nestled in a neighborhood built up mostly in the sixties. The houses were small, the lawns well kept. Sam cruised to the end of a cul-de-sac and turned around, then pulled up to the curb.

Pete Harper was clipping a hedge as Sam got out of the car. Pete was fifty-two and stocky, perfect for the lumber business, with thin, graying hair. When he saw Sam he threw the clippers down so they stuck, handles up, in the grass. He removed his gloves and stuck his hand out. "Right on time," he said. "Thanks for that."

Pete Harper led Sam into the living room. Sam took a seat on the sofa and placed his briefcase on the coffee table. Pete sat in a chair, then immediately stood up again. "Can I offer you anything? Coffee?"

"No thanks, Mr. Harper." It was apparent that Pete Harper was incredibly tense. Sam knew him to be a self-sufficient man, a hard worker, the kind who liked to control things. But litigation is inherently uncontrollable.

Janet Harper, a good-looking woman in her late forties, stepped into the living room. She pushed a wheelchair, in which sat Sarah Harper. She looked thin and wan, her head slightly bowed.

"Hello, Mr. Trask," Janet said.

Sam stood. "Hello, Mrs. Harper, Sarah."

"Please sit," said Janet. She looked at Pete. "Did you offer Mr. Trask something to drink?"

"I'm fine," said Sam. "And I really wish

you all would call me Sam. There's no need to be so formal."

"I don't know," Janet said with a lilt in her voice. "You being our lawyer and all."

Pete Harper wiped his hands on his shirt, the smile he had only seconds before commandeered by tight-lipped anxiety. No one spoke. It seemed to Sam they were all waiting for him to say something, but it didn't feel right to bring up business right away.

"You look good, Sarah," Sam said.

Expressionless, Sarah answered, "Thanks." It was forced, at once polite and pained. She wasn't looking good at all. She was, from all appearances, wasting away. The elfin face that had captivated a nation was gone, replaced by a hopeless facade. It had been more than two years since the meningitis took away her sight and the use of her leg, and substantially more. By all outward appearances, Sarah survived. Inside, something was dead.

"Sarah's been keeping up at the school," Janet said. Sam absorbed the nuance of *keeping up*. From previous conversations with the Harpers, Sam knew Sarah was not doing much at all to learn to live with her disability. Just enough to get by, apparently to please her parents. They had sacrificed years, time, and money to give their only

56

child the best in skating lessons and school tutoring. Sarah probably felt an obligation to at least go through the motions.

"I didn't know there were so many books in Braille," Pete Harper said, his hands still rubbing vacantly on his stomach. "There's whole libraries."

"What are you reading now, Sarah?" Sam asked.

"Nothing."

Janet said, "She just finished an assignment. *Lilies of the Field.*"

Nodding, Sam said, "How'd you like it?"

"It was okay," Sarah said.

"You ever see the movie?" Pete said. "With that fella, whatsisname?"

"Sidney Poitier," Janet said. "It was Sidney Poitier."

"That's right," Pete said. "Heckuva fine actor. We watched it just the other . . ." He stopped, glancing quickly at his daughter, a look of anguished embarrassment etched across his face.

"It's all right, Dad," Sarah said.

"I'm sorry," Pete said. "It's just that I don't know . . ." His voice trailed off as he looked away.

"Well, let me just explain what's going on," Sam said. "We have a settlement offer."

Across the room, Janet and Pete exchanged looks. It was almost as if they didn't want to hear it. Sam understood. It was a monumental decision for them, involving all sorts of imprecise calculations. Is the money enough? Will it truly compensate? Would acceptance mean giving up? All of these questions and more seemed to pass between Sarah Harper's parents as Sam cleared his throat and opened the folder.

"Now," Sam began, "I had a long talk with the defense lawyer. We discussed the merits of the case, the various contingencies, all of the considerations that go into these kinds of negotiations."

Again, Janet and Pete Harper looked at each other. Now they seemed confused. And I sound like a stupid lawyer, Sam thought. Drop the verbiage and get on with it.

"And the bottom line from the insurance company is a settlement offer of nine hundred thousand dollars."

Pete Harper frowned. "Nine hundred thousand?"

Sam looked up. "That's right."

"That's a lot lower than what we thought."

"It is, yes, but again, this is settlement."

Pete Harper's face showed a tinge of red. "That's not nine hundred thousand after your cut, is it?"

"Pete," Janet said with a mild rebuke.

"It's all right, Mrs. Harper," Sam said quickly. Lew had agreed to let Sam take the case for the usual one-third of the recovery. That was a big chunk, and he couldn't fault Pete Harper for feeling pinched.

"It is a settlement offer," Sam explained. "It's naturally going to be lower than what we ask for."

Pete looked out the window, saying nothing.

Sam swallowed. "Again, it's —"

"Look at my daughter," Pete said.

"Please, Pete," Janet said.

"All I'm saying is . . ." Sam hesitated, then said, "You remember back when we first met and I explained how the law is in California? Damages for pain and suffering are capped at two hundred fifty thousand."

Pete shook his head. "How can they do that?"

"They can. The real fight is over future care and earning capacity."

"And they don't think she could have earned money as a skater? As a coach? One of the best . . ."

"The insurance company put a valuation on the case, and this is what they came up with."

"Pretty easy, isn't it?" Pete stood and walked to the far wall, near a bookshelf, then spun around. "Just come up with something out of thin air. They don't see her every day. *You* don't see her every day."

"Pete, stop!" Janet Harper had a hurt yet defiant look in her eyes. Sam immediately felt like an intruder, then noticed Sarah weeping silently. Her shoulders were shaking. "Excuse me, please," Janet said, turning and wheeling Sarah out of the room.

4.

Pete Harper looked at the floor and took a deep breath. When he raised his head, Sam saw moisture in his eyes. "I'm sorry, Sam. I'm sorry." He dropped heavily into his chair, putting his head in his right hand. "It's just been so hard."

"I know," Sam said.

"I used to wake up at four thirty in the morning and make breakfast for Sarah, then take her to the rink for a couple hours' practice before school. Did that almost every day for seven years. And you know what? I didn't mind it. Didn't mind it one bit. I enjoyed every second of it, because I got to be with her. Got to be with her . . ."

A few heavy breaths came out of Pete Harper. Sam nodded, even though Pete wasn't looking at him.

"When she started winning," Pete continued, "I was so proud. Everything I taught her about sticking to it, working hard, and someday getting your dream — that all happened. Then this."

Sam said nothing.

"What hurts the most," Pete said, "is the heart it took out of her. The heart of a champion. She needs to reach down and fight and . . ." Pete rubbed his eyes. "I'm so sorry."

"Let me say one thing about this offer. It's just that, an offer. I'm obligated to report it. But we can counteroffer."

"And then they'll counteroffer, and it's just like Ping-Pong, right? A big game. With us in the middle."

"It seems that way sometimes, but eventually an agreement can be reached."

"But it'll take more time, won't it?"

"Yes."

"You tell me what you think, Sam. You tell me if you think we should take it." Pete was looking straight at him with red-rimmed eyes. That was something Sam hadn't been prepared for. In previous meetings Pete had always seemed strong and resolute. This was the first sign of vulnerability Sam had seen in him.

"When you take everything into consideration —" Sam chose his words carefully — "the length of time it takes to get to trial, the whole process of a trial, all the anxiety, the fact a jury might not see it like we do, then the benefits may outweigh the costs."

Awful. Canned. Pete Harper looked almost like he didn't understand a word Sam had said.

"We're not just out for more money," Pete said quietly. "But Sarah deserves the best care, that's all, the best chance. We're talking about the rest of her life."

"Look," Sam said, "there's no need to make a decision right now. Why not just think about it and let me know?"

"But you think we should take it?"

"I think, again, we have to consider everything. I can make a counteroffer and see what they say." Sam noted a lack of conviction in his voice.

"We'll do what you think is best, Sam."

That wasn't what Sam wanted to hear. What he wanted was a quick answer, an acceptance of the terms. He didn't want the onus thrown back on him. But there it was.

He stood up, sliding the file folder into his briefcase. "I just wanted to bring you the offer myself and let you know about it as soon as I could."

"We appreciate that."

"No problem. How about I call you to-morrow and we talk about it some more?"

"That's fine. Thanks for coming over." Pete walked to Sam, put a hand on his shoulder, and started toward the front door.

Sam took a few steps, stopped, then turned and saw Sarah Harper sitting quietly in her wheelchair down the hall. She tilted her head toward him at the sound of his feet.

"Good-bye, Mr. Trask." Her voice was weak. "Thanks for coming over."

"You bet."

Bet? They were betting on him, and he wasn't sure if the gamble was going to pay off. Not enough to give Sarah what she needed, what she deserved.

By the time he got out of the house and into his car, the day had turned a dark shade, the color of dirty ice.

5.

By Thursday, the sun was back, and LA got treated to a day of clear skies and cumulus clouds. Out on the golf course the grass was as green as a St. Patrick's Day hat. It always seemed a little greener at Bel-Air Country Club, where Lew was a member.

It was a treat to play here with Lew. Lew

loved golf and golf lore, and Bel-Air had more than its share. It was here that Howard Hughes once landed his airplane on a fairway to impress Katherine Hepburn, who lived off the fourteenth. Hughes stepped from the aircraft with clubs in hand and joined Hepburn's twosome. Club executives were so furious that Hughes resigned his membership the following day and never returned.

Sam would come back anytime, because golfing was one way to give the mind a rest, as long as you weren't a fanatic about your score. Lew was. Sam just thanked God he could hit the ball fairly straight.

But as glorious as the day was, and as good as Sam was playing, by the time they got to the par-four ninth, Sam couldn't deny the strangest feeling. Like someone was watching him. Not another golfer, not even someone from the club.

Someone like Nicky Oberlin.

Now why would he think that? It was two days since he'd met him at Starbucks, and Nicky seemed a little odd, but not wacky. Maybe it was just Sam's imagination running ahead of reality.

"You have the honors," Lew said.

"What?"

"Hey, you okay?"

"Oh, yeah." Sam teed up his ball and took one look around. At least the course was immaculate. He reminded himself it was a privilege to play here.

But as he stood behind the ball that feeling of eyes on him wouldn't go away.

He shook it off and hit a beautiful draw with a lot of roll, right into the middle of the fairway. A drive like that could take care of a lot of fretful imaginings.

As he and Lew rode toward their balls, Lew said, "So you about to wrap up the Harper deal?"

"Pushy little bugger, aren't you?"

"So?"

"Trust me, sport."

"Just asking."

"Don't worry about it, okay? I can handle everything."

"Larry Cohen called me."

Sam snapped a look at his partner. "Did he now?"

"Says you're dragging your feet on his settlement offer."

At that moment, Sam wanted to drag Larry Cohen across some barbed wire. "So what's he doing calling you? Want you to talk some sense into me?"

"That what you think I'm doing?"

"Yeah, and you can stop now."

Lew pulled the cart to a stop at Sam's ball. Sam jumped out of the cart and yanked his seven iron from the bag. Lew climbed out too.

"Settle it, Sam. Let's get out of it and —"

"And what? Take our money and run?"

"I'm just saying —"

"I say we should waive our fee, do this pro bono."

"Are you nuts?"

"No, I'm about to hit."

Sam could tell Lew was bursting a seam as he got back into the cart. It didn't help matters when Sam hit a perfect shot up onto the green.

The rest of the round was mixed with tension, but by the time they got to the clubhouse for refreshments Lew had cooled off. He gave Sam a pat on the back. "Hey, pal, let's just forget what we said out there today, huh? Tell you what. Dinner's on me. There's a great new sushi place on —"

Sam stiffened. "Oh, no."

"What?"

Sam whipped out his phone and hit Heather's key. It rang four times, then went to voice mail. Sam said, "Heather, I'm so sorry. I got hung up but I can be home in half an hour. Will you be there? Ready to go? Call me. Love you."

Lew looked at him as he sipped his gin and tonic. "Family trouble. Just what you need."

"It's not trouble," Sam said, trying to convince himself. "Just a little misunderstanding."

"Heather's seventeen."

"So?"

"That's trouble."

6.

Linda was waiting for him in the living room, sitting with her arms folded, the universal sign of spousal disapproval.

"Heather's not here?" Sam said.

"Did you expect her to be?"

"I'm just a little late."

"Like an hour. Did you just forget your dinner date, or did you not want to go?"

"Come on, Linda. I left her a message."

"I'm asking."

"What do you think? Of course I just forgot." Sam looked at the ceiling. "Was she very upset?"

"If stomping out of the house with tears in your eyes is upset, then yes, I would have to say she was."

"And you just let her go?"

"Now don't turn this around and put it on me."

Linda had her iron-eyed look, the one that let him know what was quite obvious — he was being unfair. "I didn't mean that. I'm talking about now. I want to know what she does when she goes out with these friends."

"She'll let us know when she's ready. In the meantime I suggest you start rehearsing a speech. Convince her to pronounce you not guilty."

"I just forgot. It's not like I took her iPod away. That would be a national tragedy."

"I don't think trying to be funny is going to help the situation."

"Is that really what you think I'm doing?"

"Isn't it?"

"So you think I should wallow in guilt?"

"I didn't say that."

"You didn't have to."

He stormed off to the study and closed the door with practiced finality. He didn't want to argue with Linda about Heather tonight. He just wanted everything to be normal for once.

Maybe a little work was the ticket, digging in on the FulCo case. He first went to his email.

There was another message from Nicky Oberlin. He opened it with a sense of dread.

Hey, good buddy, it was sure great seeing you and tripping down memory lane. But I feel like we just sort of scratched the surface. Let's do it again, what do you say? I know you're the big busy lawyer and all that, but hey, remember I'm the guy who can help you. You want to say same time next Wednesday? Just lemme know.

No, Sam thought. I won't just let you know. You're going to have to find some other companionship, buddy. He deleted the email without answering.

He worked another hour, then turned everything off in the study. By the time he was ready to get to bed, Heather still hadn't called. Now he wasn't just worried, he was angry. Sure, he'd been wrong about missing their dinner date. But that did not give her the right to stay out and worry her parents.

And she wouldn't answer her cell.

He decided he wasn't going to sleep after all. He turned on the TV and found an old movie. *The Asphalt Jungle.* It was the story of small-time hoods trying to make a big score. Marilyn Monroe had a small part in it.

By the end of the movie, when Sterling Hayden dies while trying to get to his child-hood home, the Trask household was still missing one daughter. He tried her cell phone again. No answer.

Linda came into the room, rubbing her eyes. "Is Heather home yet?"

That's when Sam called the police.

7.

"I can't believe you called the cops on me!"

At four forty in the morning, Heather's anger seemed to hold added emotion. The only ones in the house who were getting any sleep were Max and Buzz, who slept in Max's room. Everyone else was on the sharp edge of rage. Sam told himself to tread softly. He didn't want to lose control at this critical juncture.

"It wasn't *on* you, Heather, it was in order to find you."

"Don't be a lawyer, Dad."

"We didn't know where you were."

"You don't need to know all the time."

Her dark makeup made her seem hard, and she smelled of smoke.

"As long as you're living here I want to know where you go. We have a right to know."

Heather glared. "Then maybe I just won't live here."

"Stop being foolish." The treading softly idea was melting away like wax on flame.

"You can't stop me if I want to."

She was right. The legal wrangling that could come from a teenager seeking emancipation fell to her favor. All Heather would have to do was walk into a free legal clinic, get some forms, and file them in court. Family law in California didn't give parents many rights anymore. Then, in the months it would take to get a hearing, she'd turn eighteen.

After that she could live anywhere, do anything, without her parents' consent or even knowledge.

Sam looked at Linda, who was sitting on the sofa and seemed ready to throw in the emotional towel. It was time for another retreat. "It's late," he said. "Why don't we get some sleep and talk —"

"I'm wide awake," Heather said. "So now I want to tell you both something."

She's pregnant. Don't be pregnant!

"Sit down, Dad."

Pregnant. If it was a sit-down announcement, that had to be it. He joined Linda on the sofa. She took his hand.

Heather remained standing. "I know you guys love me and all that, but I can't keep going through this."

"Through what?" Sam snapped. Linda squeezed his hand.

"Like that, Dad. You want to control me. You guys mean well, I know that, but you just don't get me. Look, I've decided not to go to college."

It was only Linda's hand on his that kept Sam from jumping up and arguing Heather into submission. College had always been a non-negotiable with them. Her grades were good. She had a chance to get into a great school.

"I know that's rocking your boat, but I just don't like school. I want to do more with my singing. Roz wants to take the band to the next level, and we have a chance to be good. But I have to —"

"Wait a second," Sam said, unable to stop himself. "You are not going to make this band your whole life."

"You see?" Heather slapped her side. "You don't even give me a chance."

"Right. I am not going to give you a chance to do something stupid. That wouldn't make me much of a parent, would it?"

"Thank you," Heather said. "Thank you for calling me stupid."

"Not *you*. But what you're doing is —"

"Yes, you are. You think I'm stupid, you just said it. You've always thought it."

"No —"

"The Trask family sticks together. Sure! Right! So you call the cops —"

A sound from the hall turned Sam around. Now Max was standing there, squinting. Buzz, his gray and brown head cocked at the noise, was at Max's heel. "What's going on?" Max said.

Terrific, Sam thought. A real family gathering. And Heather's sarcastic comment about the family sticking together was burning inside him.

Linda said, "Can we postpone this until we're all more rested?"

"I'm tired of postponing things," Heather said, and Sam saw wet, black streaks starting to run under her eyes. "I'm tired of this whole stupid family."

She started toward the stairs.

"Wait," Sam said. But then Heather turned to the front door.

"You want to know where I am? I'm going to Roz's. And don't call me."

Then she was out, slamming the door behind her.

FOUR

1.

When the sun came up, Sam thought about driving over to Roz's and getting Heather himself. His wife talked him out of it, and he knew she was right. This thing needed some time to work itself out.

Besides, with no sleep, he couldn't be sure he'd be rational or understanding. He might end up chasing a dog down the street, or biting a mailman.

So he went into the office. But working was like slogging up a muddy hill in ankle weights. Sam tried to clear out the brain cobwebs with a triple latte, but after the early morning run-in with Heather, anything he tried to concentrate on was a boulder he could barely move.

Call me Sisyphus.

There was one thing he decided, though, and there was no going back in his mind. He finished his fourth cup of coffee and went to Lew's office.

"Hey, what's up, pard?" Lew was twiddling a pencil in his right hand as he tapped at his keyboard with the other.

"I can't do it, Lew."

"Do what?"

"Give up on Harper. I'm taking it all the way."

Lew threw the pencil on the desk. "That's disappointing."

"I'm sorry. That's just the way it's going to be."

"Just like that?"

"I've been thinking about this a long time."

"So we don't make decisions together anymore?"

"You wanted to take the decision away from me, Lew. You made the pronouncement that it was up to me, but you didn't really want me to stay on this case. But I took it on, and it's my obligation as a lawyer —"

"Will you stop with the law school ethics? You're not a One-L."

"I happen to believe in what I'm doing."

Lew shook his head. "I'm not pleased. But I think you already knew I wouldn't be." He was silent for a moment. "All right. Do what you have to do. But we are not waiving our fee. Now get out of here and go do some work, will you?"

Work. Yes. Sam would do what he always had in the past — work his tail off. He was never the smartest one in his class at law school, he knew that. But he made sure nobody would outwork him, and nobody did.

He was going to work at getting his daughter back, getting justice for Sarah Harper, and making life come out even again. Raw effort, that would do it.

As he walked back to his office his assistant, Doreen, signaled to him from her desk. She was twenty-four and had a truly expressive face. Her expression was troubled. "You have a call on line one," she said. "He wouldn't give his name. Said he was an old friend."

Sam knew who it was. He went to his office, picked up, and heard the jovial tones of Nicky Oberlin.

"Hey, I didn't hear back from you. Thought I'd give you a call, see if everything's all right."

Sam didn't want to do this little phone dance. "Everything's fine, Nicky."

"Then when are we getting together?"

"I don't know if that's going to happen. I just found out I'm going to be extremely busy for the foreseeable future. Not really going to have time."

"Time for old friends?"

"Time for a lot of things. But I've got your card and —"

"Hey, sounds like you're giving your old buddy the brush."

"It's not that."

"I think it is."

Now what? He really *was* giving Nicky the brush-off, and it was patently obvious.

"Nicky, let me just put it this way: I really appreciate the fact that you looked me up after all these years, that you wanted to get together and all that, but right now I just don't have time to fit in any new social relationships. I've got family things going on and law things going on; you know how it is. So let's just leave it at that, and remember the old times."

Pause. "You mean we'll always have Paris?"

"What was that?"

"You know, that line from *Casablanca*? Bogart says it to Bergman just before he dumps her on the plane."

"Oh, yeah. Right."

"Well, sorry, Sam. I'm not getting on the plane."

Sam's chest tightened a little. "Excuse me?"

"No brush-off."

"I don't know what you're talking about, Nicky, but —"

"Then let me make it real clear, boss. You and I are not through seeing each other. We're college chums. I didn't hold much sway in the dorms, if you'll recall. Nobody wanted to room with me, remember? I was the only guy in the dorm with a single. Not that I minded, considering all the jerks we had."

Things were starting to get seriously bent. Sam considered just hanging up but figured that would only lead to more calls, more emails. He had to settle this now.

"I don't choose to see you, Nicky, okay? That's that."

"You didn't hear me, did you, boss? You really didn't hear me. See, that's been your problem all along. You didn't hear me back in the old dorm, either. You were into yourself. You still are."

"I'm going to say good-bye now, Nicky. I wish you well, I —"

"Linda okay with that?"

"What?"

"Linda. Your wife, remember? And Heather, and little Max?"

Sam sat up ramrod straight in his chair. "You tell me exactly what you're saying."

"A fine Christian family, right, Sam? Pillars of the community and all that."

"Listen —"

"You listen. What would it do to your little family unit if they found out about that thing? That little item from back at the old alma mater? I bet you haven't told Linda about it."

"There's nothing to tell."

"I think there is."

"I'm hanging up." But he held for just a second more.

"I'm talking about your child, Sam. The one your girlfriend had. The one who's alive and well and living in good old Southern California. Did you tell Linda about the kid, Sam?"

Sam was speechless, numb.

"I didn't think so," Nicky Oberlin said.

2.

"Your dad is a little out there," Roz said, lighting a cigarette.

"He means well," Heather said.

"You want one?" Roz held out the pack of Camels. Roz smoked the unfiltered kind. She didn't want any filters in her life, of any kind. Heather shook her head.

"He just doesn't get it," Heather said.

They were sitting in the backyard of Roz's house, late morning. Roz lived with her mother in a house that backed up to the 118 freeway. Exhaust was the neighborhood perfume.

"So you in for the whole deal?" Roz asked.

"Yeah."

"We go play the Cobalt tomorrow."

"We ready for that?"

"We will maim them." Roz took another puff.

Heather said nothing. Roz was the drummer and organizer of the band. Heather sang lead and wrote most of the material. Buck and Raymond were guitar and bass. Screech Monk was only one good set away from a record deal. So went the dream.

Heather fought back tears.

"What's wrong, dude?" Roz asked.

"Everything sucks."

"Of course it does."

"I hate it."

"Use it. Write songs."

"What am I gonna do? I can't stay here forever. I have to get a place or something."

"What about school?"

"I'm not going back."

"You gonna get a job?"

"I guess."

"Or maybe we get a contract, huh? Hit it big."

"Sure."

"Think we can?"

"Why not? We're good." Pause. "Aren't we?" They *had* to be good, because singing was the only thing she cared about and knew her dad didn't approve of. They had to be good, because she had to show him she could make it. Had to prove that his way, his all-American tunnel vision was not something he could push on her.

She knew it hurt him. She didn't want him hurt. But he was like a rock you couldn't talk to when it came to certain things. They needed time away from each other.

Maybe she'd stick around long enough to see how Screech Monk did at the Cobalt. If nothing happened, she could always duck out of everything forever, out of life and the pain of it. Her family'd be better off without her existence.

3.

Steel clamps squeezed Sam's brain as he sat alone in the Chinese restaurant, the place Nicky had selected for their meeting.

One clamp was Heather. The other was what Nicky Oberlin had just laid on him.

Sam's child. His mistake. His shame.

How had Nicky found out? Sam had buried this secret long ago, even though jabs of inner pain would recur periodically, like an unwanted guest pounding on the door. He'd try to ignore them and usually they would go away. But every now and then the pounding got louder.

He once asked his pastor about this, shortly after becoming a Christian. Didn't Christ take away all that? Wasn't he forgiven? Weren't his sins washed away?

Yes, Pastor Lyle explained, but there are always consequences for sin, and one of those is the stain. We are forgiven, yes, but our souls are affected. Sometimes Satan likes to bring the past to mind, to keep us down.

Now, prompted afresh by what Nicky had threatened, Sam couldn't help thinking back to what he'd done.

Her name was Mary and he'd met her at a party in Isla Vista during his freshman year. It was a typical Isla Vista party with a couple kegs and a generous sharing of bongs. Sam was on the scope that night, trolling for a date, having broken up a few weeks ago with another girl.

His memory of the party was fuzzed by the brain cloud he'd created in himself that night with the combination of items he ingested. Was Nicky even there? He couldn't remember that, because he'd not thought of Nicky at all since leaving the dorm.

But he did remember Mary.

She was a good-looking blonde, slight in a way that made him think of Tinker Bell. They did that mutual looking across the room at each other. In the overstuffed apartment, the stereo was blaring Beach Boys and Elton and Chicago and Stones. People were gyrating in what some would call dance, but Mary was standing by the wall, looking lost.

Sam made a beeline.

"How you doin'?" His well-thought-out opening line.

"I'm looking for someone," she said.

"Here I am."

That made her smile.

"Sam Trask." He shook her hand.

"Mary Delano."

"From?"

"Austin."

"Texas?"

"You're sharp."

He liked her instantly. At least he thought he did, sotted as he was. They spent the next two hours talking, dancing, walking to Del Playa to look at the ocean and the sky. They ended up back at her dorm. Her roommate was gone for the weekend. They had the room all to themselves.

And so began a two-week romance, cut off by Sam when Mary started to get a little too serious. He put off the inevitable talk as long as he could, but eventually it had to be done. Mary did not take it well. At last it was over.

But it wasn't.

It was during a history lecture — Professor Marston on the Peloponnesian War, he would never forget — that Mary motioned for him to come outside the lecture hall.

"I'm pregnant," she said without a moment's hesitation.

In the Chinese restaurant, Sam rubbed his eyes at the memory, seeing Mary's tormented face, remembering the guilt. Now it was all coming back at him, courtesy of —

"Hey, buddy!"

Nicky Oberlin was standing at his elbow, smiling down at him.

4.

"This is it," Sam said. "You're not going to contact me anymore."

"You want some orange chicken? This

84

place has orange chicken to die for, my friend."

"I'm not your friend, okay? That's obvious."

Nicky slid into the booth like some long-lost relative. "I think you're misreading this whole thing, Sammy."

"Misreading? You threaten to tell my wife something from my past? And by the way, she would support me."

"Sure, she would. She's a great lady."

Sam felt a current shoot through his body. "You don't even know her."

"I know so much more than I used to." Nicky leaned over the table. "You sure about the orange chicken? Because —"

"What do you want from me?"

"Friendship, Sammy."

"Don't call me Sammy."

"A sort of you scratch my back, I scratch yours sort of thing."

"I told you, that's not going to happen. I don't want to have anything to do with you, especially after you threaten me."

"Threat? The sharing of information? That's the new currency, Sammy — Sam."

Nothing could sway this guy. It was like Nicky was on another channel. Sam had been reading a lot lately about the negative side of the information techno-explosion.

Studies documented the definite harm done by too much time with computers, games, iPods, whatever. They isolated people, kept them from the counterbalance of family and community.

And if a person was a loner to begin with — like Nicky appeared to be — the results could be a skewed mind that cooked bizarre thoughts.

"Nicky, let me ask you something."

Nicky shrugged.

"You have any family, anyone close?"

"That's very nice of you to ask, Sam. Thank you very much. But I'd rather talk about your family, Sam."

Undeterred, Sam kept his voice even. "What about a church family? You have a church, Nicky?"

In Nicky's eyes Sam saw the slightest flicker of something coiled and hot.

"Not a churchgoer, Sammy. I prefer to make my way on my own."

"That doesn't work."

"And you know all about what works, don't you? You have the perfect life, am I right?"

"Nothing's perfect. But I do have a family, and I have a faith I hang onto. My church is very important to me."

"What church is that again, Sam? The one

where the preacher talked at you?"

"Solid Rock Community, here in the valley —" Sam stopped on the verge of an invitation. What would Jesus do? Invite. Would he? Would he invite a peculiar guy who made veiled threats? What better action? Church was where transformation happened. It had happened to Sam, so it could happen to anyone.

Yet . . . Nicky gave off seriously creepy vibes. What if he actually said, *Sure, I'll come. Can I sit with you and your family?* Sam found the thought repellant and knew at once his faith was weak.

Invite him anyway.

Sam said nothing.

"Not that I'm not open-minded," Nicky said, "but religion just doesn't do it for me. It's all based on fear, and I think fear's for wimps."

"Fear?"

"Yeah, haven't you read Bertrand Russell? Oh no, you didn't major in philosophy. You were poli-sci."

Was there anything about college this guy didn't remember?

"It's clear that religion started with fear. Early man was afraid of the lightning and thunder, of the storms and the winds. What caused it? Must be some powerful god out there in the sky. All fear, right?"

"That's what you philosophy majors would call a non sequitur." Nicky flinched and Sam congratulated himself on a point scored. "Fear may indeed be a motivator to seek God, but it doesn't mean the reality of God is proven false."

Flashing a smile Nicky said, "By golly, you *are* a lawyer, aren't you?"

"Speaking of which, I've got to get back to the office. I think you need help, Nicky, and I would just encourage you to keep an open mind about God, and —"

"Sam, do I look unreasonable to you?"

"I wish you all the best." Sam stood up, hoping this was all finally going to be behind him. He offered his hand to Nicky.

Nicky just looked at it. "You're going to be sorry."

Sam froze, his hand hanging stupidly in the air.

Then Nicky grabbed Sam's hand and smiled. "Because the orange chicken is really, really good here."

Sam allowed himself a nervous laugh.

"Later," Nicky said, then let go of Sam's hand.

5.

"Linda, there's something I need to talk to you about."

The smell of freshly cut onions filled the kitchen. Linda looked up from the cutting board, knife in hand. "So talk."

"I need your undivided attention."

She turned to him. "What's wrong? What's going on?"

"Hold it. There's nothing wrong." He hoped. "Can we just go into the living room for a minute?"

"You want dinner? I've got sauce simmering. I don't want it to burn."

"Just a couple of minutes." He hoped again, heading into the living room. His throat was already constricting. This was going to be harder than he thought.

"So?" Linda was behind him.

"Let's sit."

"This is starting to sound serious."

"Linda, you remember when we got married, and —"

"Yes, I was there."

"— a week before the wedding I asked you if you had any doubts?"

"I remember. And I didn't."

"And I asked you once more if there was anything you wanted to know about my past."

Linda looked at her hands. "I do remember that. I asked you the same thing."

"We decided we weren't going to go into it. We both know we had other people in our lives before we met each other. And we were very different then. We were completely worldly."

"So what's this mean? You have some dark secret you have to tell me now?"

"Good guess."

She gave him a long, hard look. "Do I need to know this?"

Sam nodded.

"Why now?"

"It's come up," Sam said.

"What's come up?"

Taking a deep breath, Sam began. "When I was a freshman I got involved with a girl. And she got pregnant."

Linda didn't move.

"I offered to marry her, which was kind of old-fashioned even back then. I didn't even consider asking her to have an abortion. She didn't want one either. She was willing to marry me. But her father came out from Texas and talked her out of it. He was a big, tough guy. I thought he was going to rip my head off. He took his daughter back home with him. Later I got some papers from a lawyer. I gave up all rights to the

90

baby. She waived child support. And that's the last I ever heard."

For a long moment Linda was silent, looking away. Not a good sign. When he upset her, hurt her feelings with an untoward comment, she would look away from him, slightly and quietly. And it would take a lot of apologizing to set things straight.

He decided to start. "I'm sorry I didn't tell you this before, but we said we wouldn't."

"Yeah, little things," Linda said, her eyes still averted. "But this." She shook her head.

"This isn't any different. It's a part of my past I really regret. I thought about telling you early on, but I just kept putting it off, and finally it seemed like the best thing was to let it go."

"Until now."

"Yes, until now."

"Why?"

"It just —" He stopped himself as he was about to go on a roundabout linguistic tangent, a lawyerly avoidance. He thought better of it. "A guy I used to know back in college, his name's Nicky Oberlin, he got in touch with me."

"How?"

"He just did. Tracked me through the Internet. Said he wanted to get together with

91

me. I ignored him, but he kept emailing. Finally I met with him."

"When was this?"

"I don't know, a week ago maybe."

"And you didn't bother to tell me?"

"It didn't occur to me that there was anything to tell."

"Oh, not much."

"Linda, you're being a little unfair, aren't you?"

"Where are they?"

"Who?"

"Your former lover and child."

Sam rubbed the back of his neck. "I have no idea. Oberlin tracked her down and said they're living in Southern Cal."

"You've thought about them a lot, haven't you?"

Her barb stung. "No."

"Come on."

"What do you want me to say? That I stay up nights thinking of what might have been?"

"Do you?"

"No!"

Linda opened her mouth halfway, but words seemed to stick behind her teeth. She held like that for a moment, then buried her head in her hands.

That's when Sam saw the smoke in the

kitchen signaling an early end to dinner.

6.

Sam opened his eyes. His head was humming.

The digital clock read 3:43 a.m.

He knew he would not be sleeping anytime soon.

Usually he'd jolt awake the night before a trial. This felt different, like he was the conductor of not just one runaway train, but several. He was simultaneously outside the trains and inside, and he could only ride in one for a few moments before shooting to another. He couldn't get his hands on any controls.

His chest tightened.

All right, dude, don't have a heart attack.

Slipping out of bed, he heard Linda murmur his name. "Go back to sleep," he whispered. They'd managed to call enough of a truce to go to bed. But much more would have to be said. Sam was not looking forward to that.

He'd been unfair to Linda. He hated being unfair, because it went against the entire grain of his life. Law was about fairness, ultimately. *Fundamental fairness* was the legal term of art.

Count your blessings, he reminded himself. Meeting Linda had been his greatest blessing, and he knew it. They'd met at a little coffee house in North Hollywood. Sam was pursuing his dream of being an under-appreciated poet, and succeeding. Even then he knew he'd be going back to school someday. He just wanted to give the artist thing a flier.

He lived in a studio apartment off Vineland and supported himself waiting tables at a steak house in Toluca Lake. During the day he wrote his poetry, sending it off to underground mags and getting three free issues when something got published.

And he did readings at local venues. The Ginkgo Leaf was a place that gave home-grown poets a place to do the open-mic thing. Sam showed up one night with a couple of poems and a flask of bourbon. His writing fantasy included bouts of hard drinking. Later he'd call it his Dylan Thomas phase, in reference to the Welsh poet who died drunk at age thirty-nine.

It was while he was waiting his turn, and taking a nip, that Linda first spoke to him.

"That won't bring better words," she said.

She was holding a tray with coffee cups and cocking her head at him. It was a head with dancing hazel eyes and a cascade of long flaxen hair. She was not one of the

94

reed-thin soap actresses that sprouted like ragweed in Los Angeles asphalt. He liked that. Her look was at once more intelligent and knowing than the glimmer-eyed expressions of the actresses in waiting.

"Booze has a long history with writers." Sam winked. "Greases the wheels."

Linda — he would learn her name two nights later — shook her head. "That's a joke. Kerouac ruined himself. Dylan Thomas. Need I mention Capote?"

She knew her stuff. Fascinating. "You think Kerouac would have been Kerouac without the booze?"

"Kerouac was a tragic figure whose lifestyle is romanticized by the college sophomore. In truth, the booze killed his writing and then him."

"Where you getting all this?"

"Thinking about it. Seeing guys come in here juiced and reading their stuff and botching it and thinking they're great. Don't you do it."

"Thanks for the career advice." Sam was starting to get annoyed. He could map his own path to literary oblivion, thank you very much and see you later.

"Just a word to the wise," she said.

Sam figured he could do without her wisdom and said nothing more. Linda slipped away, but Sam kept checking on her throughout the evening. She had an athletic grace around the tables, self-possession. This only annoyed him more and he kept sipping bourbon as if to spite her until it was time for him to read. Botching it! He'd show her what real poetry was made of.

He botched it. He knew as soon as he started reading that he had overdone the drink. He'd gotten to the point where he could handle quite a bit, but in his arrogance he'd taken the proverbial one too many. There is a lag time between drink and drunkenness, just enough time for a pig-headed poet to make his way to the microphone, fumbling for his poems.

He lost his place several times. He tried to laugh it off. The audience was not amused.

When he staggered off the stage he found there was no back way out. He had to leave by the front door, so the patrons could look at him all the way. The one face he didn't want to see was hers. But she was there at the bar, facing him full-on. Through his bloodshot eyes he thought he saw more pity than scorn in her look.

He had to work the next night, pushing steaks to the studio crowd and old Burbank money. The night after he got someone to cover his shift so he could go back to the

Ginkgo Leaf and find the waitress and spoon a mouthful of crow in her presence.

She was returning a tray to the bar when he stepped in front of her. She looked startled.

"You were right," he said.

"Excuse me?"

"About drinking and poetry."

"Ah."

"So I'd like to pay you for the advice."

"I don't want any —"

"By taking you to dinner."

She smiled and her eyes crinkled at the corners. "What if I have a boyfriend?"

"Do you?"

She didn't. They went out the next Saturday. Sam chose a restaurant by the ocean on Pacific Coast Highway. He couldn't really afford it, but he was determined to pull out all the stops. There was something special about this woman.

Linda had grown up in Acton, a little burg about thirty miles east of Los Angeles proper, a desert town where people still lived close to the land. Sam's impression of the place was that the people there were strong and guileless, hanging on to a bit of the Old West ethic. That was Linda, he decided.

A month later he asked her to marry him.

She gave him a polite no. He asked her every week after that, accompanied by flowers — for which he spent half his food money. Persistence paid off. After five weeks she said yes, and he could eat again.

He gave up poetry as a profession. He felt the first real stirrings of true adult responsibility. He wanted to make a life for his wife. He wanted to make her proud.

He took the LSAT and aced it, got accepted at UCLA Law. Graduated top ten percent, went to work for the US attorney's office downtown.

By then Heather had come along, and so had Lew Newman, with a proposal to open up a two-man firm. Sam had met Lew, a Brooklyn DA, on a big RICO case involving both coasts. The two hit it off and kept in touch.

And through it all, Linda stood by him, did charity work, mothered Heather and Max.

The firm of Newman & Trask started taking off. Sure, Sam had to work long hours, but there were benefits. He and Linda bought a nice big house in Encino, up in the hills.

It was the all-American dream.

Then Linda's mother died in a car accident on Balboa Boulevard. A drag-racing kid hit her head-on. Both died instantly.

Linda went into a deep depression. It was not like her, she of the sunny optimism. Sam was concerned and almost ordered her to seek a doctor's help.

Linda found Christ instead.

Sam couldn't argue about the change. Linda started attending a small Bible study at her friend Melanie's house. One night — as Linda told him later — she was filled with what she called the Holy Spirit, calling to her, and she made her confession of Christ. The Bible study leader took her out to Melanie's swimming pool and baptized her.

All of it was a whirlwind of change in Linda, and Sam went along with it, because the depression was gone. Now he had a wife who was "on fire."

She tried to get Sam to follow along. He resisted.

He kept resisting until the night he almost hit her and had to face his own demons, and Pastor Lyle showed him the only way to defeat them was through Christ.

And life was going to be perfect after that.

Now, lying in bed, he thought of all the ways life was not perfect, and how they seemed connected to this odd blast from the past named Nicky Oberlin. He couldn't live in fear of odd people because the world was stuffed with them. But there was more to this Oberlin. He couldn't quite put his finger on it. He knew he'd be hearing from Nicky again, and he dreaded it.

The dread kept him from sleep.

7.

Sam took a shower and shaved in the downstairs bathroom, silently fetched his clothes from the bedroom, and got dressed. Then he made a pot of coffee for Linda. He left her a note saying he loved her and set it next to the coffee. Linda was still in bed when he left the house.

Sam stopped at Starbucks and took three shots in a latte. Overload, yes, but he had to be sharp this morning. Lew was counting on him. This was going to be the most important meeting with the clients yet. A rare Saturday meeting, because Allen Appleby wanted no distractions.

And what Allen Appleby wanted, he got.

Sam met Lew at the office, and they drove downtown in Lew's silver Porsche. A little class, even though the clients wouldn't see it in the bowels of the parking garage. Lew's theory was if you look good you've won half the battle. You always went in with a little more confidence.

The other half of the battle was knowing

what you were talking about, had it dead-on, and today that burden fell on Sam.

"You okay?" Lew said after they parked.

No, he wasn't. "Fine."

"You seem a little tired."

"Just a little."

"What's up?"

"Nothing's up." The edge in Sam's voice might have scratched paint. "Sorry, I didn't get a whole lot of sleep last night."

"You feel ready?"

"Yes, I'm ready. Don't worry."

But Sam had a small fist in his gut as they took the elevator to the fortieth floor of the Taylor Building. The fist punched a couple of times as they were ushered into Allen Appleby's office.

Appleby greeted them with an athletic handshake. The FulCo CEO was tall, gray-haired, and sharply suited in pinstripes. His office was all leather and teak, and large enough for a half-court basketball game. Large enough, too, to contain the massive ego of Stuart Hoch, FulCo's in-house counsel. Hoch was around Sam's age, prematurely bald, and seemed permanently sour about it. His response to Sam and Lew had always been on the tepid side.

Sam figured that was because Appleby had personally chosen Lew and Sam over

Hoch's objection. Appleby played golf with Lew's uncle, Finch Roberts, which is what sealed the deal. There really was something to the who-you-know routine. It was the mortar of professional relationships in LA.

"Let's get to it," Appleby said. He was a get-to-it kind of guy, a former Ford executive who made the cover of *Business Week* twice in the same year, once when he moved over to the top spot at FulCo.

They all sat around the shiny conference table. Even before Sam had settled into a chair, Hoch said, "So do we have standing or not?"

So that was the way it was going to be. Hoch would throw fastballs, and Lew was counting on Sam to hit them out of the park, or at least solidly up the middle.

Sam took an immediate swing. "Yes. Not a problem."

Hoch did not change his skeptical expression. FulCo was suing the federal government for breach of contract, for damages in excess of $800 million. The Feds had entered into an agreement with a major oil company for the purchase of low-sulfur fuel oil. Various subsidiaries of the oil company, relying on the contract, committed themselves to acquiring and transporting large quantities of crude. A year later, FulCo purchased the government contract from the first oil company.

The government then terminated its purchases of LSFO. The various subsidiaries had to sell their crude elsewhere, at a loss.

Sam and Lew were hired to file a breach of contract lawsuit on behalf of FulCo. But the government filed a motion for summary judgment under Rule 56 of the Federal Rules of Civil Procedure, challenging FulCo's legal standing to bring a lawsuit. The Feds were arguing that the subsidiaries of the oil company were the real parties in interest, since they were the ones with the actual damages.

If the government were to win at this stage, and get upheld on appeal, it would mean FulCo would get zip, zero.

That's why Sam had spent two weeks researching the standing issue. And he was sure of his answer. As sure as an advocate whose partnership was looking at a potential payday of around $300 million.

"Let me explain." Sam cleared his throat.

And promptly forgot everything he was supposed to say.

Sam was four when he realized his father was the biggest man in the world. He liked it that his father was so big. The man could lift him with one arm and hold him that way. As Sam grew, his father still stayed big in his eyes. And never bigger than when Sam faced one disappointment or other.

Like the time Sam freaked out on an elementary school stage when he was supposed to give a speech during a Thanksgiving play. He forgot the speech, couldn't even get started. The other kids started to laugh, especially the gap-toothed doofus, Jeffie Bogosian, known as "Booger" Bogosian to most of the kids.

Seeing Booger's face in farcical paroxysm was the last straw, and Sam screamed, "Shut up!" and ran off the stage.

Later, his dad sat him down and without any anger told him that a man didn't let things like that get to him. Everybody gets nervous or scared from time to time, and you suck it up and wait for the feeling to pass.

Thinking of Dad saved Sam this time. He very easily could have considered Stuart Hoch the latest incarnation of Booger Bogosian. Especially when Hoch sniffed, "Yes, please tell us."

Sam tried to ignore Hoch's tone, but it annoyed him. This whole setup annoyed him. It was like being called into the principal's office. All this could have been done with a memo. Yet Appleby had insisted on a face-to-face, and on a Saturday yet.

Appleby drummed his fingers on the table. Sam rifled through the files in his briefcase.

And realized, to his horror, that the memo was not there.

He'd left it in the study, intending to give it a once-over before the meeting. But in his sleepy state he'd forgotten it.

He sat up.

"Well, the general rule is that the duties arising out of a contract are due only to those with whom the contract is made." His voice sounded like a recording.

"That's black-letter," Hoch said, casting a glance at Appleby. "We all know that."

The slight angered Sam, firing up his adrenaline pump. Good. He could use the jolt. "I just want to make sure Mr. Appleby and you get the whole picture. Now if you'll hang in there, I'll explain the two theories that give us standing."

It was all coming back into focus.

"Two theories?" Hoch said. "I thought there was only alter ego."

"There's also integrated operation, so we're covered two ways. And that's a good thing."

Now Appleby looked interested. "Explain."

"There are two things we need to establish," Sam said as facts and law poured into place. "First is privity of contract. Second is foreseeability."

"Without the mumbo jumbo," Appleby said.

"Privity of contract is a legal term. It means a third party isn't entitled to the benefits of, or isn't bound by, a contract to which it is not an original party. But there are several cases, most recently out of the Sixth Circuit, which apply similar facts as we have to establish privity. We'll prevail on that."

"What about foreseeability?" Hoch said.

"I was just getting to that. The government argues that they could not have reasonably foreseen that the original party to the contract would have entered into all these subsidiary agreements, forming in effect an integrated operation. That may have been a valid claim ten years ago. But I found three cases in three different circuits, all of which predate the contract, which greatly expand the definition of an integrated operation. These cases thus gave constructive notice to the government for the kind of operation we took over."

Sam saw Appleby nod twice. "Sounds solid, but I'm no lawyer. I just want to know, bottom line, if we're going to get to court and get our money."

"We are," Sam said. Even though he couldn't, in reality, be sure how a single judge might rule on the government's motion, Appleby was not a man who liked to hear nuance.

"Good. Issue two. I'm getting hammered in the press. They've got me in with all those scofflaw CEOs. I've retained an image consultant and I want you guys to work with her, because you're going to be talking to reporters, I'm sure."

Sam didn't like that idea. He didn't want to talk to any reporters. He just wanted to do the work and stay under the radar.

"Fine," Lew said for both of them. "We'll do whatever it takes."

"Then why extend this meeting any longer?" Appleby stood. "I can still get in eighteen holes."

Hoch pulled Sam aside before he left the office. "You better be right about this."

Sam wanted to knot Hoch's tie for him, extra tight. "That's what you're paying us for, isn't it?"

Hoch looked like he wanted to do the same thing with Sam's tie. Not a good day for clothing, Sam decided, or in-house lawyers.

"We pay to get a win," Hoch said. "Make it happen."

9.

On the drive back to the office Sam said, "We're lawyers, not talking heads. I don't want to deal with this media person."

"What's the big deal?" Lew said.

"It's a distraction. Right now I don't need any more distractions in my life."

"Come on, what's it going to hurt? We go out to a nice dinner on Appleby's dime, yak it up a little, it's nothing."

"It's time. And it's not what we do."

"Hey, this is the media age, Mr. Trask. Everybody's got to do it. And when our biggest client to date tells us that's what he wants, we give it to him. I don't understand, Sam, you —"

"I'm sorry, Lew. Like I said, it's been a little distracting. Heather's going through her deal, and that's not making life more pleasant." Sam decided to hold off on telling Lew about Nicky Oberlin. No use worrying his partner too much.

"I hear you, pal," Lew said. "Girls especially, am I right?"

"I grew up with two older brothers, so it's been a real education."

"The more you know about women, the less you know about women."

"You're a real philosopher, Lew."

"Call me Lewistotle."

Lewistotle was right about women. But Sam determined he would do something radical, something he probably should have done a long time ago.

Something frightening.

He would try to understand Heather's music.

But first he would clear the air with Linda. A cool fog had descended on the home since the revelation about his out-of-wedlock child.

Nicky had done it. Managed to inject poison into his marriage. It wasn't fatal, but it was certainly a presence, the proverbial elephant in the room.

He stopped at Conroy's for some flowers. He loved the can't-miss flexibility of flowers. Good for wooing when young, apologizing when middle-aged, and decorating when you cashed in your chips. Flowers did it all, cradle to grave.

Selecting a multicolored collection that

included lilies and gerberas, Sam picked one of the nicer cards in the rack. Being a guy, Sam reflected, he usually spent as much time on a card as he did checking the rear-view mirror for traffic. Not this time. This one was for Linda, the woman he loved. More deeply, he realized, each time he did something clunky to their marriage.

He even did the hide-the-flowers-behind-the-back routine at the front door, ringing the bell. When Linda answered he smiled, then brought them out with a flourish.

They worked their magic.

"Beautiful," she said.

"Look at the card." He was particularly proud of the card.

Linda took the card out of the flowers and read it. Sam had written, *My one and only, always.*

Her eyes misting, Linda said, "A nice card."

Sam put his arms around her, then walked her inside. No need for words. They were enfolded in the silent security of twenty-two years together.

Inside, as Linda put the flowers in a vase, Sam told her about his idea of going to hear Heather's band.

"Is that crazy?" he asked.

"I think it's a great first step." Linda set

the flowers in the greenhouse window of the kitchen. The afternoon sun was starting to turn orange as it fell behind the Santa Monica mountains.

"You want to come with me?"

"I think both of us there would freak her out. Besides, I have to pick up Max at seven thirty."

"Where's Max again?"

"With his friend Todd."

"So that means I have to go to this place all by myself?"

"Why don't you just slip in the back a little after eight o'clock? And try not to look too old."

"Shall I shave my head before I go?"

"Heather would love that," Linda said. "Why don't you?"

FIVE

1.

The Cobalt Café was a venue for new bands along the Sherman Way corridor in Canoga Park. There was an alien crowd spilling out into the night street when Sam arrived. Young people, multichromatic in clothing, with piercings and heavy makeup. All smoking and trying to out-sullen one another.

Sam ached for them. They were the flotsam and jetsam of the failed social experiment of the last thirty years, the one that put a low priority on family. The culture of divorce, coupled with the decline of public schools and the endless temptations and pressures on kids, ended up with youth adrift. An ocean of lostness in the urban jungle.

But had he done all he could to keep Heather out of this despair? He and Linda had tried to get her involved with church. Didn't take. They tried to get her to go to private school, but she wanted to stay with her friends. Maybe that's when he should have insisted, drawn a line.

The only certain thing was that Heather was now part of the lost, and he had no idea what compass he could use to find her.

Maybe tonight would be a start.

He was aware of some looks through the smoky haze, but he had not worn his lawyer outfit. He had on jeans and a red knit shirt, covered by a brown leather jacket. Not exactly Goth, but not Donald Trump, either.

Inside it didn't really matter, because the place was dark as desert night. Purple lighting gave the least semblance of direction. Tables were jammed with people drinking and trying to shout over the piped music, though its resemblance to any music Sam might have appreciated was purely accidental.

"You wanna sit down?" said a voice from the darkness.

Sam saw what he thought was a young woman, though at this point he was not going to place any bets. Now he had to figure out why she asked.

"I'm here for the show," he said.

"So you wanna sit down or what?"

"Yes, I think I would."

"Ten dollars gets you a seat and a drink."

"Fine."

"Come on."

She led him through the shadows to a small round table with four chairs, three of them occupied. Sam took the empty chair with scarcely a glance from the three specters in the others.

"Whattaya want to drink?" his guide asked.

"Coke."

"What?"

"Coke!"

"Cool!"

She disappeared into the dark forest. Sam wondered how well they could check IDs in this place. They'd have to be on it, because a lot of the audience looked on the edge of twenty-one, give or take. Heather could perform under the musician's exception, a construct of California law that allowed places that served alcohol to showcase talent under drinking age.

By the time his server got back — it seemed like an hour — the first band was starting on the little stage. The noise they produced was as loud as anything Sam had ever heard, twin industrial trash compactors on either side of his head. It was everything he could do not to bolt.

But he was here. For Heather. He'd stay.

He sipped his Coke, which was more melted ice than cola, and tried to engage the music, find something to appreciate. He concluded he was totally out of it, and he might as well come to terms with that fact.

Another band eventually took the stage. When they began their set Sam started to think it would be preferable to be an Egyptian mummy — having his brains sucked out through his nose — than hear any more of this music. But through a clever use of head position, he leaned against his hand and managed to cut the noise down a little.

He ordered another Coke.

"Good stuff!" someone said.

Sam turned toward the shadow at the next table. Some guy in shades and a fedora was giving him a thumbs-up. Sam had barely heard the voice, which was shouted right over the music.

Sam nodded halfheartedly, and noticed a ponytail at the base of the fedora. Wasn't that fashion statement old school? What a laugh. Sam was positively eighteenth century here. He was an oxcart among Hummers.

The current band, featuring two scantily clad young women — *Please don't let Heather dress like that* — and two rail-thin, shirtless young men, finished after two songs. Sam had failed to pick up many of the words, except the four-letter ones.

And then it was announced that the next band would be Screech Monk. That was Heather's.

Sam's stomach took a turn on a spit.

He wanted her to do well. He wanted her out of here. He wanted his daughter to be happy, but not this way. Yet he wanted Heather to know the joy of accomplishment on her own terms.

He didn't know what he wanted.

The Coke settled his stomach a little. When the band came out, the barbeque in his gut flamed again.

Heather was dressed to accentuate her positives, though thankfully not as much as her friend Roz. This couldn't end well. This was Courtney Love revisited. His daughter was going to become a heroin addict.

Screech Monk broke into sound, loud as all the others. Heather was the only one not playing an instrument. She had the microphone. Lead singer.

Sam's palms were sweating.

Heather started to sing.

Beautifully.

She had a clear, strong, absolutely beguiling voice. Sam could even make out some of the words, and thankfully they were not offensive at all. Heather was singing about lost love. It was to a hard beat, not exactly Beach Boys. But he enjoyed it.

His daughter really could sing. Sam had no idea she could belt out a song like this.

Maybe she really did have a future.

"Great stuff there!" It was fedora man again, but this time Sam smiled and nodded vigorously.

"My daughter!" he shouted.

Fedora gave him another thumbs-up. "I'm in the business, I know whereof I speak."

Peace flickered inside Sam then. Maybe this would really all turn out okay. God was in control, right? That's what the bottom line was supposed to be. Maybe God was sending him a little message, a whisper of grace.

He'd take it.

2.

Sam told the friendly bouncer at the stage door that he was the father of Screech Monk's lead singer.

The bouncer, with shaved head and arms the size of laundry bags, told Sam to wait. Sam was not going to argue.

A moment later the bouncer motioned him through the door. Sam entered a corridor, dimly lit, and followed the man to a backstage alcove where Heather was waiting.

"I can't believe you're here." Her voice held a twinge of rebuke.

"I wanted to hear you."

"Why didn't you tell me?"

"I didn't want you to get nervous. And we haven't exactly been together on things lately."

Another band started up. Heather had to raise her voice. "So, you ready to tell me I'm heading to hell or something?"

That was a jab to the heart. "Oh, honey, no. I wanted to tell you I thought you sang beautifully."

"You're kidding, right?"

"No! You have a great voice. I mean, really great."

She looked stunned. "Wow. Thanks."

"I just wanted you to know that."

"What about the music?"

"Not my cup of Ovaltine, as you know."
"Yeah."

"But the words. You wrote that song?"
She nodded.

"Fantastic. You really have a talent."

"I still can't believe you came —"

Roz burst into the corridor. "Hey, Heather, you —" She stopped, looking at Sam. "Oh, hi."

Stay cool, boy. "Hello, Roz. I just came to say I thought you guys did great."

"No way."

"Way," Sam said. "I mean it."

"Thanks," Roz said. "I mean, thanks a lot."

The band on stage seemed to have amped up. Sam sensed someone behind him. It was the guy in the fedora, with the bouncer next to him.

"Hey," Fedora shouted to the girls. "Loved your set!"

"Thanks," Roz said, barely audible.

"So you got any contracts? Prospects?"

Roz paused, then shook her head. Sam wanted to pipe in, have the guy deal directly with him, but he held back. This was Heather's moment, and Roz's. He could give them plenty of free advice later. And no doubt would, whether they wanted to hear it or not.

Fedora shouted, "My name's Lundquist. Maybe we should talk." He turned to Sam. "Pop must be real proud of you."

Sam said, "I am."

"You sing?" Lundquist said.

Sam put his hand to his ear. "How's that?"

"Sing! You!"

"In the shower," Sam said.

"Honest truth," Lindquist said, raising his

right hand as if to swear. "I heard Dylan sing in the shower once. Worst sound you ever heard." He smiled, turned to Heather. "You guys have a website?"

She nodded.

"We'll be in touch. Again, great set."

He and the bouncer left.

Heather looked at Roz. "What do you think?"

"Who knows?"

Sam couldn't help it. "Just don't sign anything until I have —"

"Dad —"

"You don't have a lawyer for a dad for nothing. You coming home soon?"

"I'll probably stay at Roz's tonight. We want to celebrate a little."

Roz nodded.

"It's late," Sam said.

"Dad —"

"All right. But call tomorrow, will you? I get worried."

She put her hand on his cheek. "Ah, Pop, when are you gonna stop worrying about your lovely daughter?"

3.

Never.

He would never stop worrying, Sam realized as he made for his car. You're a father, it's a lifetime duty. What was the old saying? A son is a son till he marries a wife. A daughter's a daughter for the rest of your life.

He remembered the night when she was five and woke up screaming. She'd had a nightmare and he picked her up and held her and brought her into the family room. He sat in the recliner with her nestled on him and stayed there until she fell asleep. And knew then that he would do anything to protect this life. He knew he would give his own if it came to that, without any hesitation or question.

Life was sweet and good then. A daughter at five. That was the age she learned to skip. It was one of the happiest events of her childhood. Heather loved to skip when she was happy, when they went to Disneyland or just to 31 Flavors for ice cream. Always skipping.

When did she stop? It had been years, long years, since she'd done it.

Yes, she was older now, and skipping was a childhood thing. But even so, as he unlocked his car, Sam knew one thing would remain with him always. He'd protect his daughter, even if it meant his own life.

Six

1.

The next week passed in a pleasant blur. Sam got some good work done on FulCo and Harper. Heather was acting civil, even friendly at times.

But best of all, Nicky Oberlin hadn't called or emailed again. Maybe his mind games were over now. He'd gotten Sam to squirm, to dance, and now Nicky could move on to others in his pitiful pursuits.

By Saturday, Sam finally felt as if he could give some solid time to Max again. Max, who'd sort of been the odd one out in all the flurries involving Heather.

Max had a baseball game at ten, and Sam was going to go. Yes, he had a full Saturday of work to do dismantling the government's motion for summary judgment in FulCo. The law, the old saying went, was a jealous mistress. But Sam was not going to let it bat him around like the baseballs out on the field. Max needed him.

At twelve years of age, Max was in that awkward phase that had a medical term attached to it — sucky. This age was the worst. You get your first inkling that childhood is over forever, and there will be no more dipping back into the warm pool of innocence. You're not ready to look over the fence at adulthood, but you can hear the sounds, and they are sometimes fearful. You know that the people who make it over there, on the other side, are the popular ones, and that's not you.

Sam remembered well his own adolescent angst. He thought he was the most awkward doofus in the school, a guy who liked to watch old movies rather than go out with friends trying to talk a cool man into buying them Boone's Farm apple wine.

Sitting on the hard aluminum of the stands, Sam saw it was Max's turn at bat. Sam steeled himself against the death of a thousand cuts. Or, more accurately, swings. Max had never been the strongest of hitters, and when he struck out Sam felt the pain as deeply as his son. Maybe more.

The pitcher on the other team suddenly seemed the size of King Kong. Linda took Sam's hand, as if she knew exactly what he was thinking.

The first pitch came in high and near Max's chin. Max fell back on his keister.

King Kong smiled.

"Ow!" Linda pulled her hand away.

"Sorry," Sam said, realizing he'd crushed it.

"Relax."

Oh, sure. The next pitch was right down the middle, but Max didn't move the bat at all.

"Be a hitter up there, Maxie," the third-base coach yelled.

Sam wanted to shout, *Swing at it!* But that would have been the worst thing in the world for Max. Sam bit his lip.

Another pitch cut the plate in half. The umpire called strike two.

It was going to be another whiff, Sam was sure. He tried to prepare himself. Max would just have to learn to get more aggressive with the bat. He'd be able to tell him at home, he'd —

Kong went into his windup, and Sam fought not to close his eyes.

And then Max swung. Bat hit ball. Not all of it, though. The contact drove the ball into the ground and became a dribbler up the third-base line.

"Run!" Sam jumped up.

Max was on his horse toward first. The

third baseman had been playing deep and was scampering for the ball. He reached down for it barehanded, trying to make a major league pickup, but bobbled the ball.

Max crossed first. Base hit!

Sam pumped his fist as Max stepped on the bag, beaming. This was what youth sports was supposed to be about. You work, you practice, you get a result, you enjoy it. The perversion of parents driving their kids to win at all costs, the cheating coaches — not to mention the occasional mad dad who assaulted an umpire — had became a national embarrassment.

This was a small inlet of relief off the ocean of recent bad news. *Enjoy it, Sam, drink it in.*

The next batter took his stance, and Sam watched as Max took a tentative lead off first base. He was no steal threat but had an inherent quickness that could get him going at the first crack of bat on ball.

Then Max turned his head, looking at the fence along the first-base line.

What was he doing?

Sam looked at the fence and lost his breath.

Nicky Oberlin was clapping his hands and yelling something at Max.

Bill, the first-base coach, screamed at Max

to get his mind back on the game.

Sitting over on the third-base side, Sam could now hear Nicky's voice over the din of rooting parents.

"Atta boy, Maxie! 'At's the way to hit 'em, boy! You da man!"

Sam took a step down.

"Where you going?" Linda said.

He didn't answer.

2.

Only half aware of what was happening on the field, Sam threaded his way off the bleachers and around the backstop, toward the place where Nicky Oberlin stood.

And what would he do when he got there? He'd think of something, and it would flow naturally off the hot blood pounding in his head. This was so obvious, what Nicky was doing, it would have to be dealt with right here and now.

"Get out of here," Sam said.

Nicky kept looking at the field. "Be ready to go, Maxie."

Sam reached out to Nicky's shoulder and spun him. "I said get out!"

Nicky looked at him with a half smile. "Hey, I'm trying to watch a game here."

"You're a sick man. I don't want you around me or my family, understand?"

"A guy can't come to a baseball game in America anymore?"

"Not the way you're doing it. This has just become a police matter."

"Cops?"

"That's what I said, unless you —"

"And you'll tell them exactly what?"

"You're harassing me and my family."

Nicky shook his head. "And you, a lawyer. What are the witnesses going to say? I'm here, an old friend, pumping up your kid at a game, and you don't like it. Is that your legal standing?"

Hearing Nicky use legalese was disconcerting. He'd no doubt brushed up on just how far he could go with Sam. Which made him all the more dangerous.

A sudden dark wind blew through Sam at that moment. He felt himself capable of anything, of beating this man to a pulp. Pure, unreasoning animal passion.

Then a fleeting voice told him this was not the way, that vengeance belonged to the Lord. But that voice was weak and tinny and disappeared with another look at Nicky Oberlin's smiling face.

"You want to go to the mat on this?" Sam said. "You want to play with the law? I'm telling you I will go all the way on this. I will make sure your life is a living hell if you get anywhere near me or my family again."

"When did you change, Sammy? You used to be such a nice guy."

Sam made a fist at his side. His last fight had been in junior high school, one he lost when Bruce Weber caught him flush on the nose and blood streamed all over his shirt. That was when he decided fistfighting was the stupidest thing human beings could do with each other.

Until now.

"You look tense, Sammy. You should try to relax."

A loud cheer went up from the stands, terminating the confrontation for the moment. Sam looked toward the field in time to see the shortstop scoop up a grounder and throw Max out at second base.

"Now that's a shame, Sammy. Maxie was a little too distracted out there."

A fresh, hot brew of anger boiled up in Sam. If this didn't stop soon —

"You know," Nicky added, "your good-looking wife seems a little distracted too."

That burst it, the last barricade of restraint. Sam's hand shot out to Nicky's neck. He pushed him hard against the chain-link fence.

"If you ever —" Sam's words stuck in his throat, stymied by the sense that he had gone too far.

But he didn't let go.

Then he felt strong hands on his shoulders, pulling him backward, and a voice shouting, "Hey, man, take it easy."

Sam released his grip. Two other men jumped between Sam and Nicky.

"Don't pull that stuff here." One of the men pointed at Sam. "We got kids here."

Sam looked at the stands, saw the faces looking at him. At him! While the other man was saying to Nicky, "Hey, you all right?"

"I think so," Nicky said, acting the victim, rubbing his neck.

The man who had Sam by the shoulders, a large man with an American Chopper T-shirt, said, "Why don't you take off, man?"

"Let me go." Sam felt eight years old and ashamed.

The big man gave him a push away. "Go on, cool off."

3.

"What got into you?" Linda said in the car. Sam was just sitting there in the parking lot. The game was going on and he was in his car as a refuge from shame.

"It was him, Linda. That guy I was telling you about."

"Why did you attack him?"

"He was baiting me!"

"It worked."

"Whose side are you on?"

"You lost control, Sam."

"Thank you." He hated it when Linda brought up his "control issue." He hated it because he knew it was true.

"Isn't that just what he wanted you to do?" Linda said.

"So what if it was? I'm not going to let him —"

"You need to be better than that."

"Please! I'm not ten years old. He made a comment about you."

"What did he say?"

"He made a lewd comment about how good-looking you are."

When Linda didn't answer, he read into it that she was confused or frustrated. So he stayed silent too, not wanting to rip more fabric off their already fraying day.

4.

At home Sam had to face the worst part of the whole thing — explaining the incident to Max.

He'd seen the hurt look on his son's face. There was no greater parental sin than to cause a scene in front of other kids. The whole team, not to mention all the other parents in the stands, had witnessed Sam's loss of control. No doubt Max had heard it from his teammates: Your Dad freaked out. What was up with that?

When Max was dropped off at home by another parent, he went up to his room without a word.

Sam gave it a few minutes, then took the long march up the stairs. He felt like a prisoner walking the last mile. He knocked softly on Max's door.

Max was at his desk, doing something on the computer. Buzz looked up, his tail whapping the floor.

"Hey, can we talk?" Sam offered.

"It's okay," Max said without turning around.

Sam sat on Max's bed. His son's room was a mix of sports posters and black-and-white photographs. Max's hobby was photography, and he had a good eye. A sensitive eye.

Max was a sensitive soul all around. Which was what made this so hard. Sam's outburst must have really cut into Max.

"Turn around for a second," Sam said.

Sighing, Max spun around in his chair. His hair was matted and he still wore his baseball uniform. The Orioles.

Sam patted Max's knee. "You had a pretty good game today."

"Yeah."

"A nice hit."

"Uh-huh."

"You saw what happened with me and that other guy?"

Max shrugged.

"I want to explain what happened, okay?"

"You don't have to."

"No, I do. Max, this guy is someone I knew way back in college, and he's come back around to try to . . . I don't know, bother me, for some reason."

"Why?"

"I don't know. But he showed up at your game because he knew I was going to be there."

"That's creepy."

"A little, yes," Sam said, trying to keep his voice steady so it wouldn't upset Max more. "But it's nothing that can't be handled."

In the pause, Sam almost heard Max puzzling it all out in his mind.

"I'm human, Max. Maybe you figured that out by now."

Max said nothing.

"The guy pushed my button and I grabbed him. I was wrong."

"Maybe you should've punched his face in."

An odd thought coming from the normally pacifistic Max. "Much as I wanted to then, that's not the way to do things. If it gets worse, I've got the law on my side."

"What if he doesn't care?"

"About the law?"

"Yeah. What if he's a criminal?"

Good question. "Let's not worry about that. I just want you to know I'm okay, and I want to know if you're okay."

"Sure, I'm okay. I got a hit today."

Sam nodded. "Yeah, a good one. See you later, okay?"

"Dad?"

"Hm?"

"We'll be all right, right? From this guy?"

"Oh, yeah. He'll go away."

Sam was never less convinced of anything in his life.

Downstairs, Linda was waiting with an ice-cold lemonade and sandwiches. The old homestead. Safe and undisturbed.

Then the phone rang.

5.

"Mr. Trask?" The voice was official. He knew at once two things: It was the police, and it had to do with Heather.

"Yes."

"Your daughter has been picked up for driving under the influence. She's here at the West Valley station."

Sam closed his eyes against the mental vise squeezing his brain. He took a deep suck of air.

"What is it, Sam?" Linda was reading his face, her eyes wide. He put his hand up.

"Thank you," he said, then hung up.

"Tell me," Linda said.

"We've joined the happy couples who have kids driving drunk."

Now it was Linda who shut her eyes, absorbing the news. Sam let her take it in, resisting the urge to let loose with a flurry of blame-placing darts. Heather had gone out with Roz, and they drank and drove. Now could Linda see that it mattered who Heather was with?

"Can we go get her?" Linda said.

Sam thought a moment. "No."

"Sam!"

"She needs to feel this." He leaned back against the wall. "I don't know what else to do."

"I don't want her sitting in that place."

"Why not? You'd prefer she sit somewhere else, getting ripped?"

"What are we going to do?"

"Maybe we should kick her out." The moment he said it his inner world cracked wide, and he fell in. It was anger, all anger that did it. Rage was the jackhammer, and it split him.

When had he lost her? His Heather? His firstborn, a daughter, and when she'd popped her head out he fell in love with this tiny, vulnerable thing. He held her at night when she was little and scared, and took her to the pediatrician for her round of shots, holding her hand as she cried. He became her protector then, and she clung to him, and he loved her all the more.

He was there for many of the hurts that attend a girl growing up, and she'd come running to him at night when he got home.

Then she turned thirteen and started on the resistance-and-rebellion program. At the same time, Sam got busier at the firm, which meant Linda had to handle the brunt of Heather's burgeoning bad side. Marital tension was added to the plate of upheaval, and for four years their home had been painfully tense.

But this was a kind of torture, the thought of putting his daughter out of the house. Tough love, they called it. He never thought it would come to that.

"Forget it," Sam said, reaching for his

keys. "Maybe I'm a lousy father, but I want to get her home."

"You're not a lousy father, Sam."

"I wish I believed that."

6.

"I didn't mean it, Daddy." Heather was awash in tears on the sofa, her makeup running all over her face.

"What do you mean by that?" Sam was pacing. Linda sat next to Heather, trying to comfort her. Max had been ordered to stay in his room.

"Just what I said. Roz was really out of it, so I drove her car to her house."

"You were drinking. You don't know that's wrong?"

"Yes, but —"

"And then you get in a car and drive?"

"It was stupid, I know . . ." Sobs erupted, cutting off words. Heather put her face in her hands.

"More than stupid."

"Sam." Linda shook her head at him.

No, he wasn't going to stop. This had to come out now, hard. This had to be cut out of her. It had to hurt.

"Here's what's going to happen," Sam said. "Your driving privileges are being revoked."

Heather's streaked face shot up at him. "No!"

"And you're going to drop this whole band thing —"

"No! You can't —"

"And go to college in the fall. Maybe JC to start —"

"You can't make me! You can't do this!"

"In the morning, I'll call Rich Demaris to take your DUI —"

"Mom, make him stop —"

Linda pulled Heather to her chest. "It's been an emotional night. Let's wait until tomorrow."

Sam, feeling like a blood vessel might pop in his brain, threw up his hands.

7.

Oh good one, oh drunk, oh driving, and Daddy must love you for that, Mommy must be so proud.

Heather lay on the bed, looked at the ceiling, stayed there until the family was through with dinner downstairs. She could hear the sounds of routine footsteps on hardwood floor, doors closing softly, as if they thought by keeping down the noise the tension would all go away.

She lay there in silence for a long time, until it was quiet.

She got up and went to Max's door, knocked softly, and heard him say, "Come in." He was at his computer, playing chess. Buzz, lounging on the floor, looked up and wagged his tail.

"You winning?" She closed the door behind her.

"It's on beginner setting, so I'm killing it."

She looked around his room. His bed was made and there were no clothes on the floor. The opposite of her room. Max could have been the neat guy on that old show about the odd couple who lived together.

Heather sat on the edge of Max's bed, a few feet from him. "I really admire you."

"Huh?" Max turned in his chair.

"Your brain. You can do that stuff, like chess."

"I just like it."

"And I think you're a really cool brother."

He looked stunned at that. She slipped off the bed and onto her knees on the carpet. "Listen to me, will you?"

"Yeah," Max said tentatively.

"I wish I could be more like you."

"Why?"

"I just do. But look, we all have to be who we are. And I want you to remember something I tell you, okay?"

"Okay."

"No matter what happens to me or anybody, you're a great kid and you're going to be a great man. So if anything ever happens, you just keep on going and be who you are and don't ever be down on yourself, okay?"

"What's wrong?" Max said.

"I don't know." She paused. "I just love you and Mom and Dad, that's all. And I don't want anything to happen to you guys."

"Nothing's gonna happen."

Buzz came to her then, nosing her side. "And if anything ever happens to me, you'll be all right, right?"

"What's gonna happen to you?"

"I don't know."

"Dad said he'll get a lawyer —"

"I don't care about that. I'm not talking about that."

"So what then?"

"Just say you know you'll be all right."

"I guess so —"

"Say you know it."

"Why are you crying?"

She put her hands around his neck and pulled his head down so she could kiss the top of it.

"Say you know it," she said. "Know it know it know it."

8.

At 3:14 in the morning, Sam woke up fully, as if someone had slapped his head.

The blur of his thoughts pressed against his skull. He knew he was not going to go back to sleep. He'd had this feeling once before.

It was during his first big trial. All the anxieties of trial work were new to him then. The cluster of worries grew exponentially the closer he got to that first day. And then they increased as every day in court presented new challenges.

After the two-week trial there followed three days of absolute torture waiting for the verdict. Sam walked the floor at all hours, watched mindless TV in the middle of the night. He got to know some good old movies that way.

The day after the jury announced that Sam had won, he literally collapsed into bed and slept for eleven hours.

This morning he felt that anxiety all over again, only worse. Because with a trial there was always something he could do. More strategizing, more study of the law, more tactics.

But things were out of his control now. How could he stop a man who was clearly out to make his life miserable? How could he get through to a daughter who was intent on keeping him out of the most important parts of her life? How could he connect with a longsuffering wife who tended to take all the burdens of family life on her own shoulders?

Throw in a drunk-driving arrest of his daughter and you had the perfect last nail for the coffin.

Ever since Heather's birth, Sam had pursued the ideal of the perfect father and husband. He took parenting seminars. He read books as if he were studying for the parental bar exam and would only get a license to practice if he got all the answers right. He gave over his heart and mind fully to his children's good. When he'd become a Christian, he read the Bible and prayed often.

So why was God allowing this to happen? That wasn't part of the deal. *I go to church and raise my children according to your Word, Lord. You keep them from doing anything harmful. You mold them into successful citizens.*

Right? Isn't that it?

Then why was his daughter running into ruination? Why was evil intruding in his house?

Sam went to the kitchen, poured a glass

of milk, then sat in the dark. For a brief moment, the thought of having a real drink crossed his mind. He'd never been an alcoholic, though he used to drink heavily. He'd managed to quit with Linda's resolute encouragement, but that didn't remove the occasional craving.

He thought about bourbon, gave himself a little slap on the cheek, and thought about prayer.

He wanted to pray. Of course. You're a Christian, you pray. But his prayer life was a shambles. Other than meals and the group prayers at church, he didn't do much of it. Now it was as if circumstances were forcing him into it.

He closed his eyes.

He tried to recall what Don Lyle, his pastor, taught on prayer. Don did a series sometime back. He'd said something then, a method. What was it? Something about praying and Scriptures.

That was it. Pray the Scriptures. You take up the Bible and read and turn the text into a prayer. It focuses the mind, Don said. Prayer grounded in the Word could not be denied.

Sam took his milk and went to the study, flicked on a table lamp, and sat at the desk. His Bible was there, the one Linda gave him. He remembered the joy of that day. The joy seemed a distant memory now.

He picked the Bible up, looked at it. He went to the concordance to look up the passage where Jesus taught about prayer. Ask, seek, knock. It was in the book of Matthew, chapter 7:

Ask and it will be given to you; seek and you will find; knock and the door will be opened to you. For everyone who asks receives; he who seeks finds; and to him who knocks, the door will be opened.

Which of you, if his son asks for bread, will give him a stone? Or if he asks for a fish, will give him a snake? If you, then, though you are evil, know how to give good gifts to your children, how much more will your Father in heaven give good gifts to those who ask him!

A tiny window in his soul opened up, through which he sent out a flare of hope. He had never really put these words to the test. He was skeptical of the type of Christianity that taught you could ask up a Lexus if you had enough faith.

And yet there had to be something here, because Jesus said it.

Sam put his hand on the page and whispered, "Lord, I want to pray this Scripture. I want to ask you in faith for help. I feel like I'm being crushed."

He paused, waiting for a feeling that he was being heard.

Silence.

"Protect my family, Lord. I'm asking. I'm seeking. I'm knocking. I don't know what else to do, but I'm praying with everything I have now."

He stayed there until his eyes grew heavy. He lay down on the couch, and when he finally fell asleep, he dreamed. In the dream he was dressed in a suit and tie, but he wasn't in court. He was on a desolate road. Miles away from any courthouse or city, that's all he knew.

And then, from the shadowy distance, a car. Coming toward him.

A strange voice whispered in his head.

Sammy . . .

9.

He kept the prayers circulating in his head at church. Sam was exhausted but relieved — Max had been in an ebullient mood as he went off to the junior high worship. The unpleasantness at the ball field was apparently ebbing for Max. Thank the Lord for little things.

And even though Heather was still in her room at home, her issues unresolved, Sam felt he'd made some sort of faith breakthrough. He felt his early morning prayers were more honest and open than ever before.

Surely, God heard those kinds of prayers and did something about them. That was the deal, wasn't it?

He was glad to be with Linda at church. It felt like home base, the settled encampment on the treacherous mountain. Here he would regroup and begin to rebuild his family.

It was Linda who had found Solid Rock, the church at the west end of the San Fernando Valley. She'd come with a friend shortly after her conversion to Christ. The night Sam found himself listening to Don Lyle one on one, he was moved. Sam had heard a lot of great courtroom lawyers in his day, but none would have been able to touch this guy. He didn't speak with the forced emotional tones Sam heard in so many TV preachers, which rang false for him.

No, this older man's words came out of an obvious and firm conviction. His speaking seemed forged on the hard anvil of life lived and victories won, in the power of

God, over and over.

He read to Sam from the Bible, words Sam would never forget. "For though we live in the world, we do not wage war as the world does. The weapons we fight with are not the weapons of the world. On the contrary, they have divine power to demolish strongholds. We demolish arguments and every pretension that sets itself up against the knowledge of God, and we take captive every thought to make it obedient to Christ."

That text grabbed Sam in his trial lawyer's heart. Demolishing arguments was what he did for a living. Pastor Lyle went on to talk about the power of Christian thought for those who believe, but how it all seemed like foolishness to those who rejected Christ.

This was a reasonable man who could defend his beliefs, the type of Christian Sam could respect.

At the end of the two-hour meeting, Sam had decided — not really knowing when the moment of decision hit — to follow his wife into the Christian faith.

This morning Don's sermon was from Ephesians, chapter 1. He emphasized that all spiritual blessings in Christ are with Christians now. We don't have to wait until heaven.

That comforted Sam. Now if he could just keep believing it.

During the final worship song, an usher appeared at Sam's row and held something up. Sam couldn't tell what it was. The usher handed it to the person at the end of the row, and it got passed down to Sam.

It was an offering envelope with *Sam Trask* written in ink on the front. The envelope was unsealed. Sam looked inside and found a folded piece of white paper. He opened it. And his heart spiked.

On the paper was written, *I forgive you, Sam. Nicky.*

10.

"You sure you want to do this?" Roz said.

"Let's just go." Heather threw her duffel bag in the back of Roz's Mustang convertible and got in. "I just need to get away for a while."

"What about your dad?"

"He said I couldn't drive. He didn't say anything about you."

"You think just like him."

"Huh?"

"A lawyer."

"Great. I'm my old man. Just drive."

Roz put pedal to the metal and pointed

the car toward the freeway. "Where you want to go?"

"How about Mexico? Isn't that the place you go to get away from your parents?"

"We could hit Tijuana and see what happens."

"Sure," Heather said. "Get a bottle of tequila."

"And then," Roz said, "we can come back and get ready to record."

Heather looked at her. "What?"

"Yeah. Five songs."

"Where?"

"Hollywood. You remember that guy who saw us at the Cobalt? The guy who came backstage?"

"The guy in the hat."

"Yeah. Lundquist. First name Charles. Nickname Scat. I Googled him. He's done some bands."

"Really?"

"He wants to record us. Won't cost us anything. What do you say?"

Heather felt the wind in her hair. She shouldn't be doing this, just running out. She'd left a note telling her parents not to worry, but she knew they would. But this wasn't working out. She couldn't live there anymore.

Wasn't there some sort of thing she could

do to be out on her own? Some legal thing? She'd heard about it. One of her friends at school had done it. Emancipation or something.

So maybe that would be the best thing for all of them. The band was going to take off, she knew it, and she could wait tables or something to make ends meet.

"Let's do it," Heather said. "Let's make it happen."

11.

Sam whirled around.

The church was a sea of faces, probably two thousand or more.

He was here somewhere.

"What is it?" Linda said. The music stopped and the worship leader was wishing everyone a "blessed Lord's day."

"He's here."

"No."

Sam gave her the note. She looked at it and closed her eyes.

"Oh, Sam."

"This is too much." He looked around again, but saw only the exiting crowd. He got the chilling feeling that Nicky was watching him, enjoying the discomfort.

He took Linda's arm and joined the human stream heading toward the doors. The moment they hit the foyer the voice came.

"Sammy!"

Nicky Oberlin was wearing a coat and tie and an exaggerated smile.

Linda gripped Sam's arm.

Sam told himself to take it easy. He didn't want a repeat of what happened at the ball field. Not at church!

Yet his outrage was palpable. This was a denigration, an insult, a slap.

"This your wife?" Nicky said, putting out his hand.

Linda froze.

"I'm Nicky, Sam's friend from way back. Great to meet you."

One of the church greeters, Tim Wade, a tall, friendly man, put his hand on Sam's shoulder. "Morning, Sam, Linda." He looked at Nicky.

"I'm a friend of Sam's," Nicky said. He shook Tim's hand.

"Welcome to Solid Rock," Tim said.

Sam wanted to shout at Tim, at the whole church, as if Satan himself had shown up. But he also knew that was probably what Nicky wanted.

"Yeah, an old, old friend," Sam said. "From college. Good old Nicky."

Nicky barely flinched.

"Hope you come see us again," Tim said.

"Love to," Nicky said. "You have a real nice church here."

"Nicky's searching," Sam said. "He really needs the Lord."

The slightest flicker of tightness in Nicky's cheeks.

"We have a class for newcomers," Tim said. "Tuesday night. Basics of the Christian faith."

"Nicky would love that!" Sam smiled at him. "Why don't you come, Nicky?"

"I might have to take a rain check on that, Sammy. But maybe you and I could get together real soon. Yeah. For sure."

He smiled and started to back away.

"Bye," Tim said amiably. "Thanks again for coming." Then to Sam, "Nice fella."

"You have no idea, Tim."

Linda put her head on his shoulder. She was trembling. "Let's get Max and go home, Sam."

12.

Sam found the note taped to Heather's door.

I had to go. I'm not driving, so don't worry. I'll call you later. H.

"Look at this!" He screamed it. Linda came running up the stairs.

"What's wrong?"

151

He handed her the note.

"I wish she hadn't," Linda said.

"Wishing is one thing. Now what?" Now what indeed. His head was already squeezed by Nicky's little game. And oral arguments were coming up in the FulCo case. Why did Heather have to be this way now?

"I'll try calling her," Linda said.

"Good luck."

"She said she'd call us. At least she said that much."

"Always looking for the bright side."

"We have to."

He wanted to scream at her then. *No, we don't.* Why? Because God is supposed to make it bright? Then let him show himself a little. Like now.

He went downstairs to the study and shut the door. His study was neat and in order. It was a place he always felt he could regroup. Calm down, think things over.

But not this time. Peace seemed something foreign, beyond reach.

SEVEN

1.

Monday morning, Sam was more determined than ever to get lost in legal research. The upcoming hearing on the government's FRCP 56 motion for summary judgment in FulCo was the biggest moment in his legal life.

Ever since he'd been sworn into the bar, Sam indulged a little fantasy about arguing before the Supreme Court someday. It was a very long shot, of course. Not many lawyers ever get that opportunity.

If only he could. It would epitomize everything he believed about the glory of the law. The chance to stand in front of the highest court and argue, putting all his mental powers to the test, for a principle of constitutional law. He'd be standing where Thurgood Marshall stood when he argued *Brown v. Board of Education.* He'd be standing in the presence of the marble frieze depicting the Manichaean forces of good and evil in conflict, and the representation of Moses with the tablets.

Order from chaos. Light from darkness. The grandeur of American jurisprudence.

Well, even if that never happened, he could represent every client with the zeal demanded by a life in the law.

Ten minutes into his pursuit of glory he got a call. Doreen told him it was a woman named Mary Grant.

Mary.

He paused a moment, his pulse quickening. No time to prepare.

He picked up. "Hello?"

"Sam?" Her voice was soft, a little girl's voice coming over a walkie-talkie.

"Yes, it's me. How are you?"

"Bet you never expected to hear from me, did you?"

"Actually, I know why you're calling, Mary."

"What?"

"I've already heard from Nicky Oberlin."

There was a pause on the line. "Is that his name? He never gave me a name. He only whispered over the phone. He knew all about us. He said I should ask you why he was calling. Told me where you were. It freaked me out. I'm really sorry. I never

154

would have called. I'm so sorry —"

"No, it's fine that you did."

"I don't know what he wanted. I feel really strange talking to you."

"It's a very strange set of circumstances, Mary. Are you doing all right?"

"You mean in general? I can't complain."

He wanted to ask her about the boy. His boy. But the words wouldn't come.

"Sam, I don't think I can talk to you about this over the phone. I never expected to see you again and I don't want to drag you into anything. But I need to know what to do. If he calls again."

A thousand scenarios blistered Sam's brain. Quickly, before he could change his mind, he said, "If you'd like to come in and meet with me, I'm sure that would be all right. The police need to know about this."

"I don't want any involvement with police; I just want this to go away."

"Then come down to my office and —"

"I don't have a car. I mean, my car's in the shop. I suppose I could have Caleb drive me. He lives —" She stopped suddenly. "That's his name, by the way."

Caleb. A strong biblical name. Sam took a moment to catch his breath. "How . . . what's he like?"

"He's a great boy. Boy? I can hardly

believe he's twenty-eight."

"Did you ever tell him about me?"

"Sam, can we not do this over the phone? I feel so . . . I don't know."

"Let me come to you, then."

2.

Sam tried calling Linda as soon as he was on the 10 freeway heading east. She didn't answer and he didn't leave a message. This was not an item he wanted to disclose via recording. She'd understand. He hoped.

Mary lived in a modest home on a tree-lined street in Loma Linda, a little residential city in San Bernardino County. The house looked of early seventies vintage, with a two-car garage, red-brick chimney, and wooden fence to one side. Not luxury, but certainly comfortable.

Knocking on the door, Sam felt as nervous as a high school freshman picking up his first date. Though their relationship, such as it was, was a thing of the distant past, the memory of it had returned with a force that he wished would go away.

She answered the door. She looked almost exactly the same. Her chestnut hair was worn short. The blue eyes were immediately familiar. If anything was different, it was the small but visible worry line just above the bridge of her nose.

Mary offered her hand. "Good to see you, Sam."

Inside, the house was cozy and well lit. The walls were decorated with water colors and other paintings. "Did you do these?"

"Yes."

"They're nice."

"Thank you."

"You sell them or anything?"

She shook her head. "They're just for me." She looked around, her eyes not landing anyplace. "This is really strange. I'm so sorry I brought this on you."

"You didn't. It was Nicky."

"I keep thinking I've heard that name."

"He was at UCSB with us. Same dorm. Nicky Oberlin."

She frowned. "I have no recollection."

"He knows all about us, though."

"Is he dangerous?"

"I think it's just mind games at this point."

"It's working. Can I offer you something to drink?"

She brought out some iced tea and while she poured it, Sam readied the words that had been nervously bouncing around his throat.

"I have to apologize, Mary. It's been a

long time, but I was lousy to you. I'm really sorry."

She looked at him, and thankfully her eyes were full of understanding. "What did we know back then anyway? I mean, that was a crazy place to be. You're so young and they throw you together in coed dorms. We all felt free for the first time and . . . But it all worked out for the best."

Sam said nothing. His mouth was dry.

"I had Caleb. And then I met Steve Grant and we got married. He was a good father. A great father. We were very happy together."

"Were?"

"I should have mentioned. He died last January. Heart. He worked for the school district. Construction."

"I'm sorry."

Mary nodded.

"Did you have any other children?"

"Just Caleb."

"Tell me about him," Sam said.

"Oh, he's great. Married, with a lovely little two-year-old daughter. They live over in Upland."

His granddaughter. He tried to swallow. Couldn't.

"He does what his dad did," Mary said. "Good with his hands. But you know what he does early in the morning, before going to work?"

"What?"

"Writes. He wants to be a writer."

"No kidding."

"He's really good."

"I think that's fantastic, Mary."

She said, "This Nicky, what does he want from us?"

"It's me. For some reason he wants to force his way back into my life. He's just using you to get at me. Threatened to tell my wife about you."

"She never knew?"

Sam shook his head. "She does now." He paused. "Does Caleb know?"

"No, Sam. I met Steve six months after Caleb was born. I didn't want Caleb to know. I wanted him to know only one father. Do you think that was wrong?"

A small crevice cracked open inside Sam. "Not at all."

"Thank you." Mary seemed relieved, deeply, like fear of his answer had been bottled up inside her all these years. "He loved his father very much. They were so close."

For the next twenty minutes, Sam labored to reassure Mary that the law was on their side and would be utilized to the full if need be. If Nicky contacted her again, she was to make notes of the time and the content.

But Sam was certain he wouldn't be calling again, that his purpose was to get in Sam's own head.

Mary did seem reassured by then, and Sam chalked the effect up to his legal training. The point wasn't always to win cases and motions. Sometimes, just thinking issues through with someone was all they needed.

When the time for parting came, it brought a certain awkwardness. Would he see Mary again? Would they stay in touch? Would that even be a good idea?

What would Linda think about it? He would soon find out, because he was going to tell her about the meeting when he got home.

A back door slammed.

Then a voice: "Mom?"

Mary looked at Sam. "It's Caleb."

3.

When Sam didn't answer his cell phone, Linda put in a call to the office. Doreen told her Sam had gone out, but didn't say where.

Odd. He was always so careful to mark where he was. He'd called her but didn't leave a message. Odd again.

She tried to shrug it off. But shrugging didn't do it.

Yes, he was under a lot of stress. He had the big case coming up, he had Heather to deal with. They both did.

Then there was that whole thing about his having a child. It bothered her, though she knew it shouldn't. He was right about their not disclosing the past. She'd had a couple of things she wasn't anxious to share with him.

But she'd never had a baby.

Forget it, she told herself. She just didn't want the cool gap between them to grow into a distance. Sam was probably off doing something related to work, so she would do the same.

She called her business Badger Baskets. She'd always loved badgers for some reason, even as a kid. Badger in *The Wind in the Willows* was her favorite character. She rooted for the University of Wisconsin. She had two Badgers T-shirts, a couple of Badger mugs, and of course, a stuffed Wisconsin Badger mascot.

Linda made gift baskets, putting the kind of care and design into them that brought her a steady clientele. Today in her shop — a shed in the back that they'd turned into a nice work space — Linda was about to get started on one of several baskets for Mrs. Rooney at church. She was the wife of Hal Rooney, the football coach at Chatsworth High, and every year she made sure to send a nice big basket to each member of the Los Angeles Unified School Board.

It was a good gig for Linda, and she always went all out.

But as her hands unspooled the ribbon and cellophane, she saw them shaking. What was that all about?

She closed her eyes to calm herself.

4.

"Sorry. Didn't know you had company."

Sam's breath almost left him, not in a rush but in a slow, tightening reflex in the chest. The realization that he was looking at his own son almost rocked him off his feet.

Mary seemed to teeter on a narrow beam. "You startled me," she said.

"Just came to grab a couple of books." He looked at Sam. "Hello."

"This is Mr. Trask," Mary said. "This is my son, Caleb."

Caleb's handshake was firm. He had a pleasant, understated smile and blue eyes like his mother, active with intelligence and humor. He was Sam's height, with broader shoulders and short, wheat-colored hair.

Sam had to fight to keep emotion off his face.

"Mr. Trask is a lawyer," Mary said.

Caleb frowned. "Something wrong?"

When Mary hesitated, Sam said, "Someone we both knew back in college has contacted us with a proposition, and I'm handing out some free legal advice."

"You knew Mom in college?"

"Yes. We were in the same dorm."

"Cool. A blast from the past."

"Your mom speaks very highly of you."

"That's what moms are for."

"Says you're into writing?"

Caleb grinned. "Ah, I just hammer away. Trying to learn. You know."

"What writers do you like?"

"I'm a little eccentric; I like some of the older writers."

"Why is that eccentric?"

"I don't know. I'm supposed to be postmodern and cynical. But I don't respond to that. I like William Saroyan."

"*The Human Comedy*?"

"Yeah! You know him?"

"I read that book in high school. My English teacher loved it."

"And his short stories, especially in *My Name Is Aram*. In fact, that's what I'm here for, Mom. We had a paperback copy of it."

Mary said, "Check the bookshelf."

"Right. Nice to meet you, Mr. Trask."

He shook Sam's hand again and went off to the next room.

"You did a great job," Sam whispered. Then: "I better go. When this matter gets resolved, I'll let you know."

Mary nodded, and Sam thought for a moment she might be ready to cry. But she took in a breath and said, "Thank you so much for coming."

Caleb bounded into the room, holding a paperback. "Got it. Thanks. Call you later, Mom. Nice to meet you, sir." And with a wave he was gone.

Sam hardly knew what to say next. "He's obviously a good boy. Man."

Mary nodded.

"And rest assured, I'll do everything I can to keep Nicky Oberlin out of your life."

That was the least he could do for the woman he'd wronged and the son he'd never known.

5.

Sam got stuck in westbound traffic and decided there was no time like the present to call Linda. He barely got out a greeting when she said, "So where have you been all day?"

"All day?"

"I don't know, a long time. I called your office, your cell. Where did you go?"

Here we go, Sam thought. He was at the top of the luge chute in the Winter Olympics. Once he got started, it was going to be downhill, faster and faster. Better get to the finish line and be done with it.

"I went to see her," Sam said.

"Who?"

"Mary Delano."

"You *what?*"

"Calm down."

"I *am* calm. Why didn't you tell me?"

"I tried calling."

"Didn't leave a message?"

"I thought it would be better —"

"I mean, come on, this is pretty big."

"All right, I messed up."

"Yes, you did."

"Please listen," Sam said.

"I am. Go ahead."

"She called the office. Nicky Oberlin had contacted her. That's the connection. She was really upset about it. She didn't have a car, so I drove out to Loma Linda."

"You could have told me that much."

"I didn't want to worry you."

"Or was it you didn't want me thinking about you being with her?"

"I don't know what I was thinking. Maybe I wasn't thinking straight at all."

"All right." She paused. "So what happened? Did you see him? Your son?"

"He wasn't supposed to be there."

"So he was."

"He dropped by. Mary was surprised."

"I don't believe this whole thing."

Sam almost rear-ended a white Ryder truck. "Linda, please. You have to hear me. I didn't go there with any intent but to calm her down. And to get her statement about what Nicky did to her. And then Caleb came in. That's his name."

A long silence. Then Linda said, "What's he like?"

"She and her husband did a great job. He's solid. And she never told him about me. And that's the way it's going to stay."

He wanted to hold her. He thought he heard her sniffing a little. "I'm going to do a little work," she said. "I'll see you when you get home."

"You okay?"

"I will be. Because I have to be. We have to be. For Max and Heather."

EIGHT

1.

Sam met Cameron Bellamy in his office at the Van Nuys Superior Courthouse on Tuesday afternoon. Cam had been a solid prosecutor for almost twenty years, and Sam's friend since they were partnered in law school in the moot court competition.

Cam was still in athletic trim, just like in his days swimming for the UC Irvine team. Almost made the Olympics. He was about Sam's height, with sandy hair and bright blue eyes. Sam knew why juries loved this guy.

"How's life in the big money?" Cam said, offering a government-issue chair — function over comfort being the watchword. Cam's windowless office was also a study in utility and not aesthetics.

"I'm not driving a Mercedes, if that's what you mean. But we get by."

"I saw you guys in the *Daily Journal* a few

weeks ago."

"Lousy picture." The *Daily Journal* was the city's legal newspaper. They'd done a profile of Newman & Trask, but the photographer they sent out was about four feet tall. In the photo, Sam looked like he had three chins as he looked down on the diminutive picture taker.

"How's your big case against the government?"

"How is any big case against the government? Enough paper to cover the city to a depth of five feet."

Cam smiled. "You ought to come over here and work for me. Paper's a minimum, and you get into court a lot more."

"You know, that almost sounds good."

"I'm serious."

"Thanks, Cam. But I'm no criminal law expert. That's why I've come to you." He told Cam about Nicky Oberlin, all the way up to the church incident.

When he finished, Cam nodded slowly. "Sounds like you're dealing with a sociopath."

"A bad guy for sure."

"More specifically, a guy with no conscience. In the psych literature it's *antisocial personality disorder.* Means the guy does not experience guilt or qualm about what he does. He can, in short, do whatever he wants and try to get away with it."

"No conscience, huh?"

"Zip. And here's the scary part: that describes an estimated four percent of the population. I'm telling you, man, one out of twenty-five people in these good old United States are socios, and nobody knows why."

The number staggered Sam. He could hardly believe it.

Cam said, "You remember that movie with Robert De Niro and whatsisname . . . Nick Nolte?"

"Right. What was it, *Cape Fear*?"

"That's the one, where De Niro is this psycho with all these tattoos and you just look at him and you know he's evil. He's sadistic. He gets a certain pleasure out of his crimes. It's obvious. But with a sociopath, he might look as angelic as an altar boy. Like Scott Peterson."

"Oh yeah, he was a piece of work."

"He looks like Joe All-American, smiling, glad-hander. Then he kills his pregnant wife, unborn baby, as coldly as you please. And during his trial he sat there, stone-faced, no emotion. The jury hated him for that. He had no conscience. That's the really chilling part. On the outside, these types can be charming as all get out. There's no way to tag them. A sociopath could turn out to be your best friend. Before he kills you, of course."

"Just great."

"I've seen 'em right out there in that courthouse. Usually it's a guy doing his thing on a domestic partner."

"So why do you think he's after me?"

Cam shrugged. "Socios can be motivated by many things — money, excitement, sex, power. Your guy seems to be on a power trip. It's a game to him, and he aims to win at all costs."

"Is that it? It's all a game?"

"They've done studies, and in moments of candor these guys will sometimes admit feeling empty inside. They know they're missing something. But they don't sorrow over that. Instead, they're likely to target someone who does appear to have a good conscience. Someone with a spotless rep. Someone, in short, who looks very much like you."

"You're full of great news, Cam."

"And you have a past with this guy."

"Not much. We were in the freshman dorms together. I hardly knew him."

"Maybe you did something back then that ticked him off."

"And he sat on it all these years?"

"And seeing your success was the trigger point. A perfect storm of all the crud in this guy's life coming together. It's almost a random event."

"So what can you do to stop him?"

"Me?"

"The law."

"There's a stalking statute in the penal code. Section 646.9. But it requires more facts than you've got."

"More? After all he's done?"

"What are witnesses going to say, Sam? That he came to church? That he forgave you? And at the ball field. Who assaulted whom?"

That hurt, but it was the truth. He had no case to present. "So now what?"

"Can you forget I'm an officer of the court for a moment?"

"Sure."

"You have a gun?"

"No, Linda doesn't like —"

"Get one."

"Are you serious?"

"Listen to me. You have got to be prepared to meet power with power. This guy has to be convinced that he's likely to lose this power game, and that losing will hurt. Socios aren't irrational. They can still measure things by a simple cost-benefit analysis. But one thing is pretty certain: they can't be cured. They literally have no emotional alarm system. Until science figures out a way to implant one, they can do whatever they want without qualm. Including kill."

Chilled to the marrow, Sam bit his lip. "This is so bizarre, so out of reality."

"It's the reality I see every day, Sam. And you know, in the last fifteen years, I've seen it get demonstrably worse. There's something going on, I don't know what it is. Society breaking down, all that? I guess. But it's sometimes enough to make me want to get out of this business forever."

A heavy silence draped itself over them. Get a gun? Was that what this would all come to?

Cam flipped through his Rolodex. "I'm going to give you the name of a PI I know. I think it might be worth it to let him get some background on your boy."

He wrote the name and phone number on a piece of paper and handed it to Sam.

"And if this guy keeps things up, maybe I can help you get more creative."

Sam looked at him. "How's that?"

"You just keep in touch, Sam. And give my best to Linda."

2.

Sam met Gerald Case in his office on Ventura Boulevard in Encino, just across the street from Jerry's Famous Deli.

Gerald Case. A perfect name for a private investigator, Sam thought. But Case himself was not the stereotypical PI. He was around fifty, thin, wore a tie and white shirt. He could have been an accountant or estate lawyer. His graying hair was neatly clipped and combed.

And his office was neat. Sam expected something like the movies — papers strewn around empty coffee cups and a revolver or two. Instead, the dark wood desk had an immaculate glass top, a computer monitor with keyboard, a phone, a pen and pencil holder in the shape of a small red golf bag, and a framed picture. Sam couldn't see who was in it.

"Cam called me," Case said, shaking Sam's hand. "Said you were a solid guy."

"Cam's a good man."

"He is. And he's hired me a few times. I like working for the government. They pay on time."

"I hope so," Sam said. "My partner and I have a little breach-of-contract case going against Uncle Sam right now."

"Takes moxie."

"And a whole lot of hours."

Case nodded and took out a yellow legal pad from a drawer. He selected a pen from the golf bag. "So give me the 411 on your guy."

Once more Sam laid out the story. It was more painful the second time, like getting a tweak on a toothache. He threw in Cam Bellamy's idea about Oberlin's being a sociopath.

Case nodded. "I think Cam's absolutely right. In my line, I've seen a lot more of it."

"Yeah?"

"Oh, yeah. Don't know why. But in domestic cases, more and more of these guys don't have any remorse or conscience. They go out on their wives or girlfriends and think that's some constitutional right. And sometimes they end up beating or killing the women. And thinking they're in the right."

"Terrific."

"So we have to deal with the reality. I can do some background on this guy. You have a copy of the emails he's sent you?"

"I can get them."

"Get them. Is there a chance you can set up a meeting with him?"

"Why?"

"So I can follow him."

"I don't want to meet with him."

"He's going to want to meet with you. I'm guessing he's going to step it up a notch. Maybe he'll try to squeeze you for money, maybe he just wants to toy with you. We don't really know yet. But if you can set the terms, meet him somewhere, I'll be there. If that's all right with you. It's not inexpensive to do this."

Sam sighed. "Do it. I want to end this thing."

"I didn't say it would end."

"Then what —"

"I provide you with information, Mr. Trask. That's all I can do. But if you want it to stop, that's another matter."

"I've already talked to Cam about possible criminal charges."

Case shook his head. "This guy's careful. My guess is he's never going to give you something you can take to the DA."

"So what else?"

Gerald Case leaned over his desk. "How important is it to you to stop this guy?"

"It has to stop."

"Then you may need some outside assistance."

"Outside?"

"May I count on your discretion and speak freely?"

"Yes."

"There are certain people I can contact who would have a talk with this man."

Sam understood immediately. "Mr. Case, I don't want to leave the bounds of the law."

"That's fine. All I'm telling you is that the law may not solve this particular problem. I just wanted you to have all the information."

For a moment, Sam considered it. And the thought chilled him. No, he couldn't go down that path. Or could he? Given another shove, given any further threat to his family, maybe he could.

Where was his faith? It was stretched out like a thin rubber band and could hardly endure the tension of this trouble.

Sam said, "If I were to want a gun for protection, who would you suggest I go to?"

Case raised his eyebrows. "Within the law?"

"Of course."

"Just asking. There's a testing requirement, background check, ten-day waiting period, tests —"

"Tests?"

"They don't want people running out mad, getting a gun, and going back home and shooting themselves in the foot."

"Ten days may be too long."

Gerald Case spread his hands.

Sam stood up. "Thank you, Mr. Case. Do what you have to do, and send me a bill. Shall I give you something on retainer?"

"That would very nice, Mr. Trask."

3.

"Hi, Mom."

"Heather, where are you?"

"We spent the night in San Diego. I'm with Roz. We're at a motel. We're fine."

"Are you coming home?"

"Sometime."

"Heather, please."

"I'm okay, Mom. You and Dad have to be good with that."

"What are you telling me?"

"I don't know."

Heather looked at Roz, who was sitting on the bed taking a pull from a bottle of Cuervo Gold. It was sometime in the early afternoon. Heather's head was throbbing from the night before, when she'd done shooters with Roz in this dive of a place.

Life as rock stars. It wasn't all that glamorous at the moment.

"Heather, you need to talk to your father. You've got a DUI hanging over your head. You're . . ."

"What, Mom?"

"You need to come home. Let us help you."

"How's Max?"

"He's okay. He's worried about you too."

"Tell everybody not to worry, will you? Stop it."

"Heather, please —"

"Don't worry about me. I'll call you later."

When she clicked off, Roz said, "Trouble at the old homestead?" She offered Heather the bottle.

Heather grabbed it and took a long pull, the burn in her throat something to think about other than what she was doing to her family.

"Hey, easy." Roz laughed.

Heather wiped the wet from her eyes. "How much of this does it take to fall asleep and not wake up?" She looked into the bottle and the sight blurred under fresh tears.

The next thing she knew, Roz was sitting next to her on the bed, arm around her. "Hey."

"Hey *what?*" Heather snapped.

"Just . . . *hey.* Sometimes that's all a friend needs to say, okay? Hey." Roz pulled Heather close and didn't say another word.

4.

When he got home, Sam found Linda in tears in the living room.

"She's gone, Sam. I know it."

He took her in his arms as she explained the call from Heather. "What can we possibly do?" she sobbed. "Isn't there anything legal?"

Sam put his head back. "Not in California. This isn't exactly the state that upholds parental rights."

"That's crazy! What kind of a state is this?"

Sam held her close. Then his phone buzzed. Linda stepped back and said, "I'll whip something up for dinner." She kissed his cheek and headed for the kitchen.

Lew was on the phone. "How you feeling, man?"

"I'm getting by, Lew."

"No. I mean how are you feeling?"

"Fine, I said."

"You didn't say that."

"Don't play lawyer with me, Lew."

"That's what I am. And so are you, pal. Friday is big."

"You don't have to tell me how big it is. I've been working on it."

"Is that what you were doing all day?"

"Is that what this is about? You checking up on me?"

"Sam, it's no secret you've got some distractions going —"

"Lew, listen to me. I am ready. Friday I'll be ready. Will you trust me on that?"

"If you'll get a good sleep Thursday night."

"I will."

"You want to meet at the courthouse at eight thirty?"

"Sure. I'll see you there."

"Sam?"

"Yeah."

"Hang in there, boy."

Yeah. Hang.

Hang and drag. That's what life was beginning to be. You had to hang on, and you had to drag your way through work and responsibilities.

God, when will it get better?

NINE

1.

The last Friday in July beat down on Los Angeles like Lucifer's jackhammer. Sam was therefore very thankful for the favor of federal air conditioning.

The courtroom was the domain of Judge Raul Manuel. It was like the others in the downtown federal courthouse — large, majestic, wood paneled, austere. And cool. State buildings tended to be smaller, reflective of tight budgets. Summer cooling systems could sometimes be a little less than effective. The Feds were very much into refrigeration in the summer months and had the budget to do it right.

Sam and Lew took their place at the plaintiff's table. Stuart Hoch sat in the front row of the gallery, giving the pair barely a nod. He was reading a *Daily Journal* and didn't look like he wanted to be disturbed.

Of course, if Sam and Lew lost this motion, Hoch would be very disturbed. But not as much as Appleby.

Sam immediately poured himself a glass of water from the glass pitcher on the counsel table. His throat was a Sahara of uncertainty, because a motion for summary judgment under Rule 56 was a defendant's smart bomb.

The motion was a message to a judge that said there were no facts at issue. Nothing for a jury to decide. Instead, the defendant contends, the law offers no basis of recovery for the plaintiff. The plaintiff has no law on his side. Therefore, the case should be dismissed.

Blown up. Gone for good.

The government's lead lawyer, Ralph Bass, came over to shake hands. Sam had only met him once before. Bass was in his forties and wore a gray suit with understated blue tie. He was a legal powerhouse, the head of the LA office of one of DC's biggest firms. The last time he'd gone to court, late last year, he'd successfully defended a CEO who was facing twenty-five years in prison for fraud. The entire country, including Jon Stewart and David Letterman, had the CEO in stripes.

Ralph Bass didn't just hang the jury, he won an acquittal.

"Today's the day, gents," he said good-naturedly. He exuded confidence.

"You trying to talk smack to my boy?" Lew said.

"Should I? Throw him off his game?"

"He doesn't get thrown."

Bass smiled and waved at the courtroom. "Just remember, boys, this is my house."

And he walked back.

"Thanks, Lew."

"What?"

"No pressure."

"You the man. Just pretend it's the eighteenth hole at the Masters, and you have a three footer for the win over Tiger."

"Thanks again."

"Three feet! You can do it in your sleep."

Sleep was exactly what Sam needed. Only his adrenal glands were keeping him going.

Then it was time for Judge Raul Manuel to make his entrance. He was a Latino in his early fifties, had been appointed to the district court during the Clinton administration. He had the rep of leaning a little to the left, which could be good or bad. It depended on whether he felt less sympathy for big government or big business. And maybe that depended on what he'd had for breakfast.

Judge Manuel put everyone on the record

and called for statement of appearances, then asked Ralph Bass if he'd like to address the court.

He said, "No, Your Honor. We'll submit on the written motion."

Which completely took Sam by surprise. He was expecting Bass to talk a little in support of the motion, giving him time to gather his thoughts.

Instead, Judge Manuel was asking whether he or Lew was going to argue. Sam went to the podium, where he promptly dropped his notes.

They scattered on the floor.

Behind him, somewhere in the courtroom, someone laughed.

Face burning, Sam got everything back onto the podium. "Excuse me, Your Honor," he said.

"Ready to go?" Judge Manuel said.

"Yes."

But before he could say another word, the judge jumped in. "I'll tell you right now, Mr. Trask, that I'm not buying the reverse alter ego theory. That's a cute argument, that your client can pierce its own corporate veil, but I don't see it supported by your points and authorities."

"If I may, Your Honor —"

"So I don't want to hear any more on it.

You're left with an integrated operation theory, and that's what this matter is going to be about. So address your arguments to that."

Sam swallowed and felt like one of his legs had been chopped off. Now he had only one gun to fire, and it had better work.

"If Your Honor please, FulCo and its subsidiaries form an integrated operation, one unified entity. This is clear from the web of interlocking agreements to provide services and products among the companies —"

"Doesn't this just fly in the face of basic, black-letter corporate law?"

"I don't —"

"I mean, corporations are separate entities, as are the subsidiaries here. They have individual privileges, immunities, and responsibilities, including the rights to sue and be sued, on their own."

"Unless they form one family of —"

"And that's what I have yet to be convinced of."

Sam felt his throat constricting. His right kneecap started jiggling. Life was not cooperating with him. He'd never been this nervous before. Oh, maybe the first time he'd tried a case in front of a jury. But that was long ago. It was everything else —

Nicky, Linda, Heather — but he couldn't very well request a continuance to take care of family trouble.

He turned quickly in his notes to the recent Sixth Circuit case involving the integrated operation. His voice sounded like it was coming from an external sound system, piped through his body. He went around and around with Manuel for fifteen minutes, until Manuel announced that he'd had enough.

When Sam returned to the counsel table he was as spent as if he'd run five miles. He saw Hoch sitting in the first row with concern etched all over his face.

Bass was given rebuttal time. He was as smooth as Sam was nervous. Manuel hammered Bass as well, but not like he had Sam. At least that's how it seemed.

And Sam couldn't help feeling that he'd lost. Big time.

That was exactly the mood after Manuel adjourned the proceedings. Hoch hardly spoke to Sam before leaving the courtroom.

Lew tried to buck him up. "Well, good buddy, I guess those three footers are harder than they look."

2.

Sam called Linda from the office.

"We need to get away," he said. "How about you and I, together, alone, Hazlitt's?"

"Oh my, that's fancy."

"And expensive, and I want to spoil you. And I just want to have some time to forget everything else but you."

"Rough day?"

"Rough month. Rough year. What do you say?"

"What about Max?"

"I'll bring home a pizza. He hates the fancy stuff anyway."

"How can I turn this down?"

"You can't, which is a good thing. I'm not much good at arguing today."

Hazlitt's was a restaurant in Malibu, perched on a cliff overlooking the ocean. It was one of the toniest places to eat in the city, frequented by movie people and the power set.

Sam and Linda arrived at five. Sam slipped the hostess a twenty and got one of the best tables in the house — at the edge of the outdoor patio, a view to die for.

Sam ordered a dozen oysters to start.

"Ooh la la," Linda said.

"Let's go for it."

"You getting a big settlement or something?"

"I'm just praying that I didn't mess up too badly in court today."

"It's in your nature to stress. Forget it. God is in control."

"Of Heather?"

"Do you want to talk about Heather?"

"We have to do something."

"Sam, we first have to give it to God."

"You don't think I have?"

"I didn't —"

"I've been calling out to God like never before."

"That's good —"

"And not getting anything back. What am I doing wrong?"

"Nothing. You're doing it right."

"I don't see how."

"You remember that parable Jesus told, about the persistent widow?"

"Sort of."

"She kept going to this judge and demanding justice. Day after day. Finally she wore him down, and he said, 'You've got it, just leave me alone.' "

"You calling me a widow?"

"I'm telling you not to give up."

Sam lifted his glass. "I'm glad you're my wife."

"Yeah," Linda said, smiling. "You did all right."

They managed to enjoy the oysters then, and the Caesar salad mixed at the table, then two mondo lobster tails. The sun started to set, and for once, everything was just right.

Halfway through dinner Sam looked slowly around the restaurant.

"What's wrong?" Linda said.

"Nothing."

"Come on."

"It's bad. I half expected to see him here, watching us."

"Sam, Nicky is just like a thorn. We've got to let God take over."

"That sounds like . . . I don't know what it sounds like. Does prayer work?"

"If we didn't think so, we'd be in pretty bad shape."

He took her hand, kissed it. "I would not be anything without you."

His wife smiled, and once more, it all seemed right. Even more so when they shared a perfect chocolate mousse and had coffee, listening to the waves crash on the beach.

Then their waiter came up with an embarrassed look on his face. "I'm sorry, Mr. Trask, but your Visa was not approved."

"What?"

"I'm sorry."

"That can't be right. There's plenty —"

"I'm sorry. Perhaps another card?"

Sam fished out his American Express. "There's a mistake somewhere."

"Thank you, sir." The waiter seemed just as embarrassed as Sam.

"It'll work out," Linda said. "Can you call customer service?"

"Yeah." But stirrings of disquiet began to scramble his insides. He didn't want to think that someone was behind this. But the restaurant began to feel very small.

Linda took his hand. "I'm sure there's a simple explanation."

Sam wasn't sure.

The waiter returned, tight-lipped. He handed Sam the American Express card. "Sir, I'm really sorry."

"No way."

"I've asked the manager to —"

A bald, suited man appeared at the table, with the look of official business all over his face.

"I understand there's a problem —"

"Yes, and it's called fraud." Sam was aware that, indeed, people were watching him now. "Someone's messed with my cards."

The manager did not look convinced. "I'm sorry that I have to inquire about alternatives. Do you have another card?"

"No."

Linda said, "May I write a check?"

"We don't take personal checks," the manager said. "Without some form of security we —"

"Security?" Sam said. "You want me to sign over my house —"

"Sir —"

"I'm telling you this —"

"Sir, if you wouldn't mind coming to my office for —"

"This is ridiculous, this —"

"Sir —"

"Fine!" Sam's face burned. He threw his napkin on the table and stood up to march to the manager's office.

3.

"Sam, we need to talk."

Lew Newman stood at Sam's office door. Sam was midsip on his third cup of coffee, but it wasn't helping clear the cobwebs from his brain. He hadn't slept at all last night. It was starting to catch up with him.

"Come on in." Sam knew he must look like death on stilts. He had steamer trunks under his eyes.

Lew closed the door behind him. Sam didn't even try to read his expression. He couldn't read a postcard at the moment.

"I've known you a long time, pal." Lew sat in a client chair. "You want to tell me what's going on?"

Sam closed his eyes. "How much do you want to know?"

"How much do you want to tell me?"

"Can I ask what prompted this?"

"I've always been up front with you, Sam. I won't stop now. Hoch practically chewed my ear off. Says your argument was pathetic."

"Nice guy."

"He's the guy who tells the guy who writes the checks what to do."

"Is that what this is about, Lew? The old bottom line?"

"It's about you, Sam. Your health. What is happening?"

Sam paused, for a moment unable to gather his thoughts. "You're right. I'll tell you. I'm being hit hard. My daughter is determined to ruin her life and there's nothing I seem to be able to do."

"Drugs?"

"Who knows? She certainly is ripe for them. I'm worried sick. I haven't been sleeping. And yeah, it affects my work a little."

Lew said nothing.

"And then Friday night, I took Linda to dinner at Hazlitt's."

"Nice."

"Two hundred dollars worth of nice. And two of my credit cards were denied."

"What?"

"Because there's a guy out to mess up my life."

Lew frowned. "Who?"

"A guy I went to college with. He just showed up a couple weeks ago, first by email. Wants to see me. Old times and all. But then he gets weird. He won't take no for an answer. He won't stop contacting me. He shows up at Max's Little League game. Just to make trouble."

"Why?"

"I don't know! My friend, he's a DA, says the guy's a sociopath. I think he's right. And I think he got hold of my credit card numbers somehow."

"How could he?"

"I don't know. Computers? Maybe he hacked in."

"Where, at home?"

"Or here."

"We have a firewall."

193

"There are ways through anything. We're all at risk."

"I'll get our tech guy on it, he can check. Did you report this?"

"Yeah, the fraud department at both companies. I hope the FBI gets involved."

Lew stood up and put his hands in his pockets. He went to Sam's window, looked out on a hazy morning in LA. "What's this doing to you, Sam?"

Sam didn't really know. That's what he realized then. He was lost in a fog of unknowing.

"You think I'm hurting our chances with FulCo?"

Lew turned. "Sam, look —"

"No, I mean it."

After a long pause, Lew spoke slowly. "Maybe you ought to take some time off. Get away from all this —"

"But how? We're at the crucial stage."

"You don't think lawyers have breakdowns at crucial stages?"

Sam sat up abruptly. "Is that what you think? That I'm having a breakdown?"

"I shouldn't have used that word."

Sam leaned back in his chair, exhausted. This is what abject defeat must feel like, he thought. Not any little setback. The question was could he get out of it anytime soon? Could he reach down to his boot-straps, like his father always wanted him to? Dad, who was as tough as they came, ex-Marine. When he was around, he was a solid inspiration. But he wasn't around anymore, and Sam didn't know where his bootstraps were.

"Maybe I could cut back a little," Sam said.

"Sure," Lew said. "I can call the placement office at UCLA Law, see if we can find us an associate."

"You think?"

Lew shrugged. "It'll be stopgap. You just take care of you for now."

"How long?"

"Take a month."

"I should keep Harper, though."

Lew paused. "If you settle it."

Settling was probably the best idea yet. How much good work could Sam do on the case? And Lew had carried him on it, gone along all this time.

"I'll think about it," Sam said.

"Sure. It's your call. And if things get better sooner, come on back in. You have somebody you can see? A doctor?"

"What, a shrink?"

"I was only —"

"Practice law, Lew. Not medicine."

But then again, maybe seeing someone wasn't such a bad idea.

4.

"Why is there so much of this going on?" Sam asked Don Lyle. He was seated in Lyle's office at Solid Rock, which was the theological equivalent of a law office. Every available space on the bookshelf was filled, a testimony to a lifetime of learning.

Sam was glad to be here. The Monday afternoon sun cast burnt orange through the window.

"So much what, Sam?"

"People doing crazy things."

"It does seem there's been an increase in evil over the past forty years or so."

"Yeah, but there's always been evil, right? The Inquisition. The Holocaust."

"Those things were caused by a few powerful men taking control of vast machineries to do their will. What I'm talking about is the evil done by your neighbor, the guy next door. We've seen an explosion of the most horrid things. Child sexual assault and pornography. Serial killings. You remember Charlie Starkweather?"

"The guy from the fifties, went on a killing spree."

"Right. Shocked the nation. It was big

news for months. How could that have happened in our own country, people wondered. It was seen as a horrible aberration. Now something like that seems to happen each week."

"You have a theory on this? Why this is happening?"

"I do. I believe we're in what the Bible calls the days of Noah. Jesus said his return would come at such a time that the world seemed to be reliving the days of Noah."

"In what way?"

"Back in Genesis 6, before the flood, it says that God was grieved about making man, because he saw that the thoughts of his heart were wicked all the time, and that man's wickedness was great. It had, in other words, grown worse and worse. Why? Well, there was no institutional religion to restrain him. We give a bad rap to organized religion, but it serves a purpose. Man didn't have that, so he was left to his own nature. And man is ill equipped to deal with the devil on his own."

"So the devil made them do it?"

"It was more like the devil gave them the full range of options. Now look at what's happening today in the Christian West. The influence of the church is waning. Governments are eradicating Christian influence.

The churches grow fat and lazy with popular spirituality. So people are not getting the instruction and protection they need from the church."

"But most people don't go to church."

"Precisely. But the church, when it was part of culture, aided in holding back the worst sins of most men. Now that such influence is weak, man is left once again in the condition that was described in Genesis 6. It's no wonder, then, that sociopaths and psychopaths would increase."

"That's a very scary proposition."

"You bet it is."

"So does that mean Jesus is coming soon?"

"Sooner than yesterday, for certain. But this is also the point of our greatest spiritual opportunity. To rely on nothing in ourselves, and throw ourselves on the mercy of God. That's what he's always wanted, in any age."

"What do I do about this guy, then?"

"Can you think of any reason why he might be targeting you?"

"I've tried to think back, but I can't."

"What's he said to you since then? Anything in any of his conversations with you?"

Sam thought a moment. "I did try to bring religion up once, and he seemed to get quite upset. Not in a shouting way, but in a derisive way. He brought up this thing about fear being the basis of religion."

"Sure, that was a popular theory once."

"Man responded to the fear by creating manlike gods."

Don frowned. "Interesting."

"What?"

"Just a wild theory of my own, but I think the Bible backs me up. When men reject God, they end up trying, in their own way, to become tiny gods themselves. They do it in various ways, through power, pleasure, accomplishment. Sometimes crime. I wonder if your tormentor isn't trying to use fear — yours — to make himself godlike."

The thought clicked into place in Sam's mind, finding a perfect slot. "That makes sense. I have a friend who's an expert on sociopaths, and it would fit that profile."

"Have you shared this information with the police?"

"No. He hasn't done anything wrong, except a little minor harassment that doesn't look that bad. I couldn't get a restraining order on it. He's pretty clever about what he says."

"Then we need to pray for and against him."

"Excuse me?"

Don smiled. "Jesus said love your enemies and pray for them. But we also know from the Psalms that it's right to pray against further evil being done. We're going to pray that God will stop him."

5.

Linda Trask had a little secret she didn't share with the other ladies at church. In fact, she hadn't shared it with her own husband. Not yet.

And if she did now, she wondered if he might not seriously consider her a candidate for the mental ward.

The secret was that she sometimes wished she were Uma Thurman in that movie where she is a sword-wielding fighter. Linda hadn't seen it, only the previews, and she kept thinking it would be nice to be able to do that at certain, very specific times.

She'd have little daydreams about that, especially when she heard news accounts of some thug getting away with an obvious injustice. Or someone trying to bully people, like this guy trying to hurt her family.

She wondered just exactly what she would do if she ever again came face-to-face with Nicky Oberlin.

"Linda, would you mind opening us up?" Sandra Sykes said.

Linda snapped back to the moment, the women's prayer meeting at Sandra's. They'd been meeting here for three years, every Monday afternoon, a group of ten women from Solid Rock. An eclectic bunch, but all dedicated.

"I'm sorry," Linda said. "I'm a little distracted. Maybe someone else?"

"Sure," Sandra said. "But is there something going on? Something we can all pray for?"

"I don't want to take the focus . . ."

"Tell us, Linda. Please. That's what we're here for."

For some reason, Linda suddenly wasn't so sure that's what they were here for. She tried to purge the thought from her mind.

"Trust," Dottie Harris said. Dottie was a widow, eighty-five, and still wore a hat. Today's was wide-brimmed and had something like berries on it.

"Oh, I do," Linda said.

"Voice your trust," Dottie replied, her brown eyes sparkling. Dottie drank vegetable and fruit juices. Jack LaLanne was her heartthrob. "Take what's in here —" Dottie touched her head with her index finger — "and put it through here." She touched her mouth. "That way, all of us can put it here." She put her hand on her heart. "And send it there." She pointed to the ceiling.

"Thanks, Dottie. I just would appreciate it if you would hold our family up. Our daughter is going through a rebellious stage — at least I hope it's a stage — and there's a guy my husband knew in college who has come around and is acting kind of bizarre. So we could use protection."

"I like those prayers," Dottie said. "Fighting prayers. Let's do it."

6.

Walking through the door, Linda thought, Okay, it's better now. Prayed up and ready for a turning point. The next two weeks can't possibly be as bad as the last two.

Heather will come home.

Max won't take things so hard.

This Nicky Oberlin fellow will dry up and blow away.

And Sam will be fully mine again.

The house was empty. Max was at Todd's house. She was glad, actually, for some time alone. She'd make some lemonade and sit down with that Dallas Willard book she'd wanted to get to.

Time was all she needed.

In the kitchen she noticed the flowers. A beautiful arrangement in a vase, on the kitchen table. Brilliant colors.

Sam. She almost burst out crying. In all

of this he still thought of her, knew what she needed.

Thank you, God, for a husband like Sam. For this little bit of grace you've provided.

She mixed up the lemonade from the old family recipe. Grandma Trask handed it down to her personally when Linda married Sam. "Can't have it lost to the world," she'd said. The secret was in the rind, rubbing some of the oils into the pitcher.

Sam would love some when he got home. And then she'd slather him with a big, wet, lemony kiss.

Yes, all would be well.

Glass in hand, she took another look at the flowers, bent over to smell them. They smelled like love to her.

She saw a tiny envelope then, behind a white carnation. Her name on it.

She froze.

It was not Sam's writing.

All the good feeling seeped away now, out through her trembling hands. She opened the envelope, took out the card. Written in a hand she did not recognize was, *To one hot lady.*

7.

"Okay, you ready to lay this one down?"

Heather looked at Roz, who checked on the guys. They were smiling. Heather was sure Buck was high. But he could play guitar in any condition. This was going to be fun.

Charles "Scat" Lundquist sat in a control room, speaking to them through a mic. The little studio was off Santa Monica Boulevard, a rental place where Lundquist had recorded some of his best stuff, so he said.

"Let's do this ish," Roz said. *Ish* was Roz's favorite euphemism for the stuff they did, which was make music.

They made music. It was insane. Buck was all over his ax. Roz made the skins cry for mercy.

And Heather sang. She knew she could do this. She knew she could make it, and this was her chance.

When they were finished, Lundquist came out looking pleased. "That was good, real good." To Heather he said, "You got tubes, and that's no lie."

"Thanks." Heather thought this was all part of the dream. She'd tell about this when their record went platinum, how she'd had her doubts but came through in the end.

"Dinner's on me," Lundquist announced. "We're all going to a little place on Sunset and have ourselves a time." He whispered, "The bartenders don't ask for ID, if you're with me."

Roz said, "Yeah!"

Heather hesitated, but then thought about places on Sunset, and dreams. "Yeah," she said.

8.

"It has to be him!" Linda said.

Sam looked at the flowers and felt violated. Yes, it had to be Nicky Oberlin. He'd been inside their house. Left a mocking bouquet.

But how? What lock had he picked? Had anyone seen him?

Please, someone.

"I'm reporting this," Linda said. "We've got to get the police involved."

"Report it. But we need more."

"What is going on, Sam? Why isn't this stopping?"

"It's going to. It will."

As Linda was calling the police, Sam checked his email, half expecting to find something smarmy from Nicky. There was nothing.

And then Max was standing in the kitchen

door. "Cool flowers, Dad. You get those for mom?"

"No."

Max frowned.

"You have a good day at Todd's?"

"I guess. He's got XQued."

"What's that?"

"It's like the hottest game in the universe."

Sam nodded. "Oh. Yeah."

"But he kicks me all over. It gets boring."

Max took a banana from the fruit bowl, sat on a stool, and began peeling. Sam went into the study to check on Linda's phone call.

"On hold," she said. "I'm still shaking."

Sam put his arm around her shoulder. "We'll get through this." Linda took his hand and squeezed it.

"Get through what, Dad?" Max was standing in the doorway.

9.

Lundquist was right about the place on Sunset. He even had them in a private room, where the lights were low and the music loud and they could have whatever they wanted.

Heather had a beer. She didn't like beer much but thought it would be a good idea to try to like it.

Lundquist handed her a little glass. "Take this shot, chase it with the beer."

"What is it?"

"It's a very expensive Scotch whiskey. You're supposed to sip it slow, but if you down it quick and pour suds after it, it's a real gas."

Gas. That sounded funny to her for some reason, like something out of an old TV show. But Lundquist was, after all, a little older. And he knew things. Knew the way the world worked and the business. He was like a guide, a very cool one.

She took the Scotch and downed it like he said. Then took a big sip of beer. Times were good. She hoped her parents weren't too worried. Her mom had called her twice and left messages. She'd get back to them. But not now.

Roz and the guys were doing a pinball machine, screaming. It was like a giant kids' room in here, but for big kids like them.

"Having fun?" Lundquist asked.

"Oh, yeah."

"It's all up from here."

"Cool."

"So let me ask you something. You're how old?"

She paused. "Eighteen."

"You sure you're not upping that just a little?"

Her head was starting to buzz. She laughed, harder than she expected. "Maybe a little."

"How long before you become legal for real?"

"February."

"Want to know where I was when I was eighteen?"

"Sure." She giggled this time, then bit her lip. *Stop being a stupid little girl!*

"I was in New York City trying to get anybody to listen to my songs. It was a wild time back then. Punk was just getting started. Patti Smith, the Velvet Underground, the New York Dolls. It did not bode well for music. I was looking at these people and going, What is up with this? When the Sex Pistols came along, I'm going, somebody's gotta save rock, and that somebody's me."

"So you're the guy, huh?"

"You're lookin' at him." Lundquist smoothed the brim of his hat. It was a cool hat. "No, but I was writing songs that had something more to them than the world of punk, which is no world at all. And the music! Sorry, but that wasn't music, that was auto-salvage machinery pumped up."

Heather took another sip of beer, feeling adult indeed. Now he was talking about a history of which she knew so little. He was pouring knowledge into her head.

"The songs I was writing didn't turn out to be genius. But they came from the gut, so when I got into producing, that's what I was looking for. I'm still looking. I'm looking for guts and genius and somebody who can deliver it, sell it, somebody who can be the next big thing. The next Madonna."

Madonna? She was so . . . old.

"We haven't had another Madonna," Lundquist said. "What have we had? Eye candy like Britney Spears? Christina Aguilera? Assorted Simpsons? Please. I want a superstar, a megastar, a new sun around which music will circle for decades. Elvis big."

Elvis! She saw a biography of him once. He was a craze. She wondered if anybody would be that big again.

Lundquist looked over at Roz and the boys playing pinball. Then he leaned close. "You could be the one."

What was that? The room was starting to spin a little, and his words were a little jumbled. She shook her head.

"You hear me?" Lundquist said.

"Elvis?"

"You."

"With rock?"

"Elvis big."

"Really?"

"You want it?"

"There's no way. The music I do —"

"It could be done. But I want you to promise me something."

She wanted the room to stop spinning.

"Keep this between us right now," Lundquist said. "When the time is right, we'll take the next step."

Next step! She wondered if she could even walk out of there. But he'd said it, hadn't he? Elvis big. To her. Did he mean it? Was it a line? Or did she believe in herself? Was she going to go for it? The buzz was good. Forget about trying to stop the spin. Go with it.

She lifted her beer.

Lundquist lifted his. "To the King."

10.

"We don't keep secrets in this family," Sam said to Max. They were seated at an outdoor table at Tommy's. Max's favorite culinary fare was the Tommy Dog, a substantial beef wiener in a bun, covered with Tommy's famous chili. It was an indulgence Max was allowed on rare occasions, and this was one of them.

It was Linda's suggestion they come here. She knew Sam needed some alone time with Max. All she asked for was a Tommy Burger, which Sam would bring home.

"I know, Dad." Max was trying to put on a happy face, but Sam knew he was anxious. Max had a sensory system that picked up vibes, and he always seemed to be aware of tension in the home.

"So I'm going to tell you about what's going on. That guy from the game, remember? He's really trying to cause me some trouble."

"Why?"

"Not sure exactly, but he sent Mom those flowers. Just to mess with us. He's a bully."

"Is he gonna hurt you?"

"I don't think we have to worry about that." A deft, lawyerly answer. Sam was at least *concerned.* "But we need to get the police on this. We'll get it taken care of."

Max took a laborious bite of his Tommy Dog. It was impossible to eat those things without making a little bit of a mess. Chili smeared across Max's cheek. Sam felt a wave of love for his son. Life was messy too, and it would smear them all. They had to get through it with God's help.

"You remember that kid on the Dodgers?" Sam asked, referring to the team Max was on the year before.

"Peter," Max said with a grimace.

"Not a nice guy, was he?"

"He was a jerk."

"The coach's son."

"Yuck."

"He made life miserable for you guys. He was always yelling at you, and his dad never did anything about it."

"He put a dead squirrel in my bat bag."

"I remember. That's why I brought it up. There are people like that in this world, and we have to expect to meet up with them sometimes."

"Why are they like that?"

"Who knows? Sometimes they're just that way. This guy I'm telling you about, he's that way."

"What are you going to do?"

"We have the law on our side, Max. He can't keep getting away with this." Sam tried to make it sound like he actually believed that.

"When's Heather coming home?" Max said.

"I don't know, Max. Just keep praying."

TEN

1.

Tuesday ushered in an August that promised to give global-warming prophets something to scream about. For Pete Harper, though, it was his hopes that were melting, and Sam knew he was partly to blame.

"When I didn't hear from you," Pete told Sam, "I was afraid to call. I thought it would be bad news."

They were on the patio of Pete's backyard. Pete obviously took great pride in the landscaping. Said he'd done it himself. The grass was a thick green carpet, and the bougainvillea along the fence clipped and healthy. Sam couldn't help feeling the contrast between the beauty of Pete's yard and the despair he was in.

"I have to apologize for not calling sooner," Sam said. "That's part of the reason I'm here. I want to be up front with you, all the way."

"What is it, Mr. Trask?"

"I've had a couple of personal issues to deal with, and that has affected my routine."

"Nothing serious, I hope."

Sam considered his words carefully. "Not health related, if that's what you're thinking. A family issue, a couple of other things that hit all at once."

Pete nodded. "You don't have to talk to me about things hitting. I know that's what this life is made up of. You get knocked down. The only question is whether you get back up again."

"I wanted to tell you this, Mr. Harper, because I've decided to take some time off from my firm. Catch my breath a little. But I asked my partner to let me stay with your case."

"Thank you, Mr. Trask."

"But I think you have to make that decision, if you want me to continue."

"Why wouldn't we?"

"Because of what I've told you. If you don't have confidence in my ability."

Pete looked out at his yard, contemplating. He didn't speak for a long moment. "I've worked with a lot of men in my business, building things. The real question is whether you have the confidence, Mr. Trask. When I signed on with you, it was because

I had confidence in you. We sat down, I looked you in the eye, and I made my decision. I haven't heard anything today to change that. But if you think you can't handle it, then I'll have to think it through again."

He waited for Sam to answer. In that moment of silence Sam thought how much Pete Harper was like his own father. A man's man, direct and to the point and without a duplicitous bone in his body. A man to inspire confidence, which Sam now felt with a welcome jolt.

"I can," Sam said. "And I'll give it my all."

"That's good enough for me."

"And I want to do one more thing. I want to get Sarah all the compensation she deserves, and I don't want our firm to take a third of it. That's too much. I just ask for costs."

"You don't have to —"

"That's all, Mr. Harper. You let me take it from here."

2.

The talk with Peter Harper, and Pete's confidence in Sam, was a proverbial shot in the arm. It came from God, Sam had no doubt. An answer to prayer. A little grace in the dark, telling him it was going to be all right.

He didn't see how yet, but he was going to trust. This was going to be a change of direction. He was going to hang on to that hope.

Things had to get better now.

Sam called Larry Cohen's office from his car, planning to leave a message, but Cohen was in and Sam was put through.

Cohen's voice was sharp over the phone. "You ready to deal this thing?"

Deal. Sam fought hard not to snap something at Cohen. "Are you ready to settle this thing for fair value?"

"Let's not waste any time here, Sam. We'll go up to a mil five. That's our final offer."

"You really want to end up in court over this?"

"You really think you can try a case?"

There was a knowingness in Cohen's voice. Sam shook it off as paranoia. "You can call me with a serious offer," Sam said.

"Don't wait up." Cohen clicked off.

So it was going to be a trial. Sam figured that had been Cohen's plan all along. Cohen loved going to court for the insurance companies. He loved wearing inexpensive suits in front of juries, and playing the down-home working-man's lawyer.

A month ago, Sam would not have flinched in going up against Cohen in court. Especially with Sarah Harper's case.

Now he was not so sure. The stakes were incredibly high. He could lose it all. Sarah could get nothing. It was all on his shoulders.

Some faith you have there, Sam.

His cell phone rang.

"We need to meet," Gerald Case said. "I mean, right now."

3.

Linda went out to the backyard where Max was sitting on the grass, playing with Buzz.

No, *playing* wasn't the right word. Max was in the far corner of the yard and Buzz was nuzzling at him. Max petted the dog's head with one hand but was otherwise not too playful.

"Hey, kiddo." Linda knelt down, and Buzz turned his affectionate attentions to her, putting his forepaws on her knee. Linda stroked his back. "What's up?"

Max shrugged.

"You doing okay?"

No response. Getting Max to open up was a delicate process. He couldn't be forced. If she tried to pry open his inner life, he would put it on lockdown.

But he had to be encouraged to talk, or he bottled it all up until it burst out of its own accord.

"You worried about anything?" Linda said. "You want to talk about it?"

Max shook his head.

So she would have to guess and avoid the direct approach. "I was reading in the Bible about Paul the apostle. You know about Paul, right?"

Max squinted and reached for Buzz, who came obediently to him.

"Paul was the guy Jesus appeared to," she explained. "He was an enemy of Christians, then Jesus blinded him with light and told him to go to this town. And a man met him there and told him that God had chosen him to be a special messenger of Christianity. And so Paul gave up all the power he had and for the rest of his life went around making Christians out of people. Because of that, he was beaten, whipped, stoned. But he never gave up."

"Whipped?"

"Really bad."

"That stinks."

"But he kept right on going. Because he knew what God wanted him to do." Linda paused, making herself believe what she was about to say. "Your dad is like that. He's had some rough things happen to him. Like that guy at the baseball game. He told you about that."

Max nodded.

"Well, Dad's not going to let that stop him taking care of things, or us, like he always has. Can you believe that?"

He nodded again.

"You need anything right now?"

"Nah. I just want to sit out here for a while."

"Then you do that."

She got up. Max lay down on the grass so Buzz could lick his face.

Lord, protect him. Protect us all.

Instead of going through the back door, Linda walked along the side of the house, checking her garden, a reliable haven, always had been for her. Flowers were one of God's best ideas. The miracle of a blossoming rose was astonishing. Only a God of beauty could have created roses.

She passed through the gate to the front yard, where she had planted geraniums only last year. They were in full bloom now, an orchestra of color. She smiled.

And for some reason looked up.

The man was half a block away. His hair was blond and his chest and shoulders wide. He wore sunglasses and was leaning against a red car. He was looking directly at her.

He held the gaze. Intentionally.

Linda looked away and walked quickly into the house, feeling the man's eyes on her back.

Come on, she told herself. He's not watching the house. He's not —

She went to the window.

With as slight a movement as possible she pushed aside the curtain with her finger.

She looked out the window at the street.

But the man was gone. Gone too was any semblance of peace she had experienced in her garden.

4.

At four thirty, Sam met Gerald Case in the empty parking lot of a closed steak house on Balboa. The property stood slightly above Ventura Boulevard, affording a view.

Sam wanted to know why this spot.

"This used to be one great place," Case said. "Thick steaks, cold beer, gave you a sense of what the Valley used to be like. Back when there was some sense of history here. I did a lot of business in that place."

"So why'd it close?"

"The low-fat craze did it in. Funny. Red meat's making a comeback, but real-estate prices make this place a hard sell. One thing it does have is a nice high lot so you can see if anybody's around."

"Is that important?"

"From this point on," Case said, "you've got to count on being followed."

Sam took in a hard breath. "Why?"

"Let me tell you about our boy." Case took out a small flip pad and opened it. "Nicholas Oberlin. Hometown Sacramento. Odd jobs since college."

"He said he was into construction, I think."

"You see any calluses on his hands?"

"No."

"Father dead, mother still very much alive. I also imagine Mom is there to pick up his pieces."

"What's that mean?"

"In '84 he was arrested for felony battery. Beat up a guy with a baseball bat. It was going to be a big deal, according to the *Sacramento Bee.* But the case was suddenly dropped at the request of the prosecution. Lack of evidence."

"A guy getting beat up with a bat?"

"There's a dozen reasons it could've happened. Maybe the vic was the violent type. Self-defense maybe. Who knows? So the DA drops it, but the guy sues Oberlin in civil court. The case never goes to trial."

"They settled."

"Mom paid 'im off. Don't know how much, but there you go. He had two DUIs, one in '94, the other in '97. Did a couple days in jail on the second one. And all this time he's living with Mama."

"That's a little Freudian."

"A little Norman Bates-ish."

"Don't go there, please."

"I go where the information leads. Anyway, nothing in the public record, at least in California, that I can find after that. But you need to know you're not just dealing with some college chum. He's a guy with a violent past and no relationships to speak of except with his mom. That kind of profile, along with all his behavior to date, spells trouble."

Sam looked at the eucalyptus trees lining the street. They always seemed haphazard to him, these trees that were probably planted fifty years ago in the Valley. Like no one had any idea what they'd look like full grown.

"So now what?" Sam said.

"I'd like to have a look at the guy. Find out where he's hanging his hat."

"You want to see him?"

"You have a problem with that?"

"No, but how are you going to find him?"

"You're going to find him for me."

Sam shook his head.

"Set up a meeting," Case said. "Mention that you have some information to share with him, about his mother up in Sacramento. That will rock his boat."

"Where?"

"You pick the place. A park would be good. Plenty of room for me. My guess is he'll try to change the place, to be in control. He may even change it when you're on your way to see him. But I'll be following you."

"And what if he catches on?"

"He won't." Case smiled, put the pad back in his coat pocket. "Because I'm the best there is, Mr. Trask. I don't get seen unless I decide that's exactly what I want."

After Case left, Sam composed an email on his BlackBerry.

Time for us to meet again, Nicky. We need to talk about the next move. Your mom up in Sacramento must worry about you. Don't want her to. There's a way to make sure she doesn't. Two o'clock tomorrow, Lanark Park.

5.

At home, Sam found Linda wound tight. She told him about the man who was staring at her from across the street.

"You sure he wasn't scoping out something else? The house?"

"Why would he be staring at the house?"

"Could be any number of reasons. Maybe he's house shopping."

"Our house isn't on the market, Sam."

"He could have been checking out the neighborhood."

"Do you really believe that?"

Sam sighed. "I don't know what to believe. I didn't see him. I don't think this has anything to do with Nicky Oberlin."

"Why not?"

"Because Nicky's a lone wolf. That's what I think. I met with Gerald Case today, and it sounds like he's a bit of a mama's boy."

"What does that mean?"

"He's got a mother in Sacramento who always gets him out of trouble. Anyway, Case is going to follow him and figure out where he's staying."

"How is he going to find him?"

"I'm going to meet with him."

Linda stiffened. "Did he contact you again?"

"I contacted him."

"But why?"

"Honey, this is what I have to do. I have to meet with him so Case can tail him. I also want to tape our conversation. He may say something that we can take to the DA."

"Sam, what are you doing?"

"Huh?"

"You're not a detective. This is dangerous."

"I'm not about to let it go on any longer."

"What if he tries to hurt you?"

The possibility had crossed Sam's mind on more than one occasion. "If I just wait and do nothing, he could try it anyway. Linda, we've got to take action now or he won't stop harassing us. We can't let him be the one in control."

Linda laughed. It was the sort of laugh that carries sadness and hilarity at the same time.

"What's so funny?"

"Control. God's supposed to be the one in control of everything, right? This is some sort of funny control."

And then she began to cry. Sam took her in his arms and held her.

6.

"Sammy!" Nicky's voice was ebullient over the phone. "Thanks for the email, good buddy. I'd *love* to get together."

"Lanark Park. You know where it is?"

"Sure! Looked it up. Can't wait to see you face-to-face."

Gamesmanship. "Tomorrow," Sam said. "Two o'clock."

"We have *lots* to talk about." A hard tone now.

"Oh, yeah," Sam said. "You are so right about that."

Sam was shaking when he closed his phone. What was he doing? Linda was right. This was no time to play detective.

Or was it? It beat sitting and waiting.

Which is what he had to do now. The night lay ahead, and he was sure he wouldn't sleep again. Maybe he'd pop a Benadryl. That seemed to help sometimes.

Drugs.

Trust. The word popped into his mind with neon brightness.

Sure, trust. But he wasn't feeling God-trust in his body and bones. Didn't he have a book somewhere on that topic?

Sam loved books, collected too many. His bookshelves were overstuffed. When he became a Christian he dove into the study of Christianity, like he had clamped his jaws on the law. He bought books he knew he wanted to read someday, and they piled up.

He scanned the shelf and found the volume he was looking for. A simple tome entitled *Trust in the Lord,* a collection of various authors.

He took it and sat, opening to the table of contents. His saw a section written by Charles Spurgeon. He'd heard that name. Don Lyle mentioned him sometimes. He was apparently a famous English preacher from the 1800s.

Sam turned to the page.

In seasons of severe trial, the Christian has nothing on earth that he can turn to, and is therefore compelled to cast himself on his God alone. When his vessel is on its beam-ends, and no human deliverance can avail, he must simply and entirely trust himself to the providence and care of God. Happy storm that wrecks a man on such a rock as this!

Happy storm? A bit odd, wasn't it? How could anybody be happy in a storm? Maybe that was just a quaint way of putting it back then. But then there was that bit about wrecks.

Be strong and very courageous, and the Lord thy God shall certainly, as surely as he built the heavens and the earth, glorify himself in thy weakness, and magnify his might in the midst of thy distress.

Glory in weakness. Might in the midst of distress. It sounded like something only God could do.

Sam closed the book and his eyes. He wasn't sensing any glory in any of this. When he finally went up to bed, it was weakness he felt most of all. After whispering a prayer for Heather, he fell into a fitful sleep.

7.

"Sammy, what a nice gesture to want to meet me. Maybe we can end up doing some business together after all."

Nicky Oberlin wore his fake wide smile, as open as the area where they were meeting. Lanark Park was on the corner of Topanga and Roscoe. It took up an entire block, with ball fields and a pool, and a large grassy area with plenty of trees.

It was a little run-down. The city, strapped for funds, didn't keep it up as well as it used to. Sam remembered bringing the kids here when they were little. There was considerably more trash strewn about, and patches of dry ground, than in those happier times.

Heather had loved the swing set here. It was a big one, and you could go high. It was also in a wide-open space, which is why Sam chose it for this meeting. On a Wednesday afternoon, it wasn't as heavily trafficked as it would be on a weekend.

Gerald Case, parked on Roscoe, could very easily see the two of them.

"Let's cut the pretend stuff, all right?" Sam said. "You went too far when you broke into my house with that flower stunt." Sam had his micro tape recorder in his side pocket, had pressed the record button just before Nicky walked up to him.

Everything was in order, it seemed. So why was he shaking?

Because he knew Nicky Oberlin was capable of anything. But it was time to turn up the heat. The law, after all, was on Sam's side. He'd made sure of that.

"Stunt?" Nicky said. "I'm afraid I don't follow."

"You follow."

"But breaking into your house? That's a crime, isn't it?"

"You should know all about crimes, Nicky. Crimes involving baseball bats."

When Nicky didn't respond right away, Sam took comfort in a point scored. Maybe Nicky wouldn't be such a hard one to scare off after all.

"Sammy, you're talking funny for an old friend."

"Funny or not, you entered my house. Why?" He wanted to get it on tape, an admission. Something he could take to Cam Bellamy.

"You've got to get off that, Sam. I would never do anything like that to you."

"You're lying. You have a criminal record. I know all about it. I know all about your mother too."

Nicky's cheeks twitched. "You better tread lightly, Sammy. You could hurt a guy's feelings."

"I wonder if Mom knows what you've been up to down here. Maybe I ought to —"

"You best not mention my mother again."

"Oh, Mommy wouldn't like that news?"

Nicky snorted. "You're not too good at threats, Sammy."

"No, I guess you're the master, huh? That's what you want to be. You didn't make it in life, so you want to tear down those who have. Well, it's over for you, Nicky. You can't win. I know all about you and Mom and I will seriously —"

"I told you to shut up about her. You better, you hear?"

"Or what, Nicky?"

He smiled. "I will take you apart, bit by bit. You and your family."

At that moment Sam wished more than anything that he had a gun. He would have used it. The truth startled him. It was wrong, it was murder. Oh, maybe he could justify some sort of self-defense or heat-of-passion argument, but he knew his heart was pumping cold blood and he could do it right now.

"It's over for you, Nicky. This is my last warning. The DA knows everything about you now. You're persona non grata in LA. I know too many people. Better run home where it's safe. And don't show your face to me or anyone I know again."

A kid screamed on the swing set, and Sam almost jumped out of his shoes. He hoped the fright wasn't flashing on his face like a cheap restaurant sign. Nicky just stared at him.

Finally, shrugging, Nicky said, "Have it your way, Sammy. It's a real disappointment that you treat old friends this way. A real bad disappointment. Because I was willing to be friends, to let bygones be bygones. I guess human beings will always let you down. I thought you were better than that. I really did. But now I see you're just like everybody else, just like you were back at the dorm. Looking out for number one. Some Christian you turned out to be."

Nicky Oberlin shook his head derisively, then turned his back and walked toward the parking lot.

Sam watched him go and for a split second almost felt sorry for him. The guy had no life, and somewhere he'd gone diving into a pool filled with darkness.

Maybe that would be the last of Nicky in his life. But he wasn't counting on it. At least now he had a tape recording, and Gerald Case was taking things from here.

Pile up the ammo for a rainy day.

8.

Sam went to the office to box up all the files in the Harper case. He thought it more efficient to work on this at home. Doreen helped him.

"It's not going to be as fun around here with you gone, Mr. Trask."

"Fun? You'll have a blast."

"Are you okay?" She sounded like a little sister, and he was happy she did.

"I'll be fine, Doreen. I've been practicing law without a break for twenty years. Maybe I deserve some time off."

She started organizing the files in the box,

setting them in order. "You know, I was thinking of going to law school."

He looked at her. She raised her eyes, young eyes, fresh and clean. She was a good kid, Doreen. A tremendous help around the office. Working here while she finished up at Cal State at night, supporting a mother who was not doing well.

"Do you think that's a good idea, Mr. Trask? Law school? I mean, there are so many lawyers out there."

"Not all lawyers are created equal. We'll always need good ones."

"Is it worth it?"

Sam paused, leaning on the file cabinet. "How do you mean? Time and money?"

Doreen shook her head. "No, I mean is it something worth doing with your life?"

That was the big question for this generation, he thought. They were all about wanting to do something meaningful. Even Heather. She didn't want to go the college way. Maybe he should resign himself to that.

But here was one who could have been his daughter. He felt very fatherly all of a sudden.

"I wanted the same thing when I went into law," he said. "There's always been a lot of cynicism about lawyers. Remember what Shakespeare said in one of his plays? 'First thing we do, let's kill all the lawyers.' "

"That would be a lot of killing." She giggled.

"And all the lawyer jokes. Like, what do you call a thousand lawyers at the bottom of the ocean?"

Doreen laughed. "A good start."

"See that? Everybody knows 'em." He paused a moment. "But when I really started to think about what I was doing with my life, I found an old book in the UCLA library. It was a book of reflections on life and the law, and they had a quote by John Locke. He said, 'The end of the law is not to abolish or restrain, but to preserve and enlarge freedom.' I wanted to be part of that kind of thing."

"And have you been?"

He thought about all the big cases he and Lew had done over the years, the major corporate clients. The memories didn't move him. But then he thought of Sarah Harper, and her mother and father.

"Yeah," he said. "In some small way, maybe I have. And you can too, Doreen. Hang on to some idealism. It's the only thing that holds our fabric together. You remember when Hurricane Katrina hit New Orleans?"

"Of course."

"When it became apparent there was no law around, the looting started, the shootings. In the absence of law, that's what people do."

"Sheesh."

He remembered then how he felt yesterday, when he'd faced Nicky Oberlin in the park. How he had the urge to kill him right there. He wasn't so far from lawlessness himself. He decided not to share that inspirational moment with Doreen.

Sam got a page from reception. A man had a package for him. Should he come on back? He needed a signature. Sam said to send him down. He stepped out of the office into the corridor to wait.

The man was dressed in a nice blue suit and wore a pleasant smile. "Mr. Trask?"

"Yes."

"This is addressed to you." He held out a paper folded in thirds. The moment Sam took it the man said, "You've been served." Then he turned on his heel and walked away.

Lew came out of his office, watched the man exit. "What was that all about?"

Sam opened the paper and almost burst a blood vessel. "He's suing me."

"Who?"

"You have to ask?"

9.

Sam noticed the man in the red Beemer on Marquand Avenue, facing Sam's house. It was the way he was sitting, as if he had nothing else to do but watch.

And he matched the description Linda had given him.

The guy looked at Sam as he drove by. Surely there was some rational explanation for this.

Sam parked, got out, walked across the street.

The man in the car didn't move, didn't make eye contact with him. Sam heard the low tones of the car stereo as he came up on the driver's side. The window was up.

"Help you?" Sam said, loud enough to be heard through the glass.

The man looked at him, smiled, and shook his head.

"You look a little lost."

The door opened. Some urban beat thumped out of the car. The man who emerged was thick across the chest, with short blond hair and blue eyes. A Norwegian linebacker. His forearms had bulges under a long-sleeved, red linen shirt.

"You want to say something?" the man said.

Sam knew this guy could take him apart

like so many Legos. But he had to know who he was. One of the things Sam could do was size up a potential juror with a few well-chosen questions. The trick was to get him to talk.

"Just wondering if I could help you out," Sam said. "You looking for someone?"

"Sure."

"Who?"

"That's kind of a personal question, isn't it?"

"Just trying to help."

"I'm good. Thanks."

"Nice car."

"Have a nice day."

The guy got back in his car and slammed the door. And sat there.

Sam walked around the back of the car, took a long look at the license plate, then walked across the street to his house.

He decided not to tell Linda about the encounter. She had enough on her mind as it was. And she would soon have more. He sat her down in the living room and showed her the complaint he'd been served. "Oberlin's suing me."

She looked over the first page. "I can't believe this."

"It's all too believable now." He took the complaint from her. "I presume Heather's not here."

"She called me. She's looking for a place with Roz."

"Delightful. More answered prayer."

"Sam, maybe we can't see the answer yet. Heather has to go through this."

"Why? Why did God set it up this way? I'm used to knowing the rationale behind decisions. This not knowing bites."

"You sound like one of Heather's band mates."

"Please."

He walked casually by the front window, looking through the lace curtain. The red car with Mr. Linebacker was gone.

Eleven

1.

Los Angeles Daily Journal
Local Lawyer Sued for Assault

Samuel Trask, one of the name partners in the well-regarded boutique firm of Newman & Trask, is being sued for assault and battery by a former college classmate.

According to the complaint filed by Nicholas Oberlin, 47, Trask tried to choke Oberlin after an argument at a Little League baseball game on July 22.

One witness, who requested anonymity, said that Trask appeared agitated when he confronted Oberlin, who claims he was there to show support for Trask's son, who was on the field that day. "Next thing that happened, the guy grabs him by the neck and pushes him against the fence," the witness said. "Two big guys had to pull him off."

Calls to Newman & Trask were not returned.

2.

"Man, Sam, what is going on? It's like you're spinning out —"

"Forget about it, Lew."

"Did you see the *Daily Journal*?"

"Yeah. I'm a poster boy for a lawyer cracking up."

"Are you cracking up, Sam?"

"Sometimes I feel like it, I'll be honest with you. But I've got some people holding me up."

"Like me?"

"Sure, Lew. But I'm not married to you. Linda is showing her true colors. She's been a rock."

Lew was silent for a long moment. "You know, of course, that this is putting me in kind of a tight spot."

"You?"

"Us. The firm."

"Bad publicity."

"Hey, what can you do? Newspapers. Blogs. No privacy anymore. Dirty laundry gets hung out to dry and stays there."

"And we've got dirty laundry now."

"It all stinks, Sam. But maybe . . ."

"Go ahead."

"When we started out, remember, just a couple of young turks full of starch and vinegar, we agreed that if anything we did were to hurt the partnership we'd —"

"Agree to go our separate ways."

"It rips me to say that."

"I know. But you're right. And maybe it's time for me to reevaluate. I'm closing in on fifty. I wonder what I'm supposed to be when I grow up."

"Be a lawyer, my friend."

"Yeah, but what kind? Maybe God wants me to do something different with it."

"There you go. You can get it straight from the Big Guy."

Sam's heart did a slow, sad turn. "I'm not going to stand in the way, Lew. Go ahead and do up some dissolution papers and we'll go from there."

"I feel terrible about this."

"Don't."

"If you need anything, Sam, anything at all, you come right to me. This isn't the end of the friendship. And I certainly need to exact some revenge on you on the golf course."

"You can have at me, Lew, when I feel like I'm allowed to have fun again."

3.

"Cam, you have to do something to stop this guy."

"He has to break the law, Sam. He hasn't done that."

In Cam Bellamy's stuffy office, Sam felt like he was having to fight for air. Also, for Cam's attention. He seemed more than a bit consternated at Sam's presence. Sam had to remind himself that Cam was a working deputy DA, and as such had a full plate of things to do, especially on a Friday afternoon.

"He's abusing the law," Sam said, almost desperately. "He's using it to get at me. That's a crime."

"His lawyer will say he gets his day in court, and —"

"He hasn't got a lawyer. He's handling this himself."

"Then *he'll* say he gets his day in court. And the judge'll nod and look you in the snout and say, 'Are you against the legal system, Mr. Trask?' "

"Very funny."

"If I was trying to be funny I'd crack a joke."

"If you want to turn a blind eye, then why don't you —"

"Whoa, that's not what I'm doing and you

know it."

"Do I?"

"You should." Clipped and formal voice.

Sam thought about letting it go, but said, "Maybe you'll be turning a blind eye to me, returning the favor, so to speak."

"What're you talking about?"

"Nothing. Yet."

Cam pointed a finger at him. "Don't you start messing around the edges, Sam. That's not going to solve anything, and I don't want to see your can in the can."

"You threatening me?"

Thankfully, Cam Bellamy paused and allowed the heat in the room to go down a notch.

"Look how we're talking here," Cam said. "This guy's got your goat, and good. He wants you to freak, start doing crazy things. But what's he got? Nada, some half-baked assault suit. Take the offense. Counter sue. Talk to the press. You've got a solid career behind you. People won't believe this nut once you explain things."

Sam took a deep breath. His palms were sweating. Cam was right, of course. Nicky was playing him like a bass fiddle.

"There was a guy parked across from my house yesterday," Sam said. "And the day before. I think he was watching it."

"You sure?"

"Maybe ninety percent."

"What makes you think so?"

"Just instinct. I talked to him. He didn't seem very forthcoming."

"Any reason why he should be?"

Sam shrugged. "I got the guy's license plate. Is there a way you could trace it?"

"I could, if I had a reason."

"I just gave you one."

"Sam —"

"Please. We need to follow everything up. We have to find some legal grounds, anything, to get Oberlin."

"I agree with you."

Sam heaved a long, deep sigh. "Too bad we can't arrest people for what they *might* do."

"In that case," Cam said, "we'd all be locked up."

4.

Sam suggested to Linda the idea that they take Max and go up to Universal City Walk. She eagerly agreed. It was getting on toward four o'clock, and she was glad to be relieved of dinner duty.

Usually, Sam didn't like City Walk. It was always crowded and noisy. And Friday night would be the worst of it.

But today chaos almost seemed like it would be a blessing, something to drown out the interior sounds with the noise of something happening, life going on. They could have a nice dinner, maybe catch a movie. If there was anything worth seeing.

At four ten Max bounded through the door, looking remarkably happy. "I was making solid contact at the batting cage, Dad."

Sam remembered it was practice day for Max's team. One of the team dads had a batting cage at his house.

"That's great." Sam put his hand up. "High five."

Max slapped the hand. "I was keeping my head down and it made the difference. I just hope I can do that in a game."

"You will. Play like you practice, that's all."

"Wanna play catch?"

"Wanna go to City Walk?"

"Really?"

"Get something to eat, see a movie?"

"Which one?"

"We'll figure it out when we get there."

"Okay. Can we do some catch first? I want to practice my knuckle ball." Max, who was not one of the pitching prospects, had recently decided he could make it to the majors with a floater.

"Sure," Sam said. "Grab the stuff and I'll meet you out back."

Max smiled and ran up the stairs.

Linda gave Sam a kiss on the cheek. "You're a great father, you know that?"

"If I was so great Heather would be here, not out there."

"Please, don't be hard on yourself. Not tonight."

But he'd always been hard on himself, that was how he got to where he was. The idea of resting in God was still a hard one for him.

Max raced by with the mitts and a ball. "Let's go!" He was out the back door in no time.

Linda started to loosen Sam's tie. "Okay, Ace, go show off your arm."

"Right. They used to time my fastball with a calendar."

"But I bet you looked good in those tight pants."

"Oh, yeah. Looking good is the secret to the whole thing."

"Go. And don't get any grass stains on your slacks. I don't want to have to —"

A scream ripped the air.

Max.

"Mom! Dad!"

Another scream.

5.

Heather wondered if she could play with fire.

If she was going to make it in this business, she'd have to learn how. And Lundquist was definitely making sparks.

"I'm supposed to be looking for a job," she told him. They were on a bench in Ocean Front park. The sun was setting over the ocean. So cool.

"What kind of job?" Lundquist asked.

"Waiting tables, I guess."

"You're never going to have to wait tables."

"You think so?"

"You're going to do things you never even dreamed about."

She looked at him. The glow of the sun reflected off his mirrored shades. "How?"

"Let me show you."

Fire. The thrill of the drop. "Okay," she said.

"But I have to know something."

"What?"

"If you really want it. If you really want to be a major star."

"I do."

"Enough to do what I tell you?"

She started to feel the least bit hemmed in. "Within reason."

"My reasons are the only reasons. If you want this, that's rule number one. Otherwise we can call the whole thing —"

"Whatever you say. But what about Roz and the guys?"

Lundquist pulled his hat down a little farther. "You'll do an album together. But you are going to go past that. Don't worry, it happens all the time. It's inevitable."

She wanted to believe that was true. Ever since she was thirteen she wanted to be on the cover of *Teen People* or *Entertainment Weekly.* She saw herself there in a tight dress, maybe in a picture taken at the Grammys.

"You like Stacee Hartin?" he asked.

"Oh yeah, she's awesome."

"Ever seen her in concert?"

"No."

"Want to?"

"For real?"

"She's playing a one-nighter in Vegas. I might be able to score some tickets. I want you to see her. I want you to see what she does. Because you are going to do the same thing. You interested?"

Stacee Hartin. Vegas.

Vegas. With him. All right. Deal with it.

You're ready. It doesn't have to be that way.

On the other hand, what if it turns out *that way?* What if this turns into one of those pairings, where the star gets the behind-the-scenes treatment from her powerful husband?

Quit being such a wimp. He'll see it in your eyes.

Lundquist seemed to be reading her eyes anyway. "And don't worry about anything. We'll get a couple of rooms, they're cheap there. Maybe I'll teach you how to play craps. We'll have fun, we'll see a great show, and most important of all, you'll see what your future is going to be. That is, if you want it."

"I do," she said, her heart beating faster. "More than anything."

6.

Sam saw Max on his knees, sobbing loudly, his body doubled over, shaking.

"Max, what is it?"

No answer, just cries rising up in a heart-tearing wail.

Linda hit the ground next to Max. Sam saw her rock back.

And then he saw why.

In front of Max, Buzz wasn't moving.

"He's dead!" Max screamed. Sam saw his

son's eyes, wide with hot grief.

Sam stiffened, his insides cold.

Linda pulled Max to her, holding him close as he shook. Even as she did, she looked up at Sam and her eyes said, *Why?*

"Take him inside," Sam said.

Max broke free and started hitting the ground with his fists, shrieking.

Sam pulled his son up by the shoulders. Max fought against him. Sam turned his skinny body around and said, "Max, go with your mother."

"I don't want to! I want to stay with Buzz!"

"Not now, Max."

"Don't throw him away!"

"I won't, I promise." He kept his grip on Max's shoulders and waited. Max's face was drenched with tears, but he started to calm a little. "Go with Mom."

He watched the two walk toward the house. Mother and son, her arm around his body, his head against her, his world violated.

If Sam could have taken the hurt from his son and implanted it in himself, he would have. But you couldn't take another's pain.

You could, however, inflict it.

7.

Sam made sure an LAPD officer was present in the vet's office. The young vet, David, had taken care of Buzz since he was a pup.

"I can't be certain until the test comes back," he told Sam and the cop in the outer office. "But from the tongue it looks like poison."

"You got trouble with a neighbor?" the cop said. He was also young — everybody seemed young to Sam these days — a Latino with an earnest face. The silver nameplate on his chest said *Morales.*

"This wasn't a neighbor."

"You know who?"

"A guy named Nicky Oberlin."

"Why do you think it was this guy?"

"I don't think. I know."

"That's not —"

"Just write up your report," Sam said. "My dog was poisoned."

The cop didn't argue. He started filling out a form he'd placed on top of a metal note box.

David cleared his throat. "Sam, what would you like me to do with Buzz?"

"I'm taking him," Sam said. "We'll bury him at the pet park in Calabasas. Max needs that."

TWELVE

1.

"Trust me on this," Gerald Case said.

"Sure."

"Believe me."

"Fine."

Sam was driving. It was Saturday, late morning, and Sam had left his house still raging at what Nicky Oberlin had done. Killing the dog, and killing part of Max's spirit. Sam had called Case and told him it was time to kick things up more than a notch.

Case repeated, "Trust me on this."

Case had given Sam the cross streets in Reseda. The neighborhood had seen its glory days in the 1950s. It was now run-down, tired, as if it had given up the fight to look like a nice place to live. Patchy lawns in front of stucco houses testified to the misery of neglect.

"In here." Case pointed to an alley. Sam

turned into it. Case told him to pull up against a fence next to a row of city-issued trash receptacles.

"Now what?" Sam said.

"We wait."

"Wait for what?"

"The go-ahead. When it comes to illegal activity, it's best to know you're not being surveilled. You brought the cash, right?"

"Five hundred."

Case nodded. "Then as soon as Cutter thinks we're clear, we do business."

"Somebody named Cutter should be selling knives, not guns."

"Cutter sells all sorts of things."

"You know the most interesting people."

Case smiled. "You do this long enough, you don't exactly go to the social register for your contacts."

Sam looked at the weeds growing out of the asphalt near the trash cans. He thought of the future, like the one in that movie with Mel Gibson. *Mad Max.* Was this where the world was headed? Decent guys buying black-market guns because it's every man for himself?

"You want the rest of the report?" Case said.

"Please."

"Oberlin's living in an apartment on Normandie. I can give you the exact address and room number."

"Anything else?"

Case shook his head. "I want to watch his movements for a couple of days. Then we'll talk."

"I don't want to wait too long on this."

"Don't worry. He probably doesn't either."

The thought did not do a thing to quiet Sam's nerves.

"Okay," Case said, looking around one more time. "Let's go buy us a gun."

2.

Case pulled his car to a stop behind a van parked at the far end of the alley. Between a cracking cinderblock wall on one side, and high wooden fence on the other, the place was relatively hidden from prying eyes.

The van's driver-side door opened, and a guy the size of a sumo got out. Sam immediately thought this was not someone he'd like to meet in a dark alley. He wasn't too keen on meeting him in this sunlit alley.

But Case slapped Sam's knee and smiled. "There's Cutter. Come on."

Cutter leaned against the back of the van, arms folded, eyes behind dark glasses. In a sleeveless denim shirt, Cutter's arms displayed a landscape of tattoos.

"Hey, Cut, whattaya say?" Case offered his hand, which disappeared into the paw of the gun merchant.

"Hey, bro," Cutter said, in a voice that was completely out of keeping with the bodily form. It was high and . . . Sam realized with a jolt it belonged to a woman.

"This is my client," Case said. "You can call him Sam."

Cutter extended her hand. "What up?"

Sam shook hands. Cutter's grip was as firm as any man's. "Nothing much," Sam answered.

"Don't look like much of a shooter, does he?" Cutter said.

"He's a lawyer," Case answered.

"That's cool."

Sam was glad it was cool with Cutter.

"So you got the five hundred?" Cutter asked Sam.

"Yes."

"Let's see it."

Sam had the cash in his coat pocket. But suddenly found he couldn't fish it out.

"What's up?" Cutter said, looking at Case.

"I can't do this," Sam said.

Case shook his head. "What's the matter, Sam?"

"I just can't." But he wanted to. He

wanted to badly. He wanted this weapon in his hands and loaded and pointed at Nicky Oberlin's head. And he knew that was exactly why he couldn't go through with it.

Cutter said, "And why not? I don't look like somebody you can trust?"

"No reflection on you. I just have to do it another way."

"The legal way is what you're saying?"

"I guess so." Weak. But that's what it was going to have to be.

"I'm out five hundred! I got bills to pay, you know."

Case said, "Sam, think this over. You need protection."

"Legally, Gerry. That's it."

"You'll have to wait ten days. You think Oberlin cares?"

Sam peeled off a hundred dollar bill and gave it to Cutter. "For your time," Sam said.

"I knew I liked you," Cutter said. "Come back and see me sometime."

Oh, sure. Sam got another hand-crushing shake before he and Case left.

Later that afternoon, Sam bought the giant-size Law Enforcement Take Down pepper spray from Bill's Security in Canoga Park and began the process of purchasing a gun according to the laws of the State of California.

3.

"Hey."

Max didn't answer. He kept his head on the pillow.

"Time to get ready for church," Sam said.

His son shook his head slightly.

"How you feeling, bud?"

A shrug.

"I know you're still thinking about Buzz. We all are."

He saw Max squirm under the covers. He still hadn't turned his head.

"But the thing is, Max, sometimes really sad things happen like this, and that's the time you really have to let God help you." Sam was talking to himself now too. "Church is where your friends are, the people who know you and care about you."

"I don't feel like going," Max said.

"I know you don't. But it's when you don't feel like it that going's the best thing for you."

"I just don't . . ." His voice trailed off.

Sam thought about leaving it at that. Let him stay home and mourn by himself. But it didn't seem right. This was one of those defining moments when a kid had to look into the wrong end of the telescope toward grown-up status. A tiny glimpse, but also a preparation.

"Come on, Max my man. Don't let who-ever did this get you down."

"God did it."

The answer startled him. "No."

"He let it. He could've stopped it. He could've brought Buzz back to life. God can do anything but he didn't, so he killed Buzz, didn't he? What's the difference?"

Sam cleared his throat, silently praying for the right words. "Hey, what do they call the guy who comes in when the game is on the line?"

Max rolled over so his face was up. "You mean the closer?"

"Yeah. All I know, Max, is that God is the closer. And he can't be beat. We can only beat ourselves. If we hang back because we're afraid, we lose. Let's not let that happen. Let's go for it."

For a long time Max was silent, concentrating. "I'm just so sad," he finally said.

"I know."

"I'm afraid if I go to youth group I might cry or something. I don't want to be a baby."

"That's one thing you're not, Max. You want to come to church with Mom and me this time?"

He nodded as if relieved.

"Then hop in the shower and let's go."

Sam went downstairs and found Linda

staring out the kitchen window, coffee mug in hand.

"It shouldn't be like this," she said.

"How about some eggs?"

"Did you hear what I said?"

"Don't worry, Max is getting —"

"This is not *right*."

"I know." Sam put his arm around her shoulder. She tightened.

"I'm worn out from praying," Linda said. "Just so tired."

4.

Monday morning, Sam had to wait in the DA's reception area for Cam Bellamy to come back from court. He had a file under his arm and seemed distracted, and not exactly pleased to see Sam.

"You making this your home away from home?" Cam said.

Without waiting for an answer he motioned Sam to follow him inside. Cam stopped just outside his office and grabbed a Styrofoam cup from the coffee station. He didn't offer any to Sam.

"Were you able to trace that license plate?" Sam said.

Cam pushed the spout on the coffee urn, and only a small drizzle issued. "Hey, can we get some coffee made?" he said to no one in particular. Then to Sam: "Not yet."

"When?"

"Sam, I've got a full load, so just —"

"I have new information."

Cam tossed the near-empty cup into a trash can. "Come on." Sam followed the deputy DA into his office, where he threw his file on the desk.

"What new information?" Cam said wearily.

"He poisoned our dog."

Cam looked at him. "What?"

"Three days ago."

"You sure it was him?"

"Who else would it be?"

"Can you prove it?"

"You can. Get a search warrant. I can tell you where he lives. Gerald Case found the address."

"I need probable cause for a warrant."

"You can always find a way to get it."

"You watch too many TV shows."

"Then use this." Sam took his palm-size tape recorder out of his coat pocket and placed it on Cam's desk. He pressed the play button.

"Let's cut out the pretend stuff, all right? You went too far when you broke into my house with that flower stunt."

"Stunt? I'm afraid I don't follow."

"You follow."

"But breaking into your house? That's a crime, isn't it?"

"You should know all about crimes, Nicky. Crimes involving baseball bats."

"Sammy, you're talking funny for an old friend."

"Funny or not, you entered my house. Why?"

"You've got to get off that, Sam. I would never do anything like that to you."

"Forget the act. You have a criminal record. I know all about it. I know all about your mother too."

"Better tread lightly, Sammy. You could hurt a guy's feelings."

"I wonder if Mom knows what you've been up to down here. Maybe I ought to —"

"You best not mention my mother again."

"Oh, Mommy wouldn't like that news?"

"You're not too good at threats, Sammy."

"No, I guess you're the master, huh? That's what you want to be. You didn't make it in life, so you want to tear down those who have. Well, it's over for you, Nicky. You can't win. I know all about you and Mom and I will seriously —"

"I told you to shut up about her. You better, you hear?"

"Or what, Nicky?"

"I will take you apart, bit by bit. You and your family."

Sam clicked off the tape.

"It's not admissible in court," Cam said.

"You suggested I do it."

"Yes, but for —"

"I can swear to the words in an affidavit. Won't that give you probable cause for a warrant?"

After a long moment, Cam said, "All right, Sam. But I hope for your sake, and mine, we find something at this guy's place."

"How long will it take?"

"Give me twenty-four hours."

Twenty-four hours.

He could wait that long.

He hoped.

5.

"It's so obvious," Roz said.

"What is?"

"Lundquist. He wants you." Roz leaned back on the couch in her room, which was a converted garage at her mom's house in Winnetka. They had some classic Pearl Jam pumping.

"So?" Heather said. "I'm irresistible."

"You going to?"

"Going to what?"

"Let him?"

"Jeez . . ."

"You should."

Heather just stared at her.

"Think about it," Roz said. "You give it up to a record pro, no telling what he could do for us."

Us. Heather tried to keep her face impassive. She wasn't betraying Roz and the band. They'd get their names out there. But people moved on all the time. And what if she did let Lundquist be the one? Better than a lot of the grunges who wanted her.

"Let's just play it loose," Heather said.

"Let's party."

"Sure."

"Shall we call up some people?"

Heather thought a moment. "Nah. Let's hammer it out ourselves."

"Right on." Roz went to her nightstand and pulled out a drawer and came out with a big bottle of Jack Daniels. Then she brought out a pipe and baggie and matches.

Okay, this will be nice, get out of the moment for a while, get out of the dark, go flying, pass out, wake up. Do it again.

She wondered why thoughts like dark clouds kept coming. Roz took a pull straight from the bottle, then passed it to Heather, who did the same. Burning down the throat. Feeling the burn was what made the thoughts get lighter, so she kept going, and it tasted good.

6.

It was early evening, and Sam was in his study reading interrogatories in the Harper file, when Cam Bellamy called.

"Thought you'd like to know, we picked up Nicky Oberlin."

"That's great," Sam said.

"Found some pictures of you, Sam."

"What?"

"And your kids, like he had a telephoto lens."

Sam's skin prickled. "That shows he's targeting us."

"There was a handgun too. It's registered. We have just enough to try to link this up to harassment. It won't be easy, but —"

"I don't care how hard it is. Just go for it."

"He made bail. Cash. Thought you should know that too."

"Thanks."

"One more thing. I got the trace on the license number."

"And?"

"Registered to a guy named Charles Steinbring. A '98 Saturn."

"This car was a BMW."

"And Steinbring died last year. The Saturn's been in impound for four months."

"So what's that mean?"

"Who knows? You sure you got the number right?"

"I'm sure I did."

"It's possible the plates were lifted."

"So the guy was in a hot car?"

"Or a car he didn't want traced. By now there's probably new plates on it. LAPD and CHP both have the info, so if something breaks I'll let you know."

Sam thanked him and clicked off. At least the law had stepped in on Nicky Oberlin. Cam Bellamy would make sure that the full force and effect of the penal code would come crashing down on his head.

At last.

THIRTEEN

1.

For a few days life returned to a semblance of normalcy. And he needed it, as Larry Cohen was playing the paper game with him.

For litigators, the paper game had one object: to bury the other side in motions, interrogatories, formal and informal letters, and attachments galore. The heavier the paper, the better.

Cohen was a game player supreme. Sam knew that going in, and knew it was all part of the Harper case. Truth be told, Lew was right about it. When you did a cost-benefit analysis of the matter, the balance of the scales did not weigh in the favor of keeping the case open, of even getting to trial.

But Sam couldn't look at the law that way. Not anymore. So he'd meet Cohen on the playing field and deflect every move. Get him to bend, or get him in front of a jury. Nothing else would be acceptable.

The big issue would be Sarah Harper's future earnings. The California legislature had capped noneconomic damages — pain and suffering, basically — at $250,000. But there was no cap on future earnings. The key would be proving what her worth would have been.

Sam thought this would actually be the strongest aspect of his case. He had a videographer putting together a highlight DVD based on the Harpers' home videos of Sarah. They showed her skating circles around other kids at age four, and on from there.

Interspersed with this footage were a number of television sports commentators talking about her gold-medal chances, her natural prettiness, and her *spark.* That was a word that kept coming up regarding Sarah.

It was the same word that had once described American gymnast Mary Lou Retton, who became such a sensation at the 1984 Olympic Games in Los Angeles. She'd gone on to earn a ton in endorsements.

Now, with Nicky finally in legal trouble, Sam could get back to concentrating on his client. The concentrating kept him from thinking too hard about Heather, who was still resistant to communication. So Sam communicated more and more with God about his daughter.

The blowup with Max happened when he least expected it.

2.

Saturday afternoon, Sam had just come out of the study when he saw Max padding, very slowly, by the door.

"What are you doing home?" Sam said. Max had come in quietly through the front door. He was supposed to be at baseball practice, which was held two blocks away at the public park.

"I forgot my bat," Max said.

"Last week you forgot your mitt."

Max shrugged but didn't move.

"Why do you keep forgetting things?" Sam folded his arms. He had a suspicion but wanted Max to say it.

His son only looked at the floor and shrugged again.

"Because you don't want to go to practice, right?"

"No."

"Max, be up front with me."

"I am."

"Look, I know you weren't jazzed about playing fall ball. And we talked about that. But you decided to, and you made a commitment —"

"I'm going, okay? Lemme get my stupid bat!"

"Hey, don't raise your voice."

"Forget about it!" He turned toward the stairs.

"Wait just a minute —"

But Max was already running up to his room.

"Max!"

His son didn't stop. The surprise of that hit Sam in the chest. Max never ignored him. He'd always been pretty compliant. Now, suddenly, a parade of horribles kickstarted in Sam's imagination. Max ending up like Heather. Max in total rebellion.

He knew his son was still recovering from Buzz's death. But Sam couldn't let Max use that as an excuse to give up on doing the right things.

When he got to Max's door Sam saw his son sitting on his bed, his bat on his lap, his head down.

"Hey, kid, it's —"

Max's head jerked up. "Don't come in here."

"Max —"

"Don't!"

"Take it easy —"

Max jumped up. His face was flushed. He held the bat like a club. Then he burst forward.

Sam caught him at the door.

"I gotta go!" Max tried to break free.

"Let's talk about this —"

"Let go!"

Sam did let go. He let go so he wouldn't do or say something he'd regret, and keep regretting, as he had with Heather. He stood still in the doorway of Max's room, listening to his son's feet pound down the stairs.

He stood, lost.

And then angry. Not at Max, but at Nicky Oberlin. He had done this. He had come into his home just as a robber might have, and shot the place up.

If revenge is the Lord's, let it be now. And swift. And terrible.

3.

An evidentiary hearing in the matter of *People of the State of California versus Nicholas Oberlin* took place on a Tuesday morning in the courtroom of Judge Napoleon Andrews.

It was, in fact, the very same courtroom where one Robert Blake was tried on charges of murdering his wife, Bonnie Lee Bakley, in 2005. Blake was acquitted and walked out of that courtroom a free man.

Sam hoped Nicky Oberlin would not be

taking the same walk.

Nap Andrews had a good reputation, Cam said, and though he wasn't known as a law-and-order jurist, he would give them a fair hearing. Sam didn't hide a bit of disappointment at that. He wanted a judge who would skip a trial and lock Nicky up and throw away the key, a hanging judge. Old West justice.

If Oberlin had only tried to shake Sam's tree, Sam wouldn't have minded if the law meandered along in its sometimes lethargic way. But now it was different. Oberlin was going after his family. He'd hurt Max. Frightened Linda. That's why the Red Queen's edict — sentence first, verdict later — would have been just fine with Sam.

Except that it wouldn't be. If the law was good only when it was in your favor, it wouldn't really be the law. So Sam sat quietly in his theater-style seat — the design of the courtroom in the new building was a little bit Hollywood — and clenched his jaw.

"Good morning," Judge Andrews said. "We are here for a 1538.5 hearing in *People versus Oberlin*."

Sam grabbed the chair's arms like a boxing fan just before the first round: 1538.5 was the penal code section that governed motions to suppress evidence. It was the biggest potential bomb in a defense lawyer's pretrial arsenal. If a judge granted the motion, and the key evidence was held inadmissible, an entire case would be thrown out. Kaput. Finished.

A nagging thought bit at Sam's mind. What if Nicky Oberlin really did get out of this? What then? But he calmed himself — slightly — by remembering Cam's assurance that suppression was rarely granted anymore. The US Supremes had trimmed the judicial fat off the Fourth Amendment. Police evidence almost always made it through.

As the lawyers stated their appearances for the record, Sam gave the defense lawyer a once-over. His name was Blaine Jastrow, and he was a sixtieth-floor man. Expensive suit, hundred-dollar haircut, nails that would have sparkled under the right light. Lawyers on sixtieth floors were high above their street-level brethren in reputation, power, and fees.

This was Nicky Oberlin's mouthpiece, and no doubt Mama had paid for this one. He wondered where Mama was. Could she be among the spectators?

Judge Andrews said, "Mr. Jastrow, you're challenging the search warrant."

"Yes, Your Honor. The photographs found

in Mr. Oberlin's apartment must be suppressed. The items are not described in the warrant and were not in plain view. Further, the warrant was not supported by probable cause."

Cam had prepared Sam for this, assuring him that Andrews wouldn't go so far as to suppress the evidence. There were precious few times Andrews had failed to bind over a defendant for trial. This wouldn't be one of them.

"You have the burden of proof," Andrews said. "The warrant is valid on its face. It authorized a search for toxic materials, and related items thereof. You're not contesting that, correct?"

Blaine Jastrow said, "Not the face, Your Honor. We will be contesting the execution of the search and, in the alternative, the sufficiency of the affidavit."

"Call your witness, then."

"Call Officer Paul Helmuth."

A uniformed LAPD officer stood up in the back row, walked down to the rail and through the gate. He was of the overweight variety of policeman. These days, Sam thought, there were either puffy cops or hard bodies. Didn't seem to be any in between anymore.

The officer was sworn in and took the witness chair. Blaine Jastrow placed a yellow legal pad on the podium and asked, "Officer Helmuth, you served the search warrant on my client's apartment, is that correct?"

"Yes."

"Did you have a partner with you?"

"Yes."

Sam saw Jastrow roll his eyes. The officer was playing games. Police are trained to only answer the question given, but these questions were foundational only, and it would have sped things along for Officer Helmuth to just name his partner.

"Your partner's name?" Jastrow asked.

"Officer Jane Perkins."

"All right. You had the warrant in hand. Directing your attention to the face of the warrant, please read the description of the items."

Helmuth looked down with obvious consternation. "Paul Helmuth, being sworn, says that on the basis of the information contained within the Search Warrant and Affidavit and the incorporated Statement of Probable Cause, he/she has probable cause to believe that the property described below is lawfully seizable pursuant to Penal Code Section 1524, as indicated below, and is now located at the locations set forth below. Wherefore, affiant requests that this Search

Warrant be issued."

"So you swore under penalty of perjury to the Statement of Probable Cause?"

"Of course. It's required by law."

"And what is the material described in the warrant?"

"Toxic materials that may have been used in the perpetration of a crime, including, but not limited to, poisons and pest-control material."

"Is that it?"

"Yes."

"All right. What did you do next?"

"I complied with the knock-notice requirement."

"That's for the judge to determine. I asked what you *did.*"

With a sigh, Helmuth said, "I knocked on the door. Then I gave notice. I mean, I said, 'Los Angeles Police. Open the door, please.' "

"And what happened then?"

"Nothing. I knocked again, louder. I announced again. No answer. So I tried the door and it was locked."

"How long between the time of your first knock and your trying the door?"

"I don't know —"

"Your best estimate."

Helmuth looked up a moment. "Maybe

thirty seconds."

"After you tried the door and found it locked, what did you do?"

"I was about to knock again, but the door opened. The defendant opened the door."

Blaine Jastrow jotted a note on his yellow legal pad. "Did Mr. Oberlin offer any resistance to you?"

"Not at that point."

"Ah, so your assertion is that there was resistance at *some* point?"

"Verbally."

"Nothing physical?"

"No."

"After my client opened the door, he let you in, did he not?"

"After I told him we had a search warrant, yes."

"Because my client has the same right to privacy as any other citizen, right?"

Judge Andrews cleared his throat. "Why don't you move on there, Mr. Jastrow."

That was right, Sam knew. Jastrow was just needling Helmuth. There was no jury here to sway. Sam glanced over at Nicky, who was smiling at all this.

Jastrow said, "You informed my client what you were looking for, correct?"

"Yes."

"Asked him if he had any of the materials

mentioned in the warrant?"

"Yes."

"He denied it, isn't that right?"

"Yes."

"Then you started to search the apartment?"

"Yes."

"And did not find any such material, correct?"

Helmuth hesitated. "Right."

Stepping from the podium, Jastrow faced the officer like a fighter in his corner just before the bell sounds. "At what point, Officer Helmuth, did you or your partner start poking your nose into my client's drawers?"

A few of the spectators in court laughed. Sam was sure Jastrow fully intended the double entendre. Even Judge Andrews smiled.

The witness did not. "We were looking for receipts that might be directly related to the items we were searching for."

"Excuse me, Officer Helmuth, but where in the warrant is the word *receipts?*"

"It's not."

"That's what I thought."

Helmuth glared.

"You went fishing in other places too."

"We searched any place that might have papers like that."

"Including the chest of drawers in my client's bedroom?"

"Yes."

"People usually keep receipts there, don't they?"

Cam Bellamy said, "Objection."

"Sustained," Judge Andrews said.

Without a flinch, Jastrow said, "You looked in the chest of drawers and that's where you found the photographs that you seized, right?"

"Yes."

"Photographs. Of whom?"

"People."

"What people?"

"I didn't know."

"So that obviously caused you to think there was a connection between some pictures of people you didn't know and the materials for which you were authorized to search?"

This was the heart of it, Sam knew. Jastrow was trying to show that the photos had nothing to do with the warrant and shouldn't have been confiscated.

And if the judge agreed, the case would be over. Nicky Oberlin would walk out of court free as the proverbial bird.

Helmuth looked like a cornered, though well-fed, ferret. "In my training and experience, these photographs were evidence of intent. There was —"

"Let me ask you this —"

Cam Bellamy objected. "The witness didn't finish his answer, Your Honor."

"Sustained. The witness may finish his answer."

"I was just going to explain that there was nothing else in the top drawer. No clothing. The photographs were laid out in sequence. There were four different subjects in the ten photographs. From left to right, it was a man, a woman, and two minors, a female and a male. There was also a handgun in the drawer."

"Which you seized."

"Yes. Now about the pictures —"

"Did you ask Mr. Oberlin if it was registered?"

"Yes."

"Did he produce registration?"

"Yes."

"Yet you seized the weapon?"

Helmuth shrugged. "Yeah. Yes."

Jastrow jotted another note, then said, "That's all I have at this time, Your Honor."

"Very well," Judge Andrews said. "Mr. Bellamy?"

4.

Cam took his place at the podium.

"Officer Helmuth, the warrant describes cans, canisters, boxes, bags, and other similar receptacles, is that correct?"

"Yes."

"Did you think some of these items might be kept in a drawer?"

"Yes, I did. That's why I looked there."

"Why did you choose a dresser drawer?"

"Because if someone is trying to hide incriminating material, they wouldn't necessarily put it where you would expect to find it."

Cam nodded. He wasn't using notes. "Why did you seize the gun?"

"Because it looked like it was connected to the pictures. When I put it all together, I thought the defendant might be targeting those people."

"Why did you think that?"

"I asked the defendant who those people were. He said, 'None of your business.' I thought there was a risk, so I arrested him."

This was sounding thin. Sam could fill in all the blanks himself, but what would the judge think if this was the only testimony?

Cam said he had no more questions. Neither did Jastrow. Andrews asked Jastrow to make his argument on the first part of the motion.

"Your Honor," the defense lawyer said, "I think it's pretty clear what happened here. The officers did not find what they were looking for and decided they didn't like the cut of my client's jib, and went on a little fishing expedition. When they invaded his dresser drawer, a very intimate location to say the least, they found some photographs and a gun. The gun was registered. Perfectly legal. But they decided, through a wild jump of the imagination, that a potential crime might be in process. Last time I looked we didn't arrest people for crimes that haven't been committed. The arrest was clearly illegal; the seizure of this evidence was illegal. I frankly don't know what we're doing here."

Judge Andrews said, "Well, I'm glad you're unclear about what we're doing here, Mr. Jastrow, because that justifies my existence."

The comment drew laughter from the courtroom audience. The judge then invited Cam to make his argument. Sam thought Cam was starting to look a little apprehensive. Or maybe it was just Sam's anxiety coming out of his pores.

"The real issue here, Your Honor," Cam said, "is not the legality of the arrest. No evidence was seized as a result of the arrest.

The evidence was seized pursuant to the warrant, and the warrant specifically described the items to be searched for. It is clear that cans or canisters are small enough to fit in a drawer. That makes this a very simple, clear-cut matter. In serving the warrant, the officers were entitled to look in drawers, cupboards, closets, and anywhere else where one of these items might be. Opening the dresser drawer was therefore legal, and the evidence seized in plain view. Whether that evidence is indicative of a crime will be up to Your Honor at the preliminary hearing. But the evidence is clearly admissible."

Sam sure hoped so.

Judge Andrews only contemplated his decision for a moment. "On this part of the motion I agree with the People. The officers complied with knock notice, and clearly the dresser drawer was a place they could reasonably think might hold the items they were looking for. The photographs and firearm were properly seized."

Sam's sigh was louder than he wanted it to be. He sheepishly sat back in his seat and looked straight ahead. Out of the corner of his eye he saw Nicky looking over at him. He thought he detected a grin.

"Now," the judge said to Jastrow, "you

want to take up the matter of probable cause?"

"I do."

"Do you have a witness?"

"Yes. I call Samuel Trask to the stand."

Cam had also prepped Sam for this moment, though when Sam stood up he couldn't help feeling a zigzagging jolt of nerves. There were press people here, and the curious — and mostly retired — court watchers. But it was Nicky Oberlin's eyes he felt most of all. He could see that look peripherally as he made his way to the stand to be sworn.

After taking the oath and stating his name for the record, Sam readied himself for the scalpel of one of LA's top lawyers. He reminded himself that he was no legal slouch, but that was no license to be too clever.

5.

"Good morning, Mr. Trask." Jastrow smiled.

"Morning." Sam was not going to violate the two primary rules for witnesses under hostile questioning: Do not volunteer anything, and keep your answers short.

"I am placing before you the statement taken by Officer Helmuth, entitled Statement of Samuel Trask, and ask if indeed that is your statement?"

Sam took the document and gave it a cursory look. "It's a copy."

"Thank you so much for the clarification. Is that your signature — excuse me — a copy of your signature on the bottom?"

"Yes."

"There are a few things you left out of this statement, isn't that true, Mr. Trask?"

"Nothing relevant," Sam snapped.

"I was just wondering why you didn't put in the part about your assault on Mr. Oberlin."

Cam Bellamy shot to his feet. "Objection. Relevance."

"This goes to credibility, Your Honor. I want to explore Mr. Trask's state of mind, which may have colored his judgment. At the very least, it's something that should have been revealed to Officer Helmuth. I'm sure the issuing magistrate would have been very interested in knowing all the facts."

Judge Andrews pursed his lips, then nodded. "I'll overrule the objection. Witness will answer."

Sam's throat went dry. "Mr. Oberlin's lawsuit has nothing to do with the facts of his threat against me."

"Threat? Let's see." Jastrow took the statement. "You say here that Mr. Oberlin made a verbal threat to take your family apart, bit by bit."

"That's right."

"What was the context of that statement, Mr. Trask?"

"Context? He threatened me, that was the context."

"In a public park, is that correct?"

"Yes."

"At a meeting you instigated, right?"

"That's right."

"For what reason, Mr. Trask?"

"To get Oberlin to stop harassing me and my family."

Jastrow tossed the affidavit on the counsel table as if it no longer mattered. "Why, then, did you threaten Mr. Oberlin's mother at this meeting?"

In the frozen moment before Cam Bellamy's objection, Sam caught a glance at Nicky Oberlin and his look of sadistic satisfaction.

"No foundation," Cam Bellamy said.

"I'm asking the witness," Jastrow replied.

"Has to be some foundation for the question, Your Honor."

"If the DA will allow for a little fact finding, we'll find it."

Andrews put up his hand in a Solomon-like call for calm. "This is a hearing on a motion, Mr. Bellamy. I'm going to allow some leeway on this. The witness may answer."

"I did not threaten anyone's mother," Sam said.

"Did you bring up the subject of Mr. Oberlin's mother, sir?"

"I mentioned his mother, yes."

"You used a derogatory term for her, didn't you?"

"I don't recall."

"Didn't you derisively refer to her as *Mommy?*"

"I may have, but —"

"In an insulting way?"

"No."

"In an effort to intimidate Mr. Oberlin?"

"No."

"To show how macho you are?"

"Objection," Cam said.

"Sustained," Judge Andrews said.

"That's what this is really all about, isn't it, Mr. Trask?"

"Objection —"

"Your manhood?"

Judge Andrews scowled at Jastrow. "I sustained the objection, Counsel. You're not making any headway with this line."

With a nod and a smile, Jastrow said, "You have a pretty good recall of the exact words

Mr. Oberlin said to you, right?"

"I do, yes."

"How sure are you?"

"I swore to them."

"Did you write them down immediately after this meeting in the park?"

Sam turned slightly in the witness chair. "No."

"Didn't feel the need?"

"That's right."

"Didn't record them in any way?"

A trap, perfectly sprung. Jastrow was fishing, but he'd stuck the hook firmly in Sam's mouth. He couldn't lie.

"I did record them."

Jastrow had his back to Sam when he answered. Now he spun around, a look of theatrical surprise on his face. He paused, letting Sam's answer settle in the ears of the judge.

"That's very interesting, Mr. Trask. You're a member of the bar, are you not?"

"Yes."

"You must know then that private conversations are protected under California law?"

Cam Bellamy said, "Misstates the law, Your Honor."

"Confidential communications then," Jastrow said. "Which is any communication either party reasonably believes to be private."

"They were in a public park, Your Honor."

"But they weren't shouting toward the ball field, either."

Judge Andrews scowled. "This is a matter that I'll have to take under advisement. At the moment, Mr. Jastrow, I'll allow you to explore the circumstances of this recording."

To Sam the judge sounded seriously peeved, as if Sam had hidden one very important card from him. Well, he had.

"You had a tape recorder hidden when this conversation took place?" Jastrow asked.

"Yes."

"You did not inform Mr. Oberlin of this, did you?"

"No."

"You were not surrounded by people during this conversation, were you?"

"No."

"In fact, you wanted to keep things discreet, did you not?"

"Sure." Jastrow was patiently reeling him in. How much worse could it get?

"It was your expectation that the conversation would not be overheard, wasn't it?"

"Yes."

"It was Mr. Oberlin's too."

"I don't know what was in his mind."

"He was standing right in front of you, wasn't he? Same conditions applied, didn't they?"

"I don't know what was in his mind, sir."

Jastrow smoothed his tie. "We'll let His Honor draw the conclusion." He turned to the judge. "I would move that the tape be produced and admitted into evidence, Your Honor."

"Mr. Bellamy?"

"The tape is not relevant to this matter, Your Honor. The only relevance is Mr. Trask's sworn statement about what was said. That has not been challenged."

A light seemed to go off in Jastrow's head. "If I may ask the witness another question, Your Honor, perhaps we can see if the tape is relevant or not."

"Go ahead," Judge Andrews said.

"Mr. Trask, did you ever discuss this tape with Mr. Bellamy?"

Reeled in and filleted. "Yes," Sam said.

"Did you discuss taping Mr. Oberlin before you actually did?"

"Yes."

"So Mr. Bellamy knew you were going to do it?"

"No. I never said I would do it."

"Did Mr. Bellamy tell you it was illegal?"

"I believe he said it would be inadmissible."

"You believe?"

"Yes, as best as I can recall."

Jastrow raised his hands. "Too bad *that* conversation wasn't recorded."

"Move on," the judge said.

"Just so I understand this, Mr. Trask: You told Mr. Bellamy you might tape record a conversation with Mr. Oberlin, and were told by Mr. Bellamy it would be inadmissible in a court of law, is that right?"

"Yes."

"Did he tell you not to do it?"

"I don't recall that he did, no."

Blaine Jastrow looked supremely satisfied. "Your Honor, I have no further questions of this witness."

"Anything you want to ask the witness?" Andrews asked Cam Bellamy.

"No, Your Honor."

6.

"Not good," Cam told Sam in his office. Andrews had ordered a fifteen-minute recess.

"What's Jastrow going to say?"

"He's going to say the affidavit was based on an illegal tape, and therefore the search

290

warrant fails, and the evidence is inadmissible."

"And if that happens —"

"No case. Good-bye. Oberlin walks."

The prospect made Sam shiver. "Then what?"

"At the very least, we hope that he gets the message. Maybe he'll lay off after this."

"And if he doesn't?"

"We have to catch him doing something."

"Maybe he'll poison my wife. Would that do it?"

"Come on, Sam."

"Come on what? That's your job, isn't it? To stop these people?"

"No, it's not. My job is to prosecute people who commit crimes, when there's enough evidence to prove it."

"Maybe we should go back to vigilante justice."

"And lynchings?"

"In Oberlin's case, I'll give you the rope."

"You wouldn't really, Sam. I know you too well."

"I'm beginning to wonder if I know myself. You know I almost bought a gun off the street?"

"Sam —"

"Don't worry, I didn't go through with it. But I was close. Man, I was close. If he gets out of this —"

Cam looked at his watch. "We're about to find out. I'll argue the heck out of this, Sam. I just don't want you to get your hopes up."

"That's not possible at this point," Sam said.

7.

Blaine Jastrow said, "Your Honor, this is a very straightforward issue. Mr. Trask admitted under oath that he met with the district attorney before taping the conversation he had with Mr. Oberlin. Mr. Bellamy did not attempt to stop Mr. Trask from his illegal enterprise. At the very least, Mr. Bellamy knew of the potential for such an act. This information was not in the affidavit, and therefore the magistrate did not have sufficient information to rule on whether probable cause existed. This was a material omission, and thus under *Franks* the search warrant must fail and the evidence must be suppressed."

Jastrow sat down. Cameron Bellamy walked to the podium, looking like a tired insurance salesman. "Your Honor, in this case we have a warrant that was valid on its face. We would therefore argue that the good-faith exception applies. The officers who served the warrant had no reason to believe there was anything wrong with it. To suppress the evidence would be to punish the prosecution at the expense of truth."

"Very eloquent, Mr. Bellamy," Judge Andrews said. "But as you know, under *Machupa,* a search warrant based upon a previous illegal search cannot be saved under the good-faith exception. It appears that Mr. Trask illegally gathered evidence in the form of Mr. Oberlin's words."

"Even so, Your Honor, Mr. Trask is a private citizen and not part of the police arm of the justice system."

"Unless he was acting in concert with the police arm, which includes the prosecutor's office."

"He was not under any direction —"

"You knew about it, didn't you?"

"The testimony does not establish any direction on the part of the prosecutor's office."

"There does not have to be any direction. The fact is you knew about it, you didn't stop it, and you relied upon it, because that information was in the affidavit."

"We relied on Mr. Trask's recollection."

"I'm not impressed with the fine line you are trying to draw. Color me old-fashioned, but this whole thing stinks. We can't have search warrants being issued on illegal schemes hatched in the prosecutor's office, even if the prosecutor doesn't encourage them. Sitting there and letting it happen is bad enough. You profited from the illegal act upon which the search warrant was issued. Therefore I'm holding that the search warrant fails and is not saved by the good-faith exception. That being the case, all of the evidence gathered pursuant to the search warrant is suppressed. Anything further?"

"We would move to dismiss the charge," Jastrow said with barely contained enthusiasm.

Cam Bellamy sighed. "No objection."

Judge Andrews nodded. "The charge is dismissed without prejudice. Mr. Oberlin, you are free to go, sir."

8.

Sir!

Sam fought the urge to scream at the judge. *Can't you see it? Look at him. Look at Nicky Oberlin, Your Honor. How can you call him sir? You know he did it, you know it even though you kicked the search warrant. You have to know it because it's so obvious.*

Why couldn't the judge look at Nicky right now, with his smirk, looking at Sam?

Cam Bellamy turned to him also, but Sam didn't want to talk, not now. He didn't want to talk to anybody.

He charged out of the courthouse and hit the street, walking. He didn't really care which direction. He just needed to pound out the feeling of powerlessness.

It didn't help.

Sam walked by an Arby's and stepped inside to call Linda from his cell.

"They let him go," he said.

"How could they?"

"Judge suppressed the evidence."

"Sam —"

"You should have seen the look on Oberlin's face. He's not finished, Linda."

"What are we going to do? We can't just sit —"

"How's Max?"

Pause. "How do you think he is?"

"Don't tell him. I'll talk to him when I get home."

"I want to know what we're going to do. I can't go on like this, knowing he's walking around out there."

Sam clenched his jaw so tight he thought he'd chip teeth. "I'll be home later."

"Sam —"

He closed the phone. His walk back to the courthouse parking lot was strained by the feeling that every muscle in his body was taut and ready to snap. The lot was the two-story job on Sylvan across from a used bookstore. He took the stairs to the second level, which didn't have a roof. The sun was hot and threw white light on the cement. Sam hooded his eyes with his hand as he made for the last aisle where he'd parked.

And then he saw his car.

It took him a moment to convince himself he wasn't in some crazy dream. This was no dream. The two rear tires of his Acura were completely flat.

He stood there for a moment, at first unbelieving. Then on fire. One tire flat would have been an inconvenience. Two was an attack.

"Now ain't that a kick in the biscuits?"

Sam turned. And faced a smiling Nicky Oberlin.

9.

Heather woke up slowly, the burn of last night's vomit in her throat.

Was this going to be the pattern? Was it even worth it?

Not now. Death would be welcome now.

Roz was snoring on the floor. What time was it?

There was light outside. She could see a

shaft of sunlight sneaking past the black curtain. She liked things better in the dark.

For some reason, she thought of her father.

She saw him in her tired mind and he looked unhappy. She was the cause of that look, of course. But in her mind he looked sad about something more. And she thought she understood him better now.

He was just an older version of herself. He was seeing that life sucked. The whole thing with this guy who poisoned Buzz . . . Her mom had left the message and Heather called her and heard the whole thing.

"Pray for Max," her mom said.

Well, yeah, she would have if she thought it would do any good. Max was the one thing she missed at home. He was the vulnerable one in the family. She remembered saving him from one of the bigger neighborhood kids, back when he was eight or nine. She used the old line: Pick on somebody your own size. And the bully — Frankie Frisch was his name, the chubby dork — looked at her and said, "You're my size," and she ran at him and by the time she was finished he was a scratched and crying mess.

Lying on the motel bed with a sour, alcohol stomach, she thought, Well, Max, little bro, there's a lot worse stuff happening out here, and you know it now because of Buzz. You're going to have to get some rhino skin, kid. You're gonna need it.

She wished she could pray away her hangover.

Instead, she walked into the bathroom and saw the empty bottle of JD on the floor. If she shattered it, she could cut her wrists and crawl in the bathtub and it would all be over before Roz even woke up.

She turned on the faucet and threw some cold water on her face. She looked at her red-rimmed eyes — they felt like open sores.

She knelt down and picked up the bottle by the neck, held it there for a second like a hammer.

Something stop me, she said in her mind. I dare you. Give me one good reason.

At which point she realized that was as close to a prayer as she was probably ever going to get, and she sank back on the cold tile of the bathroom floor and cried.

10.

"You did this," Sam said, wondering — fearing — what he might do to Nicky Oberlin with two balled-up hands.

"Did what, Sammy?"

"You think I'm stupid?"

"You? A lawyer? You're brilliant. But you're a little paranoid, maybe. I mean, you think I did something to your car? Friends don't hurt each other like that."

"You didn't get the message, did you?"

"Somebody sending me a message?" Nicky looked at the ground as if searching for a dropped coin. "Where is it?"

"You're messing with the law."

"Me? I thought it was you the judge got mad at, you and that puppet DA who messed with the law. Why else would he throw the whole thing out like that?"

Sam looked around. They were virtually alone in the parking lot. No one to hear them.

"Restraining order comes next," Sam said.

"You don't have to do that, Sammy. Not on my account."

"You're a pathetic liar."

"Is that the Christian way? Insult your friends?"

Sam turned to the car, reaching for his keys. Saw the tires again. Now what?

"Need a lift?" Nicky said.

"Get out of here."

"Let me help you, Sammy. You need a few bucks?"

Sam considered his options, which were few. He had to call AAA and get towed to a shop. He had to buy new tires. He had to obliterate Nicky Oberlin from his life and memory.

"You don't have a tape recorder again, do you, Sammy?"

Sam said nothing.

"Nope, I don't think you do. That was a very unkind thing you did to me. I was hurt, Sammy, really hurt. And then you get me hauled into court. I had to pay a lawyer, Sam."

"You mean Mommy did."

Nicky's face went rock hard. He took a step toward Sam. "I told you about that, boy. Now you listen to me. You won't know when it's coming. You and Linda and little Maxie and that daughter of yours. You won't know when."

Let me hit him, let me crush his skull right now. Get the tire iron.

That's just what he wants you to do.

"You come near my family again and I will kill you," Sam said. "I will figure out how to make it self-defense. You understand me?"

"Aw, Sammy, that's harsh. No wonder your kids are basket cases."

If he didn't walk away now, Sam knew he'd make an attempt on Nicky Oberlin's life.

He walked past Oberlin and down the stairs, back in the sight lines of the lot attendant. He whipped out his cell and called AAA. Then he called Gerald Case and told him they had to meet.

And it had to be tonight.

FOURTEEN

1.

"When I was a cop in Arizona," Gerald Case told Sam, "our little municipality got to be a popular spot with some mob guys looking out for their health. They started coming in from Jersey and Baltimore, places like that, setting up shop, which meant porn, prostitution, narcotics. Chief got a few of us together one night and said we weren't gonna be no retirement community for a bunch of Vinnies."

The moon was gray and heavy in the sky, the air warm. Sam and Case were in the parking lot at the abandoned restaurant again. Lights were flickering in the Valley just like always, just like normal.

But nothing was normal anymore.

Case went on, "So we started hosting our own welcome parties out in the desert at a little shack in the back of a wrecking yard. We found that a few broken ribs did the trick. Once or twice we did a collarbone. But the word got out. The Feds even came down to pay us a visit. 'Good job,' they said."

"I don't want any of that stuff."

"You want this guy to go away?"

"Not like that. I can't pay for that."

"I'm asking you, you want that guy to go away?"

"Of course —"

"Then you and I didn't meet tonight. You didn't tell me to do anything. In a few weeks, you get a call from me and I say, 'Mr. Trask, how's tricks? That guy, I can't remember his name, he still bothering you?' And you say, 'Funny you should ask, but I haven't heard from him.' And I say, 'Terrific.' And out of the goodness of your heart you send me a final installment of five hundred and we're square."

"I don't know."

"Mr. Trask, I ask you to trust me. I have an interest in this case. Guys like this yank my chain. Just go home and don't think anymore about it."

"But —"

"Go home to your family, Mr. Trask."

2.

Linda looked at Sam and shook her head.

Sam put his hands on her shoulders. "I want you to take Max and go to your sister's for a while."

"Tell me why I have to do this." A note of frustration spilled into her voice.

"I told you. Oberlin's case was dismissed. He's still out there, and I don't want you to have to worry about it."

"If it's a matter of your —"

"Will you just do it, please?"

She looked at him closely. "There's something else."

"Linda, I don't want you to be concerned. I want you —"

"Now I'm *really* concerned. I know you, Sam, I know your face. What's happened?"

"He threatened me again."

Linda's jaw tightened. Sam could see the hinges clench. "Did you call the police?"

"The police can't help us."

"How can that be?"

"Will you take Max and go, please?"

"I don't want to just leave —"

"Just for a little while."

"How long?"

"I don't know."

"This is ridiculous. We have things going on. Church, and Max's baseball, and —"

"Did you forget he showed up at the game? Have you forgotten about Buzz?"

"This is a nightmare."

"Yeah, it is. And I don't want you and Max just sitting here where he knows where to find you."

"What about Heather?"

"What about her?"

"I'm not going to run out on her."

"Linda, we're not. We will call her and get her to go too. But we have to face reality. If she doesn't, we can't make her. If I could, I would."

"Would you?"

"That's a rotten thing to say."

"You weren't exactly on her side when she left."

"On her side? I did everything I could to . . ." But he hadn't done everything, and he knew it. "This doesn't change anything. I want you and Max out for a while. I'll keep in touch and —"

"No."

"Excuse me?"

"No, Sam. I'm not leaving. This is my home."

"And I'm your husband."

"And what does that make me, your property?"

"You're talking crazy now."

"I'm not going, Sam."

So there it was, Linda's line in the sand. She'd done that before, as he had. Maybe that was all part of the warp and woof of marriage, and you had to figure out when to respect those lines.

"Going where?"

It was Max, who had come to the door unnoticed.

Sam motioned him over.

"You know this Nicky Oberlin guy, who's been after me, the one who did that to Buzz? He just got let go from the criminal proceedings. He's making threats again. That's why I want you two to go away."

"But where, Dad?"

"Your aunt Nancy's."

Linda shook her head. "But if we do, that means he's won. It's what he wants us to do. To be afraid of him."

"Let's not, Dad," Max said.

"What's that?"

"He's a bully. Don't let him make us do stuff we don't want to."

Sam looked at the resolute face of his twelve-year-old. This was, quite obviously, a step of faith for Max. He was trying to show Sam something, and it seemed then more important than anything else to accept it.

"All right," Sam said. "But you two must

do everything I say. And if I hire someone to help us out, or watch the place, you'll cooperate, right?"

Linda put her arm around Max's shoulders.

"Right, Dad," Max said.

3.

Sam rushed into Judge Harry Oswalt's chambers, sweat dripping from his forehead.

"I'm sorry, Judge," he said. It was ten o'clock on Thursday and the mandatory settlement conference had completely vaporized out of Sam's mind, courtesy of Nicky Oberlin.

Larry Cohen, dressed in a cream-colored suit with purple shirt — an ensemble he'd never wear in front of a jury — sat in a leather chair. "Maybe Mr. Trask was out looking for a credible case."

Judge Oswalt smiled. He was a genial man of fifty with closely cropped, steel-colored hair. "Larry, when have you ever met an opposing advocate who had a strong hand?"

"I calls 'em as I sees 'em," Cohen said.

"Completely unbiased, of course," the judge said. He folded his hands on his mahogany desk. "Sam, is there a reason you're late with the interrogatories?"

Boom. No small talk. No niceties. Start

off with a punch to the gut.

"They'll get done," Sam said.

"Not what I asked. Mr. Cohen here has been patient in my view and hasn't filed for sanctions. Since we're all sitting here like one big happy family, let's cut through the bunk and get this thing settled."

Sam opened his mouth, but the judge cut him off. "And let's not pretend this case is going to trial. That would not be a very good use of the court's time."

Larry Cohen nodded. To Sam it seemed like the fix was in. Cohen and the judge were chummy. Tennis partners. Sam was the ball, apparently.

"If Mr. Cohen wants to make an offer that approaches the real damages, I might think about settling," Sam said. "But until —"

"I think he has," Judge Oswalt said.

"But it's not up to you, is it?"

"Doesn't pay to get huffy, Sam. You're the one who's dragging his feet around. You sure you're capable of handling this? I hear you're leaving the firm."

"Irrelevant," Sam said.

"Is it?" Judge Oswalt leaned forward. "You're going to be trying this case in front of me, and if I think you're giving less than able support to your client, I may have to step in."

"That sounds like a threat," Sam said. He didn't feel like pulling any punches at this moment. He was being backed up against the ropes, so why pretend otherwise?

"My perception is you're tired, Sam. You've got some personal issues, we all know that. The assault charge. This guy you apparently have some grudge against —"

"You don't know anything about this."

"What can you tell me that will assure me you can continue on this case?"

"I wonder if I can tell you anything." Sam was immediately sorry he said it. The smirk on Cohen's face didn't help.

"I'm disappointed, Sam. I urge you to step back and look at this objectively. If you're cracking up, get help. But don't let it infect the system."

"I don't know what arrangement you've reached with Mr. Cohen —"

"Sam, don't say anything you'll be sorry for."

"I'm only sorry I broke the speed limit to get here." Sam stood up. "This ends the conference. Mr. Cohen knows where I stand. I won't be pushed, and I won't allow my client to be pushed."

"You're acting . . . not in the best interest of your client, Sam. I don't want to have to report this."

"Report what?"

"Your conduct."

"You better spell it out for me, Judge."

"The State Bar does not look with favor on lawyers acting under mental strain so severe they accuse judges of collusion."

Sam shot a glance at Cohen, who only smiled.

"You'd send me up to Disciplinary?"

"It doesn't have to come to that," Judge Oswalt said.

Sam stood up. "This is a joke, right?"

"No joke. I'm compelled to —"

"I haven't done anything."

"That's not how it appears to us."

Us. "Oh, very pretty," Sam said. "I thought this kind of strong-arming went out with the jackboots."

Shaking his head, Oswalt said, "You are going to be very sorry you're acting like this, Sam. It's so unfortunate."

It was Cohen's face that Sam looked at as he left. It was serene. The face of a pool hustler who just took the whole stake from a rube.

4.

The drive to Harper Lumber in Canoga Park took longer than ever, and not just because of the traffic on the 101. The weight of dismay was a heavy drag, and Sam couldn't cut loose from it.

He had to cut something else loose to keep the fragile threads of the rest of his life from wrapping around his throat.

Pete Harper would have to be it.

It killed him to think of it. The Harpers trusted him. But that trust would not help them in the long run. He wasn't going to be able to take this case where it needed to go.

He should have gone to Pete's house, of course. But he couldn't face Sarah. That was one scene he could not play without cracking.

Pete was holding a clipboard and talking on a cell phone out in the yard. Stacks of lumber in various cuts and sizes created a bunker feel, as if this might be ground zero against a military attack. Sam felt besieged, and a bit like a traitor.

It hurt even more when Pete smiled at him and checked out of his call. "Sam, nice surprise."

Pete's grip was strong this time, invested with optimism. Sweat glistened on his arms.

"Moving a lot of wood?" Sam said in a feeble attempt at small talk.

"If that Valley Circle development goes through — you know the one out at the end of Roscoe — we'll move a whole bunch."

"That'd be nice."

"We could use it. Walk and talk?"

"Sure."

Pete clipped his cell phone on his belt and started walking toward the north end of the yard. "You have some news," Pete said.

"Yes."

"Good?"

"In the long run, I think it will . . ."

A forklift loaded with two-by-tens rumbled past them, drowning out Sam's words. He didn't want to shout.

Pete's face clouded. "You think we'll lose."

"No."

"What then?"

"Pete, I have to pull out."

"I thought we —"

"Something's happening to my family, Pete."

Pete nodded. "The legal thing with that guy? Listen, I don't care —"

"Thing is, I can't give my best to you because of it. I've tried, but you need somebody who can give a hundred percent."

A man in a blue work shirt and baseball hat shouted to Pete from the loading bay. "Hey, Mr. Harper, you want us to house that load of air-dried?"

"Do it," Pete answered.

"Which space?"

"Just pick one!"

Now Sam felt a double dose of guilt. He'd become a workplace irritant. "I'm sorry, Pete. I shouldn't have bothered you here."

"Sam, are you absolutely sure about this? Because if it's the matter of the fee . . ."

"That's not it. It's never been it."

"But if we have to find another lawyer —"

"I want to try to find you the best."

"Second best," Pete said.

"I'm sorry."

"I know you, Sam. I know you wouldn't do this if you didn't think it was best for Sarah."

"Thank you." But he wondered, looking at the lines on Pete Harper's face, if Pete really believed it.

In the car, Sam began putting together a mental list of lawyers to call to take the Harper case. He thought of Lew, the best litigator he knew, but ruled him out. He had never liked the Harper case, and even a standard cut wasn't going to change that. Besides, FulCo was going to be a full-time job for a while.

Ben Rosensweig was a possibility. He was a classmate who'd been kicking insurance companies all over the country. Maybe —

His phone interrupted. It was Case.

"What you got going today?" Case asked.

"One less client, if that's what you're thinking."

"Can you catch a Southwest to San Francisco?"

"Why?"

"Because that's where I'll pick you up."

"You're there?"

"I'm here. And then we drive three hours. To Burrell."

"Why?"

"There's someone I want us to talk to."

"Who?"

"Nicky Oberlin's dear old mum."

"You found her?"

"Of course. This is Gerald Case you're talking to. If you want me to handle this on my own, I'll —"

"No. I want to be there. I'm coming."

5.

Early the next morning, Friday, Sam caught a Southwest flight at Burbank Airport. Case was waiting for him at the San Francisco Airport, as promised. The car from Hertz was a Crown Victoria. "I won't put this on the expenses," Case said, "unless you like what I've turned up. And I think you will."

As they cut over the Golden Gate Bridge, enveloped in wet fog, Case said, "Ever been to Burrell?"

"No." All Sam knew about the place was that it was rural and had redwoods and a lot of old hippies, in addition to a little tourism centered on the terminus of a long-defunct nineteenth-century railroad line.

"You ought to buy some property up there," Case said. "Could be the next —"

"Tell me about the woman."

"We have three hours before —"

"Tell me."

"I traced her from Sacramento. She had a big house there, nice house, so I guess it gave her more than enough for the move. Only thing is, she's living in a dump."

"You've seen her?"

"From a distance. With binoculars. Puttering around the place. Feeding some furry little friends of the forest. She looks like a bag lady, to be honest."

"So where'd the money go?"

"Exactly. That's what we're gonna find out. Now here's the kicker. Laverne Oberlin, that's her name, was not a happy camper back when Nicky was in short pants."

"How so?"

"Called the police a number of times. Domestic. Mr. Oberlin, Nick's daddy, was apparently quite the abuser."

"How'd you find this out?"

Case smiled. "You do your job and let me

315

do mine. I know guys, okay? So back in 1970 she files a formal complaint, then immediately withdraws it. The investigating officer files a report, and it says the subject, which would be the old man, left the premises by mutual consent."

"So maybe Nicky was knocked around, or just had to watch his father take it out on his mother."

"Nicky got it too. A social worker filed an addendum. They let it go. Things were different then. Today they'd take the kid in and sort it out later. That's all I know about our boy's past."

"That's a lot."

Case nodded. "The waiting period over for your handgun?"

"Picked it up yesterday. A Browning."

"Good gun. Where is it?"

"In its case in the trunk of my car."

"Good. If it's in the trunk it doesn't fall under the concealed weapon prohibition."

"Gerry?"

"Yeah?"

"I'm a lawyer, remember?"

"I'll try to overlook it."

Eventually the scenery switched from suburbia to country, with rolling green hills and vineyards. Beautiful place, Sam thought. He'd always wanted to bring Linda here when the flowers were in bloom. He wanted to bring them all now, Linda and Heather and Max, and just lie in the sun and have nothing to do with the world.

Sam called Linda. All was quiet on the home front. Heather had even checked in. At least she wasn't in jail. Count your blessings, Sam told himself, while they last.

6.

The house was in the middle of a pine grove, with a perimeter marked by a barbwire fence. A decrepit gate made from bleached wood hung halfway open. A red No Trespassing sign, rimmed with rust, dangled from the gate.

They'd taken a dirt road about half a mile to get here. Sam noticed a few other structures in the area, but no people. He kept thinking of *Deliverance* and tried not to. He didn't need that little item in his imagination.

"Looks almost deserted," Sam said. He didn't see a vehicle of any kind around the messy yard. There was an old box spring leaning against the side of the small, squat residence. Brown paint flaked from the eaves.

"Let's go," Case said.

"You sure about this? These are Second

Amendment people up here."

Gerald Case smiled. "You've seen too many movies."

Great. *Deliverance* popped in again.

"You all right?" Case asked.

"Move."

The two walked up the dirt path to the front of the house. A birdfeeder over the small porch swung in the slight breeze. Just to the right of the front door was a folding chair, weather faded, and an empty coffee can that held about a week's worth of cigarette butts.

Charming.

Case knocked on the door.

No response.

He knocked again, more insistently.

Sam thought he heard a rustling but didn't know if it came from inside or outside. Or above. He looked up and into a pair of beady black eyes in the ugliest animal face he'd ever seen. The pointed nose was a sickly pink, set off by black ears.

He jumped back.

"What is it?" Case said.

The ugly, cone-snouted creature hissed, then disappeared somewhere on the roof.

"I don't know," Sam said. "Maybe a possum. A big rat."

"Easy, boy. We're all just creatures trying

318

to get along, right?"

Case knocked one more time. Sam got the creepy feeling all over again. He half expected to hear the thin *plunk* of a banjo string in the distance.

Instead he heard the sound of a chain unlatching behind the door.

Case looked at Sam. Sam looked at the door. It opened an inch or so.

"Mrs. Oberlin?" Case said. "May I —"

He stopped as a revolver stuck out the door.

7.

"How dare you!"

The woman was broomstick thin, her cotton dress hanging on for dear life. Her snowy hair hung down past her shoulders, framing wide gray eyes. Her hands shook as they held the gun.

Case put his hands up. "We're not here to —"

"How dare you come to get me!" the woman said.

For a brief moment Sam thought Case was a dead man. The trembling finger on the trigger, the out-of-proportion hysteria. It was a recipe for disaster. "It's about Nicky," Sam said.

The wild eyes, crazy and empty at the

same time, turned on him.

Then the woman's look transformed to worry. She kept the gun up, pointed it at Sam's chest.

"Is Nicky hurt?" she said.

"No, ma'am," Sam answered. "Let us talk to you."

"What have you done with him?"

"Nothing, ma'am. Will you put that gun down so we can talk?"

She pulled the trigger. *Click.* Sam's heart clawed into his throat.

"Not loaded," she said. "Don't tell. If you tell, they'll take me away."

And it wouldn't be a moment too soon. Sam took a deep breath. "Have you been in touch with your son?"

"Where is he?"

"Have you talked to him recently?" Case said.

"Talk?"

"To Nicky."

"Is he hurt? Is he back there?" She seemed to be drifting into another scene, another time.

"Back where?" Case said.

"I can't take it anymore."

"We'd like to talk to you."

"Have you got the pizza?"

Case looked at Sam, then back at Mrs.

Oberlin. "No pizza. We need your help."

"Help?"

"To help Nicky."

"Nicky? Where is he?" She looked out at the trees beyond the fence.

"Ma'am, would you like to come with us and talk about Nicky?"

She took a step back then, an inner flame igniting her face. "What have you done to Nicky?"

Sam looked at Case, asking with his eyes what he was doing. Case nodded assurance.

"If you come for a ride, Nicky will like that."

The woman started shaking her head, out of confusion or obstinacy Sam couldn't tell. Did it matter?

The woman's face steadied for a short beat, then she looked past them, her eyes widening again.

The sound of tires on dirt and gravel made Sam turn. Some sort of cop car with a light bar flashing skidded to a stop. Two uniforms jumped out, one with his weapon drawn.

"Don't move!" he shouted.

8.

The woman screamed and pointed her empty gun at the officers.

Sam quickly jumped in front of her, grabbed her wrist, and forced her arm down.

"On the ground!" the officer shouted.

Sam tried to take the gun from the woman's hand. She resisted. "How dare you!" she cried. "Get off my property!"

"Get down now!"

Then the woman started with obscenities, at Sam and everyone else.

"Down! Now!"

"She's crazy," Sam shouted over his shoulder. "Hold up!" He saw that Gerald Case was on his knees, hands laced behind his head.

"Get her on the ground, sir!" the officer shouted.

Sam tore the gun from Mrs. Oberlin's hand. With her other hand she went after his face, scratching the side of it. With a flick, Sam tossed the gun onto the dirt in front of the porch, then spun behind Mrs. Oberlin, holding her two spindly arms so she couldn't move.

Which did not please Mrs. Oberlin. As a stream of epithets poured from her mouth, the two deputies rushed up. The older and larger of the two, with gun drawn, saw to Case. The other, a ruddy-faced kid as nervous as Mrs. Oberlin was crazed, took out his own sidearm and looked like he didn't know who to point it at.

"Ma'am," he said, "I need you to stop —"

She cursed at him.

"Ma'am —"

"How dare you! Get out!"

Ruddy Face swallowed and looked at Sam. "Sir?"

"I'm trying to help you out here," Sam said.

"Do you have a weapon?"

"No."

"Get them on their knees!" the older one commanded.

"Please," Ruddy said, and Sam thought this must be a good kid out of his element. The rookie.

Mrs. Oberlin was providing the background noise the whole time, never stopping her full-volume tirade. In her ear Sam said, "You want to help Nicky?"

She stopped screaming. "Nicky?"

"We're here to help Nicky," he said, and in a strange way that was true. Stopping him was exactly what he needed.

"I can explain all this to you," Sam said to both deputies.

But the older deputy was already handcuffing Gerald Case.

"Whatever this is," Sam said, "it's not

what you think."

"Back away now, sir."

Sam did as ordered. Which unleashed the fury of Laverne Oberlin. Screaming like a banshee, she went for the older deputy's face. He did not treat her as gently as Sam had.

As he manhandled her to the ground and put a set of cuffs on her, the younger deputy and Sam found themselves looking at each other.

"Tough day," Sam said.

"I'm going to have to ask you to put your hands behind your back, sir."

"Son, that would be a mistake."

Ruddy hesitated.

"See, I'm her lawyer."

9.

The older deputy — Bradford, according to his name badge — managed to get the screaming Mrs. Oberlin into the back of his vehicle and close the door on her. The silence was a welcome respite.

Then he came back to confront Sam. "You have a bar card?"

Sam produced it from his wallet, showed it to the deputy. "And this is my investigator, Gerald Case."

Case said, "Can you take the bracelets off now?"

Bradford scowled at the card, handed it back to Sam. "You're aware that your client is growing marijuana in her backyard?"

"Is that what this is all about?"

"We followed you here."

"Why?"

Bradford jerked his head back toward the road. "A tip reported that rental Crown Vic out here yesterday. Said a guy with scopes was looking around."

"That would be me," Case said. "Cuffs, please?"

"Unlock him, Trace!" Bradford snapped at the younger deputy. To Sam he said, "Same guy called it in again today. Must be a neighbor. They don't like a lot of snooping around."

"I've noticed. And you thought we were here for a buy?"

"It happens. Tipster said there's cultivation going on here."

"Do you have a warrant?" Sam said.

Bradford's scowl deepened. "I told you, we got a call from an informant who gave —"

"You still need a warrant, Deputy."

"I haven't searched anything."

"An arrest warrant. You arrested my client."

"I haven't arrested her."

"What's she doing in the back of your vehicle then?"

"She was uncooperative, she —"

"She has every right to be uncooperative, unless you have a warrant or probable cause to detain her. The uncorroborated information of a tipster is not PC."

"Then we'll just take a look in the backyard."

"Not without a search warrant."

"Okay, mister lawyer sir, then I'm taking your client in for assaulting an officer. You got something to say about that?"

"Good," Sam said.

"Good?" Now Bradford looked confused.

"I'll be joining you at the station. Please give directions to Mr. Case. I'll speak to my client now."

After hesitating for a moment, Bradford indicated with his head for Trace to walk Sam to the sheriff's car.

"This is weird," Trace said.

"You have no idea," Sam said.

Trace opened the passenger-side front door. Mrs. Oberlin started with the *how dare yous* and some other colorful language.

Sam put his hand up. "We're here to help

Nicky, remember?"

She stopped her tirade and looked at Sam.

"He's in trouble and we're all going to help him," he said. "You go with these nice men and I'll be with you soon."

Looking scared now, and very tired, Mrs. Oberlin said nothing.

Sam closed the door. "She's a little out there," he said to the deputy.

"You didn't have to tell me that."

"Handle her gently."

10.

When the sheriff's car took off, Sam led Case inside the house.

"I thought you needed a search warrant," Case said.

"I'm not a police officer," Sam replied. "I'm her lawyer, remember?"

"Yeah, how'd you justify that?"

Sam turned to him. "I gave her some advice. She followed it. She calmed down. She's not in her right mind. It may be right on the edge, but it's on the edge of my representing her. And as long as I am, let's see if we can find a contact number for Mr. Nicky Oberlin."

That didn't look like it was going to be easy. The house was strewn with all manner of discarded items, some of which Sam could not identify. Nor did he want to. The place smelled like something had died. A cat maybe, or a possum.

"Sweet," Case said. "I wonder why little Nicky lets his mother live this way."

"The way she is, it wouldn't be a problem for Nicky to manipulate her. I wouldn't be surprised if he had complete power of attorney over her finances. That's going to change. I'm thinking Mrs. Oberlin needs to go to court and take back her own money."

Case smiled. "That's not going to make Nicky very happy. I love it."

"Let's check the kitchen."

It was more of the same in the kitchen, with dirty dishes piled everywhere. The smell of old food, especially ketchup, assaulted Sam's nose. Old pizza boxes were stacked like a record collection on one corner of the counter.

"Look around near the phone for an address book," Sam said.

"You'd make a good PI. How about going in with me?"

"And give up show business?"

"Isn't that what the guy who cleaned up after the circus elephants said?"

"Now you know what practicing law can be like." He sure never imagined himself scrounging around in a depressing box like this.

There were several kitchen drawers to go through. One was stuffed with old papers and receipts. It looked like Mrs. Oberlin was a pack rat. Another drawer held an amalgamation of cutlery, some of it rusted. Whatever else Mrs. Oberlin liked to do, it appeared cutting things was one of them.

With Case still scrounging, Sam opened the back door and took a look in the yard. It was less a yard than a fenced-in plot of untended ground. Pines and wild grass and bushes Sam couldn't identify. No cannabis, though. If Laverne Oberlin was growing pot, it wasn't out here.

But she wouldn't be. She was in an altered state all on her own.

"Here's our beauty," Case called from inside. Sam went back in and saw him holding up a little red book.

11.

The sheriff's station in Burrell was in the small town's idea of a strip mall, right next to the miniscule Wells Fargo Bank. If you had to have a bank here, Sam mused, being next to the sheriff's station wasn't a bad location.

As soon as Sam and Case entered through

the glass doors, they heard a screaming rant coming from somewhere inside.

"How dare you! How dare you!"

Deputy Bradford was at the front desk, looking as if he'd been waiting for them. He looked up from his Styrofoam cup and pointed at Sam. "I want her out of here."

"What seems to be the problem?" Sam said.

"She's crazy, that's what the problem is, and I don't have any inclination to lock her up and listen to her all day. So I'm going to release her to you, since you're her lawyer, and issue a citation. Then you can handle her."

"You filthy Nazis! How dare you!"

Bradford rubbed his temples. "And just so you know, we're going to go search her place."

"You won't find anything of use to you," Sam said.

"I don't really care. I have to do something to justify this. I'm getting a warrant and my advice is that you keep her away while we're there."

"Communists!"

"Who do you refer your mentals to?" Sam asked.

"Now you're making sense," Bradford said, opening a drawer in the desk. He pulled out a single sheet in a clear plastic sleeve, turned it around so Sam could read it. "This guy's in Willits. Half an hour away. I'll even call him for you, give you top priority because —"

"PACK OF ANIMALS! HOW DARE YOU!"

"Need I say more?" Bradford said.

12.

Once again, Sam was able to calm Laverne Oberlin with the thought that she could help Nicky. He spoke softly to her in the backseat as Case drove through the pines to the town of Willits. Heart of Mendocino County, the sign over the street said.

The place looked like Burrell, only with more tourists. The McDonald's in the midst of quaint shops was a dead giveaway that the place had been "discovered" and land values duly inflated. Further on, Case found a Victorian-style house that had been turned into professional space, and he pointed to one of the names on the sign: Karlin Banks, Psychotherapy, Holistic Mind Massage.

"Just what my mind needs," Case said.

Mrs. Oberlin was compliant going in, but Sam was prepared for an outburst. He happily noted that the reception area of Banks's office was almost a greenhouse of plants, offering a serene and natural feel. Laverne

Oberlin actually smiled.

Sam told the girl at the desk — and she was a girl, probably Heather's age, with a silver thing stuck through her lip — that Banks should be expecting them.

"He asked if you would go in first," she said.

Laverne Oberlin was fondling a large fern in the corner. Sam told her that he was going in to talk to the "nice man" a moment, and would return shortly with news about how to help Nicky.

Case was behind Sam. "I'm going with you," he said firmly.

"You need to keep an eye on —"

"Please."

"Sorry, Gerry. I still write the checks."

Sam went through the door alone and met a large man with gray hair, braided on two sides, standing in the middle of the office. "I am Dr. Karlin Banks," he said as if announcing his presence at some portal to the future. He wore a red-patterned dashiki shirt that brought a late-seventies Isla Vista memory to Sam, something having to do with a local hemp club. Banks wore stylish denim jeans and leather sandals. Had to be Birkenstocks.

Sam said, "I've got a very disturbed woman here who needs some help. I'd like to get a referral to a hospital for her."

"You came to the right place, my friend."

"Can I ask what you do, exactly?"

"Just what I say."

"And what is mind massage?"

"The Western mindset is very rational, cognitive. That's not bad, but it's not enough. It's like operating with one hand tied behind your back. I've also come to employ various spiritual aspects, from the Lakota community of body and spirit to Neoplatonism."

"Okay. So how long will it take?"

"As long as it does. Perhaps you should give me the initial 411."

Sam sighed, then proceeded to explain the circumstances of Mrs. Oberlin's living arrangements and her concern for her son, and her reaction to being disturbed at home. When he finished, Banks seemed not in the least perturbed.

"I'm your man," he said. "Bring her in."

Sam went back to the reception area, where Laverne Oberlin was chatting amiably with the receptionist as Case watched.

"Laverne, there's a man in the next room who'd like to talk to you," Sam said.

"Where's Nicky?"

"This man can help us all to help Nicky."

"Is Nicky in trouble?"

"If you talk to this man, we can get Nicky the help he needs."

"Yes. Help Nicky. Please."

"Come with me."

Gently, Sam took the woman's hand and helped her out of her chair. She nodded and smiled at the receptionist.

13.

Karlin Banks had prepared a soft chair in the middle of the room, now darkened with only candles glowing. He'd also lit some incense and had the sound of running water playing out of speakers. Case sat in a corner shadow.

Sam settled Laverne Oberlin into the chair and was impressed that Banks had managed to create an atmosphere that kept her quiet. Even relaxed.

Sitting cross-legged on the floor, Banks looked up at Laverne. Sam backed against the wall near Case, listening.

"Hello, Laverne," Banks said softly.

"Are you going to help Nicky?" she said.

"I'm going to help in any way I can."

"Is Nicky in trouble?"

"I want you to tell me about Nicky. But first I want you to relax. Do you feel relaxed?"

"No."

"Will you do something for me, Laverne? Will you put your head back and rest it for a second?"

"Will that help Nicky?"

"I think it will. Let's try it."

Sam watched as Karlin Banks gently spoke to Mrs. Oberlin for several minutes, the sound of his voice merging with the whisper of the water. He was good at this part, no doubt about it. Sam started to feel pretty relaxed himself.

By the time Banks was finished, it almost seemed like Laverne Oberlin was in a hypnotic trance. At the very least, she was close to sleep, yet able to talk.

"Tell me about Nicky," Banks suggested.

"Nicky is a good boy."

"How is he good?"

"He loves me. He loves me more than anything in the world."

"Of course he does. Why wouldn't he?"

"Because it's not allowed."

Banks shot a look at Sam, then went back to Laverne. "Why isn't it allowed?"

"Oh, you mustn't talk of it."

"Will something bad happen if we talk about it?"

"Oh, yes."

"What is the bad thing that will happen?"

"Mustn't talk about it. Oh no no. Hide

335

Nicky, will you?"

For all his New Age stylings, Karlin Banks looked and sounded like a man who knew exactly what he was doing.

Banks stood and circled slowly around Laverne Oberlin, looking at her from different angles. "Why must we hide Nicky?"

"So the bad thing doesn't happen."

"What is the bad thing, Laverne?"

"Mustn't talk about it."

"Where can we hide Nicky?"

"Will you, please? Hide Nicky."

"Where can we hide him?"

"Where he can't see him."

"Where who can't see him?"

"Mustn't talk about it."

Banks stopped in a position behind Laverne Oberlin. Her head was back and her eyes closed.

"Where are you, Laverne?"

"With Nicky. Shh."

"Shall I keep my voice down?"

"Yes."

"Why must I do that?"

"So he doesn't hear you."

"Who?"

"Mustn't talk about it."

Sam saw Case register frustration. With a squint, Sam told him to hang in there. At the very least Laverne was demonstrating her need for medical help. If they could get a referral to a hospital, he could get Laverne a measure of protection under the law. Sam would file for a protective order as her attorney, get a judge involved. This would force Nicky to divulge more than he was willing, and maybe something out of that could be used against him.

Karlin Banks came back to a position in front of Laverne Oberlin and lowered his substantial frame onto a big paisley pillow on the floor. He crossed his legs again.

"Now, Laverne, I want you to know that you're protected here. No one can get to you here. You're free to talk. You are safe."

"Safe?" Laverne's voice sounded the slightest bit strained.

"Yes, Laverne."

"No . . ."

"Safe, where no one can get to you."

"Mustn't talk about it . . ."

"It's all right, Laverne, it's —"

Laverne bolted upright as if zapped by a thousand volts. "No! He'll hear you! Get out! Get out!"

Banks untangled his legs and got to his knees. "Laverne —"

"How dare you! You want us killed!"

"No —"

Laverne Oberlin screamed.

14.

Roz was pounding the drums in her garage when Heather's cell phone vibrated. If it was her mom or dad, she wasn't going to answer. Not this time. Too many words going back and forth. *Just leave me alone for a while.*

But the number was one she wanted to answer.

"Hi," she said.

"Where are you?" Lundquist asked.

"Roz's."

"Is that her in the background?"

"Yeah. Good stuff, huh?"

"Good. Not great."

"What's up?" She tried to sound breezy, but inside she was waiting for him to tell her again how great she was, how much greater she would be, and whatever else was going to put her on a cloud.

"Front row is what's up."

"Front row?"

"Vegas. Stacee Hartin. Remember?"

"When?"

"Can you be ready tomorrow?"

"Um —"

"Pack something for a couple of days. We'll have ourselves a good time. Vegas is crazy."

She hesitated, her head spinning up some dimly lit imaginings, troubling. They were offset by the picture of her on a stage in a glittering dress that barely covered her as a hundred thousand screaming fans waved and shouted at her for *more.*

"You still want to go, don't you?" he said.

"Oh, yes," she said.

15.

At eight o'clock in the evening, Sam and Case got Laverne admitted into the hospital on Karlin Banks's expedited request. Not even the Navajo way could calm Laverne, and just before they left with her Banks told Sam that she had some heavy stuff under the surface, only he didn't use the word *stuff.*

It had to do with child abuse, Banks offered. He was sure of that much.

Sam didn't need any convincing, and after getting Laverne Oberlin admitted, it was time for the next phase.

Outside the hospital, Sam punched in a number from the book Case had lifted from Laverne's home.

He didn't know if Nicky would even answer, or what his reaction would be. But it only took two rings before the voice, bloated with forced jocularity, came through.

"Sam, how'd you get this number, buddy?"

"Someone very close to you gave it to me."

A hard silence fell on the line. Then Nicky said, "Why don't you tell me who that is, Sammy?"

"I think you know."

"Don't play games, not with me. I'll eat you for lunch."

"Better watch what you say, Nicky. This conversation could be monitored for quality assurance."

"You're not going to be happy about doing this, Sammy."

"How's the money holding out?"

Another silence.

"All that money you've been living off of for the last, what, twenty years?"

"You want to get to the point, bud?"

"You're the point, Nicky. You and your mother."

"You're out of your league, Sammy. You . . ."

Sam could almost hear the wheels screech in Nicky's head, the cogs of a master manipulator snagged on a wrench. "What have you done?" Nicky said.

"It's what you've done, Nicky. To your own mother."

"You better talk, right now."

"How's it feel?"

"What?"

"Getting jerked around?"

"Talk to me, Sammy, or I —"

"You what? What cards have you got left?"

"Where is my mother?"

"Where you can't get at her."

Nicky cursed, whether out of frustration or anger Sam couldn't tell. Probably both. This was a new turn for good old Nicky Oberlin.

"I'm warning you right now, you better —"

"Your warning days are over, Nick. This whole thing is over. Your mother is in need of help, and the first thing she is going to get is access to her own money."

Silence, which Sam let linger before continuing. "And then she's going to fill in the details of the story she's started to tell."

"You tell me where she is. You tell me right now. You —"

"No can do, Nick. That wouldn't be in my client's best interest."

"Client? What have you —"

"But if you follow my instructions to the letter, you can —"

A scream pierced Sam's ear. Then the line went dead. Sam pictured Nicky's cogs scattering across the courtroom, his dreams of absolute mastery up in smoke.

Sam made another call.

"Linda."

"Sam, how are —"

"Listen. I want somebody to come over."

"What?"

"Just till I get home. I need to wrap something up. Until then, Oberlin's likely to do anything. There's a guy Case knows, private security. He can use the study."

"You think we need that?"

"Just for a night. Until I can make sure Nicky won't be bothering us anymore."

"How can you do that, Sam?"

"The only way I know. Leverage."

FIFTEEN

1.

His name was Greg Wayne, and he was an ex-Marine who looked it. Close-cropped hair, wide shoulders, hands that looked like the proverbial lethal weapons. And a nice, easy smile. Linda liked him immediately, even though she was still uncomfortable about the whole arrangement.

"Don't worry about me," he told her after introductions. All he had with him was a black duffel bag. "I carry my own stores for short jobs. I won't be very noticeable." He looked around as if sizing up the place. "Bedrooms are upstairs?"

"Yes," Linda said.

"Mind if I take a look?"

"Of course not." She paused. "May I ask you a question?"

Wayne dropped the duffel bag at his feet. "Sure. Anything."

"You do this kind of work a lot?"

He nodded. "Last job was for a movie star, you'd know his name. Little guy, comes up to about here on me." Wayne put his hand just under his chin. "But on the screen, they make him look six-four. Anyway, there was a guy got it in his head that Mr. Movie Star was really doing all that physical stuff on the screen, and he wanted to take him down."

"Take him down?"

"Duke it out. Show him who was the tough guy. So, while they were getting a restraining order, I got hired to watch his back."

"And it all turned out well?"

"Oh, yeah."

"The guy never bothered him again."

Wayne smiled. "He tried."

"What happened?"

"Mrs. Trask, I don't want you to worry about anything. My job is to be here so you don't have to worry. You have a family to look out for. It's my job to free you up to do yours."

A chilly tremble snaked up Linda's spine. It wasn't for lack of confidence in this man, who seemed perfectly capable to do his job. But the fact that he was in her home at all tangled her nerves. When would this nightmare be over?

"Do you have an extra house key?"

"Sure."

Wayne nodded. "If you don't mind, I'll take that look around now."

2.

Saturday morning in Hollywood, before the shops opened and the tourists hit the Walk of Fame, was a little eerie as far as Heather was concerned. It was like being in another world, not the night life, which she knew pretty well, nor the safety of broad daylight. And here, at the famous corner, Hollywood and Vine, the long shadows of the buildings made her feel like she was in a canyon somewhere, lost.

She knew this was a famous intersection at one time. Back in the golden age of movies. What was that golden age, anyway? Black-and-white movies, she guessed. Why did anybody even go to those things?

No color, no good music, boring stories.

Life was supposed to be full color, with jacked-up sound. If it wasn't, if it was black-and-white, why stick around?

Going to Vegas was color. Lots of it.

She knew what he'd want in Vegas. So why not? There had to be a first time, so why not with a guy who could help her get what she wanted?

She almost laughed remembering that night at Starbucks, when the geekish drummer hit on her. That would have led to a lot of crud she didn't want to deal with.

This would be much, much better.

And if it didn't work out, what then? What if there was no career, no rocket to the Grammys?

Don't think about that. Get on the ride. Hold on till the end.

One thing she didn't want was to end up back here, on Hollywood Boulevard. She wasn't going to be one of those street people. Of course, she couldn't go home, because that was not her place anymore and she knew it.

So those were the options.

She heard a car horn.

Lundquist was across Vine, sitting in a silver Mustang convertible. He waved and smiled.

For one moment Heather hesitated. Something inside her said *run. Get out of there and go home. You're living in a fantasy world.*

But when he honked again she gave him a wave of her own, waited for the light to change, and crossed the street.

3.

On the plane back to Burbank, Gerald Case told Sam that now he was no longer the hunted. He was the hunter, and he needed to get ready for *the kill.*

"You mean that figuratively, don't you?" Sam said.

Case shrugged. "Whatever fits."

"Terrific."

"It's good you've got Wayne in your house until you get back. A good man. Reliable. But you can't rest. You should retain him to check on you periodically until Oberlin is a done deal."

Sam was about to ask how much this was all going to cost him but decided it no longer mattered. Getting Nicky to stop was the only thing that mattered now, even if it meant a second mortgage.

But killing him? Only in self-defense. Even then, what would that do to him?

He thought about that scene in the movie *Lawrence of Arabia,* after Lawrence has executed an Arab to show a tribe that he is willing to carry out their form of justice. His face showing inner torment, he admits to another man that he "enjoyed it."

Sam wondered if, in his heart, he would enjoy killing Nicky Oberlin. It scared him to even think about it.

"And you need to let me track him for you," Case said.

"Huh?"

"What were you thinking just then?"

"I just wandered for a second. What were you saying?"

"I said I should track him — Oberlin."

"Track him where?"

"He's not going to sit tight, now that he knows what you've done."

"Think he'll try to visit his mother?"

Case shook his head. "He knows that wouldn't be a bright thing to do. What he wants to do is disappear off your radar and hover. I want to get to him before he hovers over your house."

"How're you going to do that?"

He smiled. "I've already started."

"You know where he is?"

"I know a guy who knows."

"Who?"

"You ever read those Perry Mason books?"

"A couple maybe, a long time ago."

"Sure you did. You wanted to be a lawyer, right? Well, I read 'em too. Tons of 'em. They always had those catchy titles, you know, like *The Case of the Lucky Legs.*"

"Right."

"Only the guy I liked wasn't Mason, good as he was. It was Paul Drake."

"The detective."

"Had his own shop, like me. So anyway, whenever there was a problem Mason had to figure out, he turned it over to Drake. And Drake would either solve it himself, or turn it over to one of his operatives. I loved that. He had operatives all over the place, and all he had to do was make a call."

"Just like you, I suppose."

"That's the thing," Case said with a laugh. "Stories ain't much like life. The expenses would've killed him. But that's not to say it isn't worth it to know guys. Freelance guys. Guys you can subcontract to."

"So who's the guy following Oberlin?"

"Name's Betterson. That's all you need to know. He can follow a mosquito to a skinny guy's elbow."

"What does he do when he gets to the elbow?"

"Calls me."

"And then?"

Case winked. "I use my professional judgment."

Sam decided to leave it at that. Best, he thought, if he didn't cogitate too much. Case was like one of those Indian scouts in the B Westerns, the one that always came along with the cavalry because all those West Point trained generals and enlisted flatfeet couldn't find their way out of a covered wagon on the Great Plains. Case was like that for Sam — the advance man, the hand-to-hand combat guy. If it ever came to that.

Part of him hoped it would. Case would take care of the Nicky problem for him, and Sam wouldn't need to know the details.

4.

Heather loved the feel of the desert wind in her hair. Lundquist was driving fast, and the air was dry and hot, and it seemed like a magic carpet ride.

He had the CD player cranked up and was playing one of her favorite LA bands. It really rocked, the drummer was all over it, and everything else was reminiscent of the great Smashing Pumpkins, only with LA-style anguish you couldn't manufacture anywhere else.

Magic. Maybe it did exist. Maybe it was going to be hers after all.

Lundquist shouted something. He had his hat pulled down tight and his ponytail did a little dance in the wind.

Heather shouted, "What?"

"Listen!"

With a push of the button the music stopped. For a moment all Heather could hear was the wind whistling past her ears.

Then a new song started up, with the familiar fat, rolling bass line.

It was Screech Monk.

Their song!

Lundquist was smiling at her. "Happy birthday," he shouted.

It wasn't her birthday, but she knew what he meant. A present for her.

Her voice came in the vocal, and *she was good.*

He was really making it happen for her.

She looked at him then, trying to decide how she felt. She wasn't attracted to him physically. That ponytail was so retro it was past being hip retro. But were looks everything?

They helped.

But power was even better. You could learn to love a man who could pull strings for you. At least you could tolerate him.

Right. How much experience did she have with things like this? She wanted to think she was in control of her own destiny, but that was a crock. She needed help. Her parents had tried to convince her God could help. But here was a guy who really could, who could take her where she wanted to go.

And in return he'd want something. She knew that. So what?

Maybe she could induce him to lose the

ponytail.

"You like?" he said after the song ended.

"Oh, yeah."

He put his hand out and she took it. His grip was firm and sure.

Trust him, she thought.

The desert air hit her face with a little more heat. The long ribbon of road was part of a big nowhere. Nothing behind, nothing in front, just a strip of asphalt taking in the sun rays.

Only a few cars on the road, people going back and forth, in and out of different lives.

Okay, this was hers, the only one, and she would ride it out.

5.

Sam was home by eleven o'clock, glad to find Greg Wayne there, and that he liked him. Wayne seemed the ultimate professional and was packed and ready to leave ten minutes after Sam came through the door. He only wanted to talk to Sam for a few minutes before he checked out.

"Case says this stalker of yours is a real piece of work," Wayne said.

"That's one way to put it," Sam said. "There are a bunch of other ways, not so nice, you could say it too."

"And he says you have a weapon."

"You know how to use it?"

"Pull the trigger."

"You've got the most important part down," Wayne said with a smile. "May I suggest that when you get the gun you put it where you know you can get it quickly, and if you ever have to use it you aim right here." With his right hand Wayne made a circular motion in front of his chest. "That's the largest mass and easiest target. Okay?"

"Sure."

"You're a little nervous about that prospect."

"Shouldn't I be?"

"As long as the nerves don't freeze you. I want you to go over and over in your mind that if this guy comes into your house, you don't hesitate to shoot. You need to see that in your head beforehand. Don't wait until the moment arrives and you have to think it through."

"Have you ever shot anyone?"

"Let's just say that if I were in your shoes, and our hypothetical situation arose, it would not be a completely new experience for me to take a guy down."

"Can I ask you a personal question?"

"Shoot. To coin a phrase."

"How did it make you feel?"

Greg Wayne paused for a long moment.

He kept his eyes steady on Sam's. Finally, he said, "If you're in the right, it doesn't matter how you feel. It only matters that you do it. You've got a wife and family, Mr. Trask, and a dangerous man out there who wants to do you harm. Be ready to do him harm. I urge you to think it through now."

"I will."

"Would you like me to stay?"

"Can I call you if I need you?"

"Of course. I'll just get my stuff."

After Wayne left, Sam did think about what Wayne had said. Sam imagined facing Nicky Oberlin in his own home. He saw himself holding a gun and Nicky smiling at him, as if challenging him to do it. He tried to see himself firing. But when he did, Nicky didn't go down. He just stood there, still smiling.

6.

Sam joined Linda and Max for Domino's pizza and root beer. It was just what he wanted, simple and starchy.

Of course, the big hole where Heather should've been remained. He talked around it for a while, listened to Max trying his best not to sound nervous. Having a security guy stay in your house was not exactly the most calming thing that could happen to a sensitive kid.

The fact that Max was fighting his nervousness pleased Sam. As had become abundantly clear, there were going to be plenty of challenges in life that would require Max's courage. What was it Sam's football coach used to say? *The butterflies in the stomach are natural. Your job, gentlemen, is to make them fly in formation.*

Finally, the subject of Heather could not be avoided any longer. "Have you heard from her?" Sam asked.

Linda shook her head. "Only a message yesterday on the machine. She didn't call my cell. I guess she doesn't want to talk to us."

"Where is she physically?"

"Probably at Roz's."

"Maybe we should just go over there and walk up to the door and —"

"I don't think that would be a good idea," Linda said. "There will only be a lot of shouting."

"I'm calling her." Sam punched 3 on his cell phone, the speed-dial number for Heather. She didn't answer. He left a message asking her to please call.

"You have Roz's number?" Sam asked Linda.

"Do you think —"

"I'm not thinking anymore," Sam said. "I just want to talk to my daughter."

"You don't think I do?"

"Did I say that?"

"You implied it."

"Did I *say* it?"

"Stop being a lawyer for one second —"

"All I said was —"

"Guys," Max said. "Cut it."

Sam and Linda stopped. Max was breathing hard and his eyes were misting. His cheeks were breaking into pink.

"You're right, Max." Sam put a hand on his son's shoulder.

"When will they catch that guy?" Max said.

"Until they do," Sam said, deflecting a direct answer, "we stick together, right?"

"Yeah."

"That's what the Trask family does."

7.

"Roz, this is Mr. Trask."

"Hi."

"How are you?"

"Okay." Her voice was tentative. Maybe obstinate.

Sam calmed himself. "Know why I'm calling you?"

"You're trying to find Heather."

"I would be very appreciative if you would ask her to talk to me."

"I can't."

"Please, I'm asking you to —"

"I can't because I don't know where she is."

"Isn't she supposed to be with you?"

When Roz didn't immediately answer, Sam said, "Where is she?"

"I don't know if she would want me to tell you."

"Roz, I think I have a right to know —"

"This is kind of weird for me, to be talking to you."

"Why is it so weird?"

"I don't think you like me very much."

Sam took a deep breath. "It's true that I haven't been as fair to you or Heather as I should. I just haven't come to terms with some things. Like Heather growing up and being her own person and doing what she feels passionately about. That's wrong of me and I hope you understand that. I don't really know you and —"

"Yeah, well I guess I am a little bit different than a lot of people."

"Well, maybe below the surface we're all pretty much the same, trying to make sense out of everything, trying to make it through. All I want is to tell Heather some of that."

"Right on." Pause. "I don't really know all of what's going on. We laid down this track for a guy, a producer, and he kind of focused in on Heather, and I think she's with him."

"With him? Where?"

"I'm not sure."

"Is she . . . involved with him?"

"I don't know. Maybe."

Sam tried to fight back the hot needles under his skin. "Can you tell me where I can contact this man?"

"I have a phone number. But he's a little hard to get hold of."

"Anything you can do to help me?"

"I just don't want you to worry about her. She's a big girl. She can take care of herself."

"You really believe that?"

When Roz did not immediately answer, Sam knew she didn't.

8.

No one answered the phone at the number Roz gave him. Sam called Gerald Case and asked if he could get an address based on a phone number.

"No problemo," Case said.

While he waited Sam called Greg Wayne and requested he come over. Wayne said he'd be there in half an hour. Then Case called back with an address on Santa Monica Boulevard in Hollywood.

Sam fought ever-present traffic on the 101, getting off at Highland. He crossed over Hollywood Boulevard, then Sunset, turned right on Santa Monica. The building he was looking for was just beyond La Cienega. He found it, a modest-looking set of suites in what looked to be a converted apartment complex.

Roz had told him the producer's name was Lundquist. That's all he knew. Not all of the glass doors on the row had names. Some just had numbers. One of these, number 12, had a musical note graphic under the number.

Sam tried the door. Locked. He knocked. No answer. He looked through the glass and observed a sparse outer office. A few framed items, with some sort of record logo, hung on the plain, cream-colored walls.

There was a hair salon next door. Mancini's. Sam went in and was met by a young man with long, honey-colored hair who was five foot six or seven. He wore black bell-bottoms with silver stripes and a black leather vest over a yellow T-shirt.

"Help you?" he said, eyeing Sam's hair.

"You know the guy next door?" Sam made a motion with his thumb.

"The music guy?"

"Yeah."

"Kind of keeps to himself. I don't see a lot of him."

"Any idea where he might be?"

"I don't keep track of him. Like I said, sometimes he's around, sometimes he isn't. I can't remember seeing him in a while. Sometimes he goes on trips back east, I think. I heard him talking about some singer in New York one day, talking right outside here to one of our girls. I think he was hitting on her."

Not the news Sam wanted to hear. The man could very well be using his position as a music producer to get Heather into bed. It was a longstanding Hollywood hustle.

"Long as you're here," the little hairstylist said, "can I take a whack?"

"Some other time, maybe," Sam said. He got in his car and headed back into Hollywood traffic. The snarl was worse than ever down here. It seemed the whole city was the prisoner of gridlock these days.

Was he any less a prisoner of the gridlock of his own situation? Something had to give, and soon, or he feared he'd rear-end the limits of his capacity to carry on.

SIXTEEN

1.

Heather decided she loved everything about Las Vegas. Especially the lights at night. And the people streaming in and out of casinos and hotels, and the noise of gaming tables and music and laughing.

Action. That's what the gamblers called it, right? A lot of action. As she wandered around that first night with Lundquist, she decided this would be a great place to spend the rest of her working life, doing shows in one of the big casinos and then getting into the action wherever it was. They must have great parties here, in some of the big suites.

She loved what was happening at the crap tables. Here were a bunch of strangers circling the green felt, and when somebody got on a roll — she didn't quite understand the game, only that sometimes a person was rolling the dice real good — they all laughed and cheered and talked to each other. It was like a mini family. People just having fun, high on the action.

Of course, when somebody lost a bunch of chips they didn't look like they were having so much fun. But that was all part of it. You didn't get anything good without the risk of loss.

She knew that with Lundquist now. It was risky to be alone with him here in Vegas. But there was so much more to be gained. So much more.

And she had to admit getting front-row seats for Stacee Hartin was a perk she could get used to.

There was another perk that was nice: a high-school trick she pulled off a year ago. The famous fake ID. People always said she looked a little older than she was. Now she whipped out the ID, which came in very handy as she ordered a gin and tonic. Lundquist asked her if she really wanted to drink, and she asked him if he thought she couldn't hold her liquor, ha ha.

She let him put his arm around her when the show started. He didn't try anything else. The only thing he did was check her glass from time to time, and if it was empty he made sure she got another drink.

2.

Sam talked to Linda in the family room.

"I think Heather is with a sleazy music producer," he said.

"What do you mean, *with?*"

"Roz gave me a guy's name, Lundquist. Case found an address for him. In Hollywood. That's where I went."

"Why didn't you tell me?"

"I didn't want to worry you until I found out more."

"Worry me. Please. Don't hold out —"

"Do you want to hear about it?" Sam wanted to defuse an argument before it started.

"Yes." Linda sat on the sofa.

"All right. Roz said this guy was showing an interest in Heather. When I went down there, to the guy's office, there was a hairstylist next door who sort of knew him. Said he was the kind of guy who, quote unquote, hit on girls."

"You think Heather's with this man?"

"I don't know, but it doesn't seem out of the question."

"And if she is, she's certainly not going to answer our calls." Linda stood up. "Can we call the police?"

"And tell them what?"

"That our daughter's missing, that some

man has her."

"We don't know that."

"We know she's missing."

"Do we? She left a message saying not to worry. She's almost eighteen. The police are not going to follow this up."

"Of course they will, he's a . . ."

"What is he?" Sam said, not hiding his own frustration. "He's a guy who is using his power and influence to —"

"Take advantage of her —"

"No doubt."

"Isn't that statutory rape?"

Sam nodded. "I'll call it in. Missing person —"

"Kidnapping!"

"She went willingly."

"So what?"

"I'm just telling you what the law says."

"Oh, hang the law! This is our daughter! Just do something, Sam. Please. Do *something!*"

3.

Heather tried to suck in breath, get some air, cold air. *Please come to me.*

Head pounding, everything swirling around her.

Sensed that she was in a car, car moving,

at night.

What night was it? Saturday?

Yes. A million years ago it was Saturday morning and she was in Hollywood. And now it was a million years later and it was Saturday night and it was late and she was going to be sick.

Sick again. Oh, why was it this way? What did she do to herself?

Where was she anyway?

Night lights. Stacee Hartin.

Oh, yeah. Right. She remembered about half the show. And she better get out of this car or she was going to barf all over.

Car. Whose car?

Right. Right. Lundquist. She looked to the side and saw a vibrating shadow and she tried to open her mouth and say something, but the words were thick like pillows stuffed in her throat.

"Take it easy, there." The voice sounded like it came from outer space. How could she take it easy when her stomach felt like an overturned garbage can?

This was bad. Now she was remembering more of the night. She had been drinking a lot. She wanted to show Lundquist she could party with the best of them. She wanted to be Courtney Love and Kurt Cobain and all those classic rockers, but she was a wimp. And now she was sick and out of it and where were they going anyway?

She wanted to be at home, at least in her own bed with her mother standing over her like she used to do when Heather got sick. Just for a little while she wanted that. Then she could go back to being the star that she was meant to be.

But she wasn't magically transported to her own bed, and her mother wasn't here.

"I'm sick," she said to the shadow, hoping maybe he would have an instant remedy.

"We're almost there," he said.

"Where?"

"Where you'll feel good."

In the back of her head she heard the little voice screaming, *Idiot! You know what's going to happen, don't you?*

Oh, well, who cared anyway? She wasn't up to caring anymore.

Okay. Just let it happen. It's all part of it. You will look back on this and see it all fitting together, getting you where you needed to go.

She kept repeating that over and over to herself as the car went on. Let it happen. Let it happen.

Finally, sweet finally, the car came to a stop. It was dark everywhere. She thought for a moment they had driven into a soundproof recording studio with all the lights turned off.

Then Lundquist was helping her out of the car and into a house.

House? Where was this house?

She didn't have the energy to ask any questions. She just leaned on him as he guided her through this maze of blackness and then up some stairs. How did she make it up the stairs? Time was beginning to jump around on her.

And then she was on a bed. Soft bed. Sweet. That felt good.

Everything was swirling. She was swirling. The bed was. She could not make it stop.

And then some light. Flickering light. Candlelight. Yes, that was it. He had lit some candles.

And then she was aware of him coming to the edge of the bed. She looked up and saw him, illuminated by the candlelight. She could make out just enough of his features to know that he still had on his shades and his hat.

But something was wrong. She knew that even before he took off his sunglasses and his hat. She knew it even before he took his hand and placed it on top of his head and grabbed his hair and removed it.

No way. What was up with that? He didn't

have any hair? He was bald?

And why was he looking like that? Big, grotesque smile, and a feeling almost like he was drooling over her.

4.

Sunday was not a good day at church. Sam's insides churned like some sort of Old Testament plague, locusts devouring hope.

Now, praying in the study, Sam wondered if this was what Jacob felt like, wrestling with the angel. It seemed unfair. How do you take down an angel? How —

His cell rang.

It was Heather.

Trying to keep his voice steady, Sam opened the phone and said, "Hi, sweetie. What's going on?"

There was no response.

"Heather?"

Laughter. Crazy laughter, like she was at a party and people were drunk and she called him and then just had people laughing all around her.

"Heather, where are you?"

"I'm safe, Daddy."

Sam's throat clamped shut. It was a man's voice, pitched high like a little girl's.

"I'm happy too, Daddy. I got married!"

On Heather's phone. All capacity for

rational thought melted in the intense heat of the unimaginable. Nicky Oberlin had his daughter.

"What, no congratulations?"

Sam could hardly speak. He felt as if Nicky was watching him right now on closed-circuit TV, enjoying the spectacle of Sam squirming, completely helpless.

"We're just so happy," Nicky said. "Can you and Linda and Max make it for Thanksgiving?"

"I want to talk to my daughter."

"She can't come to the phone right now. The wedding night was really so exciting for her; she needs her rest."

"What sick thing are you talking about?"

"The wedding? That's not sick, that's a girl's happiest time! True, it was sort of my own little ceremony, it might not be entirely kosher, but boy, you should have seen her, Sammy! She was beaming! And let me tell you something else, Sammy. She is a real woman. All woman, if you know what I mean."

A cold like the hands of death gripped Sam's body. "I will find you," he said. "I will find you and kill you and if you've done anything —"

"Do you hear yourself, Sammy? Is that any way for an officer of the court to talk?

What a nasty man you have become! Now, do you want your daughter back or not? Because, Sammy, I'm not sure this relationship is going to last."

Sam listened, numb.

"I'm going to tell you what to do to come get your daughter. See, as much as I enjoy her company, it's you I really want to see, Sammy. It's you I want to be friends with. I just had to get your attention, that's all."

"Tell me where —"

"Shut it! Just shut up, Sammy, and I will talk. You will listen. Because if you don't listen I may have to spank little Heather here. Tell her what a bad man her daddy is."

Sam bit his lip, hard.

"Now here's what we're going to do. I'm going to give you directions, a little at a time. And you have to promise me something, Sammy. Are you ready to do that? To promise me?"

"What?"

"You can't let anybody else in on this. I mean cops or FBI or even your own wife. You can't have anybody listen in on your phone. Even though I've got an untraceable phone, I get kind of peeved when people snoop into my private life. When cops go searching where I live because some guy like you has a friend in the DA's office. You with me so far?"

"Yeah."

"I don't think you are. I mean, you hired a private eye. That wasn't very nice. So you're going to have to call him off. 'Cause if I catch wind he's still around, that's going to make me mad too. Like when you used my mother, like the lowlife you are."

"Just tell me what you —"

"Shut up, I said! Speak when told to. You are going to do just what I say, because if you don't, I'm afraid I can't let you see Heather ever again. Or anybody else for that matter. She'll be like that magician's assistant."

What was he talking about?

"There was that magician who used to have a beautiful assistant for his saw-the-lady-in-two act. He fired her. She now lives in Dallas and Tulsa."

Nicky cackled.

"Get it, Sammy? Saw the lady in two? Lives in Dallas and Tulsa?"

Sam said nothing. Tears of rage pooled in his eyes.

"Sammy, I asked if you got it."

"Yeah."

"Because Heather is going to end up in different parts of Nevada if you don't do just what I say."

Nevada.

"So get ready to, Sammy. Call off your dogs. Don't tell a living soul, got it? It's our little secret. And maybe, just maybe, you'll see your daughter again."

Linda chose that moment to stick her head in the study. Sam put his hand up to her, signaling for quiet.

"You got that, Sammy?"

"Got it."

"You sure? Because if you don't —"

"I have it. What's next?"

"You'll hear from me. In about half an hour. I need to attend to my wife's needs."

The connection went dead. Sam held the phone to his ear a few seconds, willing himself not to give anything away. He clapped the phone shut.

"Everything okay?" Linda said.

"Oh, there's a matter I may need to attend to."

"You sound worried about it."

"What else is new?"

She studied him. "Sam, what aren't you telling me?"

"Linda, will you let this one go? I may have to take another short trip."

"Does this have something to do with what you did up in San Francisco?"

Sam, as calmly as he could, said, "This is one of those confidential lawyer things. I'll tell you all about it when I can. All right? I'll get Greg Wayne back here while I'm gone."

"Sam, if there's anything —"

"Trust me, will you? Can you do that much?"

"Of course, but —"

"Then just do it," he said.

■ ■ ■ ■

PART II:
DESERT SOLITAIRE

■ ■ ■ ■

SEVENTEEN

1.

Driving east on Highway 15, the lights of the city illuminating the night sky like forbidden candy, Sam remembered how much he hated Las Vegas.

He'd come here with his law school classmates, each semester after finals. Five or six of them would rent a single motel room and play no-look poker to see who had to sleep on the floor. Then they'd all go down to the Golden Nugget and spread out to blackjack tables or the crap games or maybe some roulette and start on the inevitable enterprise of drinking and losing money.

Oh, what high-stakes gamblers they were too, Sam feeling the pinch if he ever lost up to twenty dollars. Then he would take a long break and walk around, cooling off before going back to the one-dollar blackjack game and more edge-of-the-seat excitement.

It was during one of those jaunts in his

third year at UCLA, to the place the veterans called "Lost Wages," that Sam finally got his fill.

He was between losing stints at blackjack in one of the downtown casinos when he wandered through the copper-smelling sea of slot machines and was engulfed by the unmistakable sounds of obsession — the ringing of coins fed into holes at the top and jangling down into the bowels of the machine, followed by the mechanical pull of the knobbed arm, then the snap upward after a hopeful letting go, followed by the tumblers spinning. Pretty pictures of cherries and lemons and eyes. And numbers. Every now and then there'd be a small payoff and a few coins would splatter into the metallic mouth at the bottom. The happy player would squeal or clap or just look at the winnings dead-eyed, scooping them up and throwing them into a cup filled with other coins. Then immediately the ritual would continue, resulting most often in loss.

Sam never could figure out the allure of the one-armed bandits. There was no skill involved, just a blind, repetitive feeding and pulling, feeding and pulling. They were even starting to put in machines where the player just punched a button. No thought involved, just plain luck, most of it bad. What was the attraction?

There was an old episode of the *Twilight Zone* in which an older man was hypnotized by a slot machine and couldn't stop losing his money to it. That's what it had to be, Sam thought. Mechanical hypnotism. No rational person would keep throwing money away in the mad hope that the machine would return a jackpot. Or would they? Was he any different tossing dice or trying to beat a dealer at twenty-one?

He was lost in such thoughts, lazily eyeing the people on the slots, when he heard a woman scream. He looked to his right and saw a woman of around sixty, dressed in a skin-tight leopard-patterned outfit — one that would have looked ridiculous even on a woman half her age — being tugged by a man in a Western shirt with a large gut overhanging an ornate belt buckle.

"Lemme go!" she yelled as the man spoke to her in low tones.

"That's enough," he said. "Come on, honey, let's go and get —"

The woman screamed in his face, "I ain't good and ready and I'll tell you when I'm good and ready and I ain't right now!" Clearly she was drunk, and she was alternating the cup of coins in her hand with a cup on the ledge next to the slot machine. That cup held beer, no doubt, which was served free to the players. That's what the casinos loved. Nothing filled their coffers faster than drunken gamblers with high hopes.

As the woman jerked away from the man, Sam saw her right hand was almost all black on the underside, the side that grabbed the arm of the slot machine. How long must she have been there to get a hand that dirty?

"Now, honey," the man said, moving in closer to the woman and reaching his arms around her body. She jerked away from him again and now the coins went flying out of the cup and she swore at the top of her voice and cried, "Now look what you did! You leave me alone and keep your big fat nose out of my business!" Then she dropped to her knees, spilling more coins as she frantically used her blackened right hand to sweep up the coins on the floor as if they were dust bunnies.

A beefy young man in a casino blazer rushed over and started to help the other man get the woman to her feet. She kept screeching, like a caged animal. She was crazy with liquor and gambling, and Sam would never forget the jiggling fat of her arms as she batted at the coins, making the whole thing seem monstrous, like a scene out of a Victor Hugo novel.

As the screaming woman was pulled up and restrained by the two men, Sam noticed a small crowd had gathered and the people were laughing, laughing at this distorted image of humanity. Sam didn't laugh. He thought how ugly it all was, this huge community of excess planted in the desert, sucking people in for no other reason than to get them to forget themselves in the vain pursuit of easy money.

He'd had no use for Las Vegas ever since, had never returned, even when one of his good friends invited him to a wedding there, promising "the party of a lifetime."

Now here he was, returning because he had to. Because the worst form of humanity was not in the casinos but somewhere out there, beyond the lights, holding hostage his only daughter and making him dance. Nicky held all the cards, as the gamblers said, and Sam had to follow his instructions to the letter.

And as the city lights got closer and brighter and more gaudy, Sam's insides shimmied, like a dancer in one of those shows in the big hotels. He saw a big, bright billboard on the right, shouting its message in gold lettering —

WELCOME TO LAS VEGAS. WHAT

2.

Heather's arms were throbbing now against the ropes. The lowlife had her on a chair, facing him. Her head was still clearing from *something.* What was he going to do to her?

How had they gotten here anyway? She had no memory of it. This was a house of some kind, but sparsely furnished and dark. She had the sense it was daytime, but the windows were all covered with heavy black drapes. The chair she was secured to was plain and hard.

Lundquist was reclining in a soft chair, his feet up on a coffee table. Above him, on the wall, was a print of a skeleton riding a motorcycle. On another table was a cage of some sort. What, the guy had pets?

She told herself not to let him get the best of her. "I have to go to the bathroom," she said.

"No, you don't."

"You want me to pee all over myself?"

"Might make a good song lyric." He smiled.

"You're pathetic."

"Not a way a wife should talk to her husband."

Heather's own stomach twisted. Was he

saying, actually saying, that he wanted her to marry him? "You are so sick."

"Honey, that wasn't your attitude last night. What happened?"

She couldn't remember last night. It was lost in a haze. Blurry pictures littered her mind. She did remember sunlight, some casino scenes, drinking during the concert — he must have gotten the drinks for her . . . yes, he had a flask — and feeling really lightheaded. Then a feeling of being awake half the night but not remembering anything.

What was it about him? He had his hat on and his shades off, and in the dim light of this place she thought she saw his eyes for the first time. They were small and dark, like a couple of black M&M's.

"You're my woman now, so I'd appreciate a little more of that lovin' feelin'," he said.

What *was* his trip? "Is this some sort of game you're into? 'Cause I'm not playing."

"No game. Don't you get the deal yet?"

She waited.

"We're married."

She scoured her mind for any memory that would prove what he just said. What was worse was not finding anything to disprove it. "You're out of it," she offered weakly.

"Got the papers and everything."

"You can't do that. You can't just get married."

"Vegas, honey."

"A person has to know what she's doing."

"I know a guy."

"I don't believe you."

He shrugged. "You're still tired from the wedding night."

Wedding night? Was he saying he had, they had . . . *No. Please, God, no.*

Lundquist smiled. "Anyway, people who've shared what we have are married in the eyes of God, right? Our love is strong. Who needs those old society conventions?"

3.

"Welcome to the Empire."

The valet was dressed in a toga and gold braids, his muscular body honed to Herculean proportions. Sam got out and left the keys in the ignition.

"Need help with your luggage?" Hercules said.

Sam shook his head and only then thought about what he didn't have with him — a change of clothes. He didn't expect to be here more than twenty-four hours anyway. He wouldn't be able to sleep, except maybe in a chair for an hour or two.

Hercules handed him a ticket and said, "Anytime you want your chariot, we'll bring it up. Enjoy your stay."

Sam walked toward the front doors. Lights assaulted him from every direction. They lit up the walk like high noon. Blinking gold bulbs popped all around the ornate but automatic front doors, which were fashioned out of glass and imitation brass. The entry could have been from one of those Italian sword-and-sandal movies of the sixties starring Steve Reeves. You didn't quite buy that it was real, but you went along with the fakery to experience the movie.

That's Vegas all over, Sam thought. You go with the fake and the phony to live the fantasy. That's why people came here and congregated in temples of sensual excess like this six-hundred-room monstrosity.

Inside the doors and to the left Sam saw, and heard, the main casino. It was instantly familiar, as was the copper smell mixed with cigarette smoke, the odor of grasping and greed. Immediately in front of him was a bank of slot machines and several zombie-like players engaged in ritual frustration. No one smiled.

God, get me out of here, Sam thought. Get me out as soon as you can with Heather next to me and Nicky Oberlin gone from our lives forever.

The people at the front desk were also made out in Greek costume, though not as revealing as the Hercules valet. No, revealing was left to the cocktail servers, who made their way back and forth from the bar near the reception area to the slots and casino. Their costumes were meant to stoke male fires, their plastic smiles to create the illusion that everyone was in a giant pleasure dome where anything — literally — could happen if you were lucky. Or had money to burn.

Without a hint of interest, Sam gave his name to a young woman at the desk. "Yes, Mr. Trask, we have your reservation. Would you like smoking or nonsmoking?"

I'd like a flamethrower, Sam thought, and free reign of the place. "Non, please."

"All right. We have you staying for one night with us. All taken care of. May I take a credit card for incidentals?"

"There won't be any," he said.

"It's just in case you —"

"I said there won't be any. Just give me my key and —"

"It's just our policy to —"

"The answer is no. My key, please."

The practiced pleasantness on the woman's face morphed into steely irritation. "If you'll just excuse me for a moment."

She turned before he could say anything more. No doubt she was going to inform her supervisor that another troublemaker was with them and would he please solve the problem? When she returned, a young man wearing a navy blue blazer — no toga for this one — and a serious look was with her.

"Can I help you, sir?" the young man said.

Sam couldn't help feeling he was talking to a couple of college students uninterested in helping him at all.

"I'm here on business, and all I want is to go to my room and sit there until it's over. I'm not going to watch movies or eat nuts or drink alcohol. As fast as I can I'm going to get out of here. I'm not interested in giving you any more of my money. May I have my key now?"

With an impassive resolve the young man said, "Please understand, we will only be taking an imprint to —"

"I understand everything that goes on here."

"Then you must know how difficult it would be to have —"

"I haven't got a credit card, Charlie. Okay? Don't believe in 'em anymore. And I don't want any of your stupid candy bars or little bottles of booze. I want to go to my room, which has been paid for, because I would hate to raise a holy stink here in the lobby and cause all sorts of upset for the people streaming in here to give you their money at the crap table. So if that's what you —"

The man in the blazer put up his hand. "That's quite all right, sir," he said with no more enthusiasm than an oyster. "We hope you enjoy your stay."

4.

At least the room was clean.

It even had a view of the lights of Vegas which, from the tenth story, actually looked benign. Most prominent in the distance was something that looked like the Space Needle in Seattle. He'd passed that on the way in, along with an ersatz Statue of Liberty, a smaller version of the Eiffel Tower, and assorted other hotel fakeries. Some of the places were familiar — Caesar's Palace and the Stardust. Others, like the Wynn, were just more of the same. A waste of girders and glass.

Sam closed the drapes and wondered what he was supposed to do next.

Wait.

He had nothing else he could do. He had his cell phone and that was it. He tossed his coat on the bed and sat in a brocaded chair. After five minutes he got up and paced.

Then he looked in the top drawer of the nightstand and found what he was looking for — a Gideon Bible.

What a throwback this was. To have a Bible available in a place like this. Sam was comforted by it.

Opening to the Psalms, he turned to the only one he had any familiarity with, the twenty-third. He knew that one even before he was a Christian. His grandmother used to recite it to him when he stayed over at her house as a boy. Once, when he was four or so, she asked him if he remembered the psalm. "Yes," he said, then stood up proudly. "The Lord is my shepherd. That's all I want."

Now, thinking back on that line, Sam thought it really was the essence of the psalm — of the Bible, in fact.

The Lord is my shepherd. That's all I want.

He read the psalm a couple of times, pausing over the table being set in the presence of enemies. He felt surrounded by enemies here at the Empire Hotel.

For an hour Sam prayed as he walked around, sometimes dropping to his knees by the bed. The thought occurred to him that maybe this whole thing was an elaborate ruse. That Nicky Oberlin was nowhere near Vegas. That he would make Sam wait and wait before calling him and telling him with a laugh that there'd been some gross misunderstanding.

The thought made him sweat.

It was ten o'clock. He tried lying down but his eyes wouldn't stay closed.

Ten fifteen.

Ten thirty.

And then a knock at the door.

Pulse quickening, Sam went to the peephole and saw a woman standing there. She was young and pretty and wore a business suit. She was holding a small briefcase. Someone from the hotel?

She knocked again. Sam opened the door.

"Sam Trask?"

"Yes."

With a smile the woman pushed by him into the room.

"Hey —" Sam said.

"Close the door," she said.

"Who are you? What do you —"

"Nicky sent me."

Sam closed the door. The woman was in her early twenties, with red hair worn up. The way she was dressed and carried herself, she looked like a lawyer or business exec. Her makeup was perfect, accentuating her full lips and green eyes. She plopped the briefcase on the bed and faced him.

"Welcome to Las Vegas," she said.

"You have a message from Oberlin?"

"Who?"

"You said Nicky sent you."

"That's right. Nicky. That's all he said."

"Why are you here?"

"Because Nicky sent me, silly. I told you that." She reached behind her head and with one motion of her hand sent her hair spilling down over her shoulders. "You are one lucky guy, Mr. Trask, to have a friend like him."

"Wait a min—"

"Call me Annabelle." She shed her coat with practiced swiftness and threw it behind her without looking.

"Not interested, Annabelle." Not interested in the sick little insult Nicky had tossed to him. "Please leave."

Annabelle put on a pouty look. "Now, sweets, there's nothing to worry about." She began to unbutton her blouse and walk toward him.

"Stop," he said.

"Do you know what a gift is?" Three buttons were undone now.

"Don't do that."

She ignored him. "I'm yours, sweets, for

the whole night."

Sam turned his back on her and went to the door, opened it, and held it open. "Get out."

"Close the door, Mr. Trask."

"Get out now. Tell Nicky to call me."

"I said close the door."

He looked back at her. Her blouse was open. He turned away again. "If you don't get out, I'm leaving you here and calling security."

"Not if you want to see your daughter again," she said.

5.

"Dad looked scared," Max said.

Linda put down the hot chocolate on the coffee table in the living room. One of them had a healthy dollop of whipped cream, the way Max liked it. They were going to watch a Wallace & Gromit DVD, but Max's observation brought her up short.

"You think he's scared?"

"Is he?"

"I don't think so. Concerned."

"Because of that guy?" There was fear in Max's voice.

"Yes. But he's taking care of it. He knows what to do."

"I don't want him to get hurt."

Linda put her arm around her son's shoulders. "He won't be."

"How do you know? You can't know."

"Of course, but —"

"I don't like him being gone."

"Max, God will watch over him."

Max shook his head. "Todd's dad died. God let him."

Joe Faulk, the father of Max's friend Todd, had been a member of Solid Rock. He was a robust, outgoing man. He was diagnosed with a virulent form of cancer and died in six months, at the age of forty-five.

"God knows," was all Linda could come up with. Lame. But what more was there? Did theologians trained in the Bible have any better explanation, when you got right down to it? Didn't their faith depend on believing God really did know, really did have the good of his people in mind?

But would that satisfy a twelve-year-old afraid for his father?

"What I mean is that we have to keep praying and believing," Linda said.

"Does that really work?"

"Yes, of course it does."

"How do you know? Todd prayed for his dad."

"Max, we don't know everything about God; we can't. He's too big. We don't know why he does some things the way he does. But we do know he tells us to pray and believe that he's good. Can you do that?"

He shrugged.

"Can you at least try?"

He shrugged again. "I wish I could do something else."

"Like what?"

"Help Dad."

"You help him all the time, Max, just by being you."

He looked at her. "I mean really help him. I don't like it when he's sad and stuff."

Linda pulled him close, searching for the right words to say to comfort and reassure, but nothing came to her. Not a word. Old answers seemed like dust on the floor. Holding Max, for the moment at least, would have to do.

6.

Forced to listen, Sam sat in a chair.

"I'm not here to make you feel bad," Annabelle said. "I'm all about good news, good feelings. That's what Nicky wants for you."

"You don't have any idea who you're dealing with," Sam said. "How much did he pay you?"

"That's not your concern, sweets. Your

concern is just to relax and have a good time."

Before he knew it she was sitting on his lap.

"Please get off."

"Now, Sam," she purred and started playing with his hair. Her blouse was off one shoulder. He put his hands on her shoulders and pushed. She slid off him and landed on the floor.

"Hey!"

Sam stood quickly. "I'm sorry." He bent over to help her up but she slapped his hand away as she clambered to her feet and unleashed a string of curses at him. Buttoning her blouse she said, "It's out of my hands now."

"Wait."

"That's it, pal." She picked her coat off the floor and started putting it on.

"What about my daughter?"

"I don't know anything."

"But you said —"

Annabelle picked up her briefcase. "It's not up to me." She took a step toward the door.

Sam stepped in front of her. "Please."

"Look out."

"Don't go."

"Now you don't want me to go? Just a

minute ago —"

"I'm desperate here. This guy who hired you, he's sadistic. He's kidnapped my daughter. He's holding her somewhere. You can help me. I need your help."

"I'm telling you, I can't."

"You can."

She tried to move past him. Sam grabbed her shoulders. He was not going to let this thread to Heather go.

"Let go."

"Please." He kept his hands on her. With a swift move she brought the briefcase up between his legs. Hot pain burst through him. Lights flickered behind his eyes as he doubled over, fell to his knees.

He heard the door open and close behind him.

So much for the hooker with a heart of gold, he thought bitterly.

He gently lowered himself to the floor in a fetal position. He stayed that way, praying for God to protect his daughter. Wherever she was.

7.

"I'm telling you, jerk lips, I have to go *now*." Heather knew she wouldn't be able to hold it in much longer.

"Talk nice," Lundquist said. "Didn't your

mother teach you how to be polite?"

"Just let me go to the bathroom."

"What's the magic word?"

Heather glared at his fat stomach. She didn't want to look at his face. "The magic word is you're a sick, stinking —"

He wagged his finger at her. "My, my, such a mouth. You know, it ought to be washed out with Dutch cleanser."

Dutch cleanser? What was that?

She had to go now. "Please."

"That's much better. Now say it like you mean it."

"Please."

"We're gonna have a wonderful life to-gether, you and me." He circled around her chair so he was behind her. She couldn't see him. All she could look at was the creepy poster of the bike-riding skeleton. The skull was smiling toothily. When she looked away from it she had the odd feeling the skull moved. Her mind was going. Had to be it. *Fight.*

She felt his hands on her neck and jolted. The ropes held her. What was he doing?

Caressing her. Oh, sick. Sick sick sick.

"Yeah," he whispered as his hands worked their way into her hair. "You and me, babe."

His hands left her. She turned her head, trying to see. Then, suddenly, a rope around her neck. Pulled snug. A noose.

No, a leash.

"I'm gonna be right behind you, honey. You just keep on being a nice girl, and everything will be fine."

She wanted to cry, cry her eyes out like she was five years old, and have her dad lift her up and rock her on his shoulder. She remembered when he did that, when she'd fallen off a bike and scraped her knee real bad. If she cried hard, she knew he'd come to her.

But she wasn't five and she was not going to cry in front of this sicko.

"Untie my hands, will you?"

"Sorry," he said. "You'll just have to make do. Hey, that's a joke. I crack myself up."

He let her into the bathroom but held the rope at the door.

"Close it, will you?"

"I want to watch."

"What shoe did you get scraped off of?"

He jerked the rope around her neck. It bit into her skin. "Not a nice mouth you have. Now do your business."

Humiliated, she couldn't wait another moment. Someday he would pay for this. Someday, some way.

She heard a phone ring. And saw a moment of confusion on his face. Or maybe disappointment.

"Do your thing," he said. "But don't get cutesy."

He slammed the door closed on the leash. She didn't know if he still had the rope in his hand or not.

Sweet relief.

She heard him, clearly, talking outside the door. "Okay. Use the address I gave you. You'll get the other five hundred tomorrow. Guarantee it, cupcake. Stick with me."

And then she heard him whistling. It was the worst sound she'd heard in a long time.

8.

Sam made it to the bed, and as soon as he was on his back his cell phone rang.

"I'm really sorry you don't like women," Nicky said. "I spent a long time picking out the right one for you."

"Where's my daughter?"

"Haven't you ever heard the one about looking a gift horse in the mouth?"

"Where is she?"

"Don't try to trace this call, Sam. I use a disposable. I'll be very upset if you waste time on that. Remember, I'm always one step ahead of you."

"What do you want from me?"

"You shouldn't have harassed my mother,

Sammy. That was a very not nice thing to do."

Sam waited, not wanting to say anything that would nudge Nicky even further off the edge of reality.

"You went too far when you did that, Sammy. Now you're going to have to do what I say."

"Then say it."

"Not now. I'm going to give you some time to think, to think about how you've treated one of your old friends. Keep your phone handy. I'll let you know what to do."

"Let me talk to my —"

But the connection was dead.

As dead as Sam's hopes that he would be getting Heather out of her terror.

9.

"You know, your daddy is a very disturbed man."

Nicky had Heather by the rope again and was leading her through the house. She kept looking for a way to break free, but with her hands tied behind her back she wouldn't even be able to open a door. "That's a laugh, coming from you," she said.

He laughed. "What do you know about life, sugar? You're still so young." He stopped and patted her cheek. She wanted to spit at him but thought she'd better not. Not yet.

"I know a pathetic piece of —"

He pulled on the rope, choking off her words, and led her to the stairs. "Come along," he said. "Like a good girl."

She didn't want him pulling her upstairs by the neck, so she complied. She looked around. It was a strange house, this. All unfinished wood. No decorations. As if it had been designed and framed, then abandoned. Was this a place he himself had built? Or maybe, her imagination conjured, he'd found a couple in here and murdered them and taken it over.

She noticed some rather obtrusive wiring along the seam where the wall met the ceiling. Even in the muted light it stuck out like a creeping vine in a haunted house. What was *that* all about?

And how alone were they?

There had to be some other houses around, but she had the sense that they were pretty well isolated. Like everything else about him, this place didn't have the right feel to it. It was a deviant growth, like a cancer.

He kept on leading her, up the stairs, then down the dimly lit corridor to the end. Through an open door. He flicked on a light and another bare bulb illuminated the room.

Which had nothing but a bed in it. A queen-sized bed with two ugly iron bedposts.

"Our honeymoon chamber," he said. "You like it?"

She couldn't speak. She looked at the bed, then his smiling face.

"I know it's not the Ritz," Nicky said, "but it'll have to do for now."

Heather shook her head as he pulled her forward.

"Lie down."

She didn't. No way was she going to allow him to . . .

With one hand he pushed her, hard. She fell backward onto the bed, heard springs squeaking.

Don't let him do this, she thought. Whatever else happens, don't let him.

"What do you have against my dad?" If she could keep him talking, maybe . . .

"Come on now, you're not ready for —"

"You afraid to tell me?"

He smiled. "You think you can play head games with me? Please."

"Then why don't you?"

"I hate women who complain! Have to hear your screeching voices —"

"You're afraid of something."

"You want me to tape your mouth shut?"

"What did my dad ever do to you? He's worth ten of you. A hundred."

That set off something in him. "You think your daddy's something, is that what you really think? Because I don't think you do. The way you talked to me about him, remember those times? You hate your father. And you're right to —"

"I don't hate him."

"Oh yes, you do. You know you do. Because he's one of those fake guys. A phony. You ever read *Catcher in the Rye?*"

She tried to remember it. She'd read it in tenth grade. It made her sad.

"It's the greatest book ever written," Nicky said. "Salinger is a god. He had vision like nobody else. That was the point of the book."

Good. Keep him talking. "It was about a kid who got sick, right?"

"No! You missed the whole deal! Holden doesn't want to live in a world with phonies. He sees them everywhere, because they *are* everywhere. So what happens to him? He ends up in a nuthouse. Because that's where the phonies put you when you call them on it."

He was talking not just to her, she sensed, but to some unseen audience.

"And they want you to fold up and die in there, give up, but I wasn't going to ever give them that satisfaction. You have to prove you're strong in the end, you have to have the will to power. And then you have to show them, you have to shove it back in their faces. Your daddy is going to get it shoved in his face."

"Psycho," she said.

His face flushed. She could see it even in the dim light. He moved over to her and put his hand on her throat.

"You're a phony too," he said.

She couldn't speak. And now she couldn't breathe. She could only look into his eyes. They were two dark orbs, cavernous. Maybe once there had been light in them, small fires of humanity. Now they were empty caves.

As he kept the pressure on, she was sure he was going to kill her. She began to flail — as much as she could with her hands behind her. She kicked out with her legs.

He crawled on top of her, keeping his hand on her throat, but using his lower body to hold her legs down.

He put his face closer to hers.

She smelled his breath. Stale mustard and tuna fish.

She gagged.

Star clusters flickered behind her eyes. Then faded. Blackness started to overtake them.

His eyes got wider, round and eager.

Forgive me, Daddy. Forgive me, God.

EIGHTEEN

1.

Sam felt like he was walking through the land of the living dead.

It was morning and he hadn't slept. He couldn't stay in his hotel room. It was a cage. He was a lab rat and Nicky Oberlin the mad scientist. The woman he'd sent was one of his creations. He had to get out before another experiment went awry.

So he walked a couple of blocks to a street that ran under a metallic awning. Like a tube. In the tube were casinos and street vendors. And a sign announcing the Fremont Street Experience.

Some experience. Dominating one side of the street was a club with a jumbo screen outside, showing videos of winking vixens in bathing suits. The banner sign hanging below the screens promised Free Topless Parties Every Evening.

People wandered along this "experience,"

going in and out of casinos as if it were nighttime. Nighttime was when the zombies should be out in force. Not in the morning light like this.

But it was twenty-four/seven here in this gaudy wasteland.

He knew there was a land of real people all around this collection of garish lights and signage. People with families who went to church and baseball games, picnics and school plays.

What an odd mix. Beauty and the Beast, only this Beast would never transform.

He walked and walked, keeping one hand in his pocket over his cell phone. All he could do was wait. It was the waiting that killed him.

He fought with himself about calling Linda. If he did, she'd hear his voice. And she'd know there was bad trouble. She always knew him.

He decided not to call. He kept on walking, dead to everything but the hope that Nicky Oberlin would call him soon and he'd get Heather out of this sunbaked netherworld, no matter what it took to do it.

2.

Fighting prayers.
That's what Dottie Harris had said that

day in prayer group. Linda wanted to fight, but she was so worn out.

So she called Dottie and asked for aid.

"Glad to do it," Dottie said. "You want me to come over?"

"No need," Linda said.

"I can bring the juicer, make some carrot-apple."

Linda smiled. "Thank you anyway, Dottie. Another —"

"Vitamin A."

"— time perhaps —"

"Beta carotene."

"Bless you, Dottie."

She felt better having Dottie Harris supporting her. After the call, she fired up the computer. She wasn't much of a surfer, but now she needed some distraction. Sam hadn't called, even an hour after she'd left a message. Her interior tape player was stuck on the trouble loop.

Distraction.

She scanned the news from her personal Yahoo! page. There was a scandal brewing in the White House, with a presidential counsel accused of lying to a grand jury in a bribery matter. Naturally, the opposition party was all over it, with senatorial blabbermouths dominating the sound bites.

She turned to the entertainment news. A

major star had made a fool of himself in a New York pub, overturning a table and causing hot artichoke dip to land in the lap of a sixty-five-year-old retired schoolteacher. Said major star had been in trouble with the law before, and it was too bad. He was one of the few really good actors working these days, but Linda couldn't stand going to his movies anymore. Apparently neither could a large portion of the moviegoing audience. His last couple of ventures tanked.

She decided to take a quick look at her email. She sifted through the junk and found a message from her friend Cheri up in Bainbridge Island. That was nice. Cheri and Ralph had completed work on a house and were inviting her and Sam and the kids to come up for a visit.

A few more messages she deleted without looking at them. Miracle drugs for men — how many could there possibly be? — were not her cup of java.

One subject line did catch her eye. *Of Interest to Mrs. Sam Trask.* She did not recognize the return address.

It was a message with an attachment. Sam had warned her about unfamiliar messages containing attachments. They could unleash viruses, still a mystery to Linda. But she could read the message at least, couldn't she? How would a spammer have put her name in the subject line?

She opened the message.

Wonder where your husband is? Take a look.

She hesitated. Then she downloaded the attachment.

It was a JPEG. A sharp digital photograph. Sam, in some sort of a hotel room, on a chair. On Sam's lap was a woman in a state of incipient undress.

She stood up and backed away from the monitor. But her eyes stayed on the picture.

A flurry of conflicting thoughts almost paralyzed her mind.

She managed to grab hold of some. Surely this was some sick setup. Sam would never do something like this. Cheat on her. Let alone be caught in a photograph doing the same.

Blackmail? Nicky Oberlin had to be behind this.

But just as quickly, doubt crept into her head. What if there was more to this than met the eye? What if Sam really *was* with another woman?

The phone rang, startling her. It was Greg Wayne.

"I'll be driving by in a little while," he said. "Everything okay on your end?"

Oh, just ginger peachy. "Nothing to report," she said.

"That's good news," Wayne said.

3.

Heather didn't know if she'd blacked out or fallen asleep.

She was on the bed, her shoulder joints aching, hands still behind her back. Her left arm was completely numb.

The last thing she remembered was his eyes.

Yes, he'd been choking her.

Why had he stopped?

Eyes.

They'd changed. As he was looking at her, as he was taking her life.

What was it he'd seen?

What was it she'd seen in *him?*

Fear? No, that wasn't it.

Desire. Yes. And the inescapable realization that he could do nothing about it. He'd failed as a man, or what he thought a man should be. Or do.

And she knew, just knew, that failure would make him more dangerous than ever.

The rope around her neck chafed. It was still secured to the iron bedpost. Her stomach rumbled.

Maybe that was the way it was going to

be. Starvation. He'd just leave her here until they found her, too late.

She told herself not to get scared. If she did, he'd win.

But try as she might, fear began to overtake her. She could feel it advancing, like lava flowing toward a village of grass huts. Willing it to go away wasn't working.

She could only talk to herself in her mind, searching. This is the time, isn't it? The time you're supposed to call out to God? But I've been dissing God like crazy for so long. Why should he listen? Why should I even think he'd do anything for me? For my dad, yeah, and for Mom and Max. But not me.

That was it, she thought. She didn't matter. Not really. Not in the big scheme. If she could accept that now, then dying wouldn't come so hard. Hadn't she wanted to go anyway? Yes, but that was because she didn't see the point in hanging around this world. Now, because she was in trouble, wasn't pulling the plug of her own accord, she was scared and wanted to live. But he was going to kill her, and believing she didn't matter might make that seem all right. Maybe the best thing. Maybe —

And then a feeling, a sense of another voice, one soft yet strong enough to hold her up for a moment longer, and it said,

You do matter, you do.

4.

It was the same dream.

Sam, alone on a road, a car in the distance. Getting closer.

He ran, but his legs were pylons stuck in wet sand. The car gaining speed.

And then an earthquake. The ground started shaking. The asphalt split down the middle with a cracking sound. The temblor was so violent he couldn't run or get any traction at all.

Then the earth opened up, and everything was falling in, the whole world, and Sam was shaking all over, his head and bones rattling, and someone was saying, *Hey!*

Sam jolted into wakefulness.

"Hey," a voice said. "Come on. Time to go."

Where was he? Lights and sounds. Casino. The smell of a lounge area.

He was in a leatherette chair. Yes, he'd been so tired. He'd ordered a Coke. Must have faded.

Sam rubbed his face. "What's that?"

"Sleep it off somewhere else, sir." It was a security guard. A young one. All decked out in a costume from security central casting.

413

"Oh, yeah," Sam said. "Sorry. I'm so tired."

"Outside, sir."

"Right."

He staggered at first, like a Vegas drunk, then found his way — the guard right beside him — to the doors. How long had he been inside this place? Judging from the light and heat, it was getting on to late afternoon.

And still no call from Nicky.

Maybe it was time to get the cops after all. The FBI, as this was an interstate violation.

Heather. Was she even still alive?

He had emerged from one nightmare only to discover he was right back in one that was worse, because it was real.

There wasn't much more of this he could take.

His phone vibrated in his pocket.

Now. Finally.

He flipped it open without even looking at the LCD.

"I'm here," he said.

"Where?"

"Linda?"

"Where are you, Sam?"

"Why are you calling me?"

"I want to know what's going on."

"I can't tell you yet, I —"

"I saw the picture."

"What?"

"The photo. With that woman. Did you know there was a photo?"

Of course. What a prize chump he was for not thinking of that, for not anticipating the lengths Nicky would go to humiliate him. The hooker probably had a camera in her briefcase. "I can explain, only not now. You've got to believe me."

"Sam, were you set up?"

"I can't talk about it now."

"Just tell me that much."

"Yes."

Silence.

"Do you believe me?" he said.

"I think so. What's he done? Where are you?"

He heard the tone for call waiting. "I have to go. Don't worry. Please."

He switched the call.

"Hello."

"Sammy! You ready to be really, really nice?"

"Where's my daughter?"

"Now there you go again. Remember when Ronald Reagan said that?" Nicky went into a whispery Reagan voice. *There you go again.* And he laughed.

Sam decided not to say another word, to

follow Nicky wherever he wanted to go. Until he got Heather back.

"So let me ask you again, Sammy. Are you ready to be really, really nice?"

"Yes."

"Good! How about another hooker?"

"No."

"No? No *what?*"

"No hooker."

"Sammy, don't try to be funny."

"I'm not."

"Listen carefully. Do you want another hooker?"

"No."

"No what?"

"No, thank you?"

"That's it! Okay, Sammy, you get to hear from your daughter. Hang on, will you?"

Silence, then the sound of something moving, like a scraping. Then a voice, his daughter's voice, crying out, "Stop! Stop!"

Oh, dear God, make him stop! Tears of sheer frustration bit Sam's eyes. Powerless, he kept the phone on his ear.

Nicky said, "She says she's fine, Sammy, and not to worry —"

"What do you want me to do? What?"

"She says you're not to worry, because you haven't lost a daughter."

"Tell me —"

"You've gained a son!"

"Tell me what you want me to do, Nicky."

"Be nice. Are you ready to be nice?"

"Yes."

"Because I'm going to let you come see her, Sammy. I'm going to be nice to you, even though you haven't been nice to me."

5.

Linda thought she ought to call the police. Right now. End of story. Maybe they had a way to trace Sam's cell phone. He was obviously in trouble, in danger of some sort. And he was stubborn too, and would try to make things right on his own.

The situation with the girl still bothered her. She wanted to believe Sam, she really did, yet there was something else going on. It was a slight fraying at the edge of her marriage. Had she just noticed it, or had it been there for a long time, unnoticed?

She had to remind herself that Sam had always been trustworthy. But how could he have even allowed himself to get into that situation?

And where? Where was that photo taken?

It seemed like her finger hovered over the phone keypad forever, waiting for instructions from her mind to call the police. Finally, she sat down heavily in the dark of the family room and just listened to the crickets outside the house.

"Mom?"

Max was in the room.

"I'm here," she said and flicked on a light.

"What're you doing in the dark?" he said.

"Just thinking."

"About Dad?"

"Yes."

Max picked at his powder blue UCLA T-shirt, the one Sam had gotten him at Pauley Pavilion last year. "Where is he?"

"He's out taking care of some things."

"But where?"

She looked into her son's persistent eyes. She knew that look well, and that it wasn't to be played with. "I don't know," she said. "But I just talked to him on the phone. I'm sure he'll be back soon."

"It's about that guy again, isn't it?"

"Probably."

"Is it wrong to wish somebody dead?"

Now there was an unexpected curveball. The tone in his voice told Linda that this was one of those questions she couldn't finesse. She prayed that whatever she was about to say would come out halfway coherent and all the way true.

"You're talking about the man who's been bothering us, right?" she said.

"Yeah," Max said.

"Then I think it's all right to pray that he stop and also for God to do whatever it takes to make sure he doesn't hurt anybody else."

"Yeah, I know. But what if you had a gun and he was trying to get at Dad or me or Heather? You'd shoot him, wouldn't you?"

She knew she would. She would not hesitate at all. "If it ever came down to that, I would protect my family."

"Is that all right with God?"

"I'm pretty sure it is."

Max went into a deep thought for a moment. Then he looked at his mother. "I think it would be okay with God, totally."

She couldn't argue with that, nor did she wish to. She put her arms out to her son and he came to her. She hugged him. "And God knows where Dad is, and we'll pray for his protection, okay?"

"Okay," Max said.

6.

Sam drove south on I-15, getting off at the place Nicky had named the last time he called.

Four times so far, Sam drove to a new spot and waited for Nicky's call. This was the game.

Nicky called two more times, and Sam continued deeper into the desert. The homes became fewer, more widely spaced. The realm of desert dwellers. People who marched to their own drumbeat.

Sam remembered camping in the Mojave desert with his father once. They thought they were all alone in the world. But one late afternoon a man in jeans approached. No shirt, about forty, with a beard and blue bandana, and a pit bull on a leash.

Oh, yes, and he had a pearl-handled revolver in a holster at his hip.

Sam's dad stood with his .22 rifle held loosely in one arm, barrel pointed at the ground. It was not threatening, but it wasn't vulnerable either.

The man without a shirt laughed and said, "Welcome, strangers. This is my place, but you're welcome to stay the night."

Sam looked around and could see only dry desert. For miles. He also saw the look in the pit bull's eyes.

The man walked away, seeming to disappear into the desert itself. And Sam's dad said they should pack up and find another spot. "You never know about these folk," he said.

Right, and as Sam drove through Nicky's hoops, he thought this was not the kind of place he wanted to tarry in for very long.

It took two hours for Sam to drive where Nicky told him. But when he was finished he wasn't two hours beyond where he'd started. He'd been driving around in a few circles.

But finally there it was, coming up out of the desert floor like an alien creature. It had an unfinished and forlorn look, as if some prefab job had been dropped here in the desert and forgotten. Isolated, like a lot of places in this part of Nevada. Owned by the sort of people who put up signs saying No Trespassing. That Means You. Killer Dogs. Only there was no fence around this one.

No power lines that Sam could see in the fading light. Could be it had its own generator. At their first meeting, Nicky had said he was in construction. So maybe he was constructing his own little fortress out here.

But for what purpose?

Had it been built for just this moment?

He stopped his car a good fifty feet from the house. As he got out the heat of desert twilight engulfed him. He considered getting the Browning from his trunk but thought better of it. If he was being watched that wouldn't be a good move.

Then again, Nicky Oberlin might not even be in the place. This could all be another ruse. Some crazy Gabby Hayes type might run out with a shotgun and tell Sam to get off his property.

No Gabby. No sound at all. Sam took a cautious step forward, then another, watching for signs of life. This was not a place where life seemed likely to prosper, unless you were a snake or a Gila monster.

Nicky Oberlin might just fit in after all.

Was Heather inside?

Sam took one more step and then heard something creak.

"Right there, Sammy. That's fine right there."

Sam stopped. Nicky was speaking through a screen door but there was no light inside. The voice came from the dark.

"Let me see Heather."

"Easy there, Sammy. You're not calling any shots. You're not the lawyer now, babe."

"Come on then, let's do it."

"Easy, buddy. I've got to make something clear. I have a real bad boy of a gun here, and it's pointed at your daughter's head. If you try anything, she's gone."

Sam's entire body chilled. Never had he felt so powerless, so bereft of options. As a lawyer he'd been trained to be able to find *something* favorable in any circumstance. Here and now, his skills failed him.

Nicky spoke again, with a playful voice. "Hey, you remember that night back in the dorm when you got drunk and started doing a Mick Jagger imitation in the hall? You remember that?"

How long was this going to take? Sam figured he had no choice but to listen until Nicky was ready to make the exchange.

"No."

"No? Come on, it was one of the great moments. You guys were having a party in your room. Keg, grass. Everybody was there. Not me. I was trying to study while everybody was out having a good time. But you were playing loud music and it was the Stones. You know I hate the Stones, Sammy? Especially that strutting Jagger. You never knew I hated 'em, did you? You never asked if you could play your music like that, did you?"

"I wasn't a nice guy back then."

"You were just into yourself, boy. You thought you were the king of everything. So I came out to see what all the noise was about and there you were, holding a bong in your hand like it was a microphone, and strutting around like Jagger while 'Sympathy for the Devil' was playing."

"Sorry."

"Hey, Sammy, were you around when

Jesus Christ had his moment of doubt and pain?"

"Can we get on with it, Nicky? You wanted me, here I am. Let Heather come out."

"First you tell me that, Sammy. Tell me you were around JC."

"I don't know what you want to hear."

"I want to hear you say what I tell you to say!"

"You want me to talk about Jesus Christ? What do you want to know?"

"Tell me he's a fake."

Sam waited.

"Tell me you renounce him as your Savior and Lord."

"Bring out my daughter. Then you can settle your accounts with me."

"Did you hear what I said? Renounce Jesus Christ."

"Not gonna happen, Nicky. Next move."

Heather screamed. Sam had to fight himself not to run forward, through the screen, and clamp his hands on Nicky's neck. But the gun . . .

"Now do what I tell you, Sammy. Renounce Jesus."

"Don't do it, Daddy!" Heather yelled. Then she screamed again.

Dear God, Sam prayed, make him stop.

"I'm coming up there," Sam said. "We're

going to settle this man to man. Stop hurting a little girl."

"Little!" Nicky cackled.

Sam took a tentative step forward, keeping his eyes on the black rectangle that was the screen door. This was going to be a deadly chess game. Chess had never been Sam's game, but he was determined not to make a stupid move.

"Not another step, Sammy."

Sam stopped. It was fast becoming night, and in a few minutes it would be pitch black. But the timing was all up to Nicky. His personal darkness was the rule now.

"Why don't you take off your coat?" Nicky said.

"I'm not carrying a weapon," Sam said.

"I told you to take off your coat. Do it now. Throw it as far away from you as you can."

Sam complied. He threw his coat vigorously to the side.

"Cell phone?" Nicky said.

"Yes, I've got a cell phone."

"I know that, dummy. I was talking to you on it. Don't go insulting my intelligence, boy. Just toss it up here on the porch."

"What can that possibly matter?" His cell phone was his only link to the outside world and he didn't want to give it up.

"Did you hear what I said?"

"Just bring Heather out and I'll give you whatever you want."

There was silence for a moment. Then Heather screamed again.

7.

Sam's heart spiked. "All right!" He unclipped his cell phone and tossed it like a softball onto the porch. It clattered up against the wood-frame house. "There."

"That's much better."

"Let me see Heather."

"It's what I wanted to do all along, Sammy. But I'm afraid we won't have any time for heartfelt good-byes. She is going to move right on past you to wherever she wants to go. Except to the police, of course. She knows what will happen to you if she opens her mouth. Tell your father you understand."

Heather's voice, swollen with fright, said, "I understand. I won't tell."

Smart girl, Sam thought. Just tell him what he wants to hear.

"Would you like to have a good look at her, Sammy?"

"Please." The word was bile in his mouth. But he was going to do anything he could to get Heather out of there. Then he would have it out with Nicky Oberlin, even though he knew Nicky must be planning some unpleasant business for him.

Just get Heather out.

"Now listen very carefully, Sammy. Because if you don't follow my instructions exactly as I lay them out, it's going to be very bad, very bad for everyone, but especially for your daughter. I'm going to let her out onto the porch. You are not to move. Not one inch. If you do I will pull her back in and kill her. Do you understand that, lawyer?"

"Yes."

"I will tell you what to do after that. If at any time you disobey me, Heather dies. You see, I learned a long time ago that you must not disobey the one with all the power. And that's what I have right now. You know that, don't you?"

Sam said nothing.

"Answer me!"

"Yes, Nicky. You have all the power."

"I wish you really meant that, Sammy. But you know, there's just part of you that's a liar. You've always been a liar. Always showing one face to the world and keeping that other face turned away, just like all the others at the old UC."

This guy was a walking psychological

disaster. He didn't belong in the world.

The screen door squeaked. It was opening. In the very last of the dark gray light, Sam saw the outline of his daughter moving slowly in front of the door. He could barely make out her form. He wanted to run up to her and hold her and comfort her, but Nicky's warning kept him firmly planted.

"He's got a rope around my neck," Heather said. Then Sam heard Heather grunt as she was yanked backward. She cried out.

A lethal mixture of rage and hate boiled inside Sam. He saw nothing but a vision of a torn and dead Nicky Oberlin.

"Looks like I have to train her, just like a doggie," Nicky said from behind the door. "Well, I never liked dogs. That kid of yours back home, he's much better off without that mutt. I'd much rather train you, Sam. So here's what we're going to do. We're going to make an exchange. But it's going to be done very carefully. You have to remember that I have a firearm pointed at your daughter's head. Are we clear about that?"

"Yes."

"Then I'm going to let you walk right up to the steps, where you will find a set of handcuffs. When you get to them you will be told what to do."

For a moment Sam hesitated.

"Come on, Sammy," Nicky said as if talking to a dog. "Come on, boy."

Clenching his teeth, Sam started toward the house. He kept his pace slow, not wanting Nicky to get nervous. He told himself it was all for Heather, he was getting closer to Heather, and they would find a way out somehow.

When he was ten feet from the front steps he could see Heather's features. She was looking at him with fear and something resembling love. He loved his daughter, and he knew that. But he felt it now as one would a fire in the bones.

I will get you to safety, he thought. If that's my last act on earth, that's what I'm going to do.

He took another step and the ground disappeared.

8.

"What are you do —" Heather's words were choked off as Nicky — she knew the guy's real name at last — pulled on the rope around her neck.

She was back inside the house. Her eyes burned with tears of rage. "You liar," she managed to say. Her hands were still secured behind her with some sort of cord. She wished she could scratch his eyes out.

"Now, now. That's a terrible thing to say to your husband."

"What did you do to him?"

He twisted the rope around her neck, burning her skin as he did, so he could lead from the front. He started tugging at her, pulling her farther into the dark house.

She resisted. He pulled harder.

"Don't be such a hard body," he said.

"I want my dad."

"I want a hit Broadway show. Can't have everything you want, honey."

Oh, please don't call me that. Don't make me more sick than I already am.

Dad.

He was taking her toward the back of the house. To do what?

All sorts of creepy pictures popped into her mind. He'd do something bad to her and then to her father.

Suffering and death.

"That's a good doggie," Nicky said as he pulled her.

God. God, be there. I'm bad and I know it, but please help my dad and me get out of this and kill this man, please, God.

"Please don't hurt my dad," she said.

"You know, I'm really tired of all this. When will you and Daddy figure it out? You can't do anything or say anything."

He stopped pulling for a moment. Darkness enveloped them. Her eyes, adjusting, could see only gloomy shapes.

"You like James Cagney movies?" he said.

"What?"

"James Cagney. *Yankee Doodle Dandy* and all that claptrap?"

"I don't know."

"You know who I'm talking about?"

"I think so."

"Yeah, he only did one movie worth talking about. *White Heat.* Ever see it?"

"No." She was starting to shiver a little.

"Oh, baby, we've got to see it sometime."

Did that mean he was keeping her alive? To be with him? Maybe death was preferable.

"See, in this movie, Cagney plays a criminal, a really good one. Nobody can tell him what to do. Isn't that sweet? Well, he does something in the movie that's really funny. Come on, I'll show you."

Pulling again. She had no choice but to follow. *Oh, God, help my dad. Don't let him be dead.*

Nicky opened the back door, the one off the small kitchen.

He was taking her outside.

His feet crunched on the dirt.

Why was he doing this?

To kill her. He wouldn't shoot her in the house. He was going to do it out here.

She held back, but he tugged her forward.

The darkness seemed to go on forever. The stars were the only light, and they were dazzlingly brilliant. But they were silent. No voice of God.

But he was there. He had to be there.

Then she heard a click.

The gun.

Nicky had just cocked his gun.

9.

His left ankle burning, Sam figured he was in a pit about ten feet down.

A trap. Nicky had played him right where he wanted him to be.

Dirt and sand, and a smell like dry plants.

It was too crazy to be real. He was in a hole like an animal. This didn't happen to men like him. He was a successful lawyer. A civilized man. Trying to be a good husband and father. People like Nicky Oberlin did not exist in real life. Not in *his* real life, anyway.

Heather. What was he doing to her now?

He felt around in the blackness. The pit was wide enough for him to almost stretch his arms wide. Unbelievable, the effort

Nicky must have put into this whole thing, his plan culminating with a staged setup just to get Sam in a hole.

Above him, the pit's opening was like a black disc dotted with pinprick lights. Stars. He waited for Nicky to show his face.

And waited.

Could he figure a way to climb out? He reached out and touched the wall of the trench. It was sandy, infirm. A clump fell as he attempted a grip. Trying to forge a makeshift ladder wouldn't work.

He was helpless.

And still no sounds from aboveground.

"Nicky!"

No answer. Sam didn't know what he was going to say to him anyway. But if he could get him talking, that would buy time. Time for what, he didn't know. It would just be more time when he wasn't hurting Heather.

"Nicky, what do you want?"

Silence.

Sam prayed as fervently as he ever had. That's all he had now.

And then he heard the gunshots.

Four in rapid succession.

Then silence again, as ominous as the darkness.

"Heather!"

No answer.

10.

The gunshots startled Heather. She jumped back two steps, stopping only because of the rope that Nicky still held in his hand.

Why had he shot his own car? He'd put four bullets holes in the trunk of his Mustang.

"Just like James Cagney," Nicky said. "In that movie I was telling you about, he put some guy in a car trunk and the guy said he couldn't breathe. So he shot air holes in the trunk. Unfortunately the guy was still in it. Ain't that a kick in the biscuits? But I didn't do that to you, did I? I wouldn't do that to my wife. I wanted you to be able to breathe too."

"What are you going to do?"

He tucked the gun into his pants, pulled out some keys, and opened the trunk.

"I'm not getting in there," Heather said.

Nicky pulled her toward him with the rope. "You will do exactly as I say."

No. She kicked him between the legs.

Nicky doubled over with a grunt.

Heather moved with a quickness that surprised her. She moved backward, calculating the length of the rope in her mind. With a final push she felt the rope grow taut on her neck, then release.

She was free of him.

But how free? He still had a gun and she was still without her hands. But she could run.

Into the night.

11.

At the top of the hole, Nicky's voice. "That daughter of yours, Sam. She's a real pistol."

"What did you do to her?" He fought back the thought that she might be dead.

"Spunky. That's what I like about her."

"Where is she?"

"Now I have to go look for her. Like she's a dog that got out of the house."

Heather was alive! "Leave her alone. Deal with me."

"Oh, I will. I just didn't want you to be lonely while I was gone."

Sam heard a latch opening.

And then another sound. It couldn't be —

Whump.

Something hit his shoulder. Sam jerked backward. The thing that hit him fell off and hit the ground.

And rattled.

12.

Dad. What was she going to do about Dad?

Heather stumbled over a rock, almost fell.

What was she going to do about herself?

She was just waiting for Nicky to shine some big light on her and hunt her down.

How far away was help? All she knew was they were deep in the desert somewhere. No sign of lights or life anywhere — except for the red-green patina on the horizon, far, far away. Must be the lights of the Strip.

Looking behind her, she had no idea how far she was from the house. Or even where the house was now. She'd have to be smarter about this. Running around in a panic wouldn't do her or her father any good. The ground was fairly flat and sandy, with a few scrubby plants scattered around. She couldn't afford to fall and hurt herself.

She kept going, thoughts colliding, pleading in her own way to God, hoping that he would show himself and help at the same time.

A sound behind her. The revving of an engine.

Then headlights.

NINETEEN

1.

Rattlesnake.

It was an unmistakable sound. In the dark he couldn't see it.

And he had nowhere to go.

The rattling got louder, faster.

Without thought, acting on pure instinct, Sam jumped and kicked out with his right foot. He wanted to get a toehold above the ground, above the snake. If he could get his foot secure, he might be able to lean across the expanse and hold himself up.

His foot went halfway into the pit's wall.

Falling back, he twisted so he could put both hands out.

And caught the other side flush. He was now hovering over the rattling sound.

But how long could he stay like this?

He calculated. If he moved upward, he risked losing the leverage he had, and falling. But if he didn't move, he'd eventually have to release.

Sam moved his right hand upward, reached out. That would be as far as he could go.

He had just one chance at this. He would have to start from the floor again. He'd have to push off with his sore left foot, dig into the dirt with his right, and give it one big push upward.

If he did this right, he might be able to get his hands over the rim of the pit. Then he might be able to pull himself out.

Might might might.

The rattling stopped. That wasn't good. Without the sound, it would be harder to calculate where to land. He could be landing on his own certain death.

Then he heard the sound of tires on gravel. Something was going on up top.

He had to get out.

He dropped to the floor of the pit.

And heard the rattle rage, just before the bite. Hot needles seared his left calf.

2.

"Heather!"

Nicky was calling her name, like she was a lost dog.

"Come home!"

The headlights were making a slow, lazy

arc. There was no way she'd be able to keep hidden.

Maybe if she could free her hands . . .

She sat on the ground, her joints burning, putting her bound wrists behind her knees. If she could slip her legs through, one at a time, she'd have her hands in front of her. She could work on the ropes then, maybe with her mouth.

The beam of the headlights was coming around her way. And the awful sound of tires crunching sand.

"Heather! I won't hurt you, dear!"

Right.

She got her left leg through the hoop of her arms, feeling like she might dislocate her shoulder.

But she was halfway there.

"Where are you, honey? This desert driving isn't doing my car any good!"

With every bit of her waning strength, she got her right leg through. She was now sitting on the ground, her hands in front of her.

The headlight beams hit her square in the eyes.

3.

As the bite ignited his left leg, Sam lashed out with his right. He stomped and stomped, as if trying to put out some phantom flame. Fear and rage welled up as he covered the ground where he thought the snake would be.

He felt a crunch and squish under his foot.

The head. He knew it, and kept pounding.

The rattling stopped.

Sam didn't. He kept up the jackhammering with his foot. Kept it up until he estimated the snake's head was jelly.

When he stopped, breathing hard, fire in his lungs, he realized the clock was ticking on his life.

He'd read about rattlesnakes a couple of years ago, helping Max on a school report. Some species were more dangerous than others. But what was the procedure when you got bitten?

He had no idea. He couldn't remember if it was a good thing or bad thing to try to suck out the venom. Didn't matter, because the bite was low on the calf and he couldn't get to it with his mouth.

He couldn't remember if a tourniquet was good or bad. He took off his belt, then decided against it.

Maybe . . . maybe if he could get out of the hole now, right now, he could get into the house and find a first-aid kit. The car sound had faded, indicating Nicky might not be inside.

But for how long?

Do it now. He'd climbed a rock wall at a church camp last year, on a men's retreat. Even with a safety harness, he felt pure macho joy in it. Okay, he told himself, you are *muy macho* now. Let's see the great escape.

Sam jumped and kicked out with his right foot. As soon as he made contact, he pushed upward.

For half a second he felt poised over nothingness. He shot his arms out. His chin hit dirt, jarring his jaw.

He fell back, scraping the wall, and when he hit the bottom his left ankle was consumed by fire.

4.

"What are you doing out here, honey?"

Nicky was still in the car, talking to her out the window.

She didn't have any good choices. She could try running again, but she'd never be able to keep away from the car. Any idea about confronting him physically again was ridiculous. He'd be more than ready for her.

"Now don't make this hard on yourself. Or your loving papa."

Dad was back there and they were out here. She didn't know if he was dead or what, but as long as she kept Nicky occupied, he wasn't hurting her father. She could give her father some time, at least.

She backed away, saying nothing.

The car sat there, idling, headlights on her.

"See," Nicky said, "if I have to come over there and get you I'm going to be very angry. I don't like to get angry. It makes me do things I'd rather not do."

Heather took another step backward, keeping it slow. Stretch this out as long as possible, she told herself.

"I got angry at my old man once, you know that? Did I tell you about that? He used to do bad things to me and my mom."

It was sickening to listen to him.

"So don't make me mad, little girl. Start walking over here. I'll let you ride in the backseat."

She started to wonder if she could avoid him until daylight. Maybe in the light of day she'd see something, or someone would see her. But the prospect was daunting.

"You better make your move right now, honey, because I'm really starting to get impatient."

Could she stay on her feet that long? She was already exhausted, propped up only by jolts of adrenaline. Lack of food made her weak.

Yet . . . maybe. She remembered that game she used to play with Max when they were little, where he'd try to touch her, and she would dodge and weave. Her brother could only touch her when she let him.

This was like that game, only now the game was deadly. She would have to dodge and weave away from a car driven by a madman.

But if she had to, she would. She would buy Dad time.

She heard the car engine rev, the sound of tires spitting sand.

Then the headlights headed straight for her, fast.

5.

Again. Sam had no other choice. *You're either going to die here — and Heather will too — or you're going to get out.*

God, get me out.

He'd failed once, which meant he knew more now. Try again.

Same procedure. Ignore the pain, just do it.

He jumped, kicked, pushed, put out his arms.

They held. Then began to slip. He flailed his legs against the pit, searching for any toehold. Rocks dislodged and fell, dirt behind them.

Sam thought he was next.

But then his right foot found security. He was stable.

For the moment.

Now his left, the one with a sprained ankle, the one with snake venom shooting through it, would have to do the work.

Come on, leg, you can do this for the team. Final seconds. You can do this.

He scraped the wall with his left foot, but only succeeded in dislodging more dirt.

Don't give up now, boy. Dig!

He tried to burrow his toe into the dirt, a million burning needles jabbing his left leg all the way to the knee.

But he found what he was looking for.

Heather's face. He saw it behind his eyes. And he pushed with both legs now and pulled with his arms. The fabric of his shirt tore, hard sand scraped his elbows.

But he was *out*.

He flopped onto his back, looked up at the sky. His left leg was throbbing. How much time did he have before the venom hit his heart?

Get in the house. Find Heather.

Kill Nicky Oberlin.

For a moment he just listened. Nothing. He rolled over onto his stomach and looked at the house. Dim light filtered through the screen door.

Getting to his knees, then standing, Sam ignored the burning in his leg and the pain in his ankle. He had to get in the house. Now.

Had to find a way to save his daughter.

At the door he waited, straining to hear any noise inside. The creak of a floorboard. Anything.

Only silence.

Slowly, he opened the screen door. Thankfully it didn't announce itself too loudly. Slipping inside, Sam quickly scanned the room. It was wooden, spare. Unfinished and cold.

Concentrating, Sam made himself put one foot in front of the other. Walking was going to be an ordeal now, but it was the only option he had.

Still no sounds.

He looked around for something to grab, some weapon. A wooden chair against one wall wouldn't do. Too heavy to carry around, too hard to break up.

His eye went upward and he saw some wires. Thick ones. They looked hastily installed. With a box of some kind — a single black box where the wires in this room terminated. Some sort of security system?

Was he being watched right now by Nicky, sitting and laughing in front of a monitor somewhere?

Anything was possible in this madhouse world he was in.

But he had to keep going, keep moving.

He had to find Heather.

6.

Heather dived.

But with her hands bound she could barely break her fall. Her face smashed into the ground. Her forehead hit a rock. She felt the gush of blood.

Behind her the car was spinning around. She could hear the tires and follow the trajectory of the lights.

She could not get up. Dazed, it was all she could do not to pass out. She was not going to do that. If she did, she was sure she'd never come out of it.

The smell of sand and blood stirred her thoughts. Max. He popped into her mind again. What would he think if he could see her now? His big sister, making a mess of her life? Max always needed someone to look out for him. She used to do that.

Max needed her. The same way she needed her father now. That was the thing about family. She wished she'd realized this a year ago.

Lights hit her again, and the sound of the car grew closer.

Get up.

She tried, struggling to her knees. Moving her body was like pushing cement bags.

The car engine was cut, but the lights stayed on her.

Her lungs fought for air.

Then she heard the sound of his steps, slowly coming near.

Maybe he had his gun out. Maybe this was it. She closed her eyes.

"Look at you," Nicky said. "What a mess. What. A. Mess. This will not do. I'm very angry now. Very, very angry."

7.

No one was inside. But Sam didn't know how long the place would stay empty.

He moved quickly as he could, dragging his left foot, through the first floor and to the door at the back. The door had a window. He looked through. Only darkness out there.

Where were they?

He found the bathroom. Like the rest of the house, it didn't have much in it. A used bar of soap sat on the sink.

Sam grabbed it and ran it under some water. He pulled up his pant leg and rubbed the punctures in his calf with the soap. It ached and stung, but he kept up the motion in the hope that he was doing himself some good. Maybe it was a fool's errand, but it was something to do.

His cell phone. Maybe it was still outside where he'd thrown it. He limped to the front door. There was no light for the porch. He got on his hands and knees and started feeling around for the phone.

Not there. At least not that he could see.

Back in the house, he decided to try upstairs. He didn't know what else to do. There had to be a way to get a signal out to somebody.

It was a struggle to get to the top of the stairs, but he made it. He couldn't help wondering at how bizarre the place was.

And the wires. What were they for?

The door to his right was open. The room was lit. He went in and saw a bed with iron posts. He got the distinct feeling that

Heather had been imprisoned here. He didn't allow himself to think that anything more had happened.

Determined to search the whole place now, he continued on to the only other door on the second floor. He opened it.

Darkness. He felt along the wall until he came to a switch, and flicked it.

Red light from a single bulb in the middle of the room offered a bloodlike illumination. But he could make out a few items.

In the middle of the floor was a mattress with a rumpled blanket. Up against the far wall was a chest of drawers and next to that some shelving. Various items lined the shelves. Square items. A cage. Boxes.

Maybe one of those boxes had a weapon. Or something else that might be of immediate use. He hoped so, because he was starting to feel a fever coming on. How much time, how much life, did he have left?

Whatever it was, he had to use it to find his daughter.

In the crimson dimness Sam crossed the room, stepping around the mattress as if it were poisonous.

He observed that the boxes on the shelf were set in a pattern. The smaller boxes, shoeboxes Sam could now see, sat on the lower shelf. Four of them. Two larger boxes were set in the middle. The top box was the size of a small TV.

Sam saw some lettering on the side of the box, leaned over and read, *Toast-All Toast'r-Oven.*

Nicky must be a regular domestic engineer, Sam thought bitterly.

He opened the box and looked inside. There was something in it that was not a toaster oven. He couldn't make it out in the shadows.

He picked up the box and carried it to the middle of the room, where he could hold it under the red light. He looked inside again.

His heart kicked his chest. He dropped the box.

The box hit his leg on the way down, tipped, spilled its contents.

Sam stepped back, unbelieving.

8.

She tried to remember some of the things her mom and dad had told her about God. She'd hardly listened to them, learned how to tune them out when they got on her about the God business. She knew more than they did. They weren't in tune at all with her life. She might as well have been a pod person who happened to land in the middle of this crazy family.

She wished she'd listened more.

God was everywhere, right? Was he here in the trunk? Or had he turned his face away from her by now?

Her head vibrated as the car rolled along.

But then there was that thing her mother had told her, that it didn't matter what you'd done, God would take you back. It was right after the first time she'd been caught drinking, when she was fourteen, and she cried. She cried because she got caught.

So there was Mom trying to explain it to her and Heather was practicing the tune-out, but that much stuck. If you wanted to go to God, he'd come running to you. That was it. Her mom said Jesus told a story about a son who left his father, but then came back and the father ran down the road to him.

That was a good story, Heather had to admit. She liked that one.

Now she hoped it was true.

Is it true, God? Are you there? Be there, be there.

9.

It was a perfectly preserved human skull.

And it was true what the horror stories

said. Skulls grin.

Sam fought for breath as he looked at the hideous find. He started backing out, keeping watch on the skull, wondering if at any moment it would jump at him.

Sucking air outside the room, he thought for a moment he might be sick. He didn't know if it was the skull or the snakebite. Whatever the cause, he doubled over and put his hands on his knees.

Who did that skull belong to? And was the next one in the box going to be his? Or his daughter's?

For a moment he was paralyzed, poised over a dark abyss with nowhere to turn. Not one choice seemed prudent. Yet if he didn't move somewhere, he was doomed.

Then he heard a car. It was coming on fast. If it was Nicky, he would check the pit. He would see that Sam was not there and then the element of surprise would be gone. If Sam could get downstairs, maybe he could grab something to hit him with, or even push him into the pit.

Sam's left leg went out from under him.

Now he was practically crippled as well.

He heard the car engine cut in what he guessed was the front of the house. No time to do anything but find a place to hide.

If he could.

10.

Heather sensed they were back at the house. Which meant Nicky would be going after her father. And there was nothing she could do. She kicked at the side of the car, as if that would do any good.

Oh, God, don't let him die. Don't let my dad die.

11.

Sam stood behind the open door, holding the skull in his hand. It was the only weapon he could come up with. He would use it to smash in Nicky's head.

He tried not to feel completely freaked by what was happening.

He heard the screen door open, then slap closed.

"Sammy?"

Sam tried to keep from breathing. He thought any sound, even a breath, would be picked up by the madman.

"Sammy, I don't know how you did it. Good one, boy. You really surprise me. Come on out and we'll talk. You want your daughter back, right?"

If she was even alive.

"I have to tell you, Sammy, you don't want to hide from me. This house is a very dangerous place."

That went without saying.

"And I hope you haven't . . ."

Nicky's voice trailed off. And then Sam heard footsteps charging hard up the stairs.

He readied the skull. He'd left the red light on, hoping to draw Nicky in.

The footsteps pounded to just outside the door.

And stopped.

A silence extended for a long, excruciating span.

Then a wicked laugh cut the air, a crazy man's laugh, chilling every inch of Sam's spine.

Nicky Oberlin stepped through the door.

In the red light his face was a clown's, contorted with perverted pleasure.

In a split second Sam saw him raise his arm, and knew his hand held a gun. Sam lunged forward and struck outward with the skull.

At the same moment he heard the crack of the gun, Sam felt the contact with Nicky's head. Bone on bone. They both went down, Sam on top.

He didn't feel a burn, told himself he wasn't hit.

He reached for Nicky's wrist, didn't find it, his hand flailing in the gloom. He knew he had to disarm Nicky before anything else.

Nicky seemed relaxed.

Sam found Nicky's right arm with his left hand, adjusted his grip to grab Nicky's wrist. It was soft, fleshy.

Then Nicky laughed again, a maniacal squeal.

"I love you too, Sammy!"

Sam raised the skull for another blow.

Nicky's own face seemed like a skull now as Sam looked into it. The eyes were hollow, the teeth smiling grotesquely.

Sam thrust the skull downward. Nicky anticipated, rolled his head left.

The skull slammed the floor.

Sam felt Nicky's left arm around his neck. Pulling him down.

"Bad Sammy," Nicky grunted.

Sam caught a whiff of Nicky's breath. It smelled like something dead.

Nicky laughed again, then shot his head forward and hit Sam's chin. Stunned, Sam dropped the skull. But he quickly followed with a right to Nicky's face. Bad mistake. Felt like he broke his hand. Stupid, he thought, even as he returned his attention to Nicky's gun.

"I love you too," Nicky said, laughing again. Pain seemed to please him. It was as if Nicky were a five-year-old who enjoyed wrestling around and getting hurt. Only this five-year-old held a weapon.

Sam raised Nicky's wrist and slammed it into the floor.

Nicky laughed.

Sam slammed it down again, and heard something metallic skitter away.

"Good one, Sam!" Nicky said, his cackling almost obscuring the words.

With a sudden burst of energy Nicky threw his right leg over Sam and turned him over. Now Nicky was on top, a chortling gargoyle, with all his weight on Sam.

"You hit me with Daddy," Nicky said. "That's funny. He hit me enough when I was a kid."

The skull. He was talking about the skull.

Sam felt his strength draining away. He had to get Nicky in some kind of hold. But Nicky was now the strong one. He had completely immobilized Sam.

"You seem a little tired, Sammy. Did Geraldine get a little taste of you?"

"Where is she?" Sam managed to say.

"Geraldine?"

"My daughter!"

"It doesn't matter anymore, good buddy. I win! That's all you have to know."

Nicky rolled off Sam, rolled like a beach ball across the floor.

He was going for the gun.

Sam struggled to get to his feet. He only reached his knees.

Then Nicky was standing against the wall, his laughter pouring out of him, and was reaching up.

For what?

Nicky pulled. Pulled the wire, that out-of-place wire Sam had noticed in the house.

He heard what sounded like a muffled explosion.

"I win, Sammy. I win everything!"

Sam was on all fours, unable to move, just looking at Nicky, who was ambling slowly toward the doorway.

Then he pointed the gun at Sam and fired.

12.

Heather heard what sounded like an explosion. Then a *bang*.

Then something else, another sound, a *whoosh*.

What was going on?

In her dark world, nothing made sense. She had to be going crazy. This was all crazy and maybe it was a bad dream.

Please let it be a bad dream, God, and get me out of it now. Wake me up and get me out and let me see that my dad is okay.

13.

The bullet hit Sam in the left thigh.

The next shot would be to his head. He had no doubt.

But Nicky didn't shoot again.

Instead he paused in the doorway.

Several things reached Sam's consciousness simultaneously.

Fire. Flames heard and seen and felt around him.

Nicky had booby-trapped the place to burn up.

Nicky laughing. And turning his back.

He was leaving Sam to fry.

A jolt of adrenaline shot through him. He got up, ignoring all pain.

He pushed off his aching legs and shot through the door.

Nicky turned around, looked shocked, raised his hand.

The gun.

Sam dove at Nicky's middle. Heard the rush of air from Nicky's mouth.

And drove Nicky back with his shoulder, back against a railing, and pushed again until Nicky fell backward, over the rail and to the ground below.

As flames began licking the walls, Sam knew he had only seconds to get downstairs.

Every step was an exercise in the raw will to live.

The fire was breaking out now, below and above. The stairs were catching flame.

Halfway down Sam stumbled, his legs no longer cooperating with his mind.

He caught himself on the rail. And looking down saw the inert body of Nicky Oberlin.

Nicky was going to burn.

Sam thought no one deserved that. At the same time he thought Nicky Oberlin did.

Using hands and arms, Sam made it to the bottom of the stairs and managed enough of a jump to get over the mushrooming fire.

He rolled onto the floor, which had not yet ignited. The walls were engulfed. Heat was increasing at a rapid rate.

Sam crawled to Nicky Oberlin, looked for the gun. It was on the floor a few paces away.

He grabbed a handful of Nicky's shirt and shook it.

No response. Sam couldn't tell if Nicky was dead or dazed.

He attempted to drag Nicky's body. But with no strength in his legs, Sam couldn't budge him.

The heat intensified.

Sam made himself stand up, made himself move one more time. He did not open the front door.

He fell through the screen.

14.

Heather heard the crackling of fire.

What was happening? Was it the whole house?

She screamed as loudly as she could.

And again.

She needed to get out of this car. She needed to know what was going on.

15.

The scream had come from the car, the silver Mustang in front of the house.

"Heather!"

He heard the muffled answer. "Daddy!"

He managed to stand and make it to the car. He put his hands out on the roof to hold himself up. He peered in the driver's-side window.

No Heather.

"Daddy!"

In the trunk. Nicky had put her in the trunk.

He opened the door, looked for the trunk release. Found it in the glove box.

Keeping himself upright by using the car, he struggled to the back, saw his daughter bound in the tiny space.

The heat of the fire, now spitting flames out the windows, was on his back as he reached over and untied Heather's hands and helped her out of the trunk.

She threw her arms around his neck, crying. Sam nearly fell, but used his left hand on the trunk's edge to stay standing.

Heather let go. "Where is he?" she said.

"Inside."

"Get me out of here, Daddy."

"Yes," Sam said, just before he blacked out.

TWENTY

1.

"Roz, you have to know where she is." Linda tried to keep her voice calm over the phone, but it was a losing battle. It was past midnight and she could not sleep. Her sense of things being terribly out of control wouldn't leave. And knowing Roz was a creature of the night, she had no qualms about contacting her at this hour.

"No lie, Mrs. Trask. She said she was gonna take off with this guy and —"

"The record producer?"

"Yeah. His name's Lundquist. He did our demo. He was hot for her. Everybody could tell."

"Do you have any idea where they are?"

"Uh-uh."

"Has she called you?"

"Uh-uh."

Linda looked at the ceiling. "Is there anything else you can tell me that would help us find her?"

"I don't think she wants to be found, Mrs. —"

"That's obvious. What can you tell us about this man, what's his name?"

"Lundquist. His first name's Charles. His nickname's Scat."

"Great. What else?"

"I don't know. He's done some producing. He seemed like a good place for us to start."

"Does he have an office? Do you have his phone number?"

"We met him at a studio on Sunset. I guess he has an office somewhere. You could Google him. I did a little bit once."

"Roz, would you mind doing that for me? I want a phone number and address. I think you can get the information faster than I can."

"I'm s'posed to go somewhere —"

"Please, Roz. We have to find her."

"I think she'll be okay, Mrs. T. She's a lot more —"

"Call me back, Roz, please."

"All right."

Linda paced and prayed. In the house, even with lights on, she felt the oppression of shadows. Sam, Heather. Something bad was happening. If she didn't have peace by the time the sun showed up, she would call the police.

Enough was enough.

Roz called back. "Whack," she said.

"What is?"

"I was going around and I found this thing, said Lundquist was going to go to Puerto Rico to set up a studio. He was leaving LA."

"He obviously didn't."

"But he never said anything. Anyway, here's a number." She gave Linda a number in the 310 area code.

"Thanks, Roz."

"Don't worry, I'm telling you."

Easier said than done.

Linda called the number. She got a recorded message, a man's voice, a little tinny and distant. "Hey, I'm gonna be outta town for a while, so just leave a message and I'll get back to you. Keep it real." *Beep.*

She clicked off.

Paced and prayed. Made herself a cup of decaf. Opened the Bible to Psalms.

At 2:35 a.m. the house phone rang.

2.

"Mama."

"Heather, where are you?"

"Mama, come get us."

"Tell me where —"

"A hospital in Vegas. Me and Dad."

Linda swallowed. "What happened? Are you —"

"Just come!"

"Which hospital, where —"

"Here!"

Another voice came on. A woman. "Mrs. Trask?"

"Who is this?"

"My name is Melba Sanchez. I'm a nurse, and —"

"What's wrong? What's happened to my husband and daughter?"

"Can you come?"

"Please tell me."

"Your husband's had an accident, but he's in stable condition."

"What happened?"

"How long would it take you to get here?"

3.

Linda and Max pulled into the medical center just after ten a.m. The dry air hit Linda like a fist of dust. Inside, smells of antiseptic and pessimism confronted her.

Sam was in a fourth-floor room, with Heather sitting in a chair next to the bed. Both faces came alive as Linda walked in.

While Max rushed to Sam's bedside,

Heather embraced her mother. No words were exchanged. They didn't seem necessary.

Linda went to Sam, who raised a hand to her. She took it. A tube ran from his elbow to an IV unit.

"Now will someone tell me what happened?" Linda said.

Sam managed a smile. "I don't even know where to start."

"Maybe I can help." The voice came from the open door. Linda turned to see a woman in a gray suit. She was tall, with nut-brown hair clipped short. On her hip was a gold star with a cityscape in the center, and the words *Metropolitan Police* in dark blue around it.

"That's Detective Powers," Sam said.

"Joan," the woman said, extending her hand to Linda.

"If it's all the same to you," Sam said to Linda, "I'd rather have her explain it all. I'm beat."

"Can we step into the visitor's room?" Joan Powers said.

"Go on, Mom," Max said. "I'll take care of Dad and Heather."

Anxious to hear the story, Linda followed Detective Powers to the visitor's room halfway down the corridor. Powers moved with a dancer's grace and seemed young to be a detective. But this was Las Vegas, so maybe it fit.

"Your husband and daughter have quite a tale to tell." Powers indicated a sofa for the two to sit. They were alone in the room, which was done up in burnt orange with a Georgia O'Keeffe print on the wall.

"Please tell me all of it," Linda said.

Detective Powers removed a small device from her coat pocket. "Do you mind if I record this?"

"What for?"

"I'll want to ask you some questions, if you don't mind. Part of the investigation."

"Investigation into what? Please —"

"All right." Powers set the micro recorder between them on the sofa. She took out a small black notebook, opened it, scanned a few pages. "Your husband told me about this man, Nicky Oberlin, who's been harassing your family."

"That's a real gentle way to put it."

"Can you tell me what he was doing to you?"

"I want to know what happened to my husband first."

"You weren't apprised by the doctor?"

"I haven't been apprised, informed, spoken to, or anything else by anyone. You know what happened?"

"I know what the medical report says. Your husband was shot in the leg —"

"Shot? By who?"

"This Oberlin guy, according to your husband."

Linda frowned. It almost sounded like the detective didn't quite buy her husband's story. Maybe she was just tired and anxious, so she let it pass. She said, "Is that all?"

"Apparently not," Detective Powers said. "He had a snakebite too."

"Snakebite!"

"Rattlesnake. At least that's what I'm told."

Linda rubbed her eyes. "And how did he get that?"

Looking at her notes, Detective Powers said, "According to your husband, this Oberlin guy had your daughter with him in this place pretty far removed, southwest of here, outside Good Springs. Very isolated. Your daughter says he was holding her there by force."

"You believe her, don't you?"

"At this point I'm trying to gather all the facts. I have no reason to disbelieve her. She says your husband showed up to try to get her out of there, and Oberlin set a trap. Your husband says he fell into a big pit. Oberlin threw a rattlesnake at him. It sounds pretty out there."

"Not if you know Nicky Oberlin. I wouldn't put anything past him. Have you caught him?"

"I'm getting to that," Detective Powers said. "Your daughter got out of the house, she says, and while Oberlin was coming after her, your husband got out of the pit. He made it into the house. At some point Oberlin came back and there was a struggle. Oberlin shot him in the leg, there was more scuffling, and your husband managed to knock him out. Did I mention the house was on fire?"

Linda just stared at the detective.

"Your husband says it was rigged. But one of our helicopters saw the flames. It was like a torch out there in the middle of nowhere. That's how we got your husband and daughter out. I'd say that was pretty lucky."

"I'd say luck had nothing to do with it."

"Excuse me?"

"Can we finish this? I'd like to go back to my husband."

"Just a couple more questions. Our CS unit's going over the place even as we speak, and that will tell us a lot."

"I hope so."

"May I just ask about the relationship

between your husband and Oberlin?"

"Relationship? There was no relationship. He just showed up one day and inserted himself into my husband's life."

"Didn't they go back to college days?"

"Well, yes, they sort of knew each other in college."

"That's what I was talking about."

"Excuse me, but am I being cross-examined here? Are you implying something?"

"As I said, it's my job to get all the facts, that's all."

"But you're not saying that my husband is in any way responsible for what happened, are you?"

"A man may be dead," Detective Powers said. "That's very serious. I'm sure you understand that."

"I don't understand your putting the burden of proof on me or my husband."

"Please, Mrs. Trask, that's not what I'm trying to do. But understand my position. I don't know anything about anybody in this case. I don't know anything about this man named Oberlin. I don't know how you or your husband or your daughter have interacted with him. If it is as you say, there is no problem. The facts will come out. But your helping me up front will prevent a lot of problems later on."

"Then let me spell this out as clearly as I can. There is no problem. Nicky Oberlin harassed our family because he had something against Sam."

"There was some bad blood?"

"Not at all. Sam had very little to do with Oberlin in college. That was over twenty-five years ago. His coming back now was all due, I don't know, to a tick in his brain. He's a psycho."

"Your husband mentioned something about a court case, a criminal matter."

"Yes, Oberlin was arrested and . . ."

"Yes?"

Linda wondered if she should mention that Nicky had filed an assault charge against Sam. It was absurd, of course, but if she didn't say anything and Powers found out later it would look bad. On the other hand, she didn't like the way this particular line of questioning was heading.

"I was just saying," Linda continued, "that a criminal complaint was filed by the district attorney against Oberlin. He poisoned our dog."

"And what was the outcome of that matter?"

"It was dismissed on a technicality."

Detective Powers didn't say anything. She

pursed her lips.

Annoying Linda. "May I go see my husband now?"

"Of course. Perhaps we can continue this in a little while."

"Perhaps," Linda said, meaning *With all due respect, no way.*

4.

Sam was smiling and holding Max's hand when Linda came back into the room.

"Did you straighten everything out for me?" Sam said.

"Yeah, right," Linda said. "Now what's this about being bitten by a rattlesnake?"

"Oh, that."

"Yes. *That.*"

"I didn't think it would bite me."

"Why not?"

"Professional courtesy."

Linda huffed and shook her head. "You're quite witty for a guy who almost died."

"The doc says they caught it in time. He says he's sure it wasn't a diamondback."

"That's a good thing?"

"Yeah. Because if it had been, I probably would be dead."

Linda closed her eyes. "When can you get out of here?"

"The sooner the better," Sam said. "Because I'm ready to leave this place and never come back."

"The hospital?" Max said.

"Las Vegas."

Heather was sitting in a chair by the window, looking out. Linda went to her, put her arm around her shoulder. Heather leaned her head against her mother's hand. Linda stroked her daughter's hair and looked out at the city below and the mountains beyond. Yes, they would leave this place and go home. They would go home to start again, and whatever horrors their family had gone through would fade into distant memory, left in the hands of God.

A few minutes later Detective Powers entered the room. "May I speak to your husband alone?" she said.

"What about?" Sam asked.

"I'd rather we do it alone."

"I'd like my family around me."

"Maybe the boy —"

"I'm staying," Max said firmly.

Detective Powers nodded. "All right. This is officially a homicide. I just got word they found the body in the burned-out house. Apparently not a pretty sight."

"Homicide?" Linda blurted. "How can you say that?"

Sam put up his hand. "All the detective means is that a human being has died. She is not saying whether there's any criminal responsibility anywhere, are you, Detective?"

"All I'm saying is somebody's dead and it wasn't by natural causes."

Yes, Linda thought. The sooner we get out of this place the better.

5.

"You don't look ready to go home," the police lieutenant said to Sam. His name was Saunders, and he was right about that. Sam should have been back at the hospital. But two nights was enough. And his family, staying in an economy motel, also had enough of Sin City.

"I'm here, let's get this over with." Sam wore a workout suit Linda had bought that morning and walked with the help of a hospital-issue cane. It was getting on toward eleven o'clock and Sam wanted to get on the road, with his daughter driving his car. Linda would take Max.

"It's just that I want to get it all straight so I don't have to be dragging you back here," Saunders said. He was thin, about forty, with a receding hairline and a lot of forehead susceptible to deep furrows. Went with the job, Sam figured.

At least the lieutenant's office wasn't intimidating. A can of Planters nuts sat on the desk next to a computer monitor and a stack of video tapes. Sam saw the official insignia *Cops* on one of the tapes. Was he a fan, or using these for training? On the corner of Saunders's desk, facing Sam, was a framed quotation: "In Valor There Is Honor — Tacitus."

The effects of the Vicodin were starting to wear off and Sam's leg was throbbing. "What isn't straight?" he said.

"How that fire started," Saunders said. "According to Detective Powers's report —"

"Didn't you find the place was rigged?"

"Yeah, but who tripped it?"

"Oberlin. Then he shot me and was going to leave me in there."

"Right. And you managed to get up, wounded as you were, and push him over a railing."

His tone sounded the slightest bit incredulous, but Sam chalked it up to police protectiveness. In this era of lawsuits and bad publicity, all public agencies were being more careful. "Yes, I pushed him over."

"And thought he was dead or knocked out?"

"I didn't really have a chance to find out.

I was a little preoccupied with the fire and the fact that I could barely move."

"So you left him there?"

"I attempted to move him. But I couldn't."

"Couldn't?"

"I physically could not move him, is what I'm saying."

The captain tapped his metallic desk with his index finger. "Right, and so you left him there."

"I had to make a decision."

"Of course."

"You understand what I'm saying, right? I tried to move him, but I couldn't, and the place was burning down, and I was bleeding and my daughter was somewhere, and frankly I place a little more value on my daughter than a sociopath who was trying to kill us both."

Saunders said nothing.

"Anything else?" Sam said.

"Yeah. Let's talk about your background with this guy. You —"

"I'm sorry. No. I'm not going to talk about him anymore. You have my statement."

"Mr. Trask, if you would just —"

Sam stood. "That's all."

"Please sit down, if you would, sir."

"Am I being held?"

"Of course not."

476

"Then the interview is over. You know where to reach me."

With a curt nod, Sam grabbed his cane and made for the door. He had the distinct feeling Lieutenant Saunders was one of those career paper pushers whose existence was justified by how much squirm he could get out of people.

Twenty-One

1.

Heather, driving, didn't speak until they were almost ten miles out of Las Vegas. The afternoon sun was bright, almost blinding. Sam was content to close his eyes and try to will his body to heal itself.

Then Heather said, "Do you hate me?"

Sam opened his eyes, turned to her.

"Do you?"

"Of course not, honey. Why would —"

"I totally messed up. I messed up my whole life."

"No —"

"I'm sorry, Dad."

Sam reached out and stroked her hair. She let him. It had been a long time. "I'm sorry too. So now we have a second chance. Both of us."

Heather said nothing. She wiped something from her eye.

"Why did he do this to us?" she said.

"That's something I ask myself a lot. There may not be any real answer to it."

"How could there not be?"

"There's a lot we don't know about how the mind works. Or what it can become when left to itself. That was him. He had no other resources or authority but his own mind. The law didn't scare him, he rejected religion. He was his own god."

"He did this weird thing." She paused. "He talked about a movie where a guy shoots a car trunk. And then he did it. Do you know what that was all about?"

"Anything else?"

"Something about heat. I think he said the actor was in *Yankee Doodle.*"

"*Yankee . . . Yankee Doodle Dandy?*"

"That's it."

"James Cagney?"

"Yeah. Know what he meant?"

"Oh, man. I think I do. *White Heat.* That's the movie. Cagney plays a guy named Cody, who's fixated on his mother. A real mama's boy who made up for it by becoming the worst criminal he could. At one point he has a hostage in the trunk of the car, and the guy says he can't breathe, so Cody shoots airholes in the trunk, killing the man, of course."

"Sick."

"He goes to prison, and when he's told his mother is dead, he goes nuts and starts tearing the place up. Nicky was fixated on his mother too. When I got to her, that really sent him off the beam."

"This is really nuts."

"At the end of the movie, he's on top of some gas tanks and he screams, 'Made it, Ma! Top of the world!' And then he shoots into the tanks and goes up in a fireball."

It all had a perverse sense of connection. Even down to the fact that Nicky Oberlin was burned to death in a house fire. Maybe he wanted it to happen, just like Cody.

Then another connection hit Sam. He knew the movie from a film series at UCSB, a tribute to James Cagney. They'd shown a bunch of his films, from *The Public Enemy* to *Mister Roberts*. Of course *Yankee Doodle Dandy* was in there, and *White Heat.*

Sam got cold as he realized Nicky Oberlin might have been sitting in Campbell Hall with him the night they showed it.

2.

Linda turned to Sam in the semidarkness. "You're worried about Heather, aren't you?"

"Am I that transparent?" Sam said.

"You should be asleep by now."

"I'm dreaming."

"About what?"

"June and Ward Cleaver."

She laughed and draped an arm over his chest. "Not the Bradys?"

"Never bought the Bradys."

"It's a good dream."

"But only that?"

"Maybe more."

Sam looked at the ceiling. "I haven't allowed myself to get comfortable in my own home yet."

"It's only been two days. After what you two went through —"

"I want it to be home. But not like before. Better."

"It will be."

"I wish I was as sure as you are. I want Heather to know God."

"Give her time. At least she's home."

Home. Sam loved the sound of the word. Of course life was not a television show. Wally and the Beav didn't live here. But the Trasks did, and Trasks stuck together.

3.

Sam took a check to Gerald Case the next morning and told him the story. When he finished, Case held out the check. "I don't feel I earned all this."

"That's your fee," Sam said.

"But if I was doing my job I would have got to him before he got to your daughter."

"You don't know that."

"I'm good, remember? I'm supposed to get those things right."

Sam refused the check. "You were part of it. You helped me force his hand. If we hadn't, who knows, maybe he would have waited for a better time. Maybe he would have taken me out."

"And he would have."

"I know."

Case nodded and folded the check. "Okay, you twisted my arm. But let me take you to dinner sometime. See, I can find anything, especially good restaurants."

4.

Now he had time to heal. With his family around him. He was even getting his legal legs back. Pete Harper had called and said he still wanted Sam to handle the lawsuit. Great news. Life had to get back to normal now even though none of them would ever be the same again.

Home was quiet this afternoon, with Max at practice and Linda taking Heather to a counselor. Robyn Caid was a member of Solid Rock and a specialist in psychological trauma. At least Heather had agreed to go. Reports after their first meeting were positive. Heather, it turned out, had not been raped by Nicky Oberlin, though he had tried. His failure was another layer in his deep and complicated profile.

Sam had also talked to Rich Demaris, a lawyer friend, who got an agreement from a deputy city attorney to reduce Heather's DUI to a wet reckless. As part of the plea, Heather would have to go through an alcohol program. That in itself was a good thing. Heather would need all the help she could get.

In his study, Sam managed to get some good research done on LexisNexis. It felt good to be back in the right kind of fight, even though he couldn't sit in the same position for too long. Not yet. His own physical therapy loomed.

His phone buzzed.

"Mr. Trask, it's Lieutenant Saunders."

"Right. What can I do for you?"

"I'm going to need you and your daughter back here."

"What? Why?"

"We have a lot more questions. We wanted to give you some time but —"

"What questions?"

"The body, Mr. Trask, the one we found

in the house —"

"Yeah?"

"It's not Oberlin."

The room seemed to telescope backward.

"We got dentals," Saunders said. "The burned guy isn't him."

Sam squeezed the phone hard, as if to force the statement back in.

"Mr. Trask?"

"I'm here."

"We thought maybe you could help us figure out who it is. We never did get a full statement from your daughter. Maybe we could set a time —"

"Where is Oberlin?"

Pause. "We don't know."

"You don't *know?* He was in the house! I saw him."

"There was only one body —"

"A car. He had a . . . a Mustang."

"No, the Mustang was still there. We think maybe he had another vehicle. There were some other tire tracks behind the place."

"I don't believe this. What are you doing about it?"

"We're looking for him."

"With how many guys?"

"What we can —"

"Find him."

"You don't have to raise your voice, sir."

New fears pinged through Sam's mind. He was out there. Nicky Oberlin was still out there. Maybe outside his house. Maybe —

"Mr. Trask, if you'll come —"

"Listen to me, Saunders. I can't help you now. I've got to protect my family."

"Sir —"

"I'll call you back if I think of —"

"Sir, if you'll just —"

"You might try one thing. The body. It might be a man named Charles Lundquist."

"Let me write that down. Who is he?"

"Low-level record producer. Had an office in Hollywood on Santa Monica Boulevard. You should be able to trace it from there. I'll be in touch."

"Wait —"

Sam clicked off and called Linda.

"Are you still at counseling?"

"No, we're on our way to the Northridge Fashion Center. We're going to —"

"Linda, listen to me. Come home. Now. I'm going to get Max."

"Sam, what is it?"

"Oberlin. He's alive."

"This time, you're all going to Aunt Nancy's," Sam told his family. "No argument."

"But what about you?" Linda said. "You can't just sit here waiting for him."

Sam opened the small case he'd brought into the living room. Opened it. Took out the gun.

"This is a Browning handgun," he explained. "If he comes here, I will use it."

Max's eyes opened wide. "Does that work?"

Heather said, "Come with us, Dad."

"I can't."

Linda touched his arm. "I don't want us to be apart."

"Just until they find him."

"What if they never do?"

A prospect Sam did not want to think about it. When Linda and Heather went to pack some things, Max said, "Can I say something?"

"Sure." Sam sat them down on the sofa. "You scared?"

Max shook his head. "That's what I wanted to tell you. I'll look after 'em, Dad."

"Your mom and sister?"

"Yeah. I'm bringing my bat with me. If he ever tries anything . . ."

Sam threw his arms around Max and pulled him close.

"I mean it," he said.

"I know."

6.

Sam was not going to leave any chance that Max would have to prove himself. As soon as Linda and the kids were off to her sister's place in San Luis Obispo, he called Gerald Case.

"The news is," Sam said, "that Oberlin is still out there. The body in the house wasn't his."

In the silence Sam could imagine Case slapping his forehead.

"I've sent Linda and the kids to her sister's. I want to hire Greg Wayne to do more drive-bys."

"I'll do them, Sam."

"No —"

"I insist. I owe you."

"You don't —"

"Consider it done."

7.

Four days dragged by. Sam managed to work, to watch, but not sleep much.

The gun was with him everywhere he

went. He hoped he was ready for anything.

He knew he couldn't continue to live like this. Apart from his family. A prisoner in his own home.

Then, on a Friday, he got an early morning call from Cam Bellamy.

"Just got off the phone with one of the homicide detectives in Vegas," Cam said. "You were right about the body they found, Sam. They made a positive ID."

"So it was Lundquist?"

"Yeah. Yesterday I had LAPD check Lundquist's office. He had an answering machine there with a message on it saying he was going out of town. Only had three messages on it."

"Anybody report him missing?"

"Not that we know of. Know what that means? Oberlin had this worked out way before he met with you. He knew all about your family, found some record guy whose identity he could take over. A guy who wouldn't be missed if he went on a long trip. That must have taken some doing."

"Why didn't he get rid of the body?"

"Listen, they think the body was under the house, and get this, covered with a resin of some kind. Which is why it burned so bad."

"Resin?"

"To preserve it. It was a trophy, Sam. That's Oberlin's profile. You know that skull you had your hands on?"

"It was his father, wasn't it?"

"How'd you know that?"

"Something he said."

"Well, you're right. The dentals checked out on that one too. Oberlin's father went missing in 1972. Sacramento cops originally thought Laverne might have offed the guy, who was a known abuser. But they ruled her out, figured she was more a victim than anything else. They concluded he had taken off and that was that. They never even looked seriously at Nicky as a suspect. He was, what, twelve years old at the time?"

"Right."

"They wouldn't have figured a kid like that could kill his father and then chop him up and bury the parts. Even less digging them up like some sort of trophies and keeping them." Cam sighed. "Sometimes I don't even believe what passes across my desk."

"Can you peg him for murder?"

"Won't be easy. We have to prove he killed Lundquist. He could claim Lundquist was a guest in the house and was there willingly, for all we know."

"What about kidnapping? Heather?"

"That's a maybe."

"Maybe?"

"She went with him across the state line. That makes it federal."

"That's good. That's life in prison."

"Probably."

"And attempted murder on me?"

"That would be in Nevada."

Sam shook his head. "This is sounding less than certain, Cam."

"We have to make a case."

"That's what I'm afraid of."

"I'd like to nail him with special circs."

"And then he gets, what, twenty years in Quentin before the needle?"

"Sam, we've only got the system we —"

"He's always managed to get around the system."

Cam paused, then spoke in low tones. "Maybe he'll get stupid and we'll get lucky, and he'll get shot."

8.

Shot would be nice, Sam thought as he drove to Beverly Hills. Take it out of the system altogether. No muss, no fuss.

But first they had to find him.

Sam needed to calm down before the business at hand. He found a parking spot on the street, across from the Connelly

Building on Camden, and listened to the radio. He had a final pretrial memo to deliver to Larry Cohen, and instead of sending it by messenger he'd decided to go himself. Maybe getting face-to-face with Cohen would convince him, finally, to give a decent settlement offer on Harper. Showing up unannounced would give Cohen less time to prepare a canned response.

The radio was playing his favorite kind of music, the most mellow kind he could find, mellow being the new watchword for his life. The tune was Larry Carlton's "Minute by Minute," which soothed like a Burke Williams masseur.

The song was just about to end when something across the street caught his eye.

And tore him right out of mellow.

It was the blond guy. The guy who had been staking out his house. Had to be. That same guy was walking out of the building doors, strolling toward Wilshire, as if he were as much a part of the fabric of everyday business as Sam and Cohen.

Slowly, Sam got out of the car, wheels turning in his head. The wheels took him across Camden and into the Connelly Building and up to reception at Cohen, Stone & Baerwitz.

"I'm here to see Larry Cohen," Sam said.

"Do you have an appointment?" snapped the young receptionist, a raven-haired ice queen.

"Yeah. I just made it."

Her face didn't crack. "I'm sorry, but —"

"Never mind. I'll let myself in."

He walked past the desk and went through the inner door, the ice queen barking something about waiting.

Sam headed for the office at the end of the corridor. He'd been in the corner digs of Larry Cohen before. No doubt this would be the last time.

He threw the door open.

Larry Cohen was on the phone. His face tightened when he saw Sam.

"I'll call you right back," Cohen said, then hung up. He stood and forced a smile. "Sam, hey, this is a surprise."

Sam ignored Cohen's hand, extended over the desk. "You wanted it too much," Sam said.

"Excuse me?"

"The W. The win. You couldn't stand the possibility that you'd get your head handed to you."

"Sam, you don't look good. You okay?"

"What I want to know is, when did it occur to you?"

"Please, sit down and —"

"Was it when I deposed the doc? Was it when we were in the judge's chambers?" Sam slapped the desk with his open palm. A small pewter statuette of a football player that sat on Cohen's desk fell over, clanking against the glass top.

"Hey, hey," Cohen said.

"I saw him," Sam said. "The Viking coming out of the building. He's your guy. You had him watching my house."

Cohen's eyes narrowed. "Sam, take it real easy."

"Who is he?"

"Sam, are you talking about one of my investigators? Because —"

"Why was he watching my house, Larry?"

"You want the Nicholson on this? Because I don't think you can handle the truth."

"Try me."

"You're unhinged, Sam. That's a legitimate part of this whole thing. So I had my guy give you a little look. So what?"

Sam looked at him long and hard. Cohen stared back, trying not to blink. Then Cohen's eye twitched.

"You knew I'd see him," Sam said. "You were rattling my cage, weren't you?"

"Please."

"You wanted me to crack."

"You have cracked, Sam. You're the only

one who doesn't know it."

"My *wife,* Larry. You scared my wife."

Cohen stood up behind his desk. "Listen very carefully, Sam. You're unbalanced. You really are. It happens. The stress."

For a second Sam thought maybe Cohen was right.

He didn't care.

"You instructed your guy to watch my house," Sam said. "And be *seen* watching my house. That's harassment. Well, you know what? I'm an expert on harassment now. I'm going to make sure you're held accountable."

Red-faced, but with a cool voice, Cohen said, "You can't prove anything. And if you were to try, to the state bar or even with some loose comment in a dinner conversation, that would be slander. I'll fight you, and I don't lose fights. With your record lately, the way you've handled yourself, who are they going to believe? You're not a rational man, Sam."

"We're going to trial, Larry. Then we'll see who's rational."

"That's a very unwise move. Now why don't —"

"Can it. I've had my fill."

9.

Sam was shaking in the car. His body was at the breaking point. He hated to give Cohen any credence, but maybe somebody looking at him would have thought the very same thing.

Crack-up.

And he knew he couldn't just will it away.

He almost hit a Caddie turning onto Wilshire. The adrenaline that kicked in put his brain into hard focus, got him on the freeway. He cruised with the light traffic to the valley. But instead of the turnoff going to the house, he found himself heading for church.

The prayer chapel was the original building on the property, a small A-frame that Solid Rock had preserved as a quiet place for prayer. Wooden pews, a stained-glass window depicting the risen Christ.

Sam went in, found he was alone.

He stayed until dark.

10.

The moment he pulled into the driveway he sensed something was wrong. The house looked as it always did, even in the darkness. And yet . . .

Sam popped the trunk where he kept the

Browning case. He opened the case and took out the weapon.

Maybe foolish, maybe not. But a live fool was the best option for his family.

He unlocked the front door and pushed it open, pausing before going in, leaning to the side like a movie cop.

Nothing.

And then a muffled scream.

11.

"When can we go home?" Max said.

"What, you don't like it here?" Aunt Nancy said.

Linda put her hand on her big sister's arm. "Of course he does. What's not to like? This is pizza central."

They were all sitting around the dining room table in Aunt Nancy's. She'd been married twenty years, then her husband left her. At least he'd left her the house, a classic Craftsman that was quaint and warm. The interior design was reflective of Nancy's eclectic artistic tastes. She had kept up her career as an artist and was doing pretty well at it.

The deep-dish pizza from Flannery's was the best on the West Coast, at least according to Flannery's itself, and this was the second night they'd had it for dinner.

Heather was eating it too. A good thing, Linda thought. Heather had found an appetite, something scarce in the last couple of years.

"I think we should be with Dad," Max said. "Even if he doesn't want us to."

"We will be," Linda said. "Soon."

"Can we call him?" Heather asked. "I didn't talk to him today."

"How about after dinner? We'll all sit around and have a good long conversation with Dad."

12.

Sam dropped to his knees, held the gun in front of him. Pain shot through his tender thigh.

Could see nothing but amorphous forms in the dark house.

He thought about hitting the lights but immediately rejected that. That would make him a perfect target.

So why wasn't he a target right now?

He was trigger-ready but frozen.

Another scream, as if into a pillow.

It was coming from the living room.

Sam heard his own breath, as loud as a steam engine.

He was sure someone was going to die, and soon.

A lamp clicked on, pouring thin light into the entryway. Sam's body tensed as he pointed the gun toward the light.

"Don't do anything, Sam. It's under control."

Case?

13.

Sam still had the gun raised when Case stepped into view.

"Don't shoot, Sam," he said. "Not yet."

Sam didn't move. "What is going on?"

"Lower the gun."

"Who screamed?"

"Your old friend."

Slowly, fighting to find a coherent thought, Sam got to his feet, left leg throbbing.

"Come in and look," Gerald Case said. "He's not going anywhere."

Sam pointed the gun at the ground but kept his hand ready. He walked to Case and looked into the living room.

Bound to a chair by yellow rope, with a knotted gag over his mouth, was Nicky Oberlin. Or what looked like Nicky Oberlin. His hair was almost entirely gone. What was left were anemic tufts hanging, like dead grass, from a scarred red landscape. The whole left half of Nicky's face was lumpy with charred skin. But nothing obscured his eyes, which glared at Sam with an otherworldly hate.

"Now listen," Case said. "Here's how it has to go down. Nicky Oberlin broke into your house tonight. Picked the lock on the back door. By the way, I've got your house key. Wayne gave it to me. So Oberlin got in, waited for you to get home. He had a knife with him. You managed to get your gun, as you have it right now, and got off a couple of shots as he came toward you."

Sam looked at him. Case's face was as cool as Sam's was hot.

"It's the only way to settle this," Case said. "It's really self-defense, if you look at the big picture. He won't stop otherwise. And you never know what will happen in court."

Nicky screamed through the linen again.

"He's not someone who can be cured, Sam. This is a war, and he's one of many players who only wants to do bad things to people. You can do this."

Sam looked at Nicky again and knew Case was right about one thing. Nicky would never stop as long as he drew breath.

Sam felt the weight of the gun in his hand.

"Don't hesitate about this," Case said.

Nicky's eyes burned into Sam.

"Take off the gag," Sam said.

"What? No. That would be the wrong —"

"Do it, Gerry, or I'll do it myself."

Case hesitated. Then he went to Nicky and untied the gag.

Nicky shook his head once, then bared his teeth in an animal smile. The left side of his mouth was little more than a jagged maw of scorched lip. He spoke out of the right side. "He's right, you know, Sammy. It ain't ever going to be over for you."

Sam approached, stopping three feet in front him. And raised the gun.

"Not so close," Case said. "And make it two to the heart."

"Why me, Nicky?"

Nicky smiled more broadly.

"Jealousy?" Sam said.

That took the hideous smile from Nicky's face. "Of you? Don't make me laugh. You're scum. You treat people like scum, because you can. You knock people up without a thought, you rip people off. And you hide behind a plastic Jesus. You're the one who should be wiped off the earth."

Knock people up . . .

"This was about Mary, wasn't it?" Sam said.

Nicky was silent.

"You had a thing for Mary, didn't you?"

"You didn't care about her. You didn't

care about anything but getting her in bed
—"

"You've carried that around all these years?"

"— and then you paint yourself as this paragon of virtue —"

"She doesn't even remember you."

"Didn't know I existed, right? But you both know now, don't you? You'll always know —"

Gerald Case said, "Don't prolong this, Sam. It has to be now."

"Yeah," Nicky said. "Do it, Sammy. And when you go to hell I'll be waiting for you."

"Now," Case said.

"Call the police," Sam said.

"No, Sam —"

"Do it."

Case took a deep breath. "You're right, of course," he said. "I'll make the call."

"Big mistake, Sammy," Nicky said. "This was your last chance."

TWENTY-TWO

1.

Los Angeles Times

A unanimous jury recommended yesterday that Nicholas Stephen Oberlin should die for the murder of local music producer Charles "Scat" Lundquist.

Oberlin, who represented himself during the trial and penalty phase, showed no reaction to the verdict reached by the jury of eight women and four men. The jurors appeared resolute as their unanimous verdict was read after a day and a half of deliberations. The panel rejected a sentence of life imprisonment without parole.

"This is a just verdict," Deputy District Attorney Cameron Bellamy told reporters afterward. "Nicky Oberlin will never hurt another human being again. And make no mistake, he would if he could."

2.

On the last Friday in May, at three thirty in the afternoon, after a grueling, three-week battle with Larry Cohen, Sam Trask concluded his closing argument on behalf of Sarah Harper.

"You all know about Lady Justice," he said to the jury, "whose statue can be seen in virtually every courtroom in the land. She is blindfolded and she holds scales in her hand. The party who has the burden of proof in a civil case, and that would be Sarah Harper today, need only provide enough evidence to tip the scales in her favor. It's not like the burden of proof in a criminal matter. I explained that to you at the opening of this case. His Honor will also go over it with you when he gives you the law you are to follow during your deliberations. But there's something else I must talk about now.

"Lady Justice holds the scales in her left hand. Do you know what she has in her right hand? A sword. It is the sword of justice, and it symbolizes her duty to cut through the distortions and the lies and see to it that the truth comes out and right is vindicated. When you march into that jury room, you are Lady Justice. You carry the sword. You have sworn to do your duty, and

I know you will.

"I'm almost finished. You've heard all of the evidence relating to Sarah's future, a future that is no longer bright because of the recklessness and unwillingness of the defendants to take responsibility. We leave the matter of damages to you now but will remind you of only one thing. Today is the one day in your life that you can take care of Sarah Harper. Two weeks from now, you can't wake up and say, 'Wait, I'd like to open this up again, I think I made a mistake.' There is no coming back. This is Sarah's one and only day in court. We are confident that we can leave the matter now in your capable hands.

"Thank you."

3.

Los Angeles Daily Journal

A jury has awarded $10 million in compensatory damages to Sarah Harper, an Olympic figure-skating hopeful who is now blind and confined to a wheelchair.

Court watchers expressed surprise at the unanimity of the jury. Most thought Larry Cohen, the noted insurance defense attorney, would continue his near-legendary string of trial victories. That all twelve jurors, five men and seven women, sided with the plaintiff's lawyer, Samuel Trask, was seen as almost shocking.

"In simple terms, Cohen got his clock cleaned," said Loren Levy, law professor at Loyola Law School and frequent commentator on Court TV. "Nobody thought that would happen. This trial makes Sam Trask the new superstar lawyer in town."

Trask, former partner in Newman & Trask of Beverly Hills, recently opened his own office in Sherman Oaks.

4.

In late June, a letter came to Sam at home, with a law-office return address. Inside was another envelope, this one with the familiar markings of prisoner mail on the outside. Under Nicky Oberlin's name was his prison number.

In an explanatory letter from Nicky's appellate lawyer, who was allowed to receive confidential communications from his client, was a professional offer to cease forwarding letters to Sam, should he so desire.

That would definitely be my desire, Sam thought. He was just about to destroy Nicky's letter without opening it, just stick it in the paper shredder without a peek, when a soft knock came at the study door.

"Come on in."

It was Heather. "Bothering you, Pop?"

"No way."

She came in, and for the first time in months she looked like his old Heather. Not the Heather of self-destruction, but the one before that. The one who had spark and optimism, even if a little confusion about her place in the world. Heather at the cusp of teen age, before the shadows got thicker.

"I had a good session today," she said.

"That's great."

"Thought you'd like to know you're not throwing your money away."

"I never think that."

Sam was in his chair, facing her. Heather remained standing, as if she hadn't quite made up her mind to stay for a while. Sam hoped she would.

"Dad?"

"Hm?"

"Can I tell you something?"

"Of course."

"I'm not gonna do that."

"Do what?"

"What that James Cagney guy did in the movie. I don't want to die. I want to live with you and Mom and Max."

Sam stood, embraced her, stroked her hair.

She didn't move and Sam didn't move.

He drank in the moment. Finally he said, "So, you want to throw the Frisbee or something?"

"Are you joking?"

"No. We used to do that."

"Yeah, like ten years ago."

"Well . . ."

She kissed his cheek. "The Trask family sticks together," she said. "But we don't always do the same things. See ya!" She bounded from the study without another word.

She's not seven, Sam reminded himself. She's close to being a woman.

They were all different now, in fact. Stronger. Their joy in each other's company deeper and more precious. Especially with the new addition to the family, the golden retriever Max had picked out and named Rocky.

Sam turned back to the letter in his hands. And found himself tearing it open.

On a thrice-folded piece of notebook paper was Nicky's childlike scrawl.

Bet you miss me, don't you, Sammy? Come on, admit it, I gave you the chance to be a real man. You felt alive, didn't you? Superior? That's what you always wanted, right my man?

Don't let that go to your head! Wouldn't want to see that happen to an old friend. Because what happened between us doesn't mean a thing. See, I actually like it here, boy. I get fed. They give me pills to keep me feeling real good and calm. And I get to think. I think about you all the time. And Heather. Mmmmm, Heather! Think you might send her up to visit? That would be a very Christian thing to do, don't you think?

Speaking of thinking, you don't have to think bad things about me, Sammy. I hold no grudge for the bad way you treated your old pal. Let's talk about it real soon, what do you say? Bury the hatchet!

Hey, send me a card at Christmas! Keep me posted on everything your cute little family is up to. I want to keep track. We're working on my appeal, and when I get out, I'll come down for a visit. Keep a light on for me, buddy!

Your forever friend from college,

Nicky

For an extended moment, like a recurring beat in a nightmare, Sam sat still. His hands trembled a little, as if he were holding a wire with a small current — not enough to do much damage on its own, but able to start a fire if a spark was near.

Then it faded, the fear. This pathetic letter was the last gasp of a dead man. Sam didn't even feel anger any longer. He was able to do what all those priests did in the prison movies of the thirties — leave the condemned man to God, and may God have mercy on his soul.

He put the letter back in the envelope, then found a place for it in the back of a drawer of his filing cabinet. He closed the drawer with a satisfying metallic thrust and walked out of the study.

Heather was leaning against the wall, a green Frisbee in her hands.

"What's this?" Sam said.

"I thought we were going to toss."

"But I thought —"

"Don't think so much, Pop."

Heather padded to the front door, turned and smiled, then motioned for her father to follow.

ABOUT THE AUTHOR

James Scott Bell (www.jamesscottbell .com) is a winner of the Christy Award for Excellence in Christian fiction and is the bestselling author of several suspense novels, including *Presumed Guilty, Breach of Promise, Deadlock,* and *Sins of the Fathers.* A former trial lawyer, Bell makes his home in Los Angeles with his wife, Cindy.